You
Can't
Hurry
Love

Also by Susan Buchanan
Sign of the Times
The Dating Game
The Christmas Spirit
Return of the Christmas Spirit
A Little Christmas Spirit
Just One Day – Winter
Just One Day – Spring
Just One Day – Summer
Just One Day – Autumn
The Leap Year Proposal

You Can't Hurry Love

SUSAN BUCHANAN

Copyright

First published in 2025 by Susan Buchanan

Copyright © 2025 Susan Buchanan
Print Edition

A CIP catalogue record of this title is available from the British Library

Paperback – 978-1-915589-04-0

Dedication

Tracy, Fiona and Heather
Thanks for being amazing friends, the excellent chat and
the endless hours of listening

About the Author

Susan Buchanan lives in Scotland with her husband, their two children and a crazy Labrador. She has been reading since the age of four and had to get an adult library card early as she had read the entire children's section by the age of ten. As a freelance book editor, she has books for breakfast, lunch and dinner and in her personal reading always has several books on the go at any one time.

If she's not reading, editing or writing, she's thinking about it. She loves romantic fiction, psychological thrillers, crime fiction and legal thrillers, but her favourite books feature books themselves.

In her past life she worked in International Sales as she speaks five languages. She has travelled to 51 countries and her travel knowledge tends to pop up in her writing. Collecting books on her travels, even in languages she doesn't speak, became a bit of a hobby.

Susan writes contemporary romance, women's fiction and romantic comedies, usually featuring travel, food or Christmas, but always with large dollops of friendship, family and community. When not working, writing or caring for her two delightful cherubs, Susan loves reading (obviously), the theatre, quiz shows and eating out – not necessarily in that order!

You can connect with Susan via her website www.susanbuchananauthor.com or on Facebook www.facebook.com/susancbuchananauthor and on X @susan_buchanan or Instagram authorsusanbuchanan.

Acknowledgements

Huge thanks to

Claire at Jaboof Design Studio for my gorgeous cover. I love my sloth! I mean, I love all of the cover, but especially the sloth!

Paul Salvette and his team at BB Ebooks for book formatting www.bbebooksthailand.com

Wendy Janes, Catherine Ferguson, Katy Ferguson, Heather Harkin, Susan Allan and Anne Pack for agreeing to beta read for me.

Mairibeth, Sophie, Vanessa, Mary, Susan – again, Victoria and Rachel – for daily motivation

The Scottish chapter of the Romantic Novelists' Association

Rachel's Random Resources for always providing such wonderful blog tours and all the amazing bloggers who take part.

Sue Baker of the Riveting Reads and Vintage Vibes Facebook group for my launch day celebration

Thanks to the following Facebook groups:

Susan Buchanan's ARC team and advance readers generally– thanks for reading early copies of my books and for sharing my social media posts – you are all awesome

Susan Buchanan's Bookworms – I truly appreciate your support and enjoy interacting with you – apologies it's sometimes so sporadic!

Lizzie's Book Group, run by the amazing Lizzie Chantree, for constant support. Thanks also for opening your online store featuring bookish clothing – saves me deciding what to wear every day www.lizzie-chantree.com

The Friendly Book Community

Chick Lit and Prosecco, run by the fabulous Anita Faulkner

To all of my super-supportive fellow authors who kindly help spread the word

Most important of all – the fam. Antonia and Luke, I love you. Antonia, thanks for helping me with writing prompts and creative ideas. Luke, thanks for distracting me with board games and keeping me sane. Tony, thanks for feeding me.

And last, and by absolutely no means least, my readers. Thank you for continuing to invest in my books. It means the world to me, as do your lovely comments. If you want to connect with me about my books, you can always email me on susan@susanbuchananauthor.com

Chapter One

Four months, three days and, ooh, two hours since I booked this holiday, and now I'm here. I stand on the balcony of our boutique hotel and admire the view. The sparkling, shimmering waters of the Pacific look so inviting, I could strip off and jump in them right this second.

By the time we arrived in Costa Rica last night it was so late we crashed out on the bed fully clothed. Costa Rica. Even the sound of it on my lips makes me happy, and being Scottish, I can trill my Rs like the Spanish, so the sound is even more melodious, richer.

I put on my playlist of Costa Rican calypso music and smile at Aidan as he turns over in bed. One of his black curls falls over his face. It's so endearing, but I resist the urge to push it out of his eyes. He hates when I do that, says I'm not his mum.

A yacht rounds the point and approaches our bay. For the fifteen minutes or so that I've been studying the ocean, Aidan has been snoring gently. One whisky too many on the plane.

I really hope he comes on some of the trips I've planned. He has already said he isn't spending his whole holiday schlepping around tourist attractions; he just wants to rest. And each to their own, but I do hope he won't pass up the chance to see the sloths and the rainforests, otherwise what was the point of coming all this way?

My main purpose for visiting Costa Rica is to see the sloths – they're my favourite animal – and I've researched the Costa Punta sloth sanctuary to the nth degree, after hearing horror stories of other sanctuaries that don't rehabilitate the sloths and are only there to bring in the tourists. Much as I can't wait to see sloths in the flesh, I want to ensure they're well looked-after and that the sanctuary I visit has their best interests at heart.

Yet I also want to kick back on the powder-white sand of Costa Rica's beaches, as well as venturing a little off the beaten track to see the national parks.

The sea-foam green of the ocean finally entices me to leave Aidan to his lie-in. I walk through the grounds, which are surrounded by lush greenery and palm trees, and pause as I first hear then spot two parakeets. They're almost completely lime green apart from a red section above their beak. Their twittering reminds me of Snow White, her feathered friends perched on her outstretched arms, and I chuckle as I stroll past the S-shaped swimming pool which leads all the way to the beach.

As I'm leaving the gardens behind, about to walk onto the beach for the first time, a uniformed hotel worker passes me and nods. '*Pura vida.*'

I try not to frown, but as far as I know, in Spanish that means 'pure life'. I mentally bookmark to check later.

'*Buenos dias*,' I say, hoping good morning works well as a response to whatever he said. He tips his hat at me and I smile and wander onto the beach.

I'm interested to see how different the Spanish used in Costa Rica is to Castilian Spanish, which I learned at school. In an effort to fully immerse myself in the culture, I dug out my old Spanish books, a few weeks before we flew here. Hopefully, I'll have the courage to brush up on my Spanish during my trip.

I glance at my watch. It's early: seven o'clock. That makes it two in the afternoon at home. If I were in Glasgow, I'd be rushing from one appointment to the other, trying to avoid losing my mind in city centre traffic, or if I were lucky, having a wee jaunt down to the Borders to visit our clients there. Apart from the speed cameras, that's a nice leisurely drive, and there's always a good tearoom to drop into. Listen to me, I sound about fifty. I'm turning thirty, I'm not collecting my bus pass just yet.

Off to my right, three divers don their suits, then pull on their tanks, adjusting their regulators and breathing apparatus. I've never dived before and would love to. The marine life here in Costa Rica must be incredible, and I envy the divers as they disappear below the water. I've packed a snorkel. Let's see how I go with that first.

Bloody hell. The water is colder than it looks. OK, it is first thing in the morning and the sun isn't very high in the sky yet, but I still didn't expect it to feel like going for a paddle at Blackpool. Brrr. No wonder the beach is deserted, and now I think about it, those divers were wearing suits. I'd half expected them to be going in with only a pair of swimming shorts and a tank of air on their back.

The tranquillity is absolute now the divers have gone. Not a soul on the beach, which I find both comforting and humbling. Whenever I take time to really look at the sea, or ocean, I always have this sense of being insignificant. Something to do with being faced with the power of nature.

I sink down onto the sand and run my hands through it, loving the texture and the slight warmth to it. It's so perfect, I almost don't want to sully it by sitting on it.

A gentle breeze picks up and it caresses my face as I close my eyes and lie back. This is bliss, and so far removed from my normal life that it's hard to believe I'm actually here.

Another member of staff approaches, identically dressed to the previous one.

'*Pura vida*,' he says in a sing-song voice, smiling and inclining his head.

I stick with the habitual '*Buenos dias*'.

My stomach rumbles, reminding me it has been a long time since dinner on the plane last night. A glance at my watch shows me I've been faffing about on the beach for half an hour. Half seven is a reasonable time to get someone up for breakfast when you're in a new country, isn't it?

'Aidan, wake up.' I shake him gently, then a little harder. 'C'mon, it's time for breakfast.'

If that doesn't move him, nothing will. Aidan likes

his food. I do, too, and I love to try new things. And where better to do so than in an idyllic part of the world like this with all its new flavours and taste sensations?

'What time is it?' Aidan's bleary-eyed face emerges from beneath the pillow he'd put over his head to block out the light.

'It's quarter to eight. Get up. We have so much to do.' I can't contain my excitement, and although I'm probably being a little naughty waking Aidan early, surely he must feel some sense of adventure about being here.

'All right, keep your hair on.' He sticks his tongue out over and over as if he's trying to get rid of a bad taste. Or perhaps he has a furry tongue from all the alcohol he consumed last night. I mean, I'm no party pooper, I had a glass of wine with dinner, too. I just didn't take it to the extremes he did.

He grabs me round the middle. 'Come back to bed.'

'Get off!' I smack him lightly on the shoulder and wriggle free of his grasp. 'Later. Now, get up, I'm hungry.'

'Fine, but let me check in with the office first.'

I stifle a groan. We're supposed to be on holiday. Sure, Aidan's heading up a huge project at the moment, worth millions of pounds, but no one can cover him when he's on leave?

Half an hour later we're in an open-air dining room, on a white wooden raised deck, gazing out at the ocean, where a couple of boats now bob in the water under a cloudless sky. The dining room looks as if it's set up for a destination wedding with its white wooden columns, white high-backed chairs with floor-length covers and silk bows. The immaculate tablecloth almost puts me off eating, I'm so scared I'll dirty it.

'Good morning, sir. Madam.' The waiter bows. 'Would you like coffee, tea or *agua dulce*?'

I chance my luck. I need coffee, but I read about *agua dulce* in my guide book and fancy trying it, too.

'Could I have coffee and *agua dulce*?' I ask.

'Of course.' The waiter beams at me then turns to Aidan.

'Coffee.' Aidan doesn't even lift his eyes from his phone.

The waiter tells us we can help ourselves to anything from the breakfast buffet and says he'll be back in a few minutes. With difficulty, I fight off the rising stab of irritation at Aidan's rudeness. I know he's under a lot of pressure at work and they're short-staffed, but would it kill him to be polite?

Whilst he scrolls through his phone, I gaze out at the ocean again. Looks like the divers are coming back in.

'Here you go, madam, and sir.' The endlessly patient waiter is the consummate professional as Aidan continues to ignore him. I school myself not to tut, even though my own patience is now paper-thin. Once again, I rail against the bad luck of my best friend, Becca, breaking her leg two weeks prior to our trip. Despite being grateful to Aidan for stepping into the breach and taking her place, I know without a second thought that I'd be enjoying myself a lot more if she were here. In fact, she would have made me stay up and party last night.

Becca lived next door to my grandfather when I was growing up and I used to go round there after school as my parents were working. We've been besties ever since. She's made no bones about not liking Aidan, and she's horrified at the prospect of us moving in together when we return, but it seemed the next logical step. We have been together for three years, after all. And despite his flaws, he has been there for me these past two years, when I've been at my lowest. That has to count for something. He didn't ditch me when the going got tough, instead staying when it mattered most.

Talking of Becca, I haven't messaged her today. I'll need to send her a few snaps shortly. Unlike my boyfriend, I am not addicted to my phone. At least, not whilst I'm on holiday, although my guide book peeks out of my bag at me accusingly, as if to say, 'You're not much better as you're always leafing through me.'

I sip my *agua dulce*. It's, well, sweet. Unsurprising given the amount of sugar cane in it, and even though it makes me gulp, I like it. I don't think I'll need any sugar in my coffee now, though.

'I'm going to check out the buffet,' I say, but I might as well be talking to myself as Aidan's eyes remain on his phone, his brow furrowed in concentration. Right, time to forget him, I'm starving.

The buffet tables are groaning with a vast variety of fresh fruit, most of which I've never seen before. I think that one's a dragon fruit. I'm sure I saw that as an answer on a quiz programme one time. And that one's guava – I gleaned that from the guide book – green with pink flesh, and I'm guessing the one next to it is its Costa Rican variant, cas, which is yellow with white flesh. The others, I honestly don't have the slightest idea what they are.

Ah, there are tiny signs underneath the baskets they're sitting on. *Granadilla*. It looks a bit like a passion fruit. *Guanabana*, which apparently translates as custard apple. Yep, never heard of that one. And the outside of it is like an avocado with spikes. Great if you're taking a masterclass in how to be attacked by your breakfast. I pass on that one and opt for the *granadilla*, some papaya, guava and then move on to the stainless-steel containers for the hot food.

First up is *gallo pinto*. It smells amazing, considering it's just rice and beans. Then I spot eggs and plantain. I've never tried plantain before either. It can't be so different from a banana, right? But I'd still be stretching my palate. I load up a plate and return to the table.

Aidan eyes my plate with interest. 'Is that banana and eggs?'

'Plantain.'

'Didn't you get me any?' he asks, frowning.

'Well, no,' I say, slightly flummoxed. 'I figured you'd want to choose your own.' I bite my tongue, not voicing that he's a grown man and well able to fetch his own breakfast.

'I suppose I'd better go grab myself some then,' he says in a surly tone. He pinches some of my guava as he passes, pops it in his mouth and moans. 'Oh, that's so good.'

I'd agree, but I haven't had a chance to try it yet. As he leaves, I tuck into my food. It's delicious, and I savour the sweetness of the fried plantain on my tongue.

You'd have loved this, Dad.

A wave of grief slams into me, and once again I wonder if I've made a mistake in coming here with Aidan.

Chapter Two

It's the third day of our holiday and I'm on the beach early, again, watching the divers. I raise my hand in greeting to the hotel worker I met when I first arrived. He must be around fifty-five or so and his face is lined and weathered from years out in the sun. I've passed him countless times and when I asked him, he kindly explained to me what '*pura vida*' means. Apart from being a greeting and also a way of saying 'you're welcome', it's more of a mantra that the Costa Ricans live by. It doesn't mean 'pure life' exactly, and it's so much more than 'the simple life', but I like the philosophy, even though I may find it difficult to implement myself straight away. Old habits die hard.

My thoughts turn to Dad as they often do. Truth is, Becca wasn't the original person I was meant to go on this trip with; it was Dad. Dad who shared his love of sloths with me when I was a young girl. Dad who showed me the photos a friend of his had taken after visiting a sloth sanctuary whilst on a cruise for his silver wedding anniversary. Something Mum and Dad couldn't afford to do for theirs. Instead, twenty of us had gone for a meal at our favourite restaurant.

From when I was knee high to a grasshopper, as

Dad used to say, we would watch all those nature programmes together. I loved learning about all the animals and their habitats, discovering the sheer number of vibrantly coloured birds to be found, the exotic places they lived. New countries. New continents. We always said one day we'd explore together. It hadn't occurred to me it was all a fantasy. As a school janitor, Dad didn't exactly earn much. That's why, when I was old enough to realise this, I resolved to change things, to ensure Dad and I could go to Costa Rica. I stuck in at school, I studied hard, determined to be a vet. I'd already chosen which veterinary course I would do. The School of Veterinary Medicine at the University of Glasgow is well known for being one of the best, so it was a no-brainer for me.

But I didn't get in. I didn't make the cut, didn't get the grades, and every so often it's like the knife of fate twists in me once again. I was so sure I would get in. I know Dad was disappointed inside, but outwardly he never let it show. He wasn't upset for himself, but for me. He knew how hard I'd worked and how much I wanted it. Going from believing I was starting at the vet school to selling pet supplies was a bit of a comedown.

I've worked my way up to area manager now, and I've been saving for a couple of years for this trip. I don't know how many times I made Dad watch the animated movie *Zootropolis* for the sloth scene. It made me laugh every time I watched it. Him too. It doesn't make me laugh any more. Not now he's gone.

Becca was devastated when she had to pull out. This trip meant so much more to me, and by extension her, than simply going on the trip of a lifetime with a friend. She was my surrogate. She knows how important it is to me. I'm not just making this trip for me, but also for Dad. For every David Attenborough programme we watched together, for every storybook he ever bought me about sloths, for every stuffed toy that sat on my bed during my childhood. I used to get a new sloth toy every birthday. It was our tradition. I still have them, although I put all but one of them in a box in my spare bedroom once Aidan started staying over, as he kept poking fun at me. I wouldn't expect him to understand. But after Dad passed away, I snuck Sammy back out. He's my favourite one. He's only five inches tall, but somehow he comforts me.

The ping of a text breaks into my thoughts and I stare down at my phone. Becca. *How's it going? How's the weather? Have you been to see the sloths yet? I miss you. God, I wish I was there xx*

I give a rueful smile. How I wish she were here, too. I type back slowly, trying to work out how honest to be, how much to tell her. Do I tell her I feel largely unimportant in Aidan's life, and that his many faults are wearing me down? How he has all but exhausted the good work and brownie points he earned by supporting me through Dad's illness and after his death? I feel so disloyal even thinking it, but I'm so confused. When we were first going out together, he was great fun, and he wined and dined me, which was nice as money was tight, although I did repay the favour, too. But as we've settled into our relationship, things have definitely changed. At first, I thought it was that the initial honeymoon phase had peaked earlier than expected, but now I wonder if it was more than that. Certainly his aggressive behaviour in the departure lounge on the way here was less than stellar. Cringeworthy is the word I'd use for his reaction at our flight being delayed, the tone he took with the ground staff, plus during our wait he barely noticed I was there, except when it came to getting a round in or being a sounding board for his complaints. I'd hoped his mean-spiritedness of late had been a blip, but now I'm concerned. Really concerned. And how does that bode for us moving in together next month, if I'm already having misgivings?

This trip, apart from being a momentous one for me, is also an emotional one because I was meant to come with Dad. Is Aidan really that oblivious? So far we haven't left the hotel grounds as he keeps saying we have plenty of time and to stop bugging him whilst he tries to relax around the pool or on a lounger at the beach. His one saving grace was finally relenting to going in the ocean yesterday. If it weren't for me, he wouldn't even have gone in. How can you go all the way to Costa Rica and not go in the water, for goodness' sake? It's the flippin' Pacific Ocean.

I hoped – stupidly, perhaps – that this trip would bring us closer together, but so far all I want to do is smack him over the head with a frying pan. A skillet. Cast iron. Or maybe a really big, heavy phone, since that's all he's interested in – talking on one.

Weather's great. How's the leg? Not been anywhere yet. Aidan wants to chill. Have decided if he won't come somewhere with me tomorrow, I'm going without him. So wish you were here x

Lightning fast, Becca's response arrives. *Leg's fine, if a little itchy, and moving around is slow-going. No sloths in the hotel grounds then? Arse. Ditch him xx*

I grin. I hope when he wakes that he has a rethink about going on an excursion today, but I'd bet my life savings he won't. One thing about Aidan, he's stubborn; once he has made his mind up about something, he doesn't go back on it.

The divers are walking towards me. I've nodded and smiled back at them the last couple of days as they've passed. I'm the only other person ever here at this time in the morning.

I start composing another text to Becca.

'Hey.' One of the guys stops beside me.

I give a start and clutch my chest. I didn't hear him approach.

He holds up his hands by way of apology. 'Sorry, I didn't mean to startle you. I just wondered if you fancied coming diving with us one morning.'

He's around my age, maybe a little younger, and his open and friendly manner disarms me. The faint tang of salt hangs in the air and I wonder if it's from his skin or the ocean itself.

'I'd like that,' I say, surprising myself, 'but I don't know how.'

His smile widens. 'Excellent. I'm Ed. Don't worry about being a novice. I'm an instructor. These are my wingmen, Nicolás and Oscar.'

'Kat.'

Once I've shaken hands with the three of them, Ed says, 'I'll be around later at the little pool, if you want to come practise.' I hesitate and he jumps in, 'Unless, of course, you have plans.'

'No, no plans today. I'll swing by later.'

'Great, I'll see you then.'

I give the three of them a little wave as they wander off, and get back to composing that message to Becca.

Well, since Aidan won't come out to play with me, I've hooked up with 3 hot guys x

Yeah, you wish. In fact, I wish that for you! xx

I laugh. *No, for real. I'm going diving with them tomorrow and Ed is teaching me to dive in the pool later x*

WTAF? Where's Aidan going to be??? And who's Ed? xx

I smile at Becca's overuse of question marks.

Ed's the instructor. The guys stopped to talk to me today as I'm always on my bloody own. You know Aidan likes his sleep. I figured I may as well try a new experience whilst I wait for him to agree to go on an excursion with me, and I've always fancied diving x

New experience? But is that Ed or diving?? Her text is followed by six winking emojis. She's incorrigible, but the banter between us has lifted my spirits. That and, of course, Ed's kind offer to teach me how to dive. There'll no doubt be a cost involved, but I don't care. There's only so much lying about, getting a tan I can do before I begin to get antsy. I've already finished two romance novels in three days.

As I pootle back into the hotel and head for breakfast, I hug to myself the fact that I have an activity today. Hurrah! And tomorrow, come what may, I'm going to see the sloths. Then I can start on the rest of my itinerary.

A few hours later, we're lying on the beach when I gather up my things. Aidan puts down his newspaper. He decided he couldn't be bothered with the sun's glare on his phone, gave in and bought an English-language newspaper.

'Where are you off to?' he asks.

'To my diving lesson, remember?' I'd told him at breakfast as he checked emails on his phone between mouthfuls of *gallo pinto*.

'What? But you don't know how to dive,' he says, his face screwed up in confusion.

I stare at him pointedly, only just stopping myself from putting my hands on my hips. 'That's kinda the point of having a lesson.'

'But when will you ever need to dive?'

My patience evaporates entirely. 'Aidan, I realise the fact may have escaped you, but we're on holiday, in Costa Rica, on the Pacific Ocean, where the water is gorgeous, warm and there is a whole host of marine life to see.'

He goes to butt in, but I hold up a hand. 'Now, I've done all I can with my little snorkel and the instructor was kind enough this morning to offer to help me practise.'

'Ha! He probably wants to take a wad of your cash, more like.'

I sigh. When did he become so mean-spirited? Was he always this cynical and I didn't notice?

'Aidan, I don't care if I have to pay. All I want is to enjoy myself, and in this case, learn something new.'

His face falls. 'And what about me?'

'What about you? You've barely looked up from

your phone since we got here. You won't come on the excursions I've waited three years to go on, despite saying you would. I came here for adventure and that's exactly what I'm going to get.' I stride off before I say something there's no coming back from.

'Kat, hi. You ready?'

'Yep, good to go.' My face breaks into a smile.

Ed's doing something with breathing apparatus as I approach. Adjusting something? Adventure and fear grip me tight all at once and I can barely breathe.

A flash of concern crosses Ed's face. 'You OK?'

'Yeah, just excited,' I fib.

'Great, so first I want you to retrieve some objects from the bottom of the pool. I need to check how good you are at holding your breath.'

Not very. Even though I used to swim competitively, holding my breath is something I've always struggled with. 'OK. Let's do this.'

Ten minutes later, I'm coughing and spluttering as I hang on to the side of the pool. 'That's harder than it looks.'

'You're doing fine. Now, let's try that with a weight belt,' Ed suggests.

I've just retrieved four objects without coming up for air. Ed has been gradually increasing the length of time I'm underwater. Apparently, it helps when it comes to using the regulator and breathing through my mouth not my nose.

Ed's eyes crinkle as he smiles. 'You're beginning to get the hang of it. Right, a little more practice then we'll get a tank on you and see if we can get you breathing through your regulator mouthpiece. You may even be able to go for a short dive tomorrow.'

The thought fills me with both trepidation and exhilaration. I steel myself. I can do this. I wanted adventure, well, here it is.

After a few more rounds of retrieving items from the bottom of the pool and Ed's patient instruction, I feel more able and more than a little reassured that I have some clue of what I'm meant to be doing.

'Good. I think you're almost there. Come here.'

I stand obediently in front of him as he shows me how the mouthpiece works and then hands it to me.

'I'll be in the water right beside you, and we'll go in the shallow end this time, to start you off.'

I read between the lines – in case I get spooked and flail about, drowning.

'Can you turn around so I can put the tank on for you? Watch out. It's heavier than you think.'

The tank is on and feels a bit odd. I'm missing some flippers, I think wryly.

'Wait, I'll adjust your weight belt a little. I think I misjudged it slightly.' He slips another weight into the belt around my waist just as a voice bellows, 'What the hell is going on here?'

Oh no! Aidan. What on earth is he doing here?

I whirl around as well as I can with the tank on my back, and Ed stands back, a frown creasing his brow.

Aidan is no longer wearing his swim shorts, but is fully dressed in a navy shirt and chinos. Has he changed his mind about us going somewhere after all? If so, typical that it would be now when I've told him I've arranged to do something else.

I grit my teeth. 'Aidan, I told you I was going for a diving lesson.'

I can't believe he is embarrassing me like this and spoiling my otherwise enjoyable afternoon.

'Is that what you call it? His paws were all over you.' Aidan's jaw is clenched.

'Steady on, mate. I'm a dive instructor. I was adjusting her weight belt,' Ed says.

Aidan glares at Ed and scowls. 'Yeah, right. And I wasn't speaking to you, *mate*.' He turns to me. 'C'mon, Kat. Time to go.' He grabs for my hand.

Apart from the fact it would be absolutely ridiculous for me to take his hand and leave, as I still have a tank of air on my back and a weight belt around my middle, I'm incensed.

'Leave? I'm not leaving. I'm just beginning to enjoy myself.'

'I bet you are,' Aidan snarls. Then he laughs. 'Do you honestly think this surfer boy is interested in you? You're far too old for him for a start. Look at you, throwing yourself at him. It's pathetic.'

'Aidan, have you had too much sun? What's got into you?' My patience vanishes completely and my voice rises a decibel or two. I've had just about enough of him belittling me.

'I won't have you embarrassing me by behaving like a tart with this amoeba.'

Oh shit.

'What did you say?' A vein pulses in Ed's neck as his eyes darken.

'I said you were an amoeba.' Aidan punctuates each

word with a pause.

'Oh, I don't care what you said about me, what did you say about Kat?' Ed's voice is dangerously soft.

'That she was behaving like a tart.' Dismissing Ed by turning his back on him, Aidan grabs me and starts to wrestle the air tank off.

'Aidan, get off me!' I try to push him away, but he's too strong, his fingers digging into my upper arms.

'She said to leave her alone.' Ed drags Aidan off me, and I gulp in a couple of stuttering breaths, my heart racing.

'Why don't you mind your own business?' Aidan shoves Ed hard in the chest.

'Why don't you cool off?' Ed pushes him hard and Aidan, arms flailing, windmills backwards into the pool. Despite the seriousness of the situation, I have to stifle a giggle.

Moments later, coughing and with hatred burning in his eyes, Aidan exits the pool, his shirt clinging to his chest, his chinos weighted down by water, almost at his hipbones. He glares daggers at us. 'You'll regret this,' he says, although it's not clear which of us his comment is directed at.

'Aidan, do you know what? I've had enough. I'm not your possession. I'm fed up with you belittling everyone – the waiter, the diving instructor, me.' I let my last word hang in the air for a second before continuing. 'We're done.' All the niggles that have been bothering me lately about our relationship rise to the surface, and I think of how much he has changed, what I've had to put up with – the walking on eggshells around him, his heavy drinking, his telling me I can't do things – but now I've had enough. I fold my arms across my chest in an attempt to both protect myself further and to show strength.

'Done? I don't think so. But you *will* pay for this.'

'I hope that wasn't a threat, Aidan, as I wouldn't want to have to report that to the hotel manager,' Ed says. 'Perhaps you can ask at reception if they have another room available whilst you review your options.'

I hold my breath, waiting for a further outburst, and flinch at the look Aidan gives me before he squelches off, presumably to change.

'Ed, I'm so sorry.' Tears prick my eyes and I wrap my arms around me to try to stop myself from shaking.

'Don't be. You haven't done anything wrong. Guys like him give men a bad name. Kat, I don't know you, but I can tell you right now, you deserve better than him. And I'm not hitting on you, by the way. I'm happily married with two kids. But that guy should not be your future.'

Sadly, I couldn't agree with him more.

Chapter Three

By the time I arrive back at the hotel room, Aidan has gone. The only hint of his presence is a two-word note, *Your loss*, and his signature. I sit down heavily on the bed, the relief overwhelming. He took me at my word. It's a bloomin' mess, but if Ed, who has known me all of two minutes, can tell me outright that Aidan is no good for me, how could I not have admitted it to myself before now? My breath hisses out of me as I pause on the thought that we were meant to be moving in together after this trip.

I'm so tired. I've been running on adrenalin since the incident at the pool. After we'd completed my lesson, I sat with Ed for a while before deciding it was probably safe to come back to the room, although he insisted on accompanying me, in case Aidan was inside or loitering nearby. Fortunately, he wasn't and now all I want to do is sleep. I barely make it to a reclining position before my eyes drift closed.

When I wake, a few hours have passed and the low glow of the light on the balcony informs me it's evening. I freshen up, and even though I'm still a little groggy from the emotion of the day and a little sad at the finality of our split, the overarching feeling is one of relief at being free.

My phone pings. Becca. *Look, you weren't meant to open it until your birthday, but you can open the smaller of the two presents I gave you, now, if you like xx*

I dig around in my backpack and pull out the little gift Becca told me to keep in my hand luggage. I wonder now if she thought Aidan might kick off and I'd need a pick-me-up as a result. Whatever the case, she's right, I do. I undo the ribbon on the parcel, carefully open the wrapping paper and remove the tissue paper to reveal a cute six-inch baby sloth plush. I can't hold back my smile. Becca knows me so well. Nearly thirty and I still love teddies. I gaze into its sweet little face and try to conjure up a name. Hope. That's perfect.

Oh, Becca, if only you knew how much I needed this right now.

I place the plush on the bed, then head downstairs to reception. It's dinnertime, but the last thing I want to do right now is eat, so I wander over to the beach bar and order myself an orange juice. I need to stay completely sober so my head is clear, just in case Aidan returns.

I'd better text Becca back, let her know what's going on. She'll be delighted we've split up, but anxious about me being out here all alone. Bizarrely, I'm not too worried about that, and surely that's telling in itself. Three days from my thirtieth birthday and I'm not fazed or afraid about spending it alone in Costa Rica. Self-pity descends for a nanosecond before I shake it off. Yes, it would have been lovely to visit all the fabulous places on my list – the national parks, the coffee plantations, and of course the sloth sanctuary – with someone special, and enjoy it together, but let's face it, that was never going to be Aidan. Why did I ever think it could be?

No, tomorrow, things will change. I have eleven days left and I intend to make every single one count. Tomorrow, I'll do what I came here to do – visit the sloths.

Next morning, I rise a little later, tired out from the previous day's events. As I dress, my phone pings. Aidan. *At the airport. Hope you're happy.*

My heart rate spikes but I force myself to remain calm. *Of course I'm not bloody happy, but I'm happier without you.* Tempting though it is to send that message, I backspace over it and don't reply.

Half an hour later, I wave to Ed, Oscar and Nicolás as I stroll along the beach towards where they're busy wriggling out of their wetsuits.

'Kat, how's things?' Ed's voice is wary.

'Good, thanks. And thank you again for yesterday.'

Ed exhales heavily. 'No worries. I hope I didn't overstep the mark.'

I shake my head. 'No, you didn't. He needed that.'

'Did Aidan get in touch?' Nicolás asks.

'Yep. He's flying home.'

Ed nods, Nicolás' eyes go wide and Oscar says, 'Good riddance,' before packing away the rest of his diving gear.

'So, what are you going to do now?' Ed asks.

I grin. 'Start enjoying my holiday properly.'

'Oh?' Nicolás raises an eyebrow.

'Yes, Aidan was holding me back, not going on the trips I'd planned to do whilst I was here.'

'Does that mean you're ready to come diving in the ocean then?' Ed smiles at me.

I wag a finger at him. 'Actually, not quite. I have something else I need to do today. Maybe tomorrow?'

'Sure. Whenever suits.'

Oscar tugs on a plain white T-shirt. 'What are your plans for today then?'

'I'm going to visit the Costa Punta sloth sanctuary. It's what I came here to do. I love their rehabilitation programme.'

'No way!' Oscar elbows Nicolás in the ribs. 'Tell her.'

I frown, then my eyes flit from one to the other. 'Tell me what?'

Nicolás rolls his eyes, but he's grinning so much two cute dimples appear at the corners of his mouth.

'My uncle Carlos and aunt Sofia own the sloth sanctuary.'

'What? Really? That's amazing. Oh my God, did you grow up with the sloths? What's it like? Do you honestly have to go by canoe to the sanctuary? How many sloths are there?' The questions tumble out of me until I realise the three of them are looking at me, then at each other, amusement dancing in their eyes and on their lips.

'Are you a sloth superfan by any chance?' Ed teases me.

'Am I ever? And I'm proud of it.'

'It shows.' Nicolás sticks his tongue out at me when

I give him a mock glare.

'Have you booked your tour yet?' Ed asks.

'Not yet. I was going to sort it after breakfast.'

'What do you think, Nicolás?' Ed raises an eyebrow at him, and the three men share a complicit smile.

Nicolás tilts his head. 'I'm sure I could sort something out.'

I haven't the faintest idea what they're talking about.

Nicolás takes out his phone as Ed and Oscar grin at me and Ed says, 'Day off for us. I haven't seen the sloths in forever. Or did you want to go alone?'

'You're kidding, right?'

These guys, whom I've known less than two days, are prepared to do this for me. I could weep with joy.

'That's settled.' Nicolás claps his hands together. 'Aunt Sofia and Uncle Carlos are expecting us later. They'll give you the VIP tour. Let's grab some breakfast and then we can hit the road.'

Two hours later, we've left Nicolás' off-roader at the car park where the road ends and the river begins.

'The sanctuary can be accessed by car, but it's much longer by road, and anyway you're in Costa Rica, you want to experience it to the max.' Nicolás' teeth gleam in the half-light of the canopied rainforest. I'm trying not to move in case I capsize the canoe. Somehow I thought it would be bigger, and I can't help worrying since Oscar helpfully mentioned there have been sightings of crocodiles in the river recently.

Finally, we bump up against dry land again, and I

heave a sigh of relief. Excited though I am about this trip, I'd rather have taken the longer road route to avoid being mauled by a crocodile in some swampy river. Since leaving the car park, it's like I've entered another world.

'Kat, look.' Nicolás points to a nearby tree, where an adult sloth is hanging from a branch, gripping on with its four-inch fingers.

'Oh my God.' I stare in amazement then catch a glimpse of a few more sloths in the surrounding greenery. I can't believe it. I really am in sloth paradise.

Nicolás grins. 'That's the adult sloth play area. Come on. I'll introduce you to Carlos and Sofia.'

We wander inside the tastefully decorated entrance to the rescue centre. It's so artfully done you barely notice when you leave the rainforest and enter the building, which almost seems to be carved out of the rainforest itself, it blends in so well. The greens and browns emulate the sloths' natural habitat. Only the wording Costa Punta Sloth Sanctuary – I'm translating from the Spanish – shows you you're no longer in the rainforest itself.

It's so much bigger inside than I expected. We're in a vast foyer with what look to be offices off to the left and an enormous exhibition area straight ahead. A sign reading Staff Only is off to the right.

¡Tía! ¡Tío! Nicolás hugs the couple who come towards us with open arms. Carlos, his uncle, has an adult three-fingered sloth clinging to him.

My eyes widen involuntarily and I want to pinch myself to check I'm not dreaming.

'Kat, pleased to meet you.' Carlos beams at me.

'And you.' I can't tear my gaze away from the grey-brown sloth which looks so at home around Carlos' Hawaiian shirt.

'Sofia.' A woman whom I'd place around early seventies with a friendly face and the twinkliest eyes I've ever seen, suggesting a fierce intelligence, greets me. I shake her hand then she notes me staring at the sloth.

'Ah, don't worry about Ferdinand. He just loves his papa. We have had him ten years. We tried to rehabilitate him, but he wouldn't go back into the wild, despite numerous attempts, and he has stuck to Carlos ever since.'

'Oh my God, I can't believe how beautiful they are up close,' I say, fascinated by the band around Ferdinand's eyes and how it makes him look half like a highwayman and half like a masked superhero. His claws are so long, and I wonder how Carlos manages to carry him around without getting scratched to pieces. I blink back tears, happy tears, as emotion overcomes me. I've waited so long to see this, my favourite animal in the whole world, and today, now, I'm achieving that long-held dream.

'I'm all he has ever really known,' Carlos explains. 'Usually, we handle the sloths as little as possible, and we do our very best to rehabilitate them, but Ferdinand's mama was struck by a car and unfortunately we couldn't save her. He was so young, only weeks old, that he had no time to learn from her what he needed to survive in the wild. So now he's one of our permanent residents.' He gazes fondly at the sloth, almost like a father with a favourite child. It's so heartwarming.

'Anyway, come, let us show you around,' Carlos says. 'Sofia, did you tell Javier they were coming?'

Nicolás leans down and whispers in my ear, 'Javier's my cousin. We grew up together. We're practically twins.'

I smile at his clear affection for his cousin.

'Yes, of course. Nicolás, boys, come with me. Carlos, you give Kat the guided tour.' Sofia shepherds them away. 'I need your help with something, Nicolás.'

She's already walking off, the boys following in her wake, and I feel completely at ease being left with Carlos and Ferdinand.

Waving me ahead of him, Carlos says, 'Come. We have much to see.' He leads me around the centre, showing me the interactive exhibits and the programmes they support to raise awareness of the sloths and the issues they face. A member of staff is holding a talk about sloths to a group of primary school-age children, and he hails Carlos as he passes.

'Ah, Carlos, can you and Ferdinand come and say hi?'

'Hi, children. This is Ferdinand.' He twists around to give the kids the best view of the sloth, which has blended in against his body.

Carlos answers the children's many questions, showing endless patience, but explaining that they must be quiet so as not to startle Ferdinand or stress him out.

'No, I'm afraid it's not possible to touch the sloths. They get scared very easily,' explains Carlos. 'Ferdinand has a special bond with me, but it's rare with humans. I am kind of like his daddy.'

As Carlos continues, he flashes me a quick smile

and gives me a 'What can you do?' eye roll, but I can tell he's in his element. Then I note his demeanour change slightly as he stares over my head. I turn to see what has caught his attention. Hello. Yeah, he caught my attention, too, although I'm pretty sure for a different reason. Another sanctuary worker is signalling to him. He's about six feet tall, has dirty blonde hair that flops over into his piercing sky blue eyes and isn't too shabby to look at, even in the khaki sanctuary uniform. Just when I thought today couldn't get any better, it has.

'Excuse me a second, Kat. My deputy manager needs to speak to me.'

'No problem.' I cast my glance back towards the gorgeous guy he's heading towards and he catches me. Oops. Busted. But his lips curve into a smile before I look away. Interesting.

I stand and listen to the questions from the school group, my brain whirring as it tries to work out some of the more difficult terms. I love that the word for sloth in Spanish is '*perezoso*' – basically 'lazy', or '*oso perezoso*' – a lazy bear. And the sloths are so sweet. It's so relaxed here I almost feel a bit '*perezosa*' myself. It's hot, though. I could do with a cold drink.

I'm suddenly aware of a delicious, spicy aftershave and I turn my head slightly to discover the gorgeous guy is now standing beside me.

'Hi. I'm Dexter. Carlos thought you might like to come and have a drink in the staff canteen. He has a minor emergency to take care of, but he'll join us shortly.'

I almost can't speak, he's so good-looking. If I'm a

seven, he's a ten. And his accent is Cork or possibly Galway. Irish anyway. I'm a sucker for an Irish accent. *Shut up, Kat, you've only just got rid of Aidan. Like, literally.*

'T-t-that would be great,' I manage. 'I'm Kat.'

He smiles and my heart flips. 'Nice to meet you, Kat. It's through here.'

We cross the foyer and disappear through the door marked Staff Only. It's like a rabbit warren through here, with rooms going off in all directions. On the right is one clearly marked Canteen, whilst on the left and further down are what appear to be the sloth-dedicated areas.

I follow Dexter into the canteen, where he fixes us both an orange juice, then we take a seat in a couple of the bamboo chairs that are on one side of the room.

'So you're not local then?' I say.

His face breaks into a grin. 'That obvious?'

When I nod, he goes on, 'I'm from Waterford, like the crystal.'

'South west?' I try to remember my Irish geography, which is woefully sketchy in places.

'South east, but at least you knew it was south.' He sips his orange juice then says, 'I don't need to guess where you're from, though. I lived in Glasgow for two years.'

'You did not!'

'Did too.' He puts his glass on the table and smacks his lips together slightly. I'm paying far too much attention to his lips, but they do look rather ... kissable? Jesus, what is wrong with me? My hormones have gone into overdrive.

'So what brings you to Costa Rica?' Dexter asks.

I opt for the short answer. 'A lifelong love of sloths.'

'Really? Me too, although my first conservation programme was with turtles. But there's something special about these little guys. This post came up a few years ago and the rest, as they say, is history.'

He blinks and the gazelle-like length of his lashes makes me gulp.

'So, you fancy yourself as a sloth enthusiast, do you?'

The way he says 'fancy' makes my heart rate increase.

I nod. 'I do, yes.'

'Hmm, I'd have to test you to be sure.'

Now he has me wondering what he has in mind.

His eyes sparkle with mischief. 'You see, I can take you behind the scenes, but we don't let just anyone go there. You've met Ferdinand, but there are a few others I can show you, if you pass the test.'

My heart swells with joy. Yes, yes, yes, I want to shout. 'I'm game.'

He raises an eyebrow and I blush, then he grabs a nearby pencil and paper as if he's going to make notes. 'OK, question one…'

His demeanour is so serious it makes me laugh. I feel so comfortable with him and I've only known him about ten minutes. I felt like that with Ed and the guys, too, but they didn't make my stomach do cartwheels. Maybe it's some strange rebound reaction to splitting up with Aidan.

'…what do sloths like to eat?'

I pause for a second to think. 'Well, they eat lots of fruit, but I've just discovered they like hibiscus flowers for dessert,' I say, hoping Dexter is impressed with my knowledge.

He laughs. 'Very good. Ten points. Question two. Can sloths a) swim, b) hang-glide or c) rock climb?'

Now it's my turn to laugh. 'I'll go with swim. And do I get bonus points for extra info?'

Dexter tilts his head to one side. 'Oh, go on then.'

With a smug smile, I say, 'They're faster in water than on land and use their long arms to propel themselves through water.'

Dexter whistles. 'You're good. Question three. Why do sloths come down to the forest floor and how often?'

'Too easy. Once a week, to poop.'

'Right again. OK, I can see I'll need to really think hard about this final question.' He waits a moment then raises his finger in an a-ha motion. 'Got it. Which country has the most sloths?'

I tap a finger against my lips as if thinking. 'Well, since Brazil has the most species of sloth and is the biggest country with sloths in it, I'll go Brazil.'

'Oh dear,' says Dexter, shaking his head, and for a moment I think I have it wrong, but then he grins. 'I thought I'd got you that time. Well, four out of four. I did promise you could meet the sloths if you passed. So, are you ready?'

'Oh yes.' I'm just about to leap out of my seat when the door opens and Carlos strolls in, more than a little flustered. 'Dexter, it's a no-go. I tried, but the circumstances are out of my control.' He shrugs and raises his hands in resignation.

Dexter's face falls but he quickly recovers. 'We'll work something out, Carlos. Don't worry. I'll look into it. OK if I take Kat to see our behind-the-scenes sloths?'

'Of course.' Carlos' worry lines are momentarily replaced with laughter lines. 'See you later, Kat.' As he wanders off, I can't help but notice Carlos' smile disappearing and a frown appearing on Dexter's face.

'Is everything OK?' I ask.

Dexter sighs. 'We've had a volunteer pull out at the last minute and Carlos is panicking a little.'

Now it's my turn to frown. 'Isn't it easy enough to get a replacement?'

'You'd think, wouldn't you, but no,' Dexter says, hand on the door. 'Hoops to jump through, and we need to actively recruit them too.' He falls silent and as he pushes the door open, I take that to mean the subject's closed.

As I follow, Dexter turns back to me. 'You're in for a treat. This is our nursery.' He stands aside to reveal a room where a woman is sitting surrounded by tiny baskets. In each basket is a baby sloth. They are the epitome of cuteness.

I stand and watch as the woman feeds milk to one of the babies through a pipette. When she has finished she dabs its adorable little mouth with a handkerchief. I so wish Dad could have seen this. My chest tightens and for a moment I can barely breathe as grief catches me unawares again.

Inside the baskets are little blankets and teddy bears. I frown in puzzlement and Dexter says, 'They're orphans. The teddy is to make them feel as if their mother is still with them.'

Oh my goodness, could this place be more wonderful?

I turn to see a slightly older pup climbing the blinds.

'That's Speedy. He keeps trying to escape, but he's not quite ready. Hopefully, we can release him back into the wild next week.'

I stare at Dexter. 'Speedy?'

Dexter grins. 'We have to get our kicks somehow.'

I smirk. 'So naming sloths is as good as it gets, is it?' Crikey, where did that flirtatious tone come from?

'Oh, I think we can do better than that, but anyway, you ain't seen nothing yet.' He points at a tiny sloth pup, asleep under a pink blanket. 'This is Rocket. We've paired her up with Bullet, another orphan.' He indicates the basket beside it, with the powder-blue blanket. They are so adorable.

He gestures with one hand to the sloth on the sofa. Yes, there's a sloth on the sofa. 'That's Zoom, and now we just have to find a name for the three-month-old sloth that came in this morning. He's being checked over right now.'

'This is incredible. How many sloths do you have here?'

Dexter does a quick calculation. 'With our new arrival today, we have twenty-five. On that note, would you like to name our new sloth? I can't take you in to visit him as he's still in pretty bad shape, but I do like to name them on the first day.'

'Oh my God, really? I'd love that.'

'Sure. The only thing is, you've seen the style of our

names for the sloths. Can you come up with something that would fit?'

That lump returns to my throat. 'Yeah, I have one that would be perfect. Flash.'

'Ha! Flash. I like it.' He writes out a name tag and tucks it into his pocket.

There you go, Dad. Gordon MacDonald, also known as Flash to his friends after Flash Gordon, will be immortalised in Costa Rica as Flash the sloth. *So even though you didn't get to make the trip, a part of you will stay behind.*

Dexter claps his hands together. 'Right, let me show you the adults.'

By the time I've met the other sloths and Dexter has filled me in on some of their backstories, I'm mentally exhausted, but also exhilarated.

'Have you eaten?' Dexter says. 'I have some tasks I have to take care of after lunch, but we could grab something back in the canteen. Sofia cooks for us and she makes some mouthwatering dishes.'

'If I'm not putting you out, that would be great. Thank you.' My stomach growls and we both laugh.

Dexter holds the door open for me. 'Your internal clock's working fine, I see.'

We walk into the staff canteen and an incredible smell assaults my senses. 'Mmm.'

'Yeah, that's *casado.* Pork today, with rice, beans, some salad and a side order of cabbage. Sound good?'

'Very.'

Sofia is standing at a serving hatch, a wide smile on her face. 'How has your day been so far, Kat?'

I give a happy little sigh. 'Unbelievable. I even got

to name the new arrival.'

Her eyes twinkle. 'Ah, a special moment indeed.' She dishes out two plates of *casado* and hands them to us.

'*Gracias*,' I say.

She smiles. '*Pura vida. ¡Buen provecho!*

I'm sure I'll enjoy it very much indeed.

Lunch is delicious, including the fried yucca, which is tastier than it sounds. Kind of like a sweet, nutty potato. As I eat, or rather savour, the food, Dexter asks me about myself, and I, in not so equal measure, grill him on how a guy from Waterford ended up in Costa Rica.

Finally, Dexter leans back in his chair and groans. 'I'm stuffed. It was so good, but I'll pay for it later.' He leans forward again and takes a sip of his drink.

I laugh. 'I think I may have overindulged, too, but same as you, it was too good not to finish it.' I sip my *agua dulce*.

'So, do you only love sloths or are you an all-round animal lover?' he asks.

'I love all animals, and in fact, I wanted to be a vet, and go to the vet school at Glasgow uni, but I didn't get in, so I've spent the past...' I wave my hand around, trying to pluck a number out of thin air '...ten years working in pet supplies sales.'

Dexter frowns. Yeah, I've lost him. It always happens when I mention my job. It's mind-numbingly boring.

'Couldn't you have done something else with animals? I mean, nothing against your current job, but you're obviously passionate about them. The very fact you applied to vet school shows that.'

'There wasn't really anything available at the time, and then I kinda fell into sales, and well, I had bills to pay. Life got in the way.' I give him a rueful smile and he returns it.

'And you've never thought of having another crack at studying to be a vet?'

'I'd love to, of course I would, but I think I've missed the boat and the competition for those courses is immense.' Something prevents me from telling him about the access course I did the past two years, eager to reignite my dream. Shame? Embarrassment that it was all for nothing?

He looks thoughtful for a moment.

'What?' I ask, wondering if I have a piece of yucca stuck in my teeth or something.

'Do you like your job?'

I shrug. 'It has its moments. I like the people I work with.'

'Yes, the people are very important.' He pauses for a moment. 'And do you have family back home?'

'Just my mum. My dad passed last year.'

'I'm so sorry to hear that. That must have been tough.' His stricken face shows me he's annoyed at himself for putting his foot in it.

'Yeah, it was. Dad and I were so close. He's who inspired my love of animals.' My voice cracks. 'He's who I was originally meant to make this trip with.'

Dexter's face blanches.

'Oh my goodness. Are you OK?' I nod then he says, 'Wait, who did you come with then?'

I smile wryly. 'My boyfriend. Now my ex-boyfriend.'

Dexter's face is a picture. 'Jesus. You *have* had a run of terrible luck. Not that your dad passing was bad luck. I mean, obviously, it was awful, but–'

'Dexter–' I rest my hand on his arm '–stop digging yourself in deeper.'

'Right. Right.' He shakes his head as if he's just woken up from hibernating all winter and is having difficulty processing what's happening.

'It's fine, really. And today Nicolás, Oscar and Ed brought me here as they knew this was my whole reason for coming to Costa Rica.'

'Your whole reason?' Dexter's eye contact is a tad unnerving now.

'Well, ninety per cent of it. Obviously, the coffee's not bad here, and it'll be cool to see the volcano and the other national parks, but yes, the sloths were my reason for coming. That and to fulfil mine and Dad's dream.' I inhale a deep breath and say, 'Dexter, this may be a little off beam, but could I be a volunteer?'

'What? You? Here?'

I'm nodding vigorously now.

'Yep, me, here. How about I take the place of the volunteer who had to drop out?' I raise my hands and shrug as if the solution is simple.

Dexter mulls this over for a second, his eyes wide as if he can't quite believe I've fallen into his lap. Actually, I can think of worse places to be, and I don't just mean the sanctuary.

'You could. We could teach you.' And then he's off on one, babbling excitedly, trying to find a reason not to and failing. A broad smile breaks across his face as my brain struggles to process everything he's saying to me. Could I really stay and work with the sloths?

Today is the happiest I've felt in I don't know how long. Caring for the sloths would be even better than going to vet school, even though it won't provide the same financial reward. It's a moot point anyway. I didn't get in, again, and I'm definitely not applying a third time.

Dare I reach for the stars, take the chance of a lifetime and become the Costa Punta sloth sanctuary's newest volunteer?

Chapter Four

'You're what?' Becca shrieks when I call her on my return to the hotel.

I allow myself a smile at the incredulity in her voice and the expression of disbelief on her face. Isn't video-calling wonderful? Becca is the most adventurous person I know and even she's gobsmacked by what I'm considering.

'Thinking about becoming a volunteer in a sloth sanctuary,' I say again.

'God, Kat, I know you can be impulsive, but this is huge even by your standards. You certainly don't do things by halves. Bust up with your about to be live-in lover one day, move to Costa Rica the next to work with your favourite animals.'

She's not wrong there. My life has gone from ordinary, to extraordinary, to off the chart in the space of only a few days. No more humdrum for me. My thoughts flit to my job at Peterson's Pet Supplies. Can I ditch the security it offers me? It's not the most exciting job, and it pays the bills, but it was always meant to be a stopgap. A stopgap that has lasted almost ten years.

'I know, Becca, it sounds crazy, but what do you really think? Honestly. Could I do it?' When she doesn't answer straight away, I prod her. 'Would you?'

She's quicker with her comeback this time. 'You know I would, if it were my sort of thing. If you stay, I'm definitely coming for a holiday.'

So not an outright no, then. Phew! I really value Becca's opinion; I always have.

'But, Kat, what about your mum? What about your job? What about the paperwork? Visa? Money? You're not me. You prefer the safer option usually.'

I mull this over as I digest her barrage of questions. 'Mum will be as fine as she ever is where I'm concerned. And maybe this is the kick up the backside I needed to leave Peterson's. I mean, it's hardly my dream job, is it?'

She murmurs her agreement.

'And as for the paperwork, Dexter says he and Carlos would sort all that for me.'

'Well, that's certainly one hurdle out of the way,' Becca says. 'But it's a volunteer post, so what will you live on? And don't you have to pay a fee to be a volunteer?'

I chew on my lip. The downside to video-calling is people can see all your facial expressions and not just have to work out what you're thinking from your tone.

'I do have some savings, but meals are paid for, and I don't need to pay any rent, obviously. They've waived the fee, as I'm helping them out of a jam, plus the other volunteer's deposit was non-refundable, and of course they didn't have to pay any travel costs for me to get here.'

Becca tilts her head to the side. 'Kat, I think you have your answer. Those were the only obstacles I could think of, and you know me, I'm a throw caution to the wind kinda person. I can already see how happy you are at the mere thought of doing this, nuts though it all may seem at the moment. Imagine how happy you'll be once you start living that dream.'

Becca's cornflower-blue eyes bore into mine then she quirks an eyebrow. 'Right?'

With a rush of resolve, and a good dollop of bravery, I decide to seize the day.

'Becca, I'm doing it! I'm going to volunteer at a sloth sanctuary!'

'Yay! An early birthday present to yourself!' She claps her hands together so hard and fast her wavy red hair bounces around her shoulders.

I've almost forgotten what day it is. Of course, two days until my thirtieth birthday and although it's going to be quite different to the day I imagined, I can't wait.

Next morning, I've just come out of the shower when my phone rings.

'Kat, it's Dexter. The answer's yes. Carlos is on board.'

'Oh, that's fantastic. You have no idea how happy that makes me.'

A tiny part of me hopes Dexter's happy about it too. I give an infinitesimal shake of my head. I'm so not ready to get embroiled in anything else, romantically, but he is easy on the eye, which is always a bonus.

'Would you be able to come back to the sanctuary tomorrow at some point to go through everything and then we can sort a start date?' he asks, with what I think is a note of hope in his voice.

I hesitate and Dexter must take this as uncertainty as he jumps in with, 'Sorry. Of course, you'll have lots to sort out in the UK, too.'

'No, it's not that. It's just, tomorrow's my birthday, my thirtieth birthday, and I fancied doing something special for it.'

'No problem. I understand. And happy birthday for tomorrow,' Dexter says. 'Would today be too soon, or how about the day after tomorrow?'

'Today's fine. I do have some things to take care of back home, but they can wait.'

'Excellent. How about I swing by and pick you up? You don't have a car, I'm guessing, so getting here is a bit tricky by public transport.'

I snort. 'I'll say. And if we can do it in a way that avoids the crocodile-infested swamp-river, I'd be ever so grateful.'

Dexter laughs. 'No problem. Yes, once is enough for the scenic route. See you in a couple of hours.'

I'm almost fizzing with happiness at the thought of working with animals, properly, not some sideline where I sell pet food supplies in the hope of one day, somehow, making the leap to working with animals again. And I won't be just working with any animals, but my favourite animals, sloths. I only wish I had someone here with me who I could share my wonderful news with. Someone who matters to me. Like Dad. I cough past the tennis-ball-sized lump in my throat.

Suddenly, I know for sure I'm doing the right thing. This is what Dad would have wanted, and although I'm doing it ninety-five per cent for me, five per cent of me is doing it for him.

Doing what he never could, what he could never have even dreamed of. Isn't life strange? Sometimes life gives you lemons – Aidan – and you can either suck it up, or make lemonade. Costa Rica and the Costa Punta sloth sanctuary will be my lemonade, and I can't wait to start.

The rest of the morning is spent making a list of all the things I need to take care of back home, as well as advising reception I'll be checking out in a couple of days, and cancelling my flight. I tap out a text to Becca first. *All done. I'm going to live in a sloth sanctuary! x*

A few seconds later, she replies. *Always said you were a lazy git!* She signs off with a plethora of emojis, including a love heart one, a PMSL one, a winking one, and ten sloths. She's mad. And I love her, and couldn't wish for a better best friend. If anyone can help me with this transition, particularly from afar, it's Becca. And I don't doubt that she'll do her best to come visit.

I've decided to put off telling Mum for a few days until I've settled in and dealt with the paperwork. I've emailed my boss, explaining the situation to him, and apologising, but laying it on quite thick about this being my dream life. I also reminded him I have four weeks' annual leave accrued, so I'm taking those holidays now. Plus, I know who will step into my shoes. Leona. And we have plenty of staff who are always looking for extra shifts. It's unnerving to realise how little I'll be missed, after ten years. I mean, I don't exactly need a carriage clock or a party in my honour, but knowing that you're just a number stings. The upside is, it makes jacking in your job a heck of a lot easier.

Lunch is a salad that I take with me down to the pool area, where I see Nicolás talking with Ed, then I spot Oscar in the water.

Ed raises his hand in salute, so I wander over with my salad and sit down beside him and Nicolás as Oscar climbs out of the pool.

'So, did Sofia and Carlos go for it?' Ed asks.

He doesn't say anything else, which I like. I can tell he doesn't want to be too pushy.

I'm unable to prevent myself from my smiling. 'Indeed they did.'

They wait expectantly for me to deliver my verdict. 'I can't wait to start! Dexter is picking me up in half an hour then we'll return to the sanctuary to go over the details and paperwork.'

Oscar beams at me. 'Oh, Kat, you'll make a wonderful volunteer.' He stands and gives me a hug, which is kind of at arm's length as he is still a little wet from his swim.

'Congratulations.' Ed grins at me. 'Lads, one more for our nights out.'

I scrunch my eyebrows. 'Nights out?'

'Yeah, you didn't think you were moving to some backwater, did you? The nightlife here rocks. And you'll have to meet my wife, Gloriana. I have a feeling you're going to have so much in common. Just don't let her talk nappies to you. Downside of having a baby and a toddler.'

Nicolás kisses me on the cheek. I'm surprised when

he doesn't kiss me on the other cheek. Maybe that's only a European thing. 'Don't listen to him. Gloriana is far more interesting than he is. I'm so happy you're going to be working at the sanctuary. I know I'm biased, as they're my family, but Carlos and Sofia are amazing.'

Ed sets his water down on the ground. 'It's true. They are. Two of the kindest people you could ever meet.'

'And Dexter's a great deputy manager,' says Nicolás. 'He's really good with people.'

Do I detect an undercurrent of something in his voice? Humour, perhaps. Whatever, I'm turning red. Hopefully, it will pass as sunburn. Sure, Dexter's good-looking, but I have literally just come out of a long-term relationship two days ago. The last thing I need is another complication. I still have that to sort out back home. At least now I can do it from a different country, no, a different continent, and somehow that makes it more palatable.

'And sloths,' says Oscar. 'Total animal lover.'

Why do I get the feeling they're trying to sell me Dexter? Not like you'd need to. Like I said, he's gorgeous, but even so, I almost feel like they're matchmaking.

Well, a new job in the Tropics I may be up for, a new boyfriend I'm not. I plan on staying resolutely single for a really long time. Almost moving in with Aidan will do that to a girl.

As I listen to Nicolás recount numerous tales of the sanctuary, I can't help wondering how Flash is faring. Hopefully, I'll find out this afternoon.

'Hi, guys, and Kat.'

I turn at the sound of Dexter's voice. He's wearing a white linen shirt and a pair of frayed cut-offs with trekker sandals. It's a definite improvement on the khaki sanctuary uniform. I sense the eyes of the other three boring into me as I turn round to greet him. Well, there'll be no show for them today.

'Dexter.' I stand. 'I'm ready to go. See you, boys.'

Dexter looks a little nonplussed, and for a nanosecond I feel guilty, but then I take in the three amigos' faces and realise I've done the right thing. Somehow, I just know they would have made little in-jokes and been winking at me behind his back if we'd stayed. Let me get this part over with, the formalities, before I change my mind. Although, as I follow Dexter, I have to admit wild horses wouldn't drag me away now. And at least now the boys won't see how red my face has become, because either my face is scarlet or I'm going through the menopause twenty years too early.

As we make the journey back to the sanctuary, Dexter fills me in a little on the history of the area. The road is a little bumpy in parts, but it's still preferable to risking my life by canoeing along the swampy river. That's not an experience I wish to repeat in a hurry, or at all.

Dexter rattles off some of the formalities, too, about various pieces of paperwork that are now in progress.

'You have to apply for a provisional visa to do volunteer work, but I don't foresee any problems. We know someone at the department, someone we usually work with when hiring volunteers, so it hopefully won't take too long.'

'That's good. And what about after that?' I ask, clutching the grab handle with one hand as the truck lists to the side slightly.

'Carlos and I will prepare the documents with you for the consulate. Once we have the provisional visa, we'll finalise the process. And if all else fails, we can always nip over to Nicaragua or Panama to satisfy the requirements.'

I give a silent sigh of relief and cough slightly at his usage of satisfy. Aren't there pirates in Nicaragua, though?

Dexter's face creases into a smile. 'Don't look so worried. It's all in hand. Promise.'

Somehow, that reassures me. I've given more thought to what I'm having for my dinner than I have this madcap move to Costa Rica. It's only natural I'll experience some level of apprehension. And since I tend to play things safe, this is a very big departure for me.

'How's Flash?' I ask, changing the subject.

Dexter nods. 'Good. He's coming along really well. He has even taken a little milk this morning. Luciana will sort him out. We'll soon have him driving us nuts hanging from the blinds like the others.'

I'm delighted to hear the little guy is OK, but it occurs to me that they must lose sloths sometimes. Surely not all of them can be saved, but I can't bring the topic up right now. It'll have to wait for another day. Today is to be a happy, if overwhelming, day.

Through the window, I note the different colours of hibiscus: yellow, orange, purple, white. The landscape is so pretty, so picture perfect, no wonder the *Condé Nast* I read on the plane named it the most beautiful country in the world. A smile curves my lips upwards. I'm going to be living here, and all I can think is '*Wow!*'

'Here we are.' Dexter finally pulls up at a tall green wooden gate. This must be the tradesman's entrance to the sanctuary. I haven't seen any signposts for it.

He jumps out and opens the gate by punching a code into a small black box to the left-hand side.

We're in a courtyard with two identical buildings opposite each other, which look like accommodation blocks, and another building, which I think may be the rear of the main sanctuary I was in yesterday. A wooden house, painted blue, with a lean-to and a wraparound veranda stands off to one side. In the centre of the courtyard there's some kind of meeting place, with several wooden garden chairs, a couple of benches and a rattan sofa around a firepit. Fresh flowers in pots are dotted around the exterior of the blue house and the blocks.

'C'mon,' Dexter says. 'This way.' He leads me down a path covered by a canopy of trees. It ends in a rather nondescript entrance with a keypad and doorbell.

As we enter, Sofia catches sight of us and comes towards us, beaming, then almost suffocates me in a bear hug as Dexter leaves me to it. 'I am so happy you are going to be part of our family.'

I smile, a little overwhelmed, but totally taken with the sanctuary matriarch.

'Me too,' I say as she fusses round me, shepherding

me to one of the offices where Dexter and Carlos are deep in discussion.

'Ah, she's here.' Carlos rises from his chair and envelops me in a hug. It's rather disconcerting being embraced in this way, but I'm sure I'll get used to it.

'I'll leave you with the boys.' Sofia casts an endearing look at Carlos, who returns it.

Dexter smiles and gives me a nod. Pity it wasn't a hug from Dexter. *Shut up. You're just out of a relationship. A messy one.* Yes, but you'd need to be blind to not admire the fine specimen that Dexter is. I park those thoughts for later as Carlos speaks to me.

'Thank you so much, Kat, for plugging this gap. I don't know what we'd have done without you.'

I gulp. He has high expectations and I have no experience with sloths. He must read my mind as he says, 'Don't worry that you haven't worked with sloths before. I trust Dexter's instincts, and from what he has told me about you, you will fit in here perfectly and look after our babies as we would.'

He has that second part right. I hope the first part will come true, too.

I glance at Dexter, who's sitting with his arms crossed, a playful but smug smile on his lips. *Thank you*, I mouth.

Suddenly, I can't wait to get started. It hits me, like a blow to my solar plexus, how real this is. I'm moving to the jungle. A week ago, if you'd told me this, I'd have laughed in your face. A week ago I'd been trying to convince our biggest client not to move to another pet supply company, and had given them a further ten per cent discount to keep their business. A week ago I had a boyfriend. A week ago I was planning to move in with him. Today, I live in the rainforest and work with sloths. A burst of joy radiates from me and my whole body fizzes with pleasure. I'm about to sign paperwork which will allow me to be here, with my favourite animals, working in close proximity with a man whom I already respect and, if I'm entirely honest with myself, could ogle much of the day as he's bloody gorgeous. Plus, I have the bonus of my bosses being total sweethearts. And I'm going to hang on to this new bout of luck with both hands.

Once we've gone through the relevant paperwork, Carlos claps his hands together. 'Right, I have some business I need to take care of. Dexter, can you show Kat to the accommodation block and where everything is?'

'Sure. Then I was thinking we could go see how Flash is doing.'

'Great idea,' Carlos and I say at the same time, then we laugh.

'See, we are in synchrony already.' Carlos pats me on the shoulder. 'Have fun with Dexter.'

Oh, don't worry. I intend to.

Chapter Five

'So this is where we hang out in the evening.' Dexter indicates the firepit I'd seen when we arrived. 'The weather's usually pleasant enough for us all to chat here after dinner. Our meals are in the canteen we were in yesterday.' He hooks a thumb back the way we've come. 'Sofia cooks for us as you know, but if you want to cook for yourself, there are facilities for that too.' He pauses. 'Victor uses them, occasionally, as he's a chef-in-the making, but honestly, with Victor and Sofia's cooking, you won't need, or want, anything else.'

I absorb all this new information, and my mind wanders to what the dynamic will be like around the firepit. I envisage someone playing folk songs on guitar, as others sway to music on the dusty makeshift dance floor.

'And here's where we sleep.'

Warmth floods me at the idea that he is including me and him in that. We'll probably be at opposite ends of the building, but the fact we're under the same roof is enough to make my heart stutter.

I follow him into the low bungalow and discover there are almost as many flowers inside as out. Their scent hangs heavy in the air – it's like a mix of honeysuckle and jasmine, with a hint of citrus, and my nostrils twitch in appreciation.

'This is the men's residence. There are five of us. I'll introduce you to everyone after we check in on Flash.' He hesitates for a second and I have a burning desire to stroke the soft stubble that graces his chin. I shake my head as if to dislodge that idea from my mind and he shoots me a quizzical glance. I wait, unable to think of any explanation. His eyes narrow and he smiles. It makes me wonder what he's thinking. Does he think I want to meet all the men? Given my reaction he could well be thinking that. Yes, I'm keen to meet everyone, but I'm not interested in romance, despite feeling more than a frisson of attraction towards Dexter. My life is currently too complicated as it is, and I still have an awful lot to unravel back home.

As we cross the courtyard to an identical block, I bat this thought away.

'And this is the women's residence. You'll be sharing this with Roisin, Ella, Mariangeles and Federica.'

This time he opens the door to the block, which takes us into a corridor with eight doors leading off of it, four on either side. It's relatively spartan, but with a few nice touches: a vase of fresh flowers, whose name eludes me; a framed print of a beach – I'm hoping that's nearby as it looks gorgeous; and a wooden map of Costa Rica showcasing the seven provinces. We're in Puntarenas now. For a moment, I thought it was going to be just like going on a school Outward Bound trip, with us all bunking up in one dormitory, rows of bunk beds and absolutely no privacy. I breathe an audible sigh of relief, and Dexter laughs. 'You thought you were going to be in for some boarding-school-type dorm, didn't you?'

I grin. 'You're not exactly right, but you're not far off the mark.'

We walk down the corridor and he explains there are five bedrooms, one rec room and two bathrooms.

'Yours is the room at the end on the right.' He passes me the key and I open the door to find a compact but sweet room, with yellow curtains covered in blue flowers. A wooden bed frame sits in the centre of the room which also houses a chair, a wardrobe with full-length mirror, a chest of drawers and a wash-hand basin. A bookcase made with some sort of hardwood with whorls in the grain stands off to the side. A glass vase filled with unusual-looking purple flowers sits on top. They're both beautiful and a little scary, with purple spikes on the outside, an aubergine inner and a yellow-green centre.

'Purple passionflower,' Dexter says as I stare at them, my brow creased.

'Really? They're rather on the prickly side.'

Dexter grins. 'A lot like some relationships.'

I relax at his easy banter and take in the room again. It's utilitarian, but has a few homely touches, and it'll do me just fine. I don't need much, just some space to reassess my life a little, and sumptuous trappings have never been my thing anyway.

'The bathrooms are right next door and across the hall on the left,' Dexter informs me.

Good. I wasn't exactly expecting an en suite, but neither had I thought that far ahead, and once again it strikes me how little consideration I've actually given to this major lifestyle change. But, hey, sometimes you need to throw caution to the wind, right?

'Why don't I give you a minute and I'll meet you outside?' His hundred-megawatt smile brightens the room further.

When he has gone, I stand in the middle of the room and imagine my few belongings that I have from home and how they'd fit in. I walk over to the bookcase and am delighted to see a few novels. Gabriel García Márquez and Isabel Allende are the only authors I recognise. Maybe I can use these books to help me with my Spanish, which it now looks like I'll need to brush up on more than ever. And here was me thinking I only needed it for a two-week trip. Once again, I wonder if I'm ready for this culture shock.

I spin around, committing the room to memory, then close the door and peek into the bathrooms, which I'm pleased to note have both shower and bath.

A minute later, I'm outside in the fresh air again, and the scent of the unusual blend of flowers inside fades before the sweet smell of hibiscus hits me.

'Suit your needs?' Dexter asks.

I sigh. 'Perfectly.'

'Good. Now, let's go see how little Flash is getting on.' He holds his arm out, gesturing for me to walk ahead of him, and we return to the sanctuary through the rear door. As he puts the four-digit code in, he says, 'Fourteen-oh-nine. You'll need to remember that. You're one of us now.'

'Fourteen-oh-nine,' I parrot back. 'Is that a special day in Costa Rica's history or something?'

'Or something. It's a special day for the sanctuary. Ferdinand's birthday.'

Aw, how sweet is that? I love this place more and more by the minute.

We head for the nursery where Luciana is busy cradling another sloth, none of those I saw yesterday, in her arms.

'Hi, Luciana. Remember Kat? She's going to be working here as a volunteer. We just came to check on Flash.'

'Nice to meet you, Kat. I'd greet you properly, but I'm a little busy.'

I wave my hand to dismiss her concerns. 'No problem. Who's this little guy, or girl?' I haven't checked his or her undercarriage so I can't tell for sure.

'Boy. This is Bolt. He's a little wary.'

Now she's said it, I can see how nervy he seems. I'm not sure how old he is exactly, but he's really clinging on to Luciana; it's clear he has no intention of letting her go. Belatedly, I note she's wearing soft leather gloves, I guess to protect herself from any major damage being inflicted upon her by her timid companion.

Dexter says, 'Bolt came to us after his mother was electrocuted on power lines. Sadly, it's one of the main reasons sloths end up here. That and them being run over on the few occasions they make it to the rainforest floor. They're safe here, but near the highways not so much. He's a little skittish, and who can blame him?'

Poor little guy. 'How old is he?'

'He's about six months. It's hard to be certain, but we try to gauge from their teeth and claws, but since their claws grow at an incredible rate, it's impossible to know for sure.'

I didn't know that. Some vet I'd have made. This is definitely going to be a learning-on-the-job role.

'Anyway, now for Flash.' Dexter walks ahead of me, through a door into the 'hospital'. 'Ah, there he is.' He points to a transparent incubator, where Flash is fast asleep.

I frown. 'Is he … is he sucking his thumb?'

Dexter and Luciana both laugh.

'He is,' says Dexter. 'Just like human babies, sloths comfort themselves by sucking their thumbs, or claws, however you want to see it.'

Dexter speaks rapidly with Luciana and I struggle to keep up, although I catch the gist of it. Seems like Flash is doing OK.

'He needs to put on quite a bit more weight, but he's stable, and as you can see, sleeping. Why don't we go get a drink and I'll explain our daily routine to you, then I'll introduce you to the team?'

'Sounds like a plan.'

We say goodbye to Luciana then walk into the main area of the sanctuary where visitors are still visible, listening with rapt attention as Carlos speaks, Ferdinand, as ever, attached to his side.

'Luciana doesn't live in the sanctuary, but the rest of us do. We work six days a week, on rotation. There's always plenty of work to do around here, but we do find some time to kick back and relax.'

Glad to hear it, although to be fair, my current idea of R&R is sitting cuddling a baby sloth. *You wouldn't mind a cuddle from Dexter, either,* a naughty little voice in my head tells me. I tell it to shut up.

'That's Alejandro.' He indicates a guy of around twenty who's busy sweeping the foyer floor.

'The thing with wild animals is, you can't tell them where to poop.'

'Indeed,' I agree.

'Alejandro, this is Kat. She's our new volunteer.'

Alejandro raises a gloved hand and lets forth a torrent of rapid-fire Spanish that I think means, 'I'd shake your hand, but I stink.'

'You can tell he's young. He needs to work on how to talk to girls,' Dexter says. When I raise an eyebrow, he says, 'I'm joking. He has them falling at his feet. He doesn't even need to try.'

I appraise Alejandro again and see what Dexter means. He's lean and lightly muscled, like an Olympic athlete in training. We leave Alejandro and head round the side of the sanctuary to where some steel cages sit like a blot on the landscape. I wince and Dexter explains, 'Wholly necessary. The cages are for those adult sloths who, if released into the wild too early, wouldn't be strong enough to survive on their own, and who could very well end up back in here for a second, longer stretch, or who may, sadly, not be lucky enough to have that second chance.'

When I frown, he says, 'Carlos and Sofia learned that the hard way in the beginning. One sloth kept trying to escape, so they decided he was ready and released him, with a little tracker on him, as they do with all the sloths, to monitor their wellbeing and see how they're getting on. Unfortunately, the sloth was hit by a car less than a week later. Victor found it on the road and fetched help, but they couldn't save it.'

A lump forms in my throat and I try to gulp it away. Poor Carlos and Sofia. I know it's all part of the cycle of life and death, but it must still hurt like hell to know you've saved an animal, only for it later to be killed.

'Ah, there's Victor. He's feeding the adult sloths today, and cleaning out their cages.' He turns and waves a hand in the air. 'Victor!'

A man wearing cut-offs and who is totally soaked from the waist down appears beside us.

'Hey, Victor. How's it going today?' Dexter fist bumps Victor, who has to be the other side of forty. He's also lucky if he's five foot three.

'Good. I only have Rapido's and Velocidad's cages to clean out and then I'm done.' He turns to me then. 'Ah, you must be the new volunteer. Do you speak Spanish?' When I say, '*Sí*,' he goes on, 'I'm sorry, I've forgotten your name.' He turns to Dexter. 'Did you tell me it?'

Dexter shakes his head. 'Not had time for a proper chat with you for a few days. This is Kat. She's from back home.'

'Ah, you're Irish then? Like Roisin? My goodness, half of Ireland will be here soon.'

'Not Irish, Scottish,' I correct gently.

'Ah, Scotland, Nessie, *Braveheart*, The Proclaimers.'

I burst out laughing. Nothing like a good stereotype to act as an ice-breaker.

'My apologies,' says Dexter. 'I just meant the UK and Ireland, or quite frankly, Europe. No offence meant.'

I smile up at him. 'None taken.' How could I take offence when he is looking at me like that?

Victor wipes his hand on his relatively clean shorts. 'Pleased to meet you, Kat. Sorry. I've been busy hosing down the cages and I'm sure I have more water on myself than on the floors.' He indicates his clothing. 'Anyway, you're going to love it here.'

We shake hands and I answer various questions Victor poses about Scotland. Do I know anyone who lives in a castle? Do I have a tartan? Have I ever eaten haggis? He's clearly warming to his theme.

Finally, he says, 'Anyway, I must get back to work, but I'll see you at dinner, Kat.'

As he wanders off, I arch an eyebrow at Dexter. 'Dinner?'

'Yes. You know, third meal of the day? You eat, don't you?'

'Of course. I just didn't realise I was invited.'

'Well, now you know. Plus, soon you'll be living here, so you may as well get into the way of things already.'

True.

'We'll meet the girls at dinner. I think Roisin and Mariangeles are in town running some errands. They were early shift this morning.' He looks at his watch. 'And if I'm not mistaken, Ella will be taking over from Luciana in the nursery shortly. Luciana finishes at four to pick up her kids.'

So many names. There's not a chance I'll remember them all, so I don't even try. I'll have plenty of time. We're going to be in forced proximity, after all, and as I glance around, I realise there aren't exactly many other things around to escape to. I've gone from living in a city to living where sloths outnumber people, well, within the sanctuary at least.

'Ah, Roisin, you're back,' says Dexter. 'Did you get everything?'

I turn, curious to meet one of my new housemates.

'We did. Dexter, a word, please.'

'Sure. But first, can I introduce Kat, our new volunteer?'

'Nice to meet you.' I go to shake hands with her, but she gestures that her hands are full of packages.

'Right. And you.' She gives me a fleeting smile, but it feels forced. 'Dexter, we need to talk.' She turns and walks away, clearly expecting him to follow her.

Dexter shoots me an apologetic glance and says, 'I'll be right back, Kat.'

I frown. What is with Roisin? Is it something I said? Or did? She definitely doesn't seem pleased to see me. Is life at Costa Punta not going to be as blissful as I first thought?

Chapter Six

An hour later, I'm sitting next to Federica, with Mariangeles on the other side of her. Neither could be lovelier to me. Federica tells me she's twenty-six, originally from Colombia and has been here two years. Mariangeles is Peruvian and arrived the day after her. You can just tell they're best friends, and they do look like two peas in a pod, not physically, but they're like an old married couple, or siblings the way they go on. It's endearing and makes me smile.

Dexter is sitting opposite me, Victor on one side, Carlos on the other. Sofia is down the other end of the table, next to Roisin, and I take a moment to assess her whilst Mariangeles and Federica engage in a non-argument to see who's right about some song that was top of the chart in 2015. Roisin is striking: jet-black hair, blue eyes, eyeliner – seriously, does she think the sloths care? – perfect white teeth, and tall. When she was standing beside me earlier, I had to look up at her. She must be five ten, at least. And she has that creamy Irish complexion but no freckles.

I wonder what her beef is with me. She seems to have taken an instant dislike to me. My thoughts are interrupted by Victor leaning across the table to ask me which part of Scotland I'm from, and if I have indeed seen the Loch Ness monster. I can't tell if he's kidding about the second thing, but I tell him I'm from Glasgow, and he then asks if that's near where the Loch Ness monster lives. I get the impression this conversation could last some time, so I excuse myself and head for the bathroom.

As I come out of the cubicle, Roisin is standing applying lipstick. Lipstick! Has she mistaken Costa Rica for Beverly Hills? Or maybe I'm just too casual, since I can't imagine tarting myself up for an informal dinner in a sloth sanctuary with my workmates. I reckon she's at least a couple of years older than me. Yes, she gives the impression of someone who looks after herself. I'm guessing thirty-five.

'Hi, Roisin. I've not had a chance to talk to you yet.'

She gives me a look which if it had a speech bubble attached to it would probably read, 'So what?'

She doesn't even acknowledge me, well, not with any words; her mouth simply closes in a firm line.

I flounder a little at her rudeness and finally say, 'Victor tells me you're Irish.'

I'm sure she said something under her breath, but I can't be certain what, although it sounded suspiciously like 'Riveting.'

Rude cow. What's got her goat? 'Anyway, I'm looking forward to us working together. See you later.'

I can't get out of the door fast enough, but I don't miss the expression on her face that quite clearly shows she isn't looking forward to working with me. Perhaps I'm being overly sensitive, but I don't think so.

When I return to the table, I focus on those who've made me feel welcome – everyone else – and we have a lovely time. The food is good – rice with *palmito*. I hadn't come across *palmito* in my guide book, but Mariangeles fills me in, as she and Federica fight over which is the best of Costa Rica's dishes, despite neither being Costa Rican.

That's when Victor decides to weigh in, as a veritable authority on Costa Rican food. As a proud Costa Rican, and being of more advanced years than the rest of us, in some cases not by much, he gives us the lowdown on what constitutes the nation's most famous dishes, as well as those that don't make the top ten in guide books, but which should absolutely make our to-try lists.

So, as Victor reliably informs me, *palmito* is palm hearts from the palm tree, and is best served with cherry tomatoes and lettuce, but it has been paired with béchamel sauce. Seriously, what's not to like? It is a taste sensation and I soon devour every mouthful, not having realised exactly how long it has been since I last ate, nor how ravenous I'd become.

I pop the final forkful in my mouth only to sense someone watching me. When I glance up, Dexter's eyes are on me.

'Good, isn't it?' he says.

Since my mouth is full, I simply nod, but as I shift slightly to reach my water glass, my gaze takes in the full length of the table and its occupants. Roisin is staring straight at me and if looks could kill … well, let's just say, I'd no longer be among the living.

Federica takes in my empty plate. 'Ah, you liked it.

Good. Mariangeles, pass me the *palmito*. Kat is empty.'

I make to protest, but Mariangeles is already passing the bowl down and then Federica piles some more *palmito* on my plate. She beams at me and I thank her.

Once she has said, 'You're welcome,' she turns away to pass the serving bowl back to Mariangeles, and I sigh and take in the heaped portion of my *arroz con palmito*. Don't they realise rice is filling? How can they all be rake-thin if they eat like this? Or maybe they just expect me, a guest, to eat like this.

'You don't need to eat it all,' a voice says.

I glance up and Dexter's eyes meet mine. 'Sorry?'

'They must think you need fattening up, but Sofia honestly won't be offended if you don't finish it.'

I blow out a breath. 'Thanks. I'll remember that, but yes, I couldn't eat another bite. I'm stuffed full.'

Silence falls over us for a few moments before Dexter says, 'So, when would you like to start? I know you have some of your holiday still to go.'

I bite my lip, thinking about how long it took me to save up for this holiday and how long I've waited, and all the wonderful places I wanted to visit. On the one hand, it goes against the grain to waste money, but on the other hand, opportunities like this never come up. I make a snap decision. 'I want to dive right in. Perhaps not tomorrow, but the day after. Would that be OK?'

'That would be perfect. But what about all the tourist things you came here to do?'

I shrug. 'I figure I'll have days off and maybe if anyone else is off that day, they'd like to come too.'

Dexter nods. 'I don't think you'll have a problem getting company, I mean, people to come with you.' He reddens slightly and it's adorable, as if I was going to misinterpret his 'company' comment, although I can't help thinking I wouldn't mind him being the one keeping me company, platonically or otherwise. For goodness' sake. Am I on heat or something? A guy throws a few nice words my way and is kind to me and I'm almost imagining him naked.

'Hey, Kat, I heard you were here. How's it going?'

I glance over Dexter's head to see Ed with a guy I glimpsed earlier, but who I wasn't introduced to.

'Great, thanks. You didn't tell me you were coming here. What've you been up to? And are you sure you actually have a home?'

Ed laughs then puts his arm around the man beside him. 'Javier and I have been fishing. Well, I say "we", Javi has been fishing and I've been taking photographs.'

He takes out his phone and shows me a few pics of brightly coloured birds. There's one of a green and red bird with a little tufty patch on its head.

'Is that a quetzal?' I ask.

'Yes, well done.' He looks impressed, as does Dexter.

I grin. 'I knew my quizzing would come in useful sometime.'

Dexter and I share a smile. I guess he's remembering, as I am, the sloth quiz he gave me to see if I was worthy enough to meet their sloths in the animal hospital.

'Did you catch anything, Javi?' Dexter asks.

'I did, indeed. A *machaca*. Three point seven kilos.'

'Wow, that's a big guy.' Dexter's eyes widen.

'Yep,' Ed agrees, 'and here's Javi with his prize.' He angles his body so he can show both of us the photo on his phone.

'Nice catch,' Dexter says. He hesitates a second. 'Javi, sorry, have you met Kat?'

Javier shakes his head. 'No, but I'm guessing you're the new volunteer Papa was talking about.'

I dip my head. 'That's me. Nice to meet you, Javi. I've heard a lot about you from Nicolás.'

'Oh no!' He covers his face with his hands. 'It's lies, all lies.'

I smile. Nicolás wasn't kidding when he said they were like brothers.

'Anyway, Kat, if you're good to go after dinner, I'll take you back, save Dexter here a trip,' says Ed.

'That would be great, thanks. Let me just say bye to Carlos and Sofia, and then I'm all yours.'

'Take your time. I'll be outside when you're ready.'

I turn to Dexter. 'So, I'll see you the day after tomorrow then.'.

He smiles and says in his delicious Irish brogue, 'Looking forward to it.'

It's almost like a physical wrench to move from the seat opposite Dexter, and for a moment it's like we're the only two people here. I'm only aware of him and me. Then the screech of a chair being pushed back knocks me out of my reverie and I stand and walk round to bid Sofia and Carlos goodnight.

After being inundated by hugs and kisses, not only from Carlos and Sofia, but also Mariangeles, Federica, Victor and Javier, I manage to disengage myself and catch Ed's eye.

As we drive back with the chirping of the cicadas around us, I can't help feeling that being driven back by Dexter wouldn't have been so bad, and I hope that my attraction to him doesn't become a problem.

Ed glances over at me. 'So it's your thirtieth tomorrow?'

'Yep, end of an era. The big three-oh.'

'Ah, that's pretty significant. Doing anything for it?'

'Well, originally I'd planned on going to the Monteverde Cloud Forest, but it might be too far and I haven't booked it.'

'A bit of an adrenalin junkie, are you?' Ed teases me.

'Not really, but I'm OK with zip wires and I just imagine that being on a mountain where you're almost in the clouds must be incredible and so much fun. And I've seen the photos. It looks amazing. But I think perhaps everything is catching up with me. I don't know if I have the energy now.'

'Are you talking about Aidan or moving to Costa Rica?' Ed prods gently.

I'm silent for a moment as I wrestle my way through my answer in my head. 'Possibly a bit of both. It's hitting me what a momentous decision I've made about moving here, in an insanely short space of time, but my gut tells me it's the right one.'

He nods, as if understanding.

'But I also know I still have to address the Aidan thing, and I haven't even told my mum I'm moving here yet. How messed-up is that?'

He remains silent, which I'm thankful for.

'I feel as if I have a lot of mental baggage to unpack before I can fully align myself with my new life.' I half-turn in my seat towards him. 'Make sense?'

'Totally. Tell you what, how about this? Have a lie-in tomorrow, have a leisurely breakfast, do whatever you fancy, and then I'll take you out diving, if you want to, that is. That way, you're still doing something momentous on your birthday, without having to go far afield.'

A smile breaks across my face. 'Really?'

Ed grins. 'Really. You've had a shitty run of luck recently. Let's make being thirty the year that changes that.'

'I'll drink to that.'

'We can do that once we've had our dive.'

I laugh and settle back against the seat as we drive on in companionable silence.

'Kat, wake up. Ka-a-at.'

My eyelids are heavy as I struggle to open them. 'What time is it?'

Ed glances at the clock on the dashboard. 'Half past ten.'

'Oh God, I'm so sorry I fell asleep. Great passenger I am.'

Ed dismisses my concerns with a wave of his hand. 'Don't worry, you were obviously exhausted.'

I nod and yawn again, a huge unsightly, unrestrained yawn.

'God, I'm embarrassing.' I rub my eyes and drag

my fingers through my hair.

'At least there wasn't much drool,' Ed says, his lips twitching.

'I drooled?' Ground open up and swallow me.

He smirks. 'Kidding.'

I bat him on the arm. 'Thanks for bringing me back, but if we're going diving tomorrow, I'd best get some sleep.'

As I close the truck door, Ed calls, 'Night, Kat. Sleep well.'

Chapter Seven

Birdsong wakes me. My eyelids are glued shut, and I struggle, disorientated, trying to work out where I am, and what day and time it is. Finally, I bolt upright. That's not birdsong, it's my mobile.

Mum.

It's my birthday. My thirtieth birthday. She'll be calling to wish me happy birthday.

'Hi, Mum.'

'Kat, what the hell is going on? What are you still doing in Costa Rica?'

What? I'm supposed to be here for another week.

'Mum. It's a two-week holiday.' And what on earth is she so angry about? I've never heard my mother use the word 'hell'. She's very conservative. The most she usually comes away with is 'fiddlesticks' or 'fluffing'. She's not one for swearing.

'Yes, a two-week holiday you're supposed to be having with your boyfriend. Do you remember Aidan?'

Oh God. He phoned Mum. How could he do this? That's a low blow. And what the heck has it got to do with Mum?

'Mum. I was going to tell you. I've just been trying to process it all myself.'

'Process it?' Mum's voice rises a few decibels. 'That boy came straight from the airport, distraught, saying you'd dumped him, and on an exotic holiday he went to when *your* friend pulled out. He was doing you a favour, and this is how you repay him?'

Thanks for being on my side, Mum. And if I get my hands on that prat of an ex of mine, I'll strangle him. Straight from the airport? Poor little Aidan. Dumped.

'And did he tell you why I dumped him?' I ask, my voice rising a few octaves to match the pitch of my mum's.

'Yes, and that's even worse. Flirting? With a dive instructor? It's so degrading.' She tuts. 'I thought your father and I raised you better than that.'

Oh no. Don't bring Dad into this. Dad didn't share your opinions on many things, Mum, and how I handled myself with men was definitely one of them. He was too sick to warn me about Aidan, but deep down I knew Dad didn't take to him.

'Thanks for assuming the worst about me, as usual, Mum,' I snap, unable to help myself. 'Why are you so keen to take his side? He's not even your family.'

'You were supposed to be moving in together when you got back, so he would've been my family eventually.'

'Well, in that case, I'm so glad we split when we did, as at least we don't have to sort out that hornets' nest.'

I know she's thinking about grandchildren, but seriously, I'm thirty, today. I'm not even a geriatric mother for another few years. I have time. She has time. But if she keeps going the way she is at the minute, she'll drive an irreparable wedge between us. There's a reason why I was a daddy's girl. Dad and I never cared about appearances or keeping up with the Joneses. We just wanted to be happy, appreciate the simple things in life.

'Katherine MacDonald, you get yourself on a flight home tomorrow and get this sorted out.'

Ooh, she's wheeled out the big guns: my Sunday name. I hesitate for a nanosecond then say, 'No.'

'Excuse me, young lady?'

'Mum, not that you've noticed, or mentioned it, although you'd think you might have recalled your visit to hospital to give birth thirty years ago today, but I'm thirty. It's my thirtieth birthday today. I don't need you to sort my life out for me, and quite frankly, you're doing a pretty poor job of it. I am not getting back together with Aidan.'

'Now, you listen to me–'

'No, Mum, you listen to me. This is my life. Aidan is a bully. He's controlling and he's mean and he has a drink problem, and I deserve better.'

'Nobody's perfect, but that boy was there for you when your father was ill.'

I laugh. 'Nobody's perfect? You're not kidding. He's far from perfect, and neither am I. But I won't be dictated to by any man. The most important man in my life never treated me like that, and I don't expect any other man to do so. And you shouldn't want that for me.' My voice is hoarse. I'm not shouting but I'm hardly whispering either.

'Your father would be so disappointed in you,'

Mum says.

I grit my teeth. 'Mum, I'm going to say this only once, "Don't ever say that to me again." Dad would never have wanted me to stay with someone who treats me the way Aidan has. You don't know the half of it. Of course he's come running to you, with his sob story. You're so gullible, you believe every word that crosses his lips. Just because he has a decent job, you think he's "good boyfriend material". Well, he's not. And we're no longer an item.'

'We'll discuss this properly when you get home,' Mum says. 'I'm not happy, and we need to have a proper chat, but I'll tell Aidan now's not the right time, and that you need some time to "process things".' She has the cheek to use my own words against me.

'Mum, you're not getting this, are you? I don't want to be with Aidan. And what's more, I'm not coming home. I'm staying.'

'Y-y-you're what?' she chokes out.

'I'm staying. I have a job lined up and I've handed my notice in to Peterson's.'

I smile. Now it feels real. I'm going to be a resident of Costa Rica for the foreseeable future.

'Kat, you can't do this. You can't take off and settle for some bar job in some godforsaken backwater. We expected more for you.'

'That's good, because I'm not working in a bar, although technically you could say I will be working in a backwater, or a swampy area, or at the very least a rainforest. I start volunteering at a sloth sanctuary tomorrow, and I couldn't be happier.'

'A sloth sanctuary. Are you out of your mind?' she

screeches. 'A volunteer? What will you live on if you're not earning? Are you having some sort of mental breakdown?'

'No, Mum, I'm having an epiphany. Now, if you'll excuse me, I have stuff to do. Oh, and, thanks for wishing me happy birthday.' I wish I had a rotary dial phone so I could slam the receiver down like you could do when my folks were young. It would be so much more satisfying. Unfortunately, technological advances and the advent of mobile phones has made that possibility obsolete. I settle for pressing the red button and imagine her face, lobster-red as she cottons on that I've hung up on her. I've never hung up on my mother in my life. I wouldn't dare. I was too well brought up. Now it's my turn to use her words.

I'm fuming. Happy birthday to me, indeed. I sit down on the bed and burst into tears.

Five minutes later, I wash my face and blow my nose. I'm not a pretty sight. I may actually have to wear some makeup today, so I don't look totally awful. I mean, I'm not one for posting on Insta or TikTok, or TokTok as my mum calls it, but I still don't want it to be obvious I've been sobbing my heart out. No, I can wipe the evidence of my self-pity away and get on with my birthday. Best to compartmentalise the showdown with Mum and take stock of the fallout tomorrow.

I turn off my phone and head down to breakfast.

I stare out at the ocean as I sip my *agua dulce* and toy with my plantain pancakes. The water is as calm as I've ever seen it, in contrast to my turbulent emotions bubbling away just beneath the surface. How dare she? How dare he? And on my birthday, too.

This move to Costa Rica really is for the best, for a multitude of reasons, but now I'm adding to it: a chance to reassess my life as a whole. How have Mum and I grown so distant from one another? I know my stronger parental relationship was always with Dad, but how did we reach this place, where she believes my boyfriend over me? Where she fights his corner, not mine? Anger flows through me at her comment that Dad would have been disappointed in me. I know it's not true, but with him gone it's not as if I can ask him. No, my gut instinct about Dad has always been right. And he always wanted what was best for me. Ironically, that's how I've ended up here. I know, in my heart, to my very core, that he would agree with all the decisions I've made this week, and I promise myself that I'll continue to make him proud of me.

After breakfast, I walk through the hotel grounds. I want to remember every detail of this incredible resort.

I spot a toucan almost camouflaged by the leaves of the tree it's hiding in, but the red stripe on its bill gives it away. I fumble in my bag for my phone and turn it on, keen to take a few shots of it. I'm no photographer, but when I finally return to Scotland, I'd like to have documented my stay here with some tangible proof.

Bing. Bing. Bing.

Messages.

Happy birthday, gorgeous girl. Thirty! You're so old. I love ya. Wish I was there. Have a ball, Becca xx

Hey, birthday girl, see you later. Get ready to swim with the fishes. I say that in a non-Marlon-Brando way.

Ed.

Happy birthday, Kat. Hope you have a wonderful day, Dexter.

Someone told me it was a special birthday for you today, Kat. Happy birthday, Sofia and Carlos.

A few more messages have come in, from friends at work, friends from school and university who've noticed on Facebook it's my thirtieth. I almost well up at everyone's thoughtfulness. So I'm not totally alone, and I have my dive today, which is exciting. It's good to know I'm in safe hands. Ed wouldn't take me out if he didn't think I was ready.

The leaves rustle in the tree beside me, reminding me of that toucan I wanted to photograph. I'm surprised he's still there, although why would he move; he has as much right to be here as I have, if not more. Even the toucans do things at a leisurely pace in Costa Rica.

I snap away, taking a few shots of him before he gets bored of his surroundings, then I meander down to the water's edge, enjoying experiencing life at a slower pace. I paddle in the sea-foam green waters, and it's bliss. I can almost taste the salt on my tongue, and the lukewarm water is so inviting, it's too much. Fortunately, I had the foresight to put my bikini on under my clothes. I peel off my shorts and T-shirt, bunch up my things, together with my phone, and set them on a lounger, then walk into the water until it's around my waist. I swim in fluid strokes for a bit before I turn onto my back and float. Happy birthday to me. Mum may not have wished me happy birthday, and Dad may no longer be around to do so, and naturally,

Aidan wasn't going to, but I have all my new friends, and I'm in this incredible location, and I'm going to enjoy every single moment.

Chapter Eight

'There she is, the birthday girl!' Ed calls to me as I approach the diving hut an hour or so later. 'All ready for your first dive?'

I tilt my head. 'Do you know what, Ed? I think I just might be.'

'Excellent. Let's get you suited up.'

Five minutes later, I'm in the ocean again and we've walked until I'm almost out of my depth.

'Now, it's a piece of cake, I promise,' says Ed. 'Just follow my lead. I'll operate your air for you this time, so you don't need to worry about a thing.'

I give him a half-smile. *Be brave. You can do this. You're thirty now. You've always wanted to do it. Think adventure.* But what comes to mind is Aidan's negativity around the possibility of me diving, as if I couldn't do it. And that spurs me on.

I follow Ed deeper into the water, put my regulator in my mouth, and practise a few breaths underwater before making a loop with my thumb and forefinger, giving him the OK sign.

We swim out into the aquamarine ocean and suddenly it's like a whole new world has opened up to me. A whole new continent. I knew the marine life was spectacular here, but I didn't expect to see it so close to shore. We can't be more than eighty metres from the beach. Not that I can see that from under the water; it's just my gut instinct.

I want to cry with happiness. Joy radiates from my every pore as beautiful fish of every size, shape and colour swim around me. It fascinates me how they know to move out of my way. It reminds me of the scenes on TV of traffic in India, where eight lanes of cars jostle to negotiate a roundabout, yet somehow don't hit each other. Incredible.

A yellow and black stripy fish, the bee of the marine world, swims past. Its colours are so vibrant, so beautiful, it's hard to put it into words. I'll have to try to remember all these fish and ask Ed their names, if he knows, or google them, or check my guide book. I want to remember every aspect of this, my first dive, because already I know it won't be my last. I have the bug, and it took me all of, ooh, two minutes.

Oh God, there's an ugly grey fish ahead and it's huge, well, compared with the pretty yellow and black one of a moment ago. Its mouth is massive. Is it a shark? I bloody hope not. I didn't think to ask Ed if these were shark-infested waters, although I do recall reading that Costa Rica has sharks. Hopefully, this isn't one of them. I may have pulled on my big-girl pants to dive today, but I don't fancy becoming a shark's amuse-bouche.

Ed swims alongside me, between me and the 'shark'. He makes the OK sign and I sigh inwardly. I guess he wouldn't do that if it were a shark.

He smiles through his mask and gestures behind

me. I turn to see a ray slicing through the water, or rather flapping its wings, as it heads towards me. It's black with white polka dots. Being down here is so humbling.

We continue to swim along and the rhythmic action of moving my flippers is so soothing. I also love the sensation of being completely weightless. Somehow that really appeals right now. Perhaps because I have a lot of baggage in my life currently. Could be my subconscious, or subliminal messaging, but whatever, I'm prepared to go with the flow.

I'm glad Ed's handling the air. I'd be panicking otherwise. Usually, I like being in control of my own destiny, but knowing I'm in the hands of an expert reassures me. From behind a cluster of coral, a skinny bright blue fish appears. It's so razor-thin it's almost unreal, and it has a long nose, or whatever fish have. God, since I'm going to live here, I had better brush up on my marine knowledge, or I'll look a complete idiot.

Ed points upwards, in the gesture he taught me for time to go to the surface.

When we break through, I wait for him to take off his mask and give me instruction, just so I know I'm doing the right thing. I mimic him and he grins. 'So, what did you think?'

After inhaling a deep breath to clear the stale air from my lungs, I say, 'When can I do it again?'

He bursts out laughing. 'Anytime, Kat. Anytime.'

My words come out in a rush as I enthuse about today's dive. Once I draw breath, Ed says, 'Do you want to grab a birthday drink? Diving can make you thirsty.'

Funny how he knows what I'm thinking before I think it. He's like the brother I never had. I always wanted a brother, a little brother, and if I'm right, Ed's a couple of years younger than me. I might be cheeky and ask him later. Ask him if I can adopt him as a brother. No, that's borderline stalker, and his wife might get the wrong idea. Hopefully, I'll get to meet her soon. She's probably already heard all about me and my sorry love life.

As we sit at the side of the pool in our shorts and T-shirts again, Ed tells me of all the really cool places to go. Some of them I'm familiar with, from my guide book, or from having googled them before I came to Costa Rica; others are undoubtedly locals' best-kept secrets. I don't care. I can't wait to explore them all.

'So, how are you feeling about starting at the sanctuary tomorrow? Sure you're ready to leave the luxury hotel behind?'

'Being honest, I baulked at throwing away this holiday after the cost of it, but I can't wait to start. Anyway, I feel the whole Aidan debacle sullied the holiday experience, plus I'm already missing Flash and Ferdinand, and Bolt and Zoom.'

'Ha! They have a way of getting under your skin. Literally, sometimes, with those claws.'

I smile. 'So, how many times have you been to the sanctuary?'

His eyes widen and he blows out a breath. 'Honestly, I have no idea. More times than I can count, though. Costa Rica as a whole is a laid-back country, but when I step across the threshold of the sanctuary, it's like entering another world.'

I nod, knowing exactly what he means, as I had the same impression myself.

'And once I met Nicolás and he took me there on one of our days off, I was hooked.'

I sip my guaro sour. 'Have you ever thought of working at the sanctuary?'

He laughs. 'Me? Work there? No. I don't have the experience. You're good with animals from what Dexter tells me. Plus, I have a family to support. I can't work as a volunteer. I need the money too much. The diving gig pays well, and I can largely make my own hours.'

'That does sound like a good deal,' I concede.

'The best.' He pauses before saying, 'Anyway, you couldn't have landed in a better place, with better people. Sofia and Carlos are like my surrogate mum and dad.'

'Yeah, they do give off that caring vibe.'

'Don't they just?' He sets down his drink. 'I have some things I need to do at home. Nicolás is having a barbecue later. Do you fancy coming?'

My heart lifts. I won't be spending the evening of my thirtieth alone after all. Yay. 'I'd love to.'

Ed smirks. 'Good, but don't try to take the barbecue tongs from him as he gets kind of territorial.'

I laugh. 'He has absolutely nothing to worry about. Even though I'm a pretty good cook, I'm too afraid to barbecue my own food in case I poison myself.' I refrain from saying that it's a similar sentiment I have towards regulating my own air when I'm underwater. He doesn't need to know that ... not yet anyway.

'So, will I pick you up about six?'

'Perfect.'

That'll give me time to make myself presentable. I have a few little dresses with me, one I'd specifically bought to wear on my birthday. It's white with red roses all over it and it's cute. And since I've decided that thirty's the year I'm going to suit myself and do exactly what I like, that's what I'm wearing.

Ed saunters off, but I stay for a while, enjoying the sun on my face. It would be so easy to just drift off, but I need to focus. My argument with Mum pops to the forefront of my mind, but I toss it away. Nope, not ruining my birthday for me. I can't believe she didn't text me to apologise, or at least wish me happy birthday. Damn, I'm thinking about it, and that wasn't part of the plan.

I know. I'll video-call Becca. It's around ten there now. She picks up on the second ring.

She starts whistling the nursery rhyme 'Five Little Ducks', and her volume picks up at the part about 'over the hill and far away'.

'Ha bloody ha. I'll over the hill, you. I'm only three months older than you. Wait until it's your turn.'

'I've decided to age backwards. Thirty is the new twenty, remember?'

'Yeah, keep telling yourself that. What are you up to? How's the leg?'

She lets out a dramatic sigh. 'Nothing. Missing you. I'm sitting here with my cocoa, pining for you.'

'Yeah, right. Perhaps if you'd replaced the cocoa with wine, I might almost have believed you.'

'Are you saying I'm a lush?' She puts her hands on her hips and her mock indignation makes me smile.

'A lush, no, a partygoer, yes. A cocoa drinker, most definitely not. Anyway, isn't there someone there to help you drown your sorrows?'

She tuts. 'It's surprisingly difficult to pull when you're laid up. Or should I say, surprisingly difficult to get laid when you're laid up.' She chortles at her own joke.

'Becca, that's awful even for you. Don't ever give up the day job.'

She snorts. 'I don't intend to. I love my job. But never mind me, you look amazing, all sun-kissed and sexy.'

'Why, thank you,' I say, but Becca continues. 'How has your birthday been? Happy birthday to you, happy birthday to you, happy birthday, dear Kat, happy birthday to you.'

'Thanks, Becca. God, I wish you were here.'

'Me too, Kat. But we'll make up for it when I come over.'

My heart stutters. 'You're coming over? Really?'

She frowns. 'Seriously? Do you think you're getting all the fun? My bestie moves to Costa Rica, and I have to stay home in Glasgow? I don't think so. Once this leg is mended, I'm checking the deals for a cheap flight.'

My soul purrs in response to her comment. How good it would be to have Becca here, even for a week. Everything has happened so fast, I haven't had time to get my head around it. I haven't even started the job at the sanctuary yet, but my whole life feels like it has been put into a cement mixer and turned on, with all my thoughts thumping around inside it.

'Becca, that would be fabulous. Oh, I love you.'

'I know. I'm amazing. So, how was your dive?'

'It was incredible. The fish were absolutely gorgeous. The colours have to be seen to be believed. You'll need to see for yourself when you come.'

'That I will.' She pans her camera to her leg. 'As soon as I can get this bloomin' thing off.'

'Yeah, you won't be able to go swimming with that cast on.' I can't curb my enthusiasm any more and return to my previous topic. 'Did you know that when you take fish out of water, they lose their colour, and it's the water that makes us see them as those colours?'

'I did, actually. Well, they'll just need to stay in the water then. What time is it there now?'

'A little after three.'

'And are you meeting Ed later?' She flutters her lashes, pouts and gives me a little knowing smile.

'I am, but not in the way you mean. Remember, he's married with two kids.'

'Ah, right, so he is. So, how come you're meeting up then?'

I stretch out my back, which is becoming stiff from sitting so long. 'Nicolás, his friend – one of the three amigos as I've now nicknamed them – is having a barbecue and Ed invited me. I guess he felt sorry for me spending my birthday alone.'

'Probably. You're a total pity case.'

She laughs as I mimic slapping her across the face.

'Just be glad you're not closer or I'd give you a Chinese burn for that comment.'

'Torture, hey, your new man might like that.'

I laugh. 'I don't have a new man, and even when I

eventually do, that won't be on the agenda.'

'You say that now…'

'Right, I'm going to go, as you've evidently been drinking a lot of that cocoa. Your brain is fried and you're talking absolute nonsense.' I pause for a second. 'Not that there's anything new with that.'

'Har de har. You're so funny. OK, have a fab time. Don't do anything I wouldn't do, and if you meet any hot guys, or rather any more hot guys, send me pics.'

I shake my head. 'You're in a league of your own, you know that?'

She winks then blows me a kiss. 'You know it. Bye, hon.'

I smile at the phone as Becca's face disappears, then I finish my guaro sour and go to put my affairs in order.

Chapter Nine

I'm glancing around reception when I hear, 'Nice dress.'

I turn around to see Ed wearing jeans and a pale blue shirt, next to a woman who must surely be a model, wearing a navy halterneck dress with a cream leaf pattern adorning it. Her ebony shoulders are toned. She definitely works out. My gaze tracks to her washboard-flat stomach then upwards to her face. Ed's wife is quite simply, stunning.

'Thanks. You don't scrub up too badly yourself.'

'Kat, this is my wife, Gloriana.'

'Hi, Gloriana. It's so lovely to meet you.'

She takes my hand and clasps it in hers. 'You too. Ed has told me so much about you.'

Great, someone else who knows about my disastrous trip.

'I cannot believe you've recently had a baby. You look amazing.'

She grins. 'It was hard work before the birth, but running around after a three-month-old and a toddler means you don't have time to eat properly, so all the baby weight has just fallen off.'

'Gloriana's a hiking guide,' Ed says. 'I had to tell

her to cool it towards the end of the pregnancy so the baby wasn't born on the top of one of our many mountains here.'

'I only listened to him so I didn't give the mountain rescue guys any extra work.' She takes his fingers lightly in hers and they exchange a look. They are such a sweet couple.

'Anyway, happy birthday. I believe today's an important one for you,' she says, 'so I thought we'd get you a little something.' She holds out a gift bag.

'Oh my goodness, you shouldn't have.' They really shouldn't have. I'm on the verge of tearing up here. These guys have known me less than a week, and in Gloriana's case, less than two minutes and they've shown me so much kindness.

'It's just a little something. I thought it'd be appropriate.'

'Thanks so much.' I take the card out of the bag, read it and then open the gift. 'Oh, wow. A waterproof camera. It's perfect.' I start prattling on about the fish we saw today and how much I loved it and Gloriana smiles.

'I knew you'd catch the bug.' She leans in towards Ed. 'He's a good dive guide and knows all the best spots. He taught me to dive, too, so if you enjoy it, you should try and go as often as you can whilst you're here. Ed tells me it's very different to back home.'

'That's for sure. I thought about diving in Oban, but it was freezing and murky. I think that was the main thing that put me off, but it's like a whole new world here.'

Ed and Gloriana laugh then Ed, his hand on the

small of Gloriana's back, says, 'Right, shall we go? I'm starving, and I did tell Nicolás we'd be there before seven.'

'Sure,' Gloriana and I say as one.

We head towards Ed's SUV and as we drive, Gloriana shows me photos of their baby, Cristina, at my request. She's adorable. Chubby, gummy and beautiful, with milk chocolate skin. She definitely won in the genes department, as did her brother, Felipe. And her eyes are the emerald green of Ed's. Ed's lips curve in a smile as Gloriana tells me all about Cristina's antics. He's smitten, with both mother and baby, and I'm so happy for my friend that he has found someone to share that kind of life with.

'Here we are.' Ed opens Gloriana's door then mine then ushers us both ahead of him towards where a calypso beat is pulsing from a terracotta-coloured villa with Roman arches and a vast marble porch.

'Wow, this is gorgeous. We'd need a lottery win back home to have something like this.'

Gloriana gives a tinkly laugh. 'Not a lottery win. His dad's an inventor. Some tech thing. Don't ask me what.'

I raise my eyebrows.

'Nicolás doesn't like to make a fuss, or boast about being sort of rich,' Ed confides.

I make a zipping motion with my fingers across my lips. 'He won't hear anything from me. Apart from how incredible his house is.'

Ed keys in the gate code – super-posh, or is it for

security? The sanctuary one, I get, but your own home? I suppose when your home is as palatial as this you may need to be careful.

A hammock swings slightly in the breeze as we pass through a courtyard towards the rear of the house. Several people greet Ed and Gloriana and ask about the children and tell Gloriana how nice it is to see her. We round the house and a fifteen-metre kidney-shaped pool greets us. A makeshift bar – or perhaps it's there year-round – stands off to one side, where a man is mixing cocktails. Two barbecues flank it. Nicolás is holding court at one, whilst Oscar is chatting to a man and woman at the other as he piles food on to their plates. The aroma of sausages and some sort of marinated chicken reaches me and my stomach rumbles.

Ed laughs. 'Someone's hungry.'

'I forgot to have lunch. I was trying to sort out my life after you left the pool bar,' I say pointedly.

'Let's get you something to eat so you don't pass out from hunger.' Gloriana takes me gently by the arm. 'I know where all the good stuff is.'

I'll drink to that, or rather I'll eat to that.

'Kat!' Nicolás sets down his barbecue tongs – they're really professional as if he has his own barbecue chef TV programme or something – then comes forward and envelops me in a bone-crushing hug. 'Happy birthday!'

I have no idea how he can hug so tight. He's whippet-thin. When he releases me, I take a moment to breathe again before saying, 'Thanks.'

Nicolás kisses Gloriana on both cheeks and tells her

that her dress looks incredible on her, then he shoulder pats Ed, and they chat for a couple of minutes before he and Gloriana go mingle.

'Make sure he feeds you,' Gloriana calls back over her shoulder.

'So, are you looking forward to the big move? Or will you miss the fluffy slippers and luxury dressing gowns too much?' Nicolás asks as he flips some burgers then waves the barbecue tongs in the air at me.

'Honestly? I can't wait. I know you'll laugh, but I miss Flash.'

He laughs. 'I hear he's quite the cutie. I haven't met him yet. I'll need to rectify that soon.' He studies me for a moment. 'My aunt and uncle are so glad you're coming to work for them. You've helped them out of a real hole.'

My eyebrows furrow. 'I'm not sure about that.' I adjust my dress, uncomfortable at the compliment, particularly when they're the ones who've done me a favour. They've helped me flip my life on its head.

Nicolás nods vigorously. 'I'm not joking. They were telling me only this morning. If they'd had to go through the recruiting process all over again – especially for Europe – it could've taken many weeks or longer to find a replacement and for them to get here.'

I mull this over and accept he's probably right on that point.

'You already being here removed that hurdle for them. Anyway, you'll love it. I used to help out in the sanctuary when I was younger. I spent quite a lot of time there after school. It has to be the best first job ever.' He grins.

'I'll bet.' Certainly beats me delivering the *Evening Times.*

'And there are so many things to do in your downtime.'

'We get downtime?' I say.

Nicolás knits his brow. 'Oh yes, of course. Here, let's get you some food, and then I can tell you all about the wonderful things within an hour's drive. Sorry, I'm a terrible host. I just get so carried away sometimes. You can probably tell I'm very proud of my country.'

I grin. 'I had noticed.'

Whilst Nicolás sorts me a plate of food, I cast my glance around the exterior of his home.

'So, is this your usual weekend get-together?' I ask.

'Sort of,' says Nicolás, expertly turning the chicken. 'I forgot to ask, what would you like to drink?'

I tilt my head to one side and tap my finger against my lips. 'What would you recommend?'

'I do a mean mojito, but then I'm not in charge of the bar tonight. My cousin is.' He calls over to him. 'Can you make Kat your best mojito, please?'

If I'd been in mainland Spain and a man had said those words, I'd have found them a little smarmy, but Nicolás is as sweet and genuine as they come. Funny, I don't know if he or Oscar have girlfriends.

'Give me two minutes. I'll do it once I finish mixing this Bloody Mary.'

'No problem, *hermano.*' Nicolás turns to me. 'He makes it from scratch, which is why it takes so long. No pre-prepared mix for him. He's an artist.'

'I can fix that for you, Kat.'

I spin round to see Dexter. He's wearing navy knee-length shorts and a Hawaiian shirt which has all the colours of the rainbow. Is he trying to outdo Carlos on the psychedelic shirt front? Has he worn it for a bet? It certainly looks like it should be in a competition, and winning first prize. My lips twitch in amusement.

'Thanks.'

He leans in. 'Nicolás bought it for me for my birthday, so every so often I wear it when I'm here. I assure you it's not part of my usual wardrobe.'

I hold up my hands. 'Oh, it's not for me to question your sartorial choices.'

His eyes crinkle. 'But you noticed, right?'

'Busted. It is kind of hard not to, though. It's a … standout shirt.'

'Very diplomatic.' He grins. 'Let me get that mojito for you, and happy birthday.'

My smile doesn't leave my face as I watch Dexter talk to the barman whilst he prepares drinks for us both. Nicolás is busy with a small queue which has formed: the hungry hordes in search of sustenance.

'Kat, your food will grow cold,' he chastises me, indicating with his tongs to my still full plate.

'Sorry, I was miles away.' Thinking about Dexter will do that to me. He looks good enough to eat tonight, never mind the barbecue food. And he smells divine. Would anyone notice if I licked him? Jeez, I need to get my libido under control. It's not as if I've been starved of sex for months – just affection, I think wryly.

I take a bite of chicken. Dexter's not the only thing that's divine; this is so flavoursome, it's like a taste explosion in my mouth. 'Mmm.' I chew a few more times. 'Mmm.'

Nicolás is staring at me.

'What?' I ask. 'Did you say something? Sorry, I didn't hear you.'

He shakes his head. 'No, I just like seeing people enjoying the food I've prepared.'

'He fancies himself as a bit of a chef,' Dexter says as he returns with my drink. 'And people moaning appreciatively over his food will definitely make him a happy boy.'

At his use of 'moaning appreciatively', I flush and my thoughts move to rather more risqué subjects where that could apply. I cough to cover my embarrassment, and then down a large sip of my mojito, which proves not to be the best choice as I splutter and cough some more.

'You OK?' Dexter asks, his eyes on mine, his hand poised over my back.

I clear my throat a few times, then tell him I'm fine.

'Oh, there's Sofia and Carlos.' Dexter waves them over.

I frown slightly as I glance over to the gate they've come through. More and more people are arriving.

I continue to chat with Dexter whilst Nicolás greets his aunt and uncle, then they both kiss and hug me as if they hadn't just seen me yesterday. I find the effusiveness of the Costa Ricans so touching, and welcome, particularly today, given I don't have my own family around me.

Whilst Dexter and Carlos fetch drinks, Sofia takes

me to one side and tells me Dexter will pick me up tomorrow from the hotel as she and Carlos are busy.

'And he will come around lunchtime. Then we can settle you in in the afternoon and you can go see the babies, spend some time with Luciana. It's a lovely way to get accustomed to everything.' She winks. 'I won't have you mucking out the cages on the first day.'

'Thanks. So, if you don't mind me asking, how long have you and Carlos been together?'

Her eyes take on a dreamy quality. 'Oh *Dios mio*, forever. Since we were fifteen. I was from a small village near San José and he was from a little town near Quepos, which as you may know is near here. Have you been yet?'

I shake my head.

'It's the nearest city to the sanctuary. We were very lucky, both of us. We may not have had much money, but we grew up in nature, surrounded by some of the most beautiful scenery in the world. Well, I imagine so. I haven't actually been out of Costa Rica.' She cackles. 'Why would I?'

Right now I have to agree with her. There's certainly no place I'd rather be, and as I catch sight of Dexter out of the corner of my eye, I convince myself it's not only because of a certain Irishman who's nearby.

'So, where did you learn Spanish?' Sofia asks, her arm partly around mine, in a gesture of familial intimacy.

'At school. It was my favourite subject.'

'You'll have noticed quite a difference here then from the pure, Castilian Spanish they speak in Madrid.'

I laugh. 'Yes, the words for "you" and the past tenses you use, although if I'm honest, I'm also trying to relearn everything too. I'm very rusty.'

Sofia wags her finger at me. 'The fact you speak any Spanish is admirable in itself. Most people who come here don't even try. Not even a few words.' She tuts, and I'm glad to have met with her approval.

'What's this about the past tense?' Dexter asks as he approaches us again.

'You were about to be, *mi hijo*, if that drink had taken any longer.' Sofia pretends to swat Dexter about the head, and he turns to me.

'She's so bossy, but don't worry, her bite is just as bad as her bark.'

This time she does swat him, but when he excuses himself to speak to some people who are arriving – there's still more? How big is this get-together? – she leans in to me and says, 'He is like another son to me. I thank *Dios* for the day he sent him to us. He has been a godsend from day one.'

I'm about to fish a little more about Dexter when Mariangeles and Luciana appear. Does everyone know everyone here? I know the world's meant to be a village, but this is ridiculous.

'Another drink, Kat?'

I blink and see Dexter holding out his hand for my empty glass. I shake my head to clear it of thoughts and mentally return to the party.

'Actually, why don't you come this way? I have something to show you,' he says.

'That sounds ominous.' My lips curve into a smile to show I'm not scared, and a frisson of pleasure darts through me. I really wish I wasn't such an open book. I even have the dry mouth. What a cliché. He could be about to show me a bear in the woods or anything and yet colour is creeping up my cheeks.

I follow him and he mixes me another cocktail then we take our drinks and meander along a path that leads to a stream. Nicolás has a stream on his property? Despite the little torch Dexter is shining ahead of us, it's properly dark now that we're away from the house and I jump at the noises coming from the bushes.

Dexter laughs. 'They're katydids.'

'Katydids?' I ask, recovering my composure.

He nods. 'That's right. You almost have an insect named after you.' His eyes crinkle and my breath catches as I note how ridiculously blue they are. We hold each other's gaze a fraction of a second too long before I blink and the moment is lost.

I gulp audibly and pray he didn't hear.

'They're loud, aren't they?' He turns towards the long grass at the side of the path.

Phew, he probably didn't hear me then. 'Yes, they are. Are there lots of them? Is that why they're making such a racket?'

'Who knows, but they're well known for being noisy little beggars.' He pauses for a second then says, 'But they're not why I wanted to bring you here.'

He wants to have his way with me; I knew it. Result! 'Oh?' I squeak.

'No, let's continue on a little.' He pads in front of me. 'Watch your step. Here.' He holds his hand out to me, and automatically, I take it as he wraps his warm fingers around mine, his grip tight but not too tight.

I'm beginning to think it wasn't an inspired idea to bring drinks down here with us, as navigating my way with two hands would surely be better than one, although given Dexter's holding my hand, you won't find me complaining.

'Here we are.' Dexter flicks off the torch.

I stop beside where the stream opens out into a slightly larger one. The lights of the house are far enough behind us that I can see Dexter and a few paces in front of me, but not a great deal else.

It takes a few seconds for me to see what Dexter is referring to, but once my eyes adjust I can't believe I didn't notice them before. Five then ten then dozens of tiny yellow and green lights illuminate the bushes, like little jewels or Christmas lights threaded through them. Fireflies. Dozens of tiny fireflies. I've never seen them like this before. I guess there's usually too much light pollution.

I turn to Dexter and he smiles. I really want to kiss him. He hesitates, then clears his throat. 'So, what do you think?'

He doesn't really want to know what I'm thinking right now. I can't exactly say, 'I want to jump you,' or 'I'd like to snog you until someone sends out a search party.' So I say, 'It's pretty special, isn't it?'

He stares at me for a long moment as if he knows I was thinking something else, but then he nods. 'Sofia showed me them the first time I was at the sanctuary, but I think the best place to see a significant number of them is here, at Nicolás'.'

'I'll need to check them out at the sanctuary,' I say, aiming to calm my galloping pulse.

'You will. But I think Nicolás was right to propose to Oscar here.'

My eyes widen. 'Nicolás and Oscar are married?'

Now it's Dexter's turn for his eyes to widen. 'You didn't know?'

'No, why would I? I didn't even realise they were … together.'

Dexter smiles. 'Well, now you do.'

'Tonight's certainly all about the revelations.'

'I'll drink to that.' He raises his glass and clinks it with mine. We sip our drinks as I take in the complete silence, apart from the katydids, and I realise I'm completely comfortable with this man. I mean, if he was an axe murderer, he has a prime location for taking me into the woods and chopping me into small pieces, as it's right on his doorstep. But I don't feel even a hint of unease. No, what I feel is full-on lust, and I need to get that under control. I guess it's my hormones, because of all the emotional upheaval I've had this week. Time to put them back in the box.

A text alert sounds and Dexter checks his phone. 'We should head back.'

I follow him back along the barely there path towards Nicolás' villa. Dexter keeps a reassuring grip on my hand, and I can't help feeling a twinge of sadness that our time alone is at an end.

Chapter Ten

As we round the final cluster of bushes, shouts of 'Surprise!' and 'Happy birthday!' greet me, and I grind to a halt as I notice a huge banner floating in the wind. 'Happy 30th birthday, Kat' it reads.

I cover my mouth with a hand. Oh my goodness. This is a surprise birthday party. This is why there are so many people here.

I turn to Dexter, whose eyes crease.

'Sorry. Nicolás told me to get you out of the way so they could finalise things.'

The ping on his phone. That was Nicolás recalling us.

'Happy birthday, Kat.' Oscar and Nicolás come over and hug me. Ed is close behind with Gloriana, who smiles. 'They're terrible, aren't they? Welcome to the club.' She hands me a glass of champagne. 'You'll need this.'

I thank her as Carlos calls everyone to order, and the forty or fifty people assembled, many of whom I now vaguely recognise from the sanctuary, fall silent. He has the magic touch.

'Kat hasn't been with us very long – in fact she doesn't officially start until tomorrow – however, you know how I feel about my gut.' He pauses and someone shouts. 'We know you like to feed it doughnuts.'

'Ha ha. Consider yourself on cage-cleaning duties for the rest of the week.'

Bursts of laughter and applause break out in response.

'As I was saying–' Carlos clears his throat '–my gut never fails me and I know Kat is going to fit right in with our little sanctuary family. Isn't that right, Dexter?'

Dexter gives a start then coughs. 'Absolutely.'

I grin at the flush that has crept up his face. Good. Not only I turn bright red when caught unawares.

Carlos beams at us all. 'So, can you all raise your glasses in a double celebration? Happy thirtieth birthday, Kat, and welcome to the Costa Punta family.'

Everyone clinks glasses and repeats the toast as my face burns and I down my drink in one.

The music changes from calypso to salsa, and Luciana and Oscar take to the makeshift dance floor to the side of the swimming pool. You can tell Luciana's the native and Oscar the learner, but wow, he would score highly on *Strictly*. I'm impressed. I've always thought salsa dancing was so sexy. I even watched *Dirty Dancing* with Becca a few times, as apparently it's a cult classic. Patrick Swayze wasn't half bad, and oh my God, did he have presence.

Even though Luciana and Oscar aren't together and since I've recently found out Oscar's with Nicolás, it doesn't detract from my enjoyment of watching them dance, although my brain is quick to replace them with me and Dexter practising the fancy footwork.

Oscar spins Luciana and she branches off on her own to riotous applause, before she ends up back in his arms, then he dips her until I feel a twinge in my back at the degree she's angled at. I don't consider myself unfit, but I certainly won't be attempting that manoeuvre anytime soon.

The track finishes and as a new one begins, Nicolás cuts in. 'My turn.' He grins at Luciana, who bows out gracefully only to immediately be accosted by Dexter, who whisks her back onto the floor as the music picks up its pace, the rhythm of their dancing increasing as the music builds to a crescendo.

Oh crap, I'm in trouble. He's gorgeous, kind, funny, can dance salsa – he's Irish, how can he dance salsa? Maybe it's innate. Maybe he's halfway related to Michael Flatley and his mentor was good at all types of dance not just Riverdance. He's also my boss.

But as he twirls and dips Luciana, I can't take my eyes off him. It's completely mesmerising. I've always found men who can dance incredibly sexy, and I don't mean those who can dance to dance music or hip hop, but to sexy, sensual salsa. I think it's the build-up. It starts slow, with the tap-tapping of the feet, until it reaches a climax, and every time I see someone dance salsa, I want to learn how to do it. It's the same with flamenco. A girl can dream, can't she? It's the brooding moodiness of the man then the passion coming out in the dance.

'Kat, you OK?' Javier asks.

I gasp and take a step back as if he has burned me.

He throws his hands up. 'Sorry, I didn't mean to

startle you.'

I shake my head. 'No, you didn't. I was just daydreaming.'

He stands, hands loosely in his pockets, but as if he is gearing up to say something.

I glance at him and arch an eyebrow, hoping that will push him on to spit out what he's trying to say, as he definitely has something on his mind.

He catches my eye then blows out a breath. 'I'm not very good, embarrassingly, but would you like to dance?'

Now it's my turn to throw my hands up. 'Eh, no thanks. I have no idea what to do.'

He grins. 'Well, that makes two of us, and since salsa is Costa Rica's number one dance and I suck at it, it's got to be more embarrassing for me than you.' He leans forward slightly. 'And I was kind of hoping that since you're not local, you wouldn't notice how terrible I am.'

His self-deprecation is endearing. I eye him suspiciously. 'You're sure you're not good?'

He nods vigorously. 'Positive.'

'Fine then.' I hold out my hand. 'You've convinced me.'

His smile lights up his face as he takes my hand. 'You won't regret it.'

I think I already am, I want to say, as he whisks me onto the dance area. I may want to dance like a native, but I'm not even good at dancing to wedding reception music, and everyone knows nobody cares how you dance to Abba, Queen or The Weather Girls.

We spin past Luciana and Dexter; the latter does a

double-take then his eyes glint their approval.

I try to hide my embarrassment with my hair, and hope the balmy night and the exertion account for my red face, and it's not clear to anyone else that I'm mortified because I have no clue what I'm doing, or that I care that Dexter is witnessing me dance so badly when he's virtually semi pro.

However, soon I dance like no one's watching, and I'm no longer even thinking of Dexter, as Javier, minx that he is, was lying. He's incredible at this and is making me feel so at ease, and as if I know what I'm doing, like I can dance, and it's powerful, amazing and I don't want it to stop. However, stop it does, and when the track finishes, he bows to me and thanks me, just as Dexter says, 'May I have this dance?'

'How very genteel.' I laugh. 'You're really good.' I nod towards Luciana, who is finally sitting down with Mariangeles, having a drink and slipping off her shoes.

He grins. 'I was rubbish when I came out here. Years of persistence from various people has paid off.'

I wonder who persisted, but unfortunately I can't ask.

The tempo of the music has slowed considerably. A ballad. Flamenco? No, simply a slow song. Oh no, and I'm dancing with Dexter. Or should that be oh yes? My heart flutters and I worry he'll be able to hear it beating as he's dancing so close to me now, not quite cheek to cheek, but our bodies are pressed close together, all in the spirit of the dance, you understand, but it's unnerving. This may be totally normal for everyone here, but it isn't for me, and I can't help being ridiculously turned on. I could be doing with being hosed down like owners sometimes do when two dogs are fighting or … yeah, you don't need to know that.

Not trusting myself to meet Dexter's gaze, I focus on those around me. Sofia and Carlos are dancing together, their eyes locked on each other; Nicolás and Oscar; Gloriana and Ed. I don't believe it. They're all couples. My breathing hitches and my heartbeat ratchets up about ten notches. Dexter clears his throat and I have no choice but to look up at him. When I do, the intensity in his gaze catches me by surprise, and I'm sure I see the same desire burning in his eyes as is burning in my loins right now.

He smiles, a lazy, sexy, knowing smile, and I inhale sharply. Sometimes lust can just catch you and you have no way of escaping it. You can have the best intentions in the world, but seriously, salsa and flamenco dancing, after all the emotion of the day and then the fireflies? I'm not a saint, and I am newly thirty. I'm in my fourth decade now. Surely I'm allowed a bit of fun. And right now, right here, with this man, I'm going to enjoy my birthday.

A few hours later, as I duck my head into Ed's car, I think what a truly incredible evening and memorable birthday it has been. The highlight, however, was definitely the trip to see the fireflies, and I can't help wondering if it was all part of the ruse to get me out of the way, or if Dexter genuinely wanted us to have a moment. Did he experience the same feelings I did? Feel the same attraction I did? Was it real, or all in my head?

Chapter Eleven

It's quite clear everyone is breaking me in gently at the sanctuary. Since I arrived a few days ago, I've been given all the good jobs: feeding the sloth pups, helping to prepare the adult sloths' meals, observing how to cater for the sloths' medical needs. Flash is coming along well. I've made a point of checking in on him as often as I can, although I've been incredibly busy. Everyone has made me so welcome, it's hard to believe I've only worked here a couple of days, and only known these people less than a week. Already I feel as if this was fated: my trip to Costa Rica, ditching Aidan, taking a stand and doing what I want for a change, thinking of no one else and to hell with the consequences. Sometimes you just have to pursue your dreams, right?

I've gelled really well with the girls and it's like having a group of sisters. Ella's by far the quietest of them all. The studious one. She reads the history of sloths, and all the scientific articles, and always has her nose in a book when she's off duty, and occasionally a sloth hanging off her arm too. She's also the youngest of us all. I'd reckon around twenty-one, but I haven't actually asked.

Mariangeles and Federica are a joy to watch. They

bounce off each other so well, and they're so funny. They remind me of me and Becca. Becca. I'm loving it here, but how I wish she were here too. Then everything would be perfect. Well, not quite everything. My, to all intents and purposes, non-existent relationship with Mum and my controlling ex-boyfriend situation could be magically sorted for me, but generally speaking, life is pretty good right now. Apart from Roisin. Do you ever feel as if someone's privy to information you're not, and somehow they've taken against you and you don't know why? Well, that's the impression I get from Roisin. She's not openly hostile towards me in front of others, although now I think about it, she has been a bit less welcoming when we've been in the women's block with the others, but certainly in front of the guys, she has been all sweetness and light.

Whatever. If she doesn't like me, that's her problem. It would be nice to get on with everyone, but life doesn't work quite like that. As long as she keeps out of my way, we'll get along just fine.

'Kat?'

I turn to see Victor gesturing towards me. 'Can you give me a hand? Are you free?'

'Of course. What do you need?'

As we walk, Victor talks. 'We've started a census to try to gauge how many sloths there are in the immediate area. By immediate area, we mean a five-mile radius.'

I frown. 'So, also outside of the sanctuary's boundaries?'

'Yep. We're trying to help the local wildlife

foundation get a handle on sloth numbers. We have special markers to record where they were sighted. Since they don't move very quickly, it's safe to say that in a month, we're looking at the same sloths.'

'How far do they travel per day then?' I smile. 'When they're not asleep, that is.'

Victor chuckles. 'Yeah, they sure like to sleep. I wish I could sleep ten hours a day.'

From the way I've seen him work, I can't imagine him sleeping at all. He's such a powerhouse.

'About thirty-five metres a day is the most they can travel, but they often choose not to do even that.'

Lazy beggars. I smile once again at the ironic names the sanctuary has given them all.

'Here, take this.' He hands me a notebook and pen. 'We'll start close to the sanctuary. You write what I find. That lets me concentrate on locating the sloths and attending to them if they need any care.'

'But how will you know if they are our sloths that are simply close to being released into the wild, or if they're sloths we haven't encountered before?'

'Ours have tiny GPS tags or collars. We release them into the wild and then we check on them a couple of times, a couple of weeks apart, to ensure they're OK.'

'I see. Well, lead the way.'

We meander through the rainforest, walking literally in circles from the sanctuary, where possible.

'There!' Victor stops suddenly. An adult sloth, possibly about three years old, is asleep in a tree. It's so well camouflaged by the trunk, I missed it. It's not Victor's first rodeo, though, and I also get the feeling little escapes him. He takes something out of his pocket. A compass?

'Write this down, please.' He gives me a series of numbers, which must be GPS coordinates. Who knew things would be so high tech here in the rainforest? Then he says, 'Male adult sloth, no visible injuries. Three to four years old.'

I note it all down.

'Right, let's go. He's fine, and as you see, asleep.'

We continue our trek, but find no more sloths until just as we're turning back, I spot one in a bush.

'Victor. Is this guy asleep?' I note he's a little on the skinny side.

Victor arrives at my side and bites his lip as he studies the sloth. 'He may be, but something's wrong. See there–' he indicates a patch on the sloth's fur '–and there.' He shows me another spot, what appears to be a scratch or a cut.

'Yeah. What is it?'

He shakes his head. 'I'm not certain, but it looks to me like he has been attacked by a dog. I'd say it's fairly recent, maybe in the past few days, and he's a little thinner than I'd usually expect. He might be dehydrated.'

Funnily enough, the exact same thing had crossed my mind.

He moves closer to the sloth. 'He's still breathing at least.'

Well, that's something. I, too, can see the gentle rise and fall of the sloth's chest.

'So what do we do?'

'I'll call it in. See if we can get Dexter here with a

medical kit to assess him properly. We really need two of us to transport him back if we have to take him in. They tend to claw at the cage, and we need gloves.'

I don't bother pointing out that there are two of us. I probably wouldn't be able to carry a sloth cage that distance.

Dexter arrives ten minutes later. The sloth hasn't moved. He checks its eyes, its fur, its claws.

He nods at Victor. 'Good call. We'll need to bring him in. He's definitely dehydrated and I don't like the look of those marks. I think that's a bite more than a scratch. Probably a dog.'

Victor sighs. 'We've seen too many of these dog attacks recently. Why can't people keep their dogs on leads when they're near an area where wild animals are prone to roaming?'

I agree, but I don't know if the Costa Ricans have the same regulations about keeping dogs on leads in certain areas the way we do back in the UK.

Dexter and Victor manage to carry the sloth effortlessly to the cage, whilst I jot down the notes they each dictate to me. I'm amazed it stays asleep. It's probably just as well as I know how stressed they get when handled. I don't fancy being near its claws when it's agitated.

A sliver of something that feels like pride shoots through me at the careful efficiency Dexter displays when dealing with the sloth. He really knows his stuff.

As we all walk back, Victor and Dexter debate further what may have happened to the sloth and discuss his initial treatment. I walk alongside, quietly, absorbing what they're saying, until my phone bursts to life. Aidan! You have got to be kidding? He can get lost. I press decline call and put my phone back in my pocket.

When we reach the sanctuary, Carlos is waiting. Whilst Dexter fills Carlos in, Victor excuses himself, explaining he needs to go muck out some of the cages.

'Do you want some help?' I ask.

Victor whirls around, his face a picture. 'You *want* to muck out the cages with me?'

To my side, I feel Dexter's eyes skim over me before he fully commits himself once again to his conversation with Carlos.

'Well, I wouldn't say I particularly *want* to clean up poo, but I kinda feel I should offer.'

Victor grins. 'C'mon then. Plenty poo for both of us.' He puts his arm around my shoulder in a gesture of camaraderie, and I like how it's almost brotherly.

As we wander off, I can almost bet Dexter is watching us. The hole I feel burning into the back of my T-shirt is caused either by his gaze, or the sun is doing a fine job today.

An hour later, I'm parched and wishing I'd brought my water bottle with me. I left it on the table in the breakfast room. This is hard work. My T-shirt is sticking to me, I can't count on two hands how many times I've shoved my bedraggled, lank hair out of my face and I'm filthy. I probably pong, too, but you know what, I'm having a fabulous time. Victor is good to chat to, and the more I listen to him, the more I feel my Spanish improving. I still find it difficult sometimes to articulate what I want to say, but we get by. Once my ear acclimatised to the differences between Castilian Spanish and the Costa Rican variant, it became easier. And it's fun. I might not be earning any money whilst I'm here, but I'm gaining invaluable experience, making friends and working with the animals I love most in the whole world. Life doesn't get better than this – minus the cleaning out poo from cages.

'Time for lunch.' Victor wipes sweat out of his eyes with a glove, then leans on his rake.

'I'll second that.' I'm starving. Breakfast was a long time ago. Anyway, I'm curious to know how the latest sloth is getting on. I also wonder what name we'll give him. We? I say that as if it's up to me, although I did get to name Flash. And just like that my thoughts turn to Dad. He'd be so proud of me, but probably not at the way I handled, or didn't handle, Mum. *He'd* be happy for me, pursuing a life out here, doing what I love, with like-minded people.

'It's my favourite for lunch. *Picadillo de Vainica.* Sofia serves it with tacos.' Victor smacks his lips together.

I raise an eyebrow. 'Sounds spicy.'

Victor shakes his head. 'Not too much. It has cumin and oregano, but its main ingredient is green beans.'

'Green beans?' I like green beans, but I think of them as a side dish, not the main event.

'Yes, fried with onions and tomatoes.' He laughs. 'You're not convinced. You'll see. Oh, and we add ground beef.'

Ah, so it's a beef dish. I thought it was a vegetarian

dish for a second. Not that I have anything against vegetarian dishes. I love a good ratatouille the same as the next person, but I'm hungry and I find that if I eat only vegetables for lunch or dinner, I'm hungry again two hours later. And this manual work, which I'm not used to, has my stomach rumbling.

When Victor opens the door to the canteen, the aroma that reaches my senses is heavenly, and I sniff the air, realising just how truly ravenous I am.

Mariangeles, Ella and Javier are already seated, chatting away animatedly, with Dexter, Roisin, Carlos and Federica at another table. I can't believe we're almost last to lunch.

As we stand plate in hand behind Alejandro, who smiles and asks how things are going, Sofia says, 'I think I've outdone myself today, *mis niños*. Tell me it isn't good.'

'I already know it will be, Sofia,' drawls Victor.

Teacher's pet! But I mean it in a good way. They clearly adore each other, and I thank my lucky stars once again that I've become part of this family. Everyone is so kind and on the same wavelength. Living here is so far removed from the life I've left back in Scotland: the commute, the driving from client to client, the pressure of sales, the tiptoeing around the controlling boyfriend; it's hard to fathom that that was my life until a little over a week ago.

I accept my plate of food from Sofia and thank her, then walk to the table Victor indicates and sit next to Alejandro, who hasn't stood on ceremony and is chowing down his food, making appreciative little moans as he does so.

'She wasn't kidding,' says Victor. 'It really is one of her best yet.'

I close my eyes after I take a bite. This is incredible. It's as if I'm visiting one of those amazing street food places you always see on cookery programmes, but I'm living here, with the cook, not having to travel to have this authentic taste of Costa Rica.

When I finish, I need five minutes to let my food settle as I'm stuffed. I note a discarded crossword puzzle book on the table to my left. I love crosswords, although I'm not sure how good I'll be in Spanish.

'Is this anyone's?' I ask, waving it around.

'It's mine,' Dexter says. 'Feel free.'

'Thanks.' I open it to a new crossword, or *crucigram*, and start reading the clues. It doesn't help that I don't understand the words of half the clues, so I enlist Victor and Alejandro's help. Before I know it, fifteen minutes have passed.

'Sorry to break up the party, but we need to get back to work.' Dexter is standing over us. He studies the crossword puzzle book over my shoulder, then raises his eyes to mine and says, 'May I?'

I shrug and say, 'Be my guest.' It's his book, after all.

He jots down an answer, then pockets the puzzle book as we all take our plates up to the hatch where I note lots of dirty dishes piled up beside the sink.

'I'll wash up, Sofia,' I say.

She waves a dishtowel at me. 'Not at all. I have a dishwasher.'

'Well, at least let me load that for you.'

She rolls her eyes as if she's indulging a favourite

child. 'If you must.'

I lift the hatch and go around kitchen-side, where I unload and then reload the dishwasher, all the while listening to Sofia as she asks me how I'm getting on.

'And I hear we have a new sloth,' she says.

'Yes, dehydrated, Dexter thinks.'

'Carlos and Dexter gave him plenty of fluids earlier. He's awake and they've attended to his cuts. Hopefully, we can rehabilitate him soon. You were doing the census with Victor, Carlos said.'

'Yes, but, well, we had to abandon it when we found the sloth.'

'Quite right. We can restart the data tomorrow. And are you settling in to your room OK?'

'I am, thank you. It's lovely, so bright and welcoming. Having all the flowers around really makes a difference.'

She winks. 'Well, why have nature on your doorstep and not make the most of it?'

I totally agree. She couldn't have any more nature nearby if she tried; she lives in a rainforest, with a swampy river off to one side and dozens of sloths all around, although we won't know exactly how many until after the census is complete.

'Kat.'

I jump. Dexter.

'Sorry, I didn't mean to startle you. I just thought you might like to see how our newest member is doing and what treatment we gave him to start his recovery.'

I nod until I probably resemble one of those nodding dogs that sit on car dashboards. Get a grip, woman! 'That would be great.' Turning to Sofia, I say,

'Lunch was lovely, thanks again. Maybe you could show me how to make it one day.'

Sofia clucks. 'Anytime. Now go see how that sloth is before Dexter combusts.'

I turn to see Dexter tapping his fingers against the door threshold. It strikes me that he sought me out, and I can't help but be pleased by that thought.

As we walk towards the animal hospital, Dexter says, 'That was noble of you this morning.'

My eyebrows scrunch up. 'Noble?'

'Yeah. Offering to help Victor muck out the cages.'

I smile. 'Well, I gathered you'd all been super kind to me the first few days and not given me any really grotty jobs, so I decided that I didn't want to take advantage and it was time to pull my weight.'

He grins. 'I like the way you're thinking.'

We enter the nursery and pass through it to the animal hospital.

'Hi, Javi. How's our newbie doing?' Dexter asks.

'I just checked his vitals and he's OK. He woke up earlier, but he's asleep again now.'

'I thought sloths sleeping all day was a myth,' I say.

'Oh, it is, but when they're indoors, they do tend to sleep more. Out in the wild, it's probably more like eight to ten hours a day. Not quite the twenty that uninformed websites tend to bandy about,' Javier explains.

'I see. That is quite a difference.'

'Yep. Anyway, are we ready to name this sloth?' he asks.

Dexter shoots me a glance. 'I am. Javi, your turn.'

'I'm between two, but I'm thinking Turbo.'

Dexter and I both laugh.

'Gotta stay in keeping with the theme,' Dexter says. 'Right, let's keep Turbo comfortable. Kat, would you like to monitor Turbo so Javi can head into town for some supplies?'

Panic rises in me. What do I do?

'No need to worry. He's not exactly fleet of foot.' Dexter smirks. 'And sloths can't jump, so he can't launch himself at you. The most he'll do is put a leisurely paw out, if he wakes. He may be a little disorientated. Give him some water through this syringe.' He smiles then pats me on the shoulder. 'You'll be fine. I promise. Have a little faith.'

'Yeah, right, I know.' I sound about as confident as someone who's terrified of heights, attempting their first parachute jump.

'OK, so, Javi, let's sort what you need in town and then I'll check in with the team,' Dexter says. He turns to me. 'Kat, I'll be back in less than an hour. Luciana's next door if you need her. Just remember, always ensure the doors are properly closed if you have to leave the room even for a second. They need to click shut.'

'OK,' I squeak. I can do this. I can do this.

The door closes behind them and the responsibility weighs heavily on me as I eye Turbo warily.

Chapter Twelve

'So, how's Turbo?' Dexter asks as he comes in, forty-five minutes later.

'Doing well, I think. He did wake up, and I did give him water through the syringe. He took it, so that's a positive.'

'Definitely. Well done. He didn't maul you?'

I can tell he's teasing. 'I changed out of my ripped-to-shreds clothes earlier. These ones happen to be my spares.'

'But seriously, Kat, give yourself a pat on the back. These are wild animals, and this is a whole new environment to you.'

'Thanks. It felt kinda nice giving him something to drink. I was still hyperaware of those claws, though.'

Dexter laughs. 'Quite right. You don't want to be caught unawares.' He eyes me carefully. 'For the record, I think you've made the right decision. You're fitting right in here.'

'You think so?' My heart rate spikes as I wonder if he means more than just as part of the team.

His top lip quirks upwards. 'Oh, I know so!'

Is it hot in here?

'Right, so ... what do you want me to do now?'

Did that sound suggestive? I know what I'd like to do now, but it's probably not something best done in public and it involves very few or no clothes. Oh my God, I've got it bad. Is this what happens when you're in a controlling relationship and you escape it? You then want to jump the first good-looking and nice guy you meet?

'Well, I thought perhaps we could feed the pups in the nursery. Luciana has to take one of her kids to the dentist, so I said she could leave early.'

Together. Us. Me and Dexter. Sitting side by side feeding baby sloths. That is my idea of heaven.

'That sounds good,' I manage, without fawning over him. Did I imagine the moment at the fireflies the other night, or when we were dancing? It didn't feel like it, but I've been so busy since moving here and learning the ropes, that I've not had time to analyse it. Maybe that's no bad thing.

We exit the animal hospital and head into the nursery, where Luciana smiles before standing and handing me a baby sloth.

'Which one is this?' I ask her.

'This is Bullet. All you need to remember is the baskets with the pink and blue matching blankets. Plus, Bullet is a three-fingered sloth and Rocket a two-fingered.'

I remember now. And the fact Bullet is greyer with the stereotypical happy face and Rocket is more beige.

'What kind of milk is this?' I ask as she hands me the pipette so I can take over.

'Goats'.'

I don't like to say that I meant full fat or semi-skimmed. Well, not really, but it didn't occur to me it was goats' milk. And here was me thinking I was up on my sloth facts. Clearly not. I'd best get stuck into my books again. In fact, I need Ella. I'll pick her brains later. Right now, I'm rather looking forward to, if a little nervous about, my baby sloth time, with Dexter.

I sit down and continue to feed Bullet, who sucks away happily.

Luciana tells us she'll see us tomorrow and closes the door. Then we're alone. Forced proximity, isn't that what they call it? Wonder how I'll cope. Parts of me awaken that should most definitely be asleep, particularly when I'm in the not-exactly-sexy confines of a sloth hangout. Words I never thought I'd ever utter, even if only in my head.

Dexter flops down on the sofa beside me, cradling another baby sloth in his arms, although it's not Rocket as the pink blanket is still in place and she's still fast asleep. I'm guessing baby sloths do sleep more than adult sloths.

As Dexter adjusts his position, trying to feed the sloth whilst wriggling around to move the cushion into place behind him, I hold out a hand and do it for him.

'That better?'

'Much,' he says. 'I should have thought to do that before I picked Zoom up.'

Ah, so it's Zoom he's holding. I smile. 'So, how am I doing so far?' God, did that sound needy, or flirtatious? I was aiming for funny, but not sure I carried it off.

'Well, you've risen to every challenge we've set you so far, and some we haven't – like the mucking out of cages.' He grins, and a tiny dimple forms on the left side of his mouth. How come I haven't noticed that before? I've known him for nearly a week, and it's quite clear that, against my better intentions, I'm into him.

'I suppose. And everyone's been really friendly.' Everyone except Roisin, who has barely exchanged two words with me. Maybe a perpetual scowl is her de facto expression.

'Yeah, they're a good bunch. It's just like one big happy family here.'

I nod, thinking again of Roisin, but then of how welcoming everyone else has been, particularly Mariangeles and Federica, who have me howling with laughter all the time.

Zoom wriggles in Dexter's arms.

'Hey, little guy, where do you think you're going?' Dexter says as he readjusts the sloth so he doesn't slip from his grasp. Zoom is so cute. His fur is cream whereas the majority of the other baby sloths are brown. I wonder if this is a genetic thing or if it's age-related. Perhaps they grow darker as they age. Certainly few of them seem to have the typical facial markings which make them look friendly and permanently happy.

Dexter's such a natural with the animals. You can tell he's been doing this a while. Makes me think he'd be good with babies, too. Hello? What the heck was that? Did I just imagine Dexter as the future father of my children? Stop right there, please, brain. I know we almost had a moment, or perhaps a missed opportunity the other night, but that's all it was. It would become incredibly complicated to get involved with my boss in the first week and be so far from home if it all went, to coin a rather inelegant phrase, tits up.

His smile disarms me. Nobody's teeth should be allowed to sparkle like that. And my stomach shouldn't drop like that at the sight of those lips. I feel like I've come down the steep incline of a rollercoaster. My throat's suddenly dry and I resist the urge to lick my lips in case he thinks I want to eat him for dinner.

We sit for a few minutes in companionable silence, with only the noise of our breathing and that of the sloths for company, the air thick with expectation, then Dexter asks me what I'd like to do in my first few months in Costa Rica. My cheeks heat. I can't tell him *that*.

'I'd really just like to explore. There are so many national parks with such varied wildlife in them, I don't know where to start.'

Dexter cradles the sleeping Zoom in the crook of his arm. 'I was overwhelmed when I first came here, felt humbled somehow when faced with the half a million different types of animals there are here.'

I can relate to that. Already what I've seen makes me feel like that sometimes, and I've barely scraped the surface.

'A few months ago, I went back to the Osa Peninsula, to Corcovado National Park. We should go there one day, too. It's incredible. I even saw a tapir.'

I try to suppress the sudden intake of breath I take as my brain homes in on his use of 'we'. Only afterwards do I register that he saw one of the few endangered Baird's tapir, and realise how magical that must have been for him.

'I had a friend over from Ireland. They were staying in an eco-lodge there, so I spent a week in the area.' He sighs, as if lost in his memories. 'I still felt like I didn't have enough time. The wildlife, the beaches, the waterfalls. I could go on.'

Please do. I could listen to him all day. It's oddly soporific as well as a huge turn-on for me listening to a man enthuse over the beauty of nature and animal life, when I'm so used to Aidan, who only wanted to talk about politics, current affairs and the economy. The phrase 'dull as dishwater' springs to mind. So apt. A far cry from the man sitting beside me. I tamp down the query over who the visiting friend from Ireland was. Male? Female? Girlfriend? A week's a long time to spend in a lodge with a platonic friend surely.

'You're making me really want to go now.'

He smiles, a lazy smile. It's so incredibly sexy and is making my insides churn like they're on a washing machine cycle.

'That's kind of the idea.'

I chuckle then startle when Bullet moves. I'd almost forgotten he was there as I listened to Dexter.

'Someone might be ready to graduate to a leaf,' says Dexter, inclining his head towards Bullet.

I hadn't realised they could eat leaves quite this young. Bullet only looks a few weeks old.

Dexter stands and heads over to a cupboard where he pulls out a small bag full of leaves.

'We replenish the bag each day. They prefer the freshest green leaves from the ends of branches, but obviously, these guys–' he gestures towards Zoom and Bullet '–are too little to go foraging by themselves right now.' He takes out a small leaf and hands it to me.

Bullet instantly perks up, interest clear in his actions. I waft the leaf near his mouth and his little claw comes up to grab it before he holds it towards his mouth, smacking his lips together. It's fascinating to watch. Again, I think who needs nightlife when you have all this at your fingertips? Becca flits into my mind and I smile. This wouldn't be her idea of a good night in. She'd be looking for the pubs and clubs. She'd happily come on holiday somewhere like this, doing the beaches, the zip wire at the cloud forest and the national parks, but she wouldn't actually want to touch the animals. The thought would terrify her.

Dexter smiles. 'He likes it.'

He does? He doesn't seem to have eaten much, if any, of it. 'How can you tell?'

'See how he's smacking his lips together? That's how a sloth trims down the leaf. And they don't eat very much per day. A baby sloth even less.'

The last part makes sense. I'm learning so much here. Dexter's good at this stuff, and evidently passionate on the subject. Again my thoughts meander towards Dexter and me, and his being passionate in a different sense. For the love of… If I were the type of girl who endorsed casual sex, I'd tell myself to have sex with him to get him out of my system, but I've had three sexual partners and I'm now thirty. Each of them I've been with for three years of my life. Not exactly casual – and those timescales are pointedly similar.

Dexter puts Zoom back in his cot and checks on some of the other sloths, who've been remarkably, or perhaps not so remarkably, silent, and still, whilst we've been chatting.

He turns back to me and hesitates. What? He's clearly on the verge of saying something. He runs a hand across his five-o'clock shadow, which I long to reach up and brush my fingers across. I almost have to sit on my hands to stop myself, but that's out, as I'm still holding Bullet.

'Kat, I was wondering if you fancied going for a walk later.'

In the swampy undergrowth around the sanctuary? Surely not.

I clear my throat. I would like to go for a walk, but I don't trust myself to speak in case I come across as an overexcited puppy at the mere mention of the word 'walk'.

Dexter rushes on, 'We'd drive to the beginning of the walk. We wouldn't start from here.'

My stress levels return to normal. The thought of sinking into the murky, swampy river water by mistake freaks me out.

I look out of the window. I couldn't afford to come to Costa Rica in high season, so I'm here in July, during the official rainy season, although September and October are the wettest months. I'm glad it hasn't rained too much since I've been here, and I've noticed it tends to rain more in the afternoon and early evening. Right now, it's chucking it down.

Dexter jumps in. 'It'll stop raining before then. I've checked the forecast.'

Interesting. He's organised and the walk was … premeditated. No, that makes it sound like he's going to murder me. Prearranged.

'Sure.' I try to keep my tone casual. 'Where did you have in mind?'

'I was thinking we could go down to Manuel Antonio National Park.'

'I'll trust your judgement.'

Dexter grins. 'You're in good hands.'

A cough has us turning our heads towards the door. Roisin. It had to be Roisin. Did she hear our exchange? I don't want everyone knowing Dexter and I are spending time alone. It's private and no one else's business.

'Roisin?' Dexter flushes. Perhaps he's concerned she overheard too. Maybe it looked like the boss was making a play for a member of staff.

'Carlos asked me to come and relieve you,' she says in clipped tones, but somehow she still manages to imbue the words with a suggestive undercurrent. 'He needs to speak to you in his office.'

'Oh, right. Sure.' Dexter turns, a myriad of emotions crossing his face as he turns back to me. Uncertainty. Regret. Excitement. 'Kat, we'll pick this up again later.'

I know exactly what he's referring to, but does Roisin? I nod to him and as the door closes behind him, the scowl on her face leaves me in no doubt that she did. The atmosphere in the room has become almost unbearable in the space of only a few seconds. She really doesn't like me, and have I finally touched on why? The look of loathing she gave me when she turned back after Dexter left proves one thing: she likes Dexter. Well, tough, if he likes her, he can do something about it. And if he likes me, ditto.

I don't want any trouble, but I'm not going to roll over and let some self-absorbed little upstart rain on my parade. I'm going for a walk with Dexter later, and I'm hopeful we can pick up where we left off at Nicolás'.

Chapter Thirteen

I didn't know how to dress for our walk, nor indeed at exactly what time Dexter intended for us to set off, but at dinner he mentioned wearing long trousers and taking a hoodie.

It was difficult to curb my enthusiasm for an evening spent in Dexter's company, alone. He hadn't mentioned anyone else, so I assumed it would just be the two of us, and I liked the sound of that. I liked the sound of that very much. As Mariangeles and Federica chattered away, with Ella chipping in occasionally and Roisin seated as far away from me as possible, but still glaring daggers at me at every opportunity, I hugged to myself the fact I'd soon be in Dexter's company, and only Dexter's company. I prayed the anticipation wasn't misplaced.

I excuse myself from the table and go to the bathroom. As I freshen up, dragging a brush through my unruly mass of curls, the door opens and Roisin swans in. Of course she does. I nod in acknowledgement. But again, because we're alone and there's no one to witness her surliness, she acts as if I'm not even there, before entering a toilet cubicle, but not before I notice how much more makeup than usual she's wearing. I cough as her cloying perfume, which she has applied rather more liberally than advisable tonight, hits the back of my throat. I put my brush back in my bag and leave before my eyes start streaming. I've always been oversensitive to strong smells, well, manufactured ones – for some reason cow poo, or sloth poo, doesn't have the same effect. As I walk back to the table, I reflect on what Roisin was wearing – skinny jeans encasing her endless legs, a top with a tight corset-like bodice and a few jangly bracelets. Not really the sort of apparel you'd think to wear for dinner with colleagues and friends in a sloth sanctuary. My jaw clenches involuntarily. She's up to something.

After taking a few minutes strolling round the exhibition area to order my thoughts, I return to the table, then glance down at what I'm wearing– a navy T-shirt and grey cargo pants. Not the sexiest, but then Dexter did advise me to wear a hoodie, so I wasn't going to get out the Dolce & Gabbana dress – nor do I own one.

As I approach the table, I inhale sharply. Roisin is sitting beside Dexter, off to the side. I say sitting, she's practically perched on his lap and her arm is draped around his shoulders. To be fair, Dexter readjusts himself, shrinking away from her attentions, but she only homes in on him more. No one else has noticed. I pretend not to have seen and sit back down with Mariangeles, where I half-listen to the current topic: the decline of howler monkeys in the region. As Ella imparts that spider monkeys are the most at risk as they're actually endangered, Roisin gives a tinkly laugh then trails a finger down Dexter's cheek. He jerks back, reddens and actively tries to engage Sofia in their conversation, but she has her back to him as she's talking and laughing with Victor and Alejandro in rapid-fire Spanish, clearly relating some anecdote, and doesn't hear him.

I continue to half-listen to the conversation in my group, unable to actively contribute anything as I'm wound so tight at what's unfolding in front of me.

At the screech of a chair being pushed back hurriedly, I glance up. Only I notice. Everyone else is too involved in their conversations. Dexter strides off, a grim set to his jaw. He doesn't even see me.

Relief surges through me. I hate to admit it, but for a second I was worried Roisin was going to succeed in getting her mitts into him. I finally join in the conversation at my table, risking a surreptitious glance at the next table. Roisin is sitting ramrod straight, staring into space. Unattractive lines crease her forehead. I'm sure she wouldn't be happy if she knew how she was feeling was having that effect. Suddenly, she whips around and I don't quite disguise my interest in time. Busted.

For the next five minutes, I sense her penetrating gaze on me. It's so unnerving, eventually, I sit back and tell Mariangeles and Ella, 'I'm full. I'll see you later.'

I stroll out into the courtyard and gulp in the not exactly fresh air. For a moment, I long for the freezing cold air I was able to draw into my lungs daily back in Scotland. The humidity in Central America takes some getting used to.

'You had enough too?'

I startle. 'Jesus, you scared me, Dexter.'

He laughs and the sound is both melodious and comforting.

'Sorry,' he says, not sounding remotely sorry, a smile playing on his lips.

God, I'm done for. I don't want to go for a walk, I want to drag this man into bed and do lots of naughty things to him, and have them done to me. Is it that I've forgotten what to be in lust is? Certainly I never felt this way about Aidan. It would have been hard to; he's so rigid, unswerving, never spontaneous.

I want to kiss Dexter so much, it gives me a physical pain beneath my breastbone.

'You ready for our walk?' he says into the darkness, jolting me out of my thoughts.

'Yeah,' I breathe.

We hold each other's gaze for a few seconds too long then I break the spell as otherwise I'm going to take the initiative and snog this man senseless right here, right now, in this courtyard, without caring who's here to witness it. 'Shall we go?'

Dexter stutters for a moment as if he too was caught up in the moment then he leads the way to the truck as I try to calm my racing heart and marshal my thoughts.

'I have to be honest. This is not what I was expecting.'

Dexter laughs. 'What were you expecting?'

'I thought for some reason we'd just go for a pad about.'

'That's not always advisable here.' He grins. 'All

sorts of things come out at night, but then that's what we're here for, with a guide, of course.'

Ramón, the guide, asks if we're ready to set off. There are six of us on this night tour of the jungle. I still find it strange that it's completely dark by half past six. And the sun sets so quickly here, unlike back home, where it doesn't get properly dark straight away and is a much more gradual process. Here the darkness is heavy and all-encompassing and never more than when you're in the middle of a rainforest with its unusual sounds and potential for threat around every tree trunk.

Dexter steadies me with a hand on my upper arm when I stumble as I follow Ramón deeper into the rainforest. I confess to being a little spooked at the total silence and darkness, broken only every so often by the cry of something unidentifiable. I thought the nature programmes Dad and I used to watch would have been of more use to me, but I'm in the dark – pun intended – as to what to expect and what many of these noises and smells are, although the pervading dampness isn't hard to identify. I guess with all the rain here in the rainy season, that's inevitable.

A rustling in the trees overhead has me peering upwards at the natural canopy created by the mesh of branches. I startle at the sound, because I know that monkeys aren't nocturnal, and that's what I'd mainly expect to find in the trees, in the daytime. Then a high-pitched chirp starts up, some kind of call. Ramón turns to us.

'Red-eyed tree frog.' He beams. 'Something's after him.'

I whirl around. What's after him? How big is it?

You don't get jaguars in this part of the jungle, do you?

Dexter puts his hand on my shoulder. 'Don't worry. It'll just be a snake or a bat.'

'A snake?'

'Yeah, there's quite a lot of snakes here. Didn't you notice the way Ramón is bashing some of the foliage with his stick as he carves a path through for us?'

I shake my head.

'That's because there are snakes and we don't want any surprises. They're more scared of us than we are of them.'

I'm not sure that's strictly true, but now may not be the time to mention that. Despite wanting to be a vet, snakes are not high on my to-nurture list. It's the scales and the fact they shed their skins. They don't have pythons here, do they? I decide to ask.

'I don't think so. I've never seen any. Anyway, most of Costa Rica's snakes aren't venomous.'

'That's good to know as I panic after I'm bitten, wondering if it's one of the venomous ones or not,' I mutter.

Dexter laughs. 'Do you really think I'd bring you somewhere dangerous?'

I breathe out. 'No.'

'There you go then.' He smiles. 'I'd hardly want to put myself in danger either, would I?'

Again no.

'No, what we're looking for tonight are coatis, armadillos, ocelots and of course, sloths.'

Although I'm surrounded by sloths daily now, the idea of seeing them in the wild at night still thrills me.

We continue to follow Ramón as he literally cuts us

a path through the dense jungle. How does he know where he's going? How will we find our way back? We've strayed from the path, or rather, we weren't ever part of the main tourist trail. From what Dexter says, this is private land, and the busy, vibrant Espadilla beach, with its many bars and restaurants, seems a world away, despite being nearby. I may want to visit the beach another day, as I've heard from Federica that it's a lot of fun and the food is amazing, but for now, I'm happy to soak up the atmosphere of being on this tour with Dexter, and the other four, who have now begun to chat in earnest to Ramón. I'm already thinking if a predator does come, all I have to do is outrun the others. We've only just met. For once, I'd need to be selfish. Self-preservation, you understand.

Another rustling, this time from the bushes straight ahead. And then I see it. An anteater, or an armadillo? No, definitely an anteater; it has hair and no armour.

Ramón indicates for us to back up. He whispers something low to Dexter, who nods.

'What did he say?' I ask.

'He says they can be aggressive when cornered, so it's important we give it space.'

This trip is worrying me more and more as the night goes on. So much for wanting to be a vet. Maybe I'm only meant to observe wild animals like this from afar – by that, I mean on TV. Yet as my panic rises again, I stare in wonder, watching this odd-looking animal shuffle about on the ground, its elongated snout snuffling along, searching for its next meal.

'I can't believe the size of its snout,' I whisper to Dexter.

'It has a two-foot-long tongue, too.'

I try not to laugh. I can just imagine what smutty response Becca would have made to that comment.

Once our long-nosed friend disappears off into the undergrowth again, I exhale the breath I was holding, part from fear, part out of awe.

'You OK?' Dexter asks, his eyes brimming with amusement.

'I'm fine, thanks,' I reply rather snootily, which makes him burst out laughing until Ramón shushes him. Then I hear it again, the call of the tree frog.

'There!' I point. A red-eyed tree frog is less than two metres from us, and I can just about pick out all of its features, even with our torches lowered to the ground so as not to startle it.

'He really is bug-eyed, isn't he?' I say.

One of the tourists overhears – an American, or perhaps Canadian – and snorts.

'He sure is,' he agrees. He takes a few photos with his impressive-looking camera – I guess it works better than my phone, which is completely useless at taking night-time photos – everyone and everything has red eyes when I do so. Now it's my turn to snort. It wouldn't matter in this case, as it's a red-eyed tree frog. Maybe I'll use my phone camera after all.

Dexter eyes me quizzically, staring at me until I feel I have to explain. He gives that lazy, sexy grin again and I gulp.

We settle back into walking again, Ramón in the lead, turning back every now and then to ensure we're OK and haven't been savaged by the non-existent jaguars in the jungle.

'Aargh!' The American woman jumps back in fright, and I career into Dexter, almost knocking him flying. This time it's me who tries to right him before he ends up on the floor – the jungle floor, but as I catch hold of him, I only succeed in toppling over, too, and I land most inelegantly on top of him. 'Oof!' I say as all the air goes out of my lungs.

Dexter gazes up at me, his sky blue orbs burning into mine. 'You know, if you wanted to get horizontal with me, you only had to say.'

I swat him as best as I can with my hand, from the position I'm in, which doesn't prove very effective. I sit up, colour rushing to my cheeks, and it's partly embarrassment at what he said, and which I didn't deny, and partly at the feel of his body so close to mine, in such an intimate position. Were we not on the floor of the jungle and surrounded by five anxious faces, I'd be more inclined to remain 'horizontal' with him.

As I brush down my clothes, I meet his gaze again, but this time there's a steely determination in me, and I detect humour and something else behind his eyes: lust? I do recall what it looks like, despite it being forever since anyone looked at me like that. And I find I'm quite enjoying the feeling.

'I'm so sorry,' the woman interrupts. 'I saw something, something big, and it frightened me. It hissed at me.'

She's still trembling as Dexter explains, 'It was a raccoon.'

The woman's husband tilts his head. 'A raccoon?'

'Yeah, we get them here too. They're pretty active at night,' Dexter explains.

The man nudges his wife and laughs. 'A little ol' raccoon scared you, darlin'. We get those in the back yard.'

They both giggle at this and laugh at how silly she was to be so scared.

Dexter and I exchange a look and await Ramón's instructions.

'That was amazing – terrifying, but amazing,' I say when we return to the starting point of the tour and we've said goodbye to everyone. 'I've had a lovely evening, Dexter. Thank you.'

'All in a day's work.' He gives a goofy grin. 'But we're not done just yet.'

I raise my eyebrows. 'We're not?'

'Nope. C'mon.'

In the truck, he won't tell me where we're going, and I realise only when he pulls into a lay-by that we're at the beach. How are we going to be able to see? Does he intend to have his wicked way with me on the sand with the lapping of the waves as our soundtrack? I don't like sand getting everywhere. And it does get everywhere.

'What are we doing?' I ask.

Dexter's lips curve into a smile as he gets out of the truck. 'You'll see.'

Intrigued, I follow him. Part of me loves surprises, part of me loathes them. I'm hoping, and praying, I like this one.

We step down onto the sand and Dexter catches my hand in his. 'Just so you don't stumble. We can keep each other upright. We've both been a bit clumsy, or is it unlucky, tonight in that respect.'

As he holds my hand, I can't help but think how lucky I am. I'd happily stumble over and over with him. However, it is hard to see in front of me once we round a bend and lose the lights from the beachfront cafés and bars. Now we only have the torch from one phone to see by; Dexter was quite insistent on that. Enough for us not to go flying, but not enough to illuminate things too much. I'm paraphrasing what he said, but I'm close, and I must admit, I'm more curious than ever to see what he has in store.

He stops so suddenly I almost run into the back of him. 'Here we are.'

'What?' I look out towards the ocean, but I can't see anything.

Dexter takes hold of my other arm so he's swinging me round the other way and then I gasp. The ocean is filled with tiny pinpricks of light – blue light – and it's magical. It's the only word to describe it. I'm actually speechless. It's so beautiful, tears threaten behind my eyes. I'm here in the dark, with this gorgeous man, with these stomach-churning feelings inside me, witnessing this incredible sight. I'm so honoured, so lucky, and so humbled.

'Bioluminescence.'

I turn in his arms to face him. 'I've heard of it, but I've never seen it before in real life. It's beautiful.'

Dexter scans my face, his eyes searching mine. 'You're beautiful, Kat. So I wanted to bring you to this beautiful place and tell you so.'

Emotion overwhelms me and I struggle to keep

myself in check until Dexter, still studying my face, lowers his mouth to mine, and I bring my lips up to meet his. And it's every bit as good as I imagined it would be. And more.

Chapter Fourteen

'So, are you coming to the cloud forest next time we go?' Ella asks me next morning in the women's rec room as we prepare to face the day. 'We're trying to figure out who wants to go so we can work out who needs to change shift with who, to allow that to happen.'

'Wouldn't miss it for the world,' I say as I slip on my trainers.

'I've been once before.' She goes all starry-eyed, then focuses back on me. 'There really are no words to describe it.'

That's how I often feel about my life here in Costa Rica. Both the night-time jungle tour and that incredible kiss with Dexter – and what happened after. No, I didn't sleep with him, but let's just say there was more than one kiss. I wonder how we'll behave around each other today. Will it be all secret, knowing smiles or will we act almost as if nothing has happened? I really hope he doesn't act as if *nothing* has happened. That would be awful, not to mention awkward. Once again, I remind myself why getting involved with not only another sanctuary worker but my boss isn't a good idea. But I like him – a lot – and I think he likes me.

Well, if the way he conducted himself last night is anything to go by, he does. Wait until I tell Becca. She'll be buying bridal magazines and choosing her bridesmaid dress. I'm kidding, but she will be ecstatic that it underlines Aidan is but a not-so-distant memory.

'I'm on administration of meds to the sloths this morning, for those who need it. You want to tag along, see how we do that, and what protocols we need to follow?' Ella asks.

'That would be great.' I really need to start feeling as if I'm contributing here. I know I'm still learning and it's early days, but I hate being on the back foot. I hate starting new jobs, even when it's a job I love, in a place I love. My inner voice says 'with a man you love'. I tut. It's a bit early for that. My inner voice sniggers.

After breakfast, I follow Ella to the hospital and we check on the patients. Flash is my first port of call. As Ella chats with Carlos, who enters the room just after us, I give my attention over to Flash, who looks to be healing nicely. A couple of other sloths are still in the hospital wing. I don't know their names. I'll need to ask.

'Right, so here's where we keep the medication,' Ella says. She pats a cupboard to her left. 'Here are the forms we need to fill in detailing which animal has had which medication and at what time. We also have different forms for medications that we note are running low.' She points those out, and as she continues to talk me through the processes of how the medical side of things are run, I give her my full attention. Ella is so easy to listen to, and she really knows her stuff. I admire that in one so young. Listen to me. I'm doing it again – I'm only thirty. There's only nine years between us. But what I mean is it's rare for someone her age to be so knowledgeable and mature, and Ella is both, but lovely and modest with it.

She's not preachy either, which is a welcome change. It's clear she simply loves her job, her life, and she wants everyone else to feel the same, or at the very least know how to care for the sloths as well as she does.

When the door opens and Dexter appears, I take an involuntary step backwards. He seems to fill the room. It isn't exactly a huge room, the hospital, despite its grandiose title, but Dexter, at over six feet, leaves little room to manoeuvre, literally, once he's inside the room with us.

'Hey,' he says to both of us.

Ella lifts her head from where she's making notes on one of the sloth's profiles. 'Oh, hi, Dexter. I was just showing Kat how we administer and account for the meds, and the reporting logs we fill in.'

'Good idea.' He turns to me. 'Kat, you have a phone call.'

I knit my brows. 'A phone call?' Absent-mindedly I pat the pocket of my cargo pants where I put my mobile earlier. Nope. Still there.

'On the sanctuary line,' Dexter says pointedly.

I frown. 'On the sanctuary line?' I parrot back to him.

He nods again, but a tick pulses in his cheek.

'But hardly anyone knows I'm here, and no one knows this number.'

'Clearly someone does,' he says drily.

'Back in a sec, Ella.' I walk past Dexter and out into the foyer, where I cross to Carlos' office. Surely Immigration isn't trying to deport me already.

I nod a hello to Sofia, who is sitting at the desk sorting some paperwork. 'Dexter told me there's a call for me.'

She waves in the direction of the phone on the other desk. 'Yes. Apparently, they couldn't get you on your mobile.'

Fear clutches at my heart. Has something happened back home? Is Mum all right? Despite our argument on my birthday, and the fact we often don't see eye to eye, she's still my mum and I'd be devastated if anything happened to her, especially after losing Dad.

'Hello?'

'Thank God. I've been out of my mind with worry.'

Aidan. You have got to be joking. If I didn't have a phone to my ear, I'd be putting my head in my hands or hitting it off of the desk right now. Was I not clear enough?

'Aidan, I can assure you there's nothing to worry about.' I try to keep my tone measured, but he brings out the worst in me and my words have a spiky edge to them.

'How can you say that?' he splutters. 'You "dump" me and then don't even come home when you're due to return.'

I hear the quote marks in his tone, which somehow also manages to ooze condescension.

I turn my back to Sofia, unsure how much English she speaks, and unwilling to involve her in my drama.

Already I'll have to apologise for this intrusion. How dare he! How dare he!

'Aidan, let's be clear on one thing, I didn't "dump you", I dumped you. We are no longer together. We will not be together again. Finito.' I almost say 'Capisce?' but I think it would make me sound like some mafia heavy.

'Kat, you can't just end things like this. We were about to buy a flat together.'

'That's right, Aidan,' I almost screech. 'About to. We didn't, thankfully. End of.'

'You know, you can be very cruel sometimes.'

I almost laugh. Says the controlling boyfriend. No, I will not let myself be manipulated – again.

'Not something you'll have to worry about any more,' I bark. 'Now, if you don't mind, I have work to do.'

'Work? You're working over there? But what about your job? You can't give up your job. How will you pay–?'

'Aidan, that's no longer your concern. I can, and I have, and I'm perfectly happy where I am. Please don't call me again.'

'Well, I'll need to let your mum know the latest. She's been talking about coming over to talk some sense into you.'

Panic flows through me then, and I ball my hands into fists. Thank God neither of them is here. I'm not a violent person, but my God, I want to punch them both right now.

'I'm thirty. I don't think I need my mother to talk sense into me. I've made my decision. I'm staying here,

Aidan. Feel free to convey that to Mum. Goodbye.'

I hang up the phone as my breathing becomes ragged. I need some water. My head aches from the build-up of pressure in it, and a sharp pain behind my eyes causes me to wince. I'm so angry.

'Sorry, Sofia, for the interruption. It won't happen again.'

She waves my apology away. 'It's no trouble. Is everything OK?' Her eyebrows shift upwards and her forehead visibly tightens.

I give her a small smile. 'It will be, thank you.'

Once I've left the office, I head for the ladies' loos, check there's no one in them and promptly burst into tears.

I know we'd put a reservation fee down on a new-build flat, but the deposit hadn't been paid yet, the missives hadn't been concluded and all in all, both Aidan and I are in a position we can extricate ourselves from relatively easily. Why can't he see that? Because he's a narcissistic power-hungry passive-aggressive control freak who wants everything to go exactly the way he planned, when he says so. Phew! Glad I got that off my chest.

I sigh with relief that the blinkers finally fell from my eyes and I had the courage to stand up to him. Who knows, if I hadn't befriended Ed and decided to take up diving that day, I could be back home in Scotland, signing legal documents at the solicitor's, linking Aidan and me for the foreseeable future. I've had a lucky escape.

The door to the ladies opens. I hold my breath. Please don't let it be Roisin. I just know my face is tear-stained. I'd kind of hoped to have a chance to splash water on it before I head back out to work. The last thing I need is to see her scowling face full of disdain for me.

Then I hear humming. From the tunefulness, I recognise Federica's voice, and breathe more easily again. When the cubicle door next to me closes, I compose myself and open my door.

I'm drying my hands on a paper towel when Federica comes out. I glance in the mirror at her. 'Hi.'

'Hi, how's your day going? I heard Ella was going to go through the med rituals with you.'

'She did. I've been enjoying learning about it all.' I ignore her question.

'I was wondering…' she says as she washes her hands, her eyes flicking to mine '…would you practise English with me?' When I don't immediately respond, because that's not what I was expecting her to say, she rushes on. 'Only, I'm trying to do a course online, since with my hours here, it's not so easy to attend a class in person. And it's not equal.'

'Of course I'll help you.' I pat her arm lightly. 'I'd be delighted to.'

She smiles and it lights up her whole face. 'Thank you. Dexter is helping me, too, but I figured if I can understand his Irish accent and your Scottish one, then hopefully I can understand any English accent. You guys speak so fast.'

I laugh and switch to English. 'We do. Well, there's no time like the present,' I say slowly.

She laughs. 'My English is not so good yet, but I know some basics. I did some English at school.'

'Where did you go to school?' I ask her.

'In my home town in the north of Peru. A place called Chiclayo. Do you know it?'

I shake my head. 'No, but I'll look it up. I'm always keen to learn more about new places.'

'Well, it's very popular with Peruvians for vacation. There are mountains, beaches, as well as the adobe pyramids, not to mention gorgeous cathedrals and a palace.'

'Sounds wonderful. Sold!' I say.

Federica grins. 'I am extremely passionate about my country.'

'I can tell,' I say, mirroring her grin.

As we return to the foyer, she tells me roughly what she has covered in her online course. Personally, I think she has done a lot. She just lacks confidence and the opportunity to chat face to face with native speakers or the chance to speak with a teacher and classmates.

Federica has taken me under her wing, and now it's my turn to return the favour.

When I return to the hospital, Dexter is there, checking on Flash.

'How's he doing?' I ask.

Dexter glances up, but his face doesn't bear any trace of warmth, unlike the man whose ardent kisses last night gave me stubble rash this morning, which I then had to cover with makeup, something I haven't worn since I arrived at the sanctuary.

Whatever. Maybe he's not a morning person.

'His cuts have healed. I've also weighed him and he has gained a little weight, which is great news.'

So why does Dexter sound so pissed off? Surely he's

not annoyed about Aidan calling.

'Once Ella has finished with you here, can you take over from Luciana in the nursery? She has a meeting and there was a mix-up with the dates. They've just called to tell her it's today.'

'Of course.' I'm still wondering why he's so off, as Federica comes in.

'Ah, there you are, Dexter. Delivery. Oh, by the way, Kat's agreed to help me with my English, too. Now I have two teachers, I'll be able to learn so much faster.'

Dexter glances at me. I can't quite make out what's going on with him. I'd have sworn that was a hint of admiration in his eyes, but he still looks narked about something. No matter.

'That's great.' Dexter smiles warmly at Federica.

Where's my warm smile? I'm starting to feel a little put out. Dexter snogged the face off me last night and today is as warm as Siberia. I hope he's not regretting our encounter. I'm not, or rather, I wasn't. I don't do hot and cold, though. I can't be bothered with game-playing. You're either into someone or you're not.

'Yes, I'll have an Irish-Scottish accent. I can't think of anything better,' says Federica.

Dexter and I both raise a smile at that, and once again our eyes meet, but I can't fathom quite what is going on behind his. One thing's for sure, I'll find out later. I'm done with men messing me about or messing with my head. If he wants something to happen between us, I need us to be open and honest with each other.

'Let's check on that delivery then.' Dexter strides

out of the room without so much as a backward glance.

Half an hour later, I'm done and relieve Luciana of her duties. Speedy is clambering over the sofa. Funny how I'm beginning to recognise the different sloths. He has a little dark spot just above his eye which distinguishes him from the others, and his fur is denser than that of the younger sloths. I guess he must be around seven months old. I'll miss him when he goes.

One of the younger sloths is climbing on a rocking chair, which I now realise is the perfect training material for him. Trees would be outside of his area of expertise still.

Luciana fills me in on which sloths have been fed and which still need a little milk or leaves. She opens the door from the nursery that leads to the outdoor covered area where the sloths can play safely without being able to escape and which helps prepare them for surviving on their own. I recall seeing a similar set-up in the area for the older sloths.

I settle in happily, watching the sloths' antics – those who are awake – and give a little milk to Nimble, whose chart says he has only been here ten days. He also looks only a few months old.

I've just worked out it's Bolt climbing on the chair when Carlos comes in. He smiles and sits down beside me. 'Have I missed Luciana?'

'Yes, she left about twenty minutes ago.'

'Ah. I'll catch her later.' He gestures to Nimble. 'He likes you.'

My heart leaps. 'Really? How can you tell?'

'He's very relaxed, and sloths can be such tense animals. That's why we don't let anyone except the sanctuary workers touch them.'

I nod. I knew that sloths didn't like to be touched, but I'm definitely learning more about these cute little guys every day.

Carlos regards me earnestly. 'Kat, I just wanted to say I'm so happy with how you've settled in.'

I sigh. 'Carlos, it's like a dream for me here. I love animals, always have, and sloths are my favourite.' I glance down at Nimble, taking in his little cream-coloured face, in contrast to the trademark darker stripes beneath each eye. 'Who couldn't love them?'

'I feel exactly the same way. Anyway, I wanted you to know I'm very happy with the work you've done so far. I hear you've been studying the medicines they receive, today.'

'Yes. Ella has been great.'

'She's an asset to the sanctuary, that's for sure. We'd be lost without her.'

I smile at the fondness in his voice. Carlos certainly seems to think of all his workers as his family. Sofia does too, from the way she treats us all. It's so touching.

'So, would you like to come with me to one of the other sanctuaries later this week? We share information about the sloths, learn from each other, discuss numbers, that sort of thing. Taking care of sloths is still a relatively new thing. Only a few decades, so we're always learning from other people's studies.'

'Absolutely. Thanks, Carlos.'

'Right, I'll let you know the details. See you later.'

Once he's gone, I hug to myself just how much I'm integrating into this new way of life. I'm almost tearful as I think of all the years wasted working in pet supplies, when I could have been braver and come and done something like this. But then Dad was still around, so I'd never have left Scotland back then. The grief catches me unexpectedly again. I take a few deep breaths and have just managed to compose myself when the door opens. Roisin.

Well, I was right about the scowl. Either it's permanent or she reserves it solely for me.

When she remains standing in the doorway, I raise my eyebrows in a question.

'Where's Luciana?'

Ah, no preamble. No chit-chat. No pleasantries.

'At a meeting. Will I tell her you're looking for her when she gets back?'

'No. I'll text her.' She turns and leaves as quickly as she appeared, the door swinging to behind her.

I roll my eyes. I suppose not everyone can be good-natured, but does she have to be so goddamned horrible? She couldn't be any more obvious if she came up and said, 'I don't like you,' and punctuated each word by a jab of her long, bony fingers to my chest.

I put Nimble down in his cot and move to the outside area of the nursery to check on the three sloths who're in there, hanging from the trees, moving along the man-made canopy and dropping into their little swimming pool.

I giggle as one of them lets go of the branch he's climbing on and lands with a splash in the pool. I note the mats around the pool. I can imagine everything would be soaked otherwise. I'm also not stupid and don't go too close in case they soak me. The sloth swims seamlessly through the water. He's a better swimmer than me, and I made the school team. He looks so happy. I mean, I know sloths *look* permanently happy, but he's definitely enjoying himself. Splash! I startle as another joins him and then the third. Pool party for three.

I stand and watch them for a little while, enjoying the camaraderie they're displaying, then I return to the main nursery, where the sloths are sleeping like, well, babies, or playing on the rocking chairs. I'm about to sit down to observe them when my phone rings in my back pocket.

Becca.

Guilt swamps me. I haven't called her for a good few days now, and I haven't texted much either.

I answer. 'I know, I know, I'm sorry, how are you? I've been a little caught up with my new sloth lifestyle.' I'm waiting for her to speak but there's silence.

'Hello, hello?' I repeat.

'Katherine Imogen MacDonald, your father would be turning in his grave right now at your behaviour.'

Bile rises in my throat, both at the fact Mum has tricked me into answering the phone by involving Becca, and at the way she has used Dad against me, again.

I try to speak but no words come out. It doesn't matter anyway as Mum has no intention of letting me talk. She's off on one. 'If you won't see sense, I'll come over there.'

She had better be kidding.

'Mum, I don't want you coming over. There's no need. I have a new life here. I'll visit at Christmas. I'm doing well over here. I love it.'

My staccato-like sentences are intentional. I want to make it easy for her to understand this is how I want my life to be. I don't need her meddling in it.

'I gave you a chance, Kat. I had Aidan call you when you wouldn't listen to me before.'

I pace the room, venturing into the outdoor area again, trying to calm the panic building within me. I don't want her coming here. I don't want her spoiling things for me. The realisation saddens me, but it's true. She's no Dad. Even if she wanted to, she couldn't replace him. They always were poles apart. It was no surprise that I gravitated towards Dad. Mum and I had, and still have, little in common, and that was only further emphasised after Dad's death.

I'm trying to get a word in edgeways, intermittently sighing and rolling my eyes, when the door opens and Luciana returns. I mouth 'Sorry' at her, but she's frowning. She seems distracted. I try to wrap things up with Mum as I smile at Luciana, who's now flitting from cot to cot, checking in on each one's occupant.

Now it's my turn to frown. Doesn't she trust me? She pushes past me into the recreation area where the three sloths are still swimming.

She rounds on me. 'Kat, where's Nimble?'

'In his cot. I've not long finished feeding him.'

'Kat, he's not in his cot and the door was open.'

The door was open? How could the door have been open? It takes a second for my brain to catch on. Roisin. My phone slips from my hand. I don't even stop to pick it up or check if it's broken as it hits the floor. Instead, I dash out the door. Please let Nimble be OK.

Chapter Fifteen

Panic claws at my heart. Nimble's missing? But how? I'd have seen him. He's so little. The pool. I was watching the sloths playing in the pool. Luciana said the door was open. Could a baby sloth have fitted through the gap? I didn't see that the door was open, that Roisin had left it open, so I have no idea by how much it was open. Was there room for him to slip through? That hadn't even occurred to me. Both Dexter and Carlos were very clear when I first arrived that we all had to ensure the doors clicked shut, to avoid exactly this sort of incident. And now it has happened, and on my watch. It wasn't my fault, but right now, that doesn't matter. I have to find Nimble.

'Luciana, it's possible he's still here. You stay here, and I'll check the foyer and the other rooms.'

'OK, but if you don't find him in five minutes, I'll need to raise the alarm.'

I nod. Five minutes. It's more than I could have hoped for. The disappointment in Luciana's eyes causes a physical pain in my chest, not only because Nimble is missing but because I'm being silently blamed for something I didn't do.

I open the door, close it firmly behind me and, like

a stealth ninja, head out into the foyer. Fortunately, the school group isn't due to arrive until this afternoon, so the sanctuary doesn't have many visitors. I'd like to think they'd have told someone if they'd seen a baby sloth on its own, but you can never be sure.

Since Nimble's only little, I don't need to look overhead initially, although my eyes are drawn automatically upwards. He couldn't climb anything larger than the practice rocking chairs at the moment. I don't think, anyway. Knowing my luck, this will be the first time a baby sloth of his age climbs the equivalent of a redwood. I bat the idea away. I try not to jog across the foyer, but I need to make sure the external doors are shut. My absolute worst nightmare would be if he managed to get out into the wild again. It's too soon. He wouldn't be able to fend for himself yet. I'm terrified he may be run over by someone in the car park. He can't have gone far. Sloths don't move quickly. The irony of a sloth escaping isn't lost on me, and maybe tomorrow or next week I'll look back on this and laugh, but right now the danger feels very real indeed.

After I confirm that the external door is locked, I hunker down to check low to the ground, under tables, desks, chairs, then on chairs, behind curtains, plant pots, the toilets, everywhere I can think of. Five minutes passes quickly. I must be running out of time. Luciana opens the door to the nursery. Oh no, it's time. My short career at the sanctuary is about to be over. Dread pools in the pit of my stomach. I don't want things here to end like this and it's so unfair. I'll deal with my anger at Roisin's carelessness later.

Carlos walks out from his and Sofia's lounge area, one of the two rooms I haven't checked yet, the other being his office. He smiles at me, but I hesitate in my reply, then give him a wan smile back. He shakes his head slightly, then enters his office. I walk towards Luciana, knowing this is it.

'Kat!'

Carlos' voice startles me. I turn to see him cradling Nimble.

'Is this who you were looking for?' His voice holds none of his earlier warmth and his eyes are steely.

I sigh with relief. 'Yes.' I can address the fact he's probably going to fire me later, but for now I'm just thankful Nimble is OK.

'Yes. Thank you.' I hold my hands out to take him from Carlos.

'Luciana will put him back. Why don't you come into the office?'

He passes Nimble to Luciana as Dexter enters the foyer, followed by Victor.

'Hey, Carlos, you got a minute?'

'Sure. Kat, can you wait in my office, please?'

Dexter stiffens then shoots me a glance. He knows something's up.

I go into Carlos' office and sit down, then put my head in my hands. I want to bawl, I want to rail against the injustice of it, but most of all I want to throttle Roisin. She's the one who caused this, but I can't exactly say so. I'm not a snitch. And it's not as if she left the door open on purpose. I take my hands away from my face. Or did she? Cogs whirr in my brain. Could she have? She wouldn't. Would she?

Nausea swirls in my stomach as the realisation she may have done it intentionally to get me into trouble slots into place. I grit my teeth. I need to find out. I have to clear my name. OK, I'm getting ahead of myself. Perhaps Carlos isn't about to give me my marching orders, but I need to know.

The minutes until Carlos returns are interminable. I fidget and cast my eyes around the room what feels like a thousand times. I consider what I'm going to say to him without dropping Roisin in it. I also think that would look worse, if I suggested someone else was to blame. I don't see any way out of it. I'll just need to accept whatever fate he metes out to me.

Carlos enters his office and sits down heavily behind his desk, his expression grim.

'Carlos, I'm really sorry,' I begin, but he holds up a hand.

'Kat, maybe I was too quick to accept your offer of help and taking on someone untrained like you was a mistake. I thought you'd fit in here perfectly, save us having to go on a huge recruitment campaign which would mean weeks or months before we had another volunteer here.' He draws breath and sighs. 'These animals are my life. Them and the people who work with me. If anything bad happens to them, it's as if something has happened to one of my children.'

Absent-mindedly, I wonder how Javier feels about that.

He rubs a hand across his face then goes on. 'Today you endangered one of our most vulnerable sloths. Nimble is only young. He could not survive at this point in the wild without his mother. That's why he's undergoing rehabilitation and we have a schedule in place for his release back into the wild. Anything that interferes with that upsets the delicate balance between nature and nurture that we strive so hard to put in place.'

He pauses again. 'I was very clear from the outset that it was of paramount importance that the doors were always closed securely to avoid just this type of situation.'

I nod, not trusting myself to speak, and fully cognisant of the fact Carlos doesn't want me to; he wants to get his speech off his chest. I gain the impression this isn't something he enjoys doing. He's such a cheerful, happy person that coming down hard on someone mustn't come easily to him.

Beads of perspiration form on his forehead and my heart goes out to him, even though he's at best giving me a dressing-down, at worst leading up to sacking me.

'I'm a great believer in second chances, generally, but not when it comes to the animals.'

My heart almost stops. This is it.

Carlos blows out a breath. 'However, Dexter has convinced me to give you a second chance.'

Wait, what? Dexter? After the way he was so curt with me this morning? Maybe our encounter yesterday did mean something. I smile a little at this, but just a little, I don't want Carlos to think I'm being blasé about being off the hook.

'Thank you, Carlos. I don't know what to say.'

'Don't thank me, thank Dexter. I like you, Kat, but the animals come first. This is your final chance.'

'I understand. I won't let you down.' I want to give

him a hug and beg forgiveness, even though I did nothing wrong, but I resist. I don't think it would be well-received right now.

'Make sure you don't. Now, I want you to shadow Dexter and the others for the next week or until Dexter is happy for you to work on your own.'

I bat away the thought that nothing would give me greater pleasure, but simply thank him again and make a quick exit. Colour had already risen in my face as Carlos chastised me for carelessness, but the mention of shadowing Dexter has my colour ratcheting up to postbox-red, I'm sure. It certainly feels like it. I'm boiling now, and I don't think it has anything to do with the heat.

As soon as I leave Carlos' office, I let out a long, low breath. I'm exhausted. And relieved. No one will ever look after the sloths with more care and attention now than me. But really I know it's not my care of the sloths that's questionable; I know what I need to be wary of is Roisin trying to sabotage me.

'You OK?' Ella stops in front of me. 'I heard about Nimble.'

I sigh. 'Yeah, and, I know. I'm sorry. It won't happen again.'

Her eyes go wide. 'Carlos didn't fire you?'

I shake my head. 'He's given me a second chance.'

If possible her eyes go even wider. 'A second chance?' she parrots back at me. When I nod, she says, 'Then you're very lucky indeed, Kat. The sloths are Carlos and Sofia's life. He never gives second chances where they're concerned. He didn't with Maite.'

The air goes out of my lungs and I realise just how

much I've dodged a bullet. 'Maite? Who's Maite?'

She frowns for a second. 'Dexter's ex, who used to work here.' She waves a hand to end the discussion. 'I've got to go. I need to pick up some supplies in town. We've run out of one of the medicines and can't wait until the next delivery.'

'OK. I'll see you later then.'

She turns to go then whirls back around. 'Kat?'

'Yes?'

'For what it's worth, I'm glad he gave you a second chance.' She leans forward and gives me a brisk hug, which I return.

'Thanks, Ella,' I whisper in her ear. 'That means a lot, especially right now.'

She clasps one of my hands in hers. 'Just … be careful.'

'I will.' I give her a half-hearted smile. I'm sure this wasn't my fault, well, almost sure.

As Ella walks through the foyer to the front door of the sanctuary, I stand watching her, dazed. Everything has happened so fast, I feel wrung-out and a little bit overwrought.

With Carlos telling me he wants me shadowing Dexter and the others, after retrieving my fortunately undamaged phone from the floor of the nursery, I go in search of Dexter for further instructions, but draw a blank.

I'm heading outside when I spy Roisin walking my way, and duck back indoors, where Sofia spots me as she comes out of the kitchen.

'Ah, Kat. Come. It's almost lunchtime and I need a taster.'

I speed-walk towards her, in an attempt to avoid the inevitable confrontation with Roisin until I can at least order my thoughts.

'I'm your woman,' I say to her and feel a warm glow inside when she rewards me with a huge smile.

'Kat, I know what happened this morning. I have a good feeling about you. We're not going to talk about it any more. I know you'll take care of our sloths.'

I nod vehemently. 'I will. You can rest assured I'll be on the ball from now on.'

She shoos me into the kitchen. 'Now come. Taste. Lunch is in ten minutes.'

The smell as I enter the kitchen is heavenly. 'Mmm,' I say, my nose in the air like a Labrador at the first sign of food.

'*Sopa de pejibaye*,' explains Sofia before she proffers a spoonful of it for me to try.

That's easy for her to say. I got that it's a soup, and I can see that from what's on the spoon, but other than thinking it looks like pumpkin soup, I have no idea what it is, apart from another phrase to add to my Spanish repertoire.

I blow on the spoonful then put it in my mouth. Wow! I may not know what this is, but it's bloomin' good. It's not pumpkin. I'll need to check the dictionary on my phone later. It's rich, thick and creamy. Same colour as pumpkin soup, though.

'This is delicious. You have quite the gift, Sofia.'

She grins. 'Lots of practice with all the workers to feed.'

I smile at her. 'What's *pejibaye?*

She bites her bottom lip for a second and tilts her

head to one side. 'Palm fruit?'

'Well, it's really tasty.'

To think that all these palm trees I've seen around provide this bounty.

Sofia dips her head. 'Good enough for lunch?'

'Oh yes, definitely good enough for lunch.'

'Would you like to help me serve up?' she asks. 'The hungry hordes will be here in a few minutes.'

'I'd be honoured.'

We've only just prepared everything: the plates, the cutlery, the bread, the drinks, when the door opens and one after another, my team files in.

'Yay! *Sopa de pejibaye.*' Federica claps Mariangeles on the back.

Mariangeles sighs, slumps down on her chair, takes out her wallet and passes Federica a one-thousand colon note. I do some mental arithmetic. I think that's about a pound fifty.

Federica explains in English – she really is taking this practising her language skills with me seriously. 'She lost the bet. Once a week we bet what dish Sofia will serve. Mariangeles thought it would be *pozole*, but I was right.'

At my blank expression, she says, '*Pozole* is a stew. You have that to look forward to.' She leans in towards me and whispers, 'I may have to coerce Sofia into making it next week as Mariangeles is bleeding me dry.'

I chuckle. They really are the dream tag team. I slide in beside them with my own bowl and tear off some of the *pan casero*. Its slightly sweet taste marries surprisingly well with the soup and the flavour of the coriander garnish, or *culantro* as they like to call it here.

My spoon is halfway to my mouth when the door opens and a laughing Roisin enters, followed by Dexter. Her eyes glint with mischief and her hand pats Dexter possessively as if he has just cracked the world's funniest joke. His gaze meets mine and he gives me an infinitesimal nod, but it's enough for Roisin to detect a change in him as she whirls round to face the room, ostensibly looking for a free table, but as soon as she sees me, her posture stiffens and her sharp intake of breath is almost audible. Busted.

There's no longer any doubt in my mind that she left that door open on purpose. Knowing this makes me initially feel relieved that it definitely wasn't down to me being negligent, but then disgusted at the fact a human being, particularly someone meant to be enough of an animal lover to want to work in a sloth sanctuary, would stoop so low, endangering an animal, a baby no less, to suit her own twisted agenda.

I imagine she wasn't expecting to see me still here. Well, ha ha, the very man whom she has been flirting with immediately before lunch is the reason I'm still here. You've got to love the irony.

I hold her gaze, letting her know I know what she did. She glances away, evidently not enjoying the heat being on her. She caught me out once; it won't happen again. I'll be on my guard. And if she thinks she's getting her claws or paws or whatever into Dexter, she can think again.

After lunch, Dexter stops by my table. 'We're going for a drive shortly.'

I think back to our drive last night and what that and then the walk culminated in, and I can only be cheered. Plus, I still need to thank him for convincing Carlos to give me a second chance.

Diagonally opposite me, Roisin bristles, despite the fact she's supposedly in a conversation with Victor and Javier. Eavesdropping. What a surprise.

I nod to Dexter. 'OK. Just tell me when.'

'Meet me in the car park in ten minutes.'

'Fine by me.' I start clearing up and quickly excuse myself to the others at the table, all the while sensing Roisin's eyes boring into me. Well, tough. Stuff her. She has done enough damage for one day.

Chapter Sixteen

When I arrive at the truck, Dexter is standing with his back against the rear door, texting. In profile, he is just as devilishly handsome. His tanned legs are encased in those ever-present khaki shorts and he has changed into a sea-green T-shirt. Rugged. Dishevelled. Sexy. I lick my lips, which have suddenly become drier than the Mojave Desert.

How did he get a chance to change? And where are we going that he felt it necessary? He didn't give me a heads-up about changing. I look down at my khaki sanctuary uniform. It's not exactly doing me any favours. Not that I expect to be attired like a supermodel, but hey, some civvies would've been good.

Dexter turns when he sees me and a languorous smile crosses his lips. Good start. I try but fail to drag my eyes away from those lips, until they stop smiling and Dexter's 'Ahem' breaks into my thoughts.

'Ready?' I say, overbrightly.

He nods, for a second his eyes not leaving mine. If only I could read his thoughts.

Once in the truck, he puts on some music. At least that'll help with any awkward silences, although I am wondering now why we needed to take a drive. Does he have something to show me, somewhere we need to go, or does he want to talk?

It's not long before he sighs then says, 'Kat, I like you, a lot.'

After hesitating for a millisecond, as that's so not where I thought this conversation was going, I reply, 'I like you too.'

Then I hold my breath, anxious about what's coming next.

'But I don't want to get in the middle of something.' When I frown he goes on, 'Your ex-boyfriend calling?'

Relief mixed with anger at Aidan once again messing with my life courses through me before I say, 'No. You've nothing to worry about there. Definitely ex. Emphasis on the ex.'

His eyes crinkle at the corners as his smile lights up his face. 'That's very good news.' Then he pauses as if steeling himself. 'So, now can we address what happened today?' He pauses again, then says, 'That was careless with Nimble.'

I say nothing, because I'm not admitting to something that wasn't my fault.

'I don't want you to stay at the sanctuary solely because I *like* you like you, but because I genuinely think you're a valuable addition to the team. I have good intuition about these things and I can see how much you love it here, both the place itself and being with the sloths. You glow, Kat.' He pauses at a junction and gives me a long look. Again, I wish I knew what was going through his mind.

'And I've never stuck my neck out like that for

anyone – and I know you didn't ask me to – but I felt it was the right thing to do. So all I'm asking is, please be ultra careful. These animals are so precious to us, not just to Carlos, but to all of us. When something happens to one of them, it's like a personal loss, like losing a family member.'

All the blood drains from my face and my body starts to tremble.

Dexter looks at me, concern written all over his face before realisation dawns. 'Oh my God, Kat, I can't believe I said that to you. I'm so sorry.' He jerks the truck over to the side of the road and gets out, striding round to my side.

When he opens the door and puts his arms out, I almost collapse into them. I know what he meant, but it's nothing like losing your father, nothing like losing the person you were closest to in the world, who you looked up to, who was on the same wavelength as you, who got you.

Tears roll down my cheeks, probably wetting his shirt, but he holds me close until I stop trembling.

He holds me away from him slightly and peers into my eyes. 'It hasn't been a good day, has it?'

Mutely, I shake my head as the tears continue to fall. He wipes them away with his fingertips, then gently kisses me on the cheek, which almost has me breaking down again.

'Kat, I think we need some time out.'

My heart plummets. Does he mean time apart? We've only just got together, if you can call it that. My back goes rigid and I tense beneath his hands.

'Sorry, let me clarify, I meant we need time away

from the sanctuary and the stresses there. You've been thrown into all this so quickly. Let's go back to the park, but this time in the daytime. It's hard to feel sad when you see all the monkeys playing.'

I smile and nod before finally mumbling, 'Sounds like a plan.'

Just as I'm about to get back into the truck, Dexter lowers his lips to mine in the sweetest of kisses. It doesn't stay that way for long, though, and by the time we get back in the truck, I think both of us are all hot and bothered, and more than a little turned-on.

It doesn't help when some seductive salsa music comes on the radio, with rather risqué lyrics. I glance at Dexter and discover that his chest is heaving with laughter. The sight sends me into fits of the giggles, and as we arrive at Manuel Antonio National Park, I'm still laughing.

What a wonderful end to a terrible day. After we saw so many monkeys at the park – I failed to keep track of the numbers – Dexter insisted on texting the sanctuary to tell them we wouldn't be back for dinner and that he was taking me out to show me the sights. We had ceviche on the seafront of Espadilla beach. The sea bass was so fresh it almost took my breath away, and the saltiness made me wonder if I was tasting the salt from the ceviche or because it was in the air. The zesty lemon, the sweetness of the red bell pepper and the onion made for sensory overload. I do like my food.

We walked on the beach whilst it was still light, holding hands and shrieking as the waves covered our sandals and threatened to drench us. It felt so right being with Dexter. I know we were in a little bubble, far from the sanctuary and the stress of today, and the unknown to all but me stress of Roisin and her antics, but I was happy to just *be* today with him. I've never been with someone who after knowing me for such a short amount of time was prepared to put his reputation on the line to protect me.

When we return to the sanctuary, Dexter parks the truck, then takes me by the hand and steers me away from the main rear entrance to a door I've never even noticed before. It leads into the back of the accommodation blocks, but bypasses the firepit arena.

'I fancied some more time alone,' he says, meaningfully. 'Does that work for you?'

As his kisses graze my neck, I try not to moan. Does that work for me? Does it ever. If I don't get to touch this man sometime soon, I will combust.

Mumbling, a lustful 'Uh-huh,' I allow him to lead me by the hand round the side of the accommodation block.

'Your place or mine?' He waggles his eyebrows.

I try not to burst out laughing. Can't have it spoiling the mood, which I have to say is red-hot at the moment.

'Which is more likely to have fewer occupants?'

With no hesitation, Dexter says, 'Yours. The girls are always chatting at the firepit late into the night.'

'Let's go then.'

We tiptoe round to the entrance to the women's block, using the trees as cover.

As we slip inside undetected, a whoosh of air goes

out of me, then adrenalin kicks in. We've made it. Giggling like naughty teenagers, we kiss once before I manage to get the key in my door, which I promptly lock behind me. Don't want to be interrupted, do we?

And then we're kissing and touching and shedding clothes, and I gasp at the delicious sensation of Dexter's skin on mine. This feels so right. I haven't felt like this before. Is this what it's meant to be like? I'm not even talking about sex, or the potential of it, but just this general air of wonderfulness. I can't think how else to describe it. As we topple over onto the bed, giggling some more, I'm sure of only one thing – I don't want this feeling ever to end.

Chapter Seventeen

'She must be in, the truck's back.' Federica.

Oh God. They can't find us together. Or rather, I don't want them to find us in bed together, or quite so quickly. I'd rather escape the furtive, knowing looks. Let them think I've gone to sleep and I'm a deep sleeper. Drat! I told Ella I wake at the drop of a hat.

A gentle knock comes at the door, then a whispered, 'Kat, are you asleep?' Ella.

Dexter, beside me, is doing his utmost not to howl with laughter. He actually has a hand clasped over his mouth so he doesn't give himself away. I hold a finger to my lips, ensuring he stays silent.

Another knock, then when I don't answer, footsteps trailing away. I breathe a sigh of relief, then startle, my hand flying to my chest when my phone pings really loudly next to my ear. I exhale in a rush and Dexter grins.

'It's not funny. It scared me half to death.'

'How about I take your mind off it?' he suggests as he kisses my neck, then my lips…

At five forty-five, I shake Dexter awake. He's gorgeous

even in sleep. 'You need to go.'

'Hmm?' he replies groggily. He doesn't even have morning breath. How is that possible?

'You need to get up,' I whisper, 'unless you want to do the walk of shame.'

He bolts upright, rubbing his beautiful sky blue eyes. He yawns then after blinking a few times, he's compos mentis enough to take in his surroundings.

'Oh! I fell asleep here. Crap. I'd better go.'

My lips curve into a smile as he hops around the room, trying to put on his clothes with minimal fuss and minimal noise. He's mostly successful.

He kisses me goodbye at the door, then says he'll see me later. His hand is on the handle, ready to turn it, when he lets go.

I frown and he puts a finger to his lips.

Federica's voice wafts down the corridor, followed by that of Mariangeles. Oh, great. How are we going to sneak him back out now?

I tiptoe to the door and press my ear against it. Footsteps, moving away. How many sets? Two? The voices fade away. They must have closed the rec room door.

Dexter looks at me, his eyes searching mine to see if the coast is clear.

I point with a finger, indicating now is the time to go. He creaks open the door and tiptoes out then hares it across the courtyard to the men's accommodation block.

I stifle a smile at us behaving like teenagers having an illicit rendezvous. We're adults, for goodness' sake, but for our own reasons, right now, we don't want anyone to know that we're dating. Are we dating? Hopefully, last night wasn't just a wham, bam, thank you ma'am thing for Dexter. It certainly wasn't for me. And it could get kind of awkward if one of us was less invested in this than the other.

For once, I take Becca's advice and stop overanalysing. Becca. Mum. I groan as I recall that with everything that's happened in the past twenty-four hours, I haven't managed to call Becca back. I was too caught up in Nimble's escape. Something to add to today's to-do list. But for now, I'm going to have a shower and reflect on an amazing night with an incredible man, and I'm not only talking about the closed-door part. I really like him, and if there is such a thing as 'the one', vomit-inducing though it might sound, I think he might be it.

'Thank God she couldn't get flights. Let's hope, that being the case, and them being so expensive when flying at short notice, that'll put the kybosh on it.'

'I did my best, Kat. I'm so sorry,' says Becca.

'Listen, I know what Mum's like. I'm just furious that she's taking Aidan's side. How can she be so blind to his faults? You saw through him straight away.'

Becca gives a ghoulish laugh. 'I have the power.'

I smile at that. Everything always feels better when Becca's around. 'Sorry I didn't call back. I had a bit of a sloth emergency and things have been a bit full-on.'

'Don't worry. I get it. So, everything's all right?'

I give a devilish grin and wink. 'It's better than all right.'

'Oh, that good, huh?'

I nod, unable to prevent the smile that just about splits my face in two.

'You dirty stopout!' Becca shrieks. 'Yay! Way to get Aidan out of your system.'

My eyebrows knit. 'Becca, that's not why we … you know.'

'Course not, but it helps. God, I wish I could tell him, to his face. I detest that man.'

'I'd kinda guessed,' I say drily. 'And no, you can't tell Aidan I've slept with someone else. Even though we're no longer together. He already sees me reneging on us moving in together as some twenty-first-century breach of promise case.'

Becca was in the middle of taking a sip of her drink and splutters liquid everywhere. When she regains her composure, she says, 'Thanks for that.'

'You're welcome. Didn't you know that Pepsi coming out of your nose was attractive these days?'

'You're not funny.' She makes a face. 'I'm genuinely happy for you, hon, and as soon as I get this cast off, and can find a flight that won't cost me two months' salary, then I'm coming for a visit.'

'You'd better. Right, I've got to go. I'm on mucking out cage duty this morning.'

'Rather you than me. Love you.'

'Love you too.'

Yes, Dexter dropped that little nugget on me last night during our post-amorous snuggles.

Is it odd that I've had a very satisfying morning

mucking out cages with Victor, even though some were filled with sloth poo? Victor may be a country boy, but simple he's not and he knows food like no one I've ever met, so much so my stomach has been rumbling and I've been salivating all morning, despite me having a hearty breakfast of *gallo pinto*. Sofia doesn't believe on sending us out to work on an empty stomach. She really is like a mother hen with her chicks. Even the black sheep – me currently – gets clucked over. I know I'm mixing my metaphors but who cares?

Some surreptitious glances were cast my way, and I'm sure Dexter's, too, this morning in the canteen, but I kept my head down, deep in conversation with Alejandro and Victor, deciding shying away from the girls was the best course of action so as not to invite comment on my whereabouts last night.

Dexter popped in, but grabbed something to go. I've never seen him do that. I'm guessing he didn't fancy being interrogated either, so took the coward's way out.

But now it's time for lunch and I think we're both going to have to toughen up, or develop a poker face, depending on the way the conversation goes, as I'm sure the girls, in particular, won't let it lie.

I'd imagine gossip is currency here. Unless they go into town, with such a small pool of people to choose from, when anyone does anything remotely interesting, it has to be that day's news.

When I enter the dining room, everyone is already seated except Dexter. Ha, he's continuing with his cowardice, is he? Hopefully not avoiding me. I bat the unwelcome thought away and allow myself a slight smile. Given the way we were last night and this morning, I'd like to think not. And although I got it wrong with Aidan, I'd say I'm generally a good judge of character.

I peer at today's lunch as Sofia hands me a plate. Anticipating my question, she says, '*Tamal asado.*'

I nod, as if that means something to me. It doesn't.

She beams at me. 'Cornmeal on banana leaf, with chicken and vegetables.'

'Sounds amazing.'

She flushes with pride. 'I added some olives too. A tip my mother gave me.'

I thank her and choose to brave the gauntlet, sitting between Mariangeles and Federica.

'How is everyone?' I ask. Ella and Luciana are there. Funny, I've just realised Roisin rarely, if ever, eats at this table. I wonder if that's my influence or if she doesn't like sitting with the other women. Or perhaps they don't like her sitting with them. The latter's unlikely as they're so friendly. Plus, she seems only to have an issue with me.

'Good. I was bathing some of the sloths today,' says Ella.

'Oh, that sounds like a great job.' I grin. 'Definitely better than mucking out cages with Victor.'

Everyone groans. 'We hate doing that,' confides Mariangeles. 'Victor must have no olfactory nerves or something. He's immune to the stench.'

I think to how Victor talks about food and figure that can't be the case.

'I love bathing the sloths, especially the young ones. They seem to enjoy it. It's like playtime for them.' Luciana stares off into the middle distance, dreamily. You'd almost think she was dreaming of some hot beau rather than reminiscing about giving sloths a bath. I mean, I might have that look were I thinking of being in a hot tub naked with Dexter, but...

'Talking of playtime,' Mariangeles says, 'you and Dexter were late back last night. Did you have a good time at the beach?'

I nod as I feel colour rising in my cheeks. 'Yeah, it was really good. I saw the howler monkeys at the park – boy, are they loud – and the sloths, of course. It's quite different from at night.'

'I didn't realise you'd been to the park already,' Federica interrupts.

'Especially not at night.' Mariangeles' lips twitch in amusement.

'Yeah, the night before.' I don't rise to the bait. 'Anyway, we had ceviche at Langostino. Dexter had been before, and then we had ... a walk around.'

Smug looks pass between Mariangeles and Federica. Ella remains resolutely quiet. She's keeping out of it.

'We thought you'd have joined us at the firepit once you got back.' Mariangeles stares at me, challenge in her eyes, as if she's daring me to lie my way out of this one.

'Yes. I was keen to practise my English with you ... with you both,' Federica says.

I shake my head. 'I was shattered and decided just to hit the sack. All this rainforest air is really taking it out of me.'

Even Ella raises her head and then her eyebrows at this.

'I didn't even hear you get back,' Mariangeles prods.

She's enjoying this. It's like having an annoying big sister quizzing you after your very first date.

I shrug. 'Well, I didn't want to burst in when I was going to go straight to bed anyway.'

Mariangeles grins. I know what at, too, so I jump in with, 'And let's face it, if I came to join you lot, you'd never have let me escape and I'd have been up for hours.'

'Ah, we can't have you being kept up for hours.' Mariangeles' eyes flick to the door.

Dexter walks in, his eyes searching the room until they settle on me. A smudge of dirt is on his nose, and his hair is mussed from whatever activity he has been doing today, or perhaps he has just been yanking at it whilst poring over paperwork. Who knows? Although I can recall his hair being pretty mussed last night, but that was for a whole other reason. Now who's daydreaming?

Mariangeles coughs and none too subtly digs Federica in the ribs. Federica splutters as she takes in Dexter's arrival, and presumably his reaction to me. I glower at them both and keep my gaze trained studiously on the table.

I make small talk with Ella, although honestly I'm not even sure what about, until Dexter pulls up a chair opposite Mariangeles and next to Ella, so as he's diagonally opposite me.

I mutter a hi, but don't participate in the conversation which ensues. Every nerve ending in my body is tingling at the sight of him. Plus, I'm trying not to smile, in case it's obvious we slept together last night, and it's not like I make a habit of sleeping with men not long after I meet them. Maybe it's the fact I'm in a foreign country, a strange continent, that I'm being so blasé, but my time with Dexter has felt so right from the moment I met him. It doesn't feel as if I've only known him just over a week. So caution was duly thrown to the wind. Well, some caution; we did take *pre*cautions. Doing otherwise would have been taking my new devil-may-care attitude too far.

After lunch, which was quite frankly torturous, I make a hasty exit and then realise I'm not sure what I'm supposed to do next, so I gravitate towards the hospital to see how Flash is faring. Carlos is standing over him, a pencil in one hand, a notebook in the other. His gaze is faraway.

'Hi, Carlos. How is he?'

He regards Flash with affection. 'I think maybe in the next month or so he'll be able to be rehabilitated. His cuts are starting to heal, but I'd like him to put on a little more weight first.'

If only the real Flash had been able to heal. Maybe I shouldn't have suggested we name him Flash. His name reminds me too much of Dad and the pain of losing him, especially given the not exactly warm relationship I enjoy with Mum. That reminds me, I still need to sort that nonsense out.

'That's great news.' But inside, a little part of me feels as if I'll lose Dad all over again. Crazy, I know, but when does grief ever make sense?

'Talking of rehabilitation, how would you like to accompany me this afternoon to release one of our sloths back into the wild?'

I gasp. 'Really?' I'm taken aback that he would ask me, or suggest something so wonderful after the Nimble debacle, but I'm excited too. 'Who's being released?'

'Velocidad. Let me just tell Sofia we're going and we can prepare the crate for him. Can you go tell Victor I need him? He's in the outdoor adult sloth play area.'

'Sure.' I zip off to tell Victor, eager to see my first sloth rehabilitation.

Chapter Eighteen

Victor helps us prepare Velocidad for transport. A lump forms in my throat. Velocidad is one of the sloths I've spent the least amount of time with, but even so, it pains me that he won't be among us any more. I know it's silly to think like that, but I can't help it.

Carlos tells Victor some GPS coordinates and Victor taps them into the sat nav, then we're off, Victor driving Carlos' jeep as we rattle along the bumpy road until we reach the highway.

'We're heading for Platanillo,' says Carlos.

He's sitting in the front of the jeep with Victor, I'm in the back, but he turns his body round as far as his seat belt will allow. 'It's important that we return the sloth to the exact location it came from, or as near as possible to it, if we're not entirely sure, or if we weren't the ones to bring it in.'

Ah, now I understand why he gave Victor GPS coordinates. 'Why's it so important for them to be returned to the same exact spot?'

'Because the habitat in each location is slightly different; the biodiversity varies. There's still little to no research on how sloths survive in the wild once they leave the sanctuaries, but what little has been done shows that the sloths have a significantly lower survival rate if they're rehabilitated in a different area to where they were found.'

'Oh, right. I hadn't realised that.'

Carlos gives a sad smile. 'Most people don't. In fact, that's why we do a campaign every few months advising people not to bring sloths to us, but to call us and tell us where they are, so *we* can get to *them*. That way we have a confirmed location so we can ensure later we rehabilitate the sloth to where it originally came from.'

I nod. 'I can imagine how much harder that is if people just take them, in good faith, from the roadside to try and get them help, not taking into consideration, or necessarily remembering, where they found the sloth.'

'Exactly. We encounter this problem all the time. Fortunately, with Velocidad, we're relatively confident of where he's from, as the couple who found him called us and didn't try to bring him in themselves. As luck would have it, they'd seen one of our ads on a billboard only the week before.'

My eyes go wide. 'That was lucky.'

Carlos smiles. 'I like to think of it as serendipity.'

Victor cuts in, 'And now, since we've been using radio telemetry to monitor the sloths and collect data, we have a much better idea of what they're up to, how they're faring, where they go.

'It's also why we work so closely with the foundations who arrange these cutting-edge studies. We, and other sloth sanctuaries and rescue centres, share information. It's a steep learning curve. Not a great deal is known about sloth rehabilitation, but we're finding out more all the time.'

Much of this I didn't know, and I'm fascinated. I want to help. I feel so privileged to witness Velocidad's release and also to join Carlos next week, if he still takes me, to one of the other rescue centres.

Soon we arrive at the site. It's an emotional moment, for all of us, I'm sure. I'm keen to see what Velocidad will do. Will he immediately blend into the jungle? Climb a tree? Scour the rainforest floor? Refuse to leave the cage?

My mouth dries as the anticipation builds. What will Velocidad do? True to form, he doesn't move very quickly. Carlos and Victor have to coax him out of the cage, where he looks like he'd happily stay. Finally, he ventures out and after a tense ten minutes, he chooses a tree to climb.

Whilst it's touching, it almost makes me want to laugh, too, which I feel is highly inappropriate at this key moment. He's not exactly a monkey scampering off and swinging through the trees. Instead, Velocidad takes over five minutes to climb about nine metres.

Carlos breaks into my thoughts. 'I think he's going to be just fine. He'll be very happy back in the water apple tree.'

'This is the exact tree you found him at?'

Carlos nods. 'Look.' He shows me pictures on his phone, and I see from the flora around the image that we are indeed at the foot of Velocidad's original tree.

'Of course, he may have come from somewhere else before he was found, but I suspect he fell through a gap in the tree canopy. Do you see the rope above us between those two trees?'

I squint in the sun, trying to focus without blinding myself. Yes, I do.

'Is it blue?'

Carlos nods. 'That's it. Well, after Velocidad came to us, we worked with the other rescue centres, raised some funds and added the rope bridge. We knew we'd need to rehabilitate Velocidad here, and we also figured if he had issues crossing the gap, then others were bound to, too.'

Makes sense. I feel so humbled at how much work Carlos and his team, and the other rescue centres, put into rehabilitating the sloths. It's truly a labour of love.

When we return to the sanctuary and get out of the jeep, I say, 'Thanks for letting me be a part of this. What you do here is truly amazing.'

Carlos pats one of my hands with both of his. 'You're welcome, but remember, you are also one of those who do this work now. I sense your passion to help animals, Kat. It's no surprise to me you ended up here with us.'

I smile at him. 'Thanks, Carlos.'

He returns my smile. 'Kat, do you believe in fate?'

When I nod, he says, 'Well, I believe fate brought you to us. And I hope you stay here for a very long time. I see a kindred spirit in you.' He releases my hand as Victor wanders towards us. 'Now, let's eat.'

Dexter is conspicuous by his absence at dinner, but I decide not to tempt uninvited questions by querying his whereabouts. He'll be around somewhere. I just hope he's not avoiding me.

I regale everyone at my table, the same crowd as at lunch, with the story of Velocidad's release, then they each tell of their first experience releasing a sloth back into the wild.

'I cried,' confesses Ella. 'For ten whole minutes.'

Mariangeles puts her palm to her chest. 'When we released Enero, I nearly had to be physically restrained from going after him to bring him back.'

'Enero? January?' I ask.

She nods. 'We went through a period of naming them after months of the year. We'd already done days of the week.' She falls silent for a second, remembering. 'Domingo was my first sloth.'

'Sunday. Was it a Sunday that you found him or that he came here?'

Mariangeles' brows knit for a second and she rests a hand on her head, thinking. 'No, it was a Wednesday, but we were starting from the first day of the week. Domingo was so sweet. I almost felt as if he was showing me affection. I was gutted when Carlos told me they're totally indifferent to humans.'

'Yeah, I remember wondering how that could be the case, when they're always smiling,' I say.

We laugh and they all share more sloth stories, but Dexter still doesn't appear. No one else comments on his absence. I wonder if he's unwell, or if he had some time off and went somewhere. Somehow that pains me, if after what we shared last night wasn't enough for him to want to spend time with me today, supposing he had the free time to do so.

We all gravitate outside to the firepit as is our

night-time ritual. Alejandro arrives with his guitar, which makes me stifle a smile as I think back to how I imagined evenings would be spent after dinner here. Folk music, guitar playing, singing haunting songs. I'm nothing if not romantic in my ideas, although actual romance in my life seems to have gone out the window in the past twenty-four hours. Where is he?

I glance round. Everyone's here except Dexter – and Roisin, who said she was going into town with a friend. Should I sneak off now when they're all busy, engrossed in the conversation, feign a headache, but somehow slip into the men's accommodation block? I managed to slip into the women's block last night – with Dexter, undetected. Can I repeat that?

I catch Alejandro's eyes resting on Ella as he plucks the first few notes on his guitar, and I smile. Well, at least romance may, eventually, be on the cards for someone.

Mariangeles and Victor are involved in a heated discussion about which country has the best salsa music. When Ella joins in with them, Federica turns to me. 'Is it OK if I ask you some more questions about English?'

She's so enthusiastic and earnest, how can I refuse, so we spend a good fifteen minutes or so going over verb conjugation and I test her on some homophones – she had a tiny English grammar book in the pocket of her cargo pants. She's really quite dedicated and determined, and reminds me of how I felt when learning Spanish. When we wrap things up, I say, 'I'm beat, guys. I'm going to call it a night.'

'Night, Kat,' everyone says, then returns to their

conversations, Federica joining the salsa discussion. I see my chance to slope off without anyone paying me any attention, ducking behind the giant mango tree that separates the courtyard from the accommodation blocks.

I walk in the direction of the women's residence, then scoot over to the men's, inching open the main door so it doesn't squeak.

The others' laughter reaches me from outside. I grin. Good, they haven't noticed where I went. When I reach Dexter's door, I hesitate. I can't just walk in. I know we slept together last night, but I can't exactly flounce in unannounced, so I tap the door. No answer. I tap again. Still no answer. Perhaps he's in a deep sleep, or maybe he isn't here after all. Only one way to find out. I turn the handle and go in. The blinds are drawn, the room in semi-darkness, the only light coming from a small table lamp, but it's more than enough for me to witness the horror before me and I recoil as if I've been slapped across the face.

Roisin is reclined in a seductive pose on Dexter's bed in a barely there black mesh bodysuit which leaves very little to the imagination. If we weren't in the Tropics she'd be freezing, I can't help thinking. She's also wearing a blindfold. My stomach lurches. Thank God she can't see me.

'Finally,' she purrs. 'I thought you'd never get here. Do you like what you see?'

I dash out of the door, then sprint out of the accommodation block, not caring who sees me, into the women's block, where I just make it to the bathroom before I promptly throw up into the toilet bowl.

How could I have got it so wrong? I honestly thought he liked me. But clearly I'm only one of a string of women. So much for my intuition, my being a good judge of character. Ha! And Roisin? I groan. Anyone but her. She's a total bitch. It's the only word for her.

Rage swirls inside me. She knew Dexter and I were getting closer, although she probably hadn't realised quite how close, and she pulled out all the stops. Is that why he's been avoiding me today? Or was I simply of no consequence? What the hell have I done? I've packed in my job – even though it wasn't my dream job or anything – and moved over five thousand miles away, shagged the boss and now I'm just a notch on his bedpost. I want to scream. I grit my teeth, then pad across to my room, let myself in, sink down onto the bed and sob my heart out. Damn you, Dexter.

Chapter Nineteen

It takes all my strength, both emotional and physical, to get out of bed next morning. I'm lucky if I slept ten minutes. I didn't take myself for gullible, but it turns out I am. I have no idea how I'm going to face Dexter or Roisin today. I haven't checked myself in the mirror yet, but I must look dreadful. I can hardly see out of my slits for eyes. My T-shirt was soaked from all my tears last night. I didn't even get changed for bed, just lay on top of the covers and buried my head into my pillow so no one would hear me crying.

Of course I heard the others come back last night. How could I not? As everyone else drifted off, doors closing quietly, crickets chirping in the background, I lay awake thinking about everything, reliving that awful scene with Roisin. The only saving grace is that she doesn't know I was there. God, I feel sick again. At least once I'd thrown up, I was physically OK, but emotionally I don't know if I'll ever be. I can't unsee it. The seductive tone of her voice, the pout of her full lips, the swell of her chest; the way she'd let herself into his room, tarted up like that for him, makes me want to heave. Something has been going on between them, but the question is, was he seeing her at the same time as me?

I didn't think Dexter was like that, but the evidence speaks for itself. Is that why he missed dinner last night? He was readying himself for a secret rendezvous with Roisin? Why couldn't he keep it in his pants? Maybe Roisin is that kind of girl, but I'm not. I'm only intimate with someone if it really means something to me. I thought I meant something to Dexter. I mentally slap myself for being so naïve.

Yes, I'm gutted at the possibility of something between Dexter and me being a thing of the past now, but I'm more worried over my future here at the sanctuary. How can I sustain that now?

When Federica knocks on my door to tell me it's time for breakfast, I pull myself together a little and call through the door that I overslept and I'll meet them there. I need to limit the amount of time for chit-chat with them and I especially need to ration the torturous time I spend in Dexter's company. At some point I'll have it out with him, I'm fed up being trodden on, but it won't be today. I'm still too raw.

At breakfast, the girls have saved me a seat, and I reflect on how grateful I am that they readily accepted me into the fold, and how they look after me. Already I feel a part of the family here, but how long will that last now? At the moment, that saddens me more than anything else. I don't want to be torn away from these wonderful women, nor the animals I love so much. How could I have been so stupid? Part of the reason I'm upset is because I feel I've let myself down. I've just got rid of Aidan, and now I've fallen straight into this 'thing' with Dexter, no-holds barred, and for what? To have him crap on me from a great height, that's what.

I shove my *chorreadas* around my plate. Usually, I'd be wolfing these pancakes down, but right now I'd choke if I tried. With some difficulty, I manage a few sips of coffee, all the while hoping it doesn't come back up.

Out of the corner of my eye, I catch Federica and Mariangeles exchanging concerned surreptitious glances. I'll have to tell them what has happened, but I can't get the words out just yet. I have no idea why I bothered coming for breakfast, other than it would look weird if I didn't. I only hope Sofia doesn't notice I haven't eaten much. I don't want to cause offence, or have her worrying over me.

Roisin hasn't appeared and neither has Dexter. Probably still wrapped around each other. I push back my chair so fast it screeches.

'Excuse me,' I manage before I dart across the canteen and out into the foyer where I spot Roisin just before I bolt into the bathroom, slam the door and retch into the toilet bowl. This is becoming something of a habit.

I'm still trying to compose myself when the door creaks open. It had better not be bloody Roisin. That's all I need. It would be just like her to come rub salt in my wounds. Then I remember she doesn't know I saw her.

'Kat?' Mariangeles. 'Kat, are you OK?'

The gentleness of her tone and the concern in her voice make me want to weep.

'Yeah,' I say.

'Is something wrong or are you just feeling off-colour?'

Deciding it's better to get this over with, painful though the words will be, I open the door.

Mariangeles' eyes widen. 'You don't look so good. Do you need to sit down?'

I shake my head, although that then makes me feel rather faint. I brace my arms on either side of the sink, then finally turn on a tap, wash my hands and splash water over my face.

The water cools my skin, which was red-hot only a moment before. Eventually, I'm able to talk.

Mariangeles has stood silently waiting for me to speak as I freshened up.

I turn to her. 'Dexter's sleeping with Roisin.'

'What?' A mix of incredulity and shock crosses her features. 'No.' She shakes her head. 'No way.'

I nod sadly. 'Yes way.'

She shakes her head again. 'Dexter barely tolerates Roisin.'

That's not the way I've read it when I've seen them together, well, mostly. I think back to how uncomfortable he looked when Roisin was all over him in the canteen. But was that purely because I was there too? And it's certainly not what I witnessed last night in his room. No one puts on a display like that for someone who 'barely tolerates' them. Do I tell Mariangeles the whole truth? What I saw?

I settle for, 'I have proof.'

She continues to shake her head. 'No, *chica*, there must be some mistake. Dexter isn't like that. He would never … not with *her*.'

I frown. 'Why are you so sure? I know what I saw.'

Mariangeles' brows knit. 'You saw them together?'

I heave a sigh. 'Not exactly.'

'What did you see?' Mariangeles presses.

'Enough to know they're sleeping together.' I expel all the air out of me in one huge whoosh. 'Enough to know there's no coming back from it, for me and Dexter.'

'No, Kat, you're wrong.'

But I've stopped listening. I'm not wrong. My eyes didn't deceive me. That image will be imprinted on my memory possibly for the rest of my life, certainly for the rest of my time in Costa Rica, however long that may be.

As Mariangeles reassures me, I shift to autopilot. I'm still on autopilot when she guides me out of the door five minutes later, and I wait like a naughty schoolchild outside the headmaster's office, this time Carlos', whilst Mariangeles speaks in hushed whispers to him. I groan, praying she doesn't mention Dexter. When she comes out of his office, I glare at her.

'Don't worry, I told him I needed you today, but not why. That way we can steer clear of everyone for a bit. A bit of good, hard labour will help. We're going to chop down some wood–' my eyes go wide with alarm at this '–for the play area for the youth sloths. There are a few more of them now, so we need a couple more stimulation areas.' She grins. 'They're not good at waiting their turn for a branch to swing from.'

I exhale heavily. Thankful though I am for Mariangeles' diversion, it's only delaying the inevitable confrontation with Dexter. And the smug look I'll receive from Roisin when she has confirmation she has split Dexter and me up before our relationship could really take off. Although not before it could get to the next level. I mentally kick myself for sleeping with him so soon. But if felt so right. I worry at a ragged fingernail, my once well-cared-for nails reduced to shreds. I'm surprised they're not bleeding from the savage way I've treated them the past few hours.

There's a reason men usually do this work, I think as I stretch my back and set down the axe I've been wielding for the past thirty minutes, but which feels far longer. My feminism has gone out the window. What I wouldn't give for a deep-tissue massage right now. I'd always thought I was in fairly good shape, relatively fit, but now I feel about a hundred and two. Plus, I'm soaked in sweat. Nice. Whilst I enjoy the weather being lovely here, I could do without the humidity being as high. I'll pay for this workout tomorrow, if I can get comfortable in bed at all tonight. Bed. Best not to think of that right now. The only good thing is that it's satisfying work, and Mariangeles assuaged my concerns about cutting down trees by advising me we have a permit to do so, and we only cut in certain areas and we always replant, but we do need some materials and this is where we take them from.

She also told me to steer clear of the manchineel trees. I thought they looked pretty and even that they carried fruit, like some kind of Latin American apple, but it turns out they're one of the most toxic trees in the world. Just as well Mariangeles was here to keep me right. The last thing I need is my life worsening in any way right now, or ending from me touching the tree's milky white sap. I file away the info for later, mindful never to eat anything from the trees without first asking what it is.

The sun is merciless on our backs, however, and for every five swings of the axe, I feel as if I'm having to take one swig of water. That doesn't stop me needing to wipe the sweat from my brow every few minutes, and it also runs in rivulets between my breasts and down my back. This is stay in the shade or by a pool weather, not chop logs to build a play area for sloths temperatures.

I'm sticky and uncomfortable, yet there's something therapeutic about the rhythmic thwack, thwack of the axe hitting the tree, despite my inner conservationist wanting to apologise for chopping it down.

When we make our way back towards the main building for lunch, Federica and Ella are hefting boxes out of one of the trucks.

'Here, give me one of those,' I say to Ella, whose ponytail bounces as she tries to readjust a box which is slipping from her grasp.

'Where did you two get to?' Federica asks. 'What's going on?'

Mariangeles shoots me a look, and I nod for her to relay the details of this unhappy chapter in my life.

Once Mariangeles has apprised them of the situation and after much swearing by all three in Spanish, Federica lowers the box she's carrying to the ground and comes towards me, closing her arms around me in a mummy-like hug that the Egyptians would be proud of. Her long chestnut hair swings over my shoulder, partially obscuring my face, and it's all I can do not to break down as I hide behind it.

When we break apart, Ella is hanging back, her brow creased in confusion. 'I don't understand. That's not who I thought Dexter was. Plus, he's never really seemed that friendly with Roisin. I always had the impression that of us all, he liked her the least.'

I nod. 'Maybe so, but she's tall, leggy, bewitching obviously and clearly experimental in bed.'

As I say that last part, I remember I didn't get around to telling Mariangeles the whole story. At her quizzical look, I sigh. 'Never mind.'

I should have skipped lunch. As everyone else digs in to Sofia's latest ecstasy on a plate, I twirl pieces of mine on the fork and barely manage one or two bites. I honestly don't even know what it is, and for once, I don't have the urge to ask.

At least Dexter has the decency to avoid me. He must feel a little bit awkward coming into a room with two women he has slept with on consecutive nights. I wonder if it would matter to Roisin if she knew for certain I'd slept with Dexter. Probably not. I've met her type before, and they're all about winning. Well, she can take home the prize. I'm a fair person, but I don't like to share. Not boyfriends anyway. And whilst I know it's ridiculous to think of Dexter as my boyfriend, since we've only known each other just over a week, the fact that we slept together was that pivotal moment when a casual thing moves into something more meaningful. It was real for me; I thought it was for Dexter, too. Unfortunately, he seems to like it real with more than one person at a time. I groan again. Roisin. It had to be her.

I'm taking a sip of my *agua dulce* when Dexter strolls into the room, looking, goddamn it, even sexier than ever. His stubble is thicker and the creases around his eyes are a little more pronounced, but the confident way he strides into the room has my breath catching in my throat, despite myself.

I stare down at my drink, fiddling with my napkin. It takes all my composure not to burst into tears.

'Hey,' he says, stopping by my chair. 'I missed you last night.'

What the actual...? Did I hear him right? Is he seriously doing this?

I raise my eyes to meet his and he recoils, taking a step back.

Hushed voices reach my ears – Mariangeles and Federica whispering. I stifle a half-smile. They'll be worried things are about to kick off, but they needn't worry. I won't give him the satisfaction, certainly not with an audience. That conversation is for another time.

His handsome face crumples. 'Is everything OK?'

I do everything in my power to keep my tone even, but my 'Fabulous,' comes out as a snarl.

Ella gets to her feet. 'Sorry, Dexter. Luciana needs Kat to relieve her from the nursery so she can have lunch.'

I glance gratefully at Ella. 'Oh, gosh, is that the time? Thanks for the reminder.' Turning to Dexter, I say, 'Excuse me,' and bolt for the door before I knee him in the balls.

As I tell Luciana she can go for lunch, I sit on the sofa and watch two sloths climb on the rocking chairs – their favourite game. Even their comical antics can't cheer me up today, though. How dare he? How dare he pretend he missed me when he had that tart in his bed. I will never trust my instincts about anyone ever again.

I'm still seething five minutes later when Mariangeles enters the nursery. She sits down beside me and gives me a hug. 'What are you going to do?'

It takes real effort to unclench my teeth. 'Well, I was hoping it would dawn on him that something was amiss, but obviously I've given him too much credit.'

Mariangeles gives a sad smile. 'I just can't believe it.' Her eyes flash. 'I've always thought of Dexter as one of the good guys.'

'Yeah, I thought so too.'

My phone pings a text message. Becca. As I go to read it, Mariangeles says, 'I'll see you later.'

Hi, Kat. How's tricks with the delectable Dexter? xx

Oh, Becca. Your timing couldn't be worse. My fingers hover over the keys, but I can't do it. I need some time before I admit that I've failed once again. That I've got it wrong once again.

I've fed the pups, tidied the nursery and counted the number of leaves in each packet about a hundred times before the workday is finally over. I do compose a rather noncommittal reply to Becca eventually. I can't face the truth just yet. As I walk back to the women's accommodation block, lost in my thoughts, a familiar voice makes me stop.

'There you are. Have you been hiding from me? I thought I'd never get you on your own.' Dexter smiles at me as I turn towards him. His smile soon falls away as I dredge up every ounce of vitriol within me, everything I've been keeping inside all day and say, 'Are you for real? You *missed* me last night? Hardly! Was your Irish counterpart not enough for you?'

Dexter frowns. 'What? Of course I missed you last night.' He hesitates. 'Irish counterpart? What are you talking about?'

His hesitation is all the proof I need. 'Let's just say I don't believe you missed me at all, given you were otherwise occupied last night.'

Dexter's frown deepens. 'I was otherwise occupied, you're right.'

'Hah! You're not even denying it. Well, do you know what? She's welcome to you. You disgust me.' I storm off, trying to put some distance between us.

'Wait! Kat!' He puts his hand on my arm. 'I don't know what you think happened, but I think we're at cross purposes here.'

I shrug off his arm. 'I don't think so. I saw it all too clearly. Unfortunately.'

Dexter follows me until he's level with me again. God, I wish he didn't have such a long stride. I can't outrun him.

A vein pulses in his neck. 'What did you see?' His voice has risen ever so slightly. Someone doesn't like being caught out.

I stop and square my shoulders at him. 'Do you

really want me to say it? Are you honestly that cruel?'

He looks … mystified. 'Cruel? Kat, spit it out. What did you see?'

I study him, unable to believe he's making me do this. 'Dexter, the reason I don't believe you missed me last night is because I *saw* Roisin spreadeagled on your bed, waiting for you, wearing nothing but a skimpy bodysuit. Happy now?' Then I turn and flee for the women's block before he sees the tears streaming down my face, and before I break down in front of him.

Chapter Twenty

I'd thought I had no tears left after finding Roisin in Dexter's bed, but the crumpled-up tissues and the empty box are testament to the fact I shed a few more bucketloads after my run-in with Dexter last night. At least he hasn't plagued me with texts. Although should I be more upset that I didn't matter enough to him to even merit an apology? Not that it would have made anything any better. I'm still trying to work out how best to move forward and whether I should cut my losses and go back home, but I don't want to make any knee-jerk decisions, plus I've made friends here.

As I pad across the courtyard and sit down at the empty firepit, the sound of wheels scattering gravel breaks into my thoughts. Please don't let it be Dexter out on some early morning mission for Carlos. But it's Javier and Nicolás. Javier has five or six red fish slung over his shoulder.

'You're up early,' Javier says with a smile as he closes the gate behind him. 'Coffee?'

I could kiss him. 'Yes, please.'

He lopes off to the kitchen whilst Nicolás sits down beside me.

'What time did you go fishing?' I ask.

Nicolás stifles a yawn and reclines slightly on the rattan sofa. 'About eleven last night.'

'Last night? You must be exhausted. Surely you didn't fish all that time.'

He rubs a hand over his face. 'Not all the time. I was shattered after being away with Dexter the night before.'

I stiffen and my blood runs cold. 'Dexter?'

'Yeah, Carlos sent us over to Limón.'

'Limón?' I'm aware I keep parroting what he's saying, but I can't stop myself.

'There's a sloth rescue centre over there that we're working with, and as chance would have it, they also had a spare radiator for the truck. Carlos bought it off the owner.'

Beads of perspiration form on my neck, and I wipe my sticky palms on my shorts. 'And you went too?'

He grins. 'Well, you didn't want the boy to go all alone, did you? It's a long journey, so it was a great way for us to catch up and the owner and his wife were very friendly. Although Dexter snores. I'm not sharing a room with him again.'

I hold on to the side of the sofa, feeling as if I may keel over at any second. Limón. Nicolás. Dexter. Radiator. They shared a room.

My eyes flutter closed as my brain tries to process what Nicolás is telling me. If Dexter was in Limón with Nicolás, he couldn't have been waiting for Roisin. A momentary glimmer of hope shoots through me. Dexter wasn't with Roisin. It's all in her head. I bat away the possibility that something still may be going on between them. For the moment I focus on the fact he couldn't have been about to arrive for a prearranged rendezvous with Roisin, because he was on the other side of the country, with Nicolás, and stayed there overnight.

I groan. What have I done? I accused him of sleeping with Roisin without even waiting around to hear his side of the story. And I bad-mouthed him to Federica, Mariangeles and Ella. Oh God, ground open up and swallow me. Now I have a whole host of different problems to those I had when I woke up this morning.

I sink my head into my hands.

'You OK?' asks Nicolás, his voice threaded through with concern.

'Never better,' I mumble. He doesn't need to know the extent of my stupidity.

'You did what?' says Becca when I call her later.

'I know. I've screwed up. And I realise you're probably at work and this isn't the best time to ask you for relationship advice, Becca, but I really like him, and I think I was so afraid, after the whole Aidan thing, that it would go wrong, that I saw it go wrong when there was actually nothing wrong at all.'

'Kat, can you use simple sentences, please? I'm not at work, I'm on annual leave, but I'm still in bed and honestly, I'm also a little hungover. I was out for cocktails last night and I overindulged a tad.'

'You need coffee,' I say.

'I do. So, let me get this straight. You found Roisin offering herself up on a plate to Dexter, understandably assumed the worst, told everyone he was a shit and then discovered he may not have known anything about it and wasn't even at the sanctuary, but five hours' drive away.'

Shame fills me and I feel colour rise in my cheeks. 'Yeah,' I mumble.

'Sorry?'

'Yes! That's about the size of it. Becca, what am I going to do?'

She shrugs. 'Eat humble pie for a start.'

'Gee, ta. That was really helpful.'

'Kat, you are one of the most easy-going people I've ever met, but when you blow, you blow. To be fair, finding someone almost stark naked in the bed of the man *you'd* been stark naked with the night before is a reasonable defence.'

'Not helping,' I mutter.

'I'm sorry, but if you like Dexter as much as you say you do, you have to swallow your pride and go apologise. Hopefully, it'll be enough.'

'That's what I'm worried about – that it won't be.'

'Well, you won't find out if you don't go and speak to him. You never know, he may see the funny side of it. This time next week, you may both be laughing about it.'

'Or I might be on a flight home,' I say under my breath.

Becca tuts. 'Kat, much as I would love to have you home, I don't want you back under those circumstances. And I suggest you clarify things with your friends, too, before Dexter gets wind of the fact you've told them an inaccurate version of events.'

My heart plummets. Great.

When the workday starts, I steel myself for running into Dexter, but it seems once again he isn't around. Isn't he meant to be the deputy manager? He doesn't do a great deal of managing, just swans around a lot. Right, getting arsey about things isn't going to win me any brownie points with Dexter, or have him accept my apology. Grovelling will probably work best.

Mariangeles strolls round the side of the main building, carrying a pair of hedge trimmers.

'Aren't we in the rainforest?' I ask.

'Yeah, but we still need to keep the front entrance clear so people can see our signage.' She gestures to the main sign, which does indeed have quite a bit of foliage growing under and over it.

'Point taken.' I exhale heavily. 'Listen, Mariangeles, I need to tell you something.'

Her eyebrows shoot up. 'Again? I'm still reeling from the last revelation.'

I smile. 'I promise I won't make a habit of it.'

'Don't. I think I'm in Dexter's bad books as I tore a strip off him this morning.'

What…? Oh no! My face crumples.

'Hey, you OK? Sorry, I didn't mean to bring him up. But the more I thought of the way he'd treated you, the angrier I became. I'm not having him treat my *hermana* like that.'

I'd smile at her calling me her sister, and I love the way she has considered me one of the family from the moment I arrived, but she's already spoken to Dexter?

This just gets worse and worse.

I groan. Well, it's more of a whimper really.

'What's wrong?'

My words shoot out of me. 'Dexter was in Limón with Nicolás the night I saw Roisin in his room almost naked, trying to pull him with her tawdry seduction routine. He couldn't have had a prearranged "appointment" with her. I got it wrong.' Finally, I draw breath, certain I'm turning purple from forgetting to pause.

Mariangeles' eyes go wide. '*Mierda!*

'My thoughts exactly. And now I need to go and apologise to Dexter. And tell Ella and Federica that he didn't do what I thought he did with Roisin.'

Mariangeles is silent for a long moment then she starts to laugh, and keeps laughing, then bends over, putting her hands on her knees, barely able to catch her breath.

'What's so bloomin' funny?' I ask.

Mariangeles straightens up and wipes tears from her eyes, then rubs her nose and coughs. 'Can you imagine Roisin lying on Dexter's bed, ready to play the temptress, and no one turns up?'

My lips curve upwards and I chuckle. 'I wonder how long she was lying there like that.'

Mariangeles shakes her head. 'I don't know. She's pretty determined and resilient. Couple of hours?'

I snort. 'She must have been uncomfortable and freezing.' My hand flies to my mouth. 'Do you think she now knows Dexter was in Limón?'

Now Mariangeles' shoulders are shaking. 'Well, if she doesn't, she either thinks Dexter did an about-turn and avoided her by not even venturing into his room, after finding her there, or she knows someone else saw her. Oh, *Dios mio*, how embarrassing!'

I cringe, inwardly and outwardly. Much as I don't particularly like Roisin, mainly because she has been frosty as hell towards me, I wouldn't wish that crushing realisation on anyone. Not even someone who has designs on the man I've fallen for.

In my peripheral vision I catch sight of the woman herself making her way over to us, and manage to blurt out a, 'Later, Mariangeles,' before I hotfoot it inside to avoid having to be in Roisin's company.

Now to locate Dexter. And then find somewhere private to have a seriously humiliating conversation. I mean, I don't think I was unreasonable in coming to the conclusions I did: that Dexter and Roisin were bumping bones, but maybe I should have tackled the subject more indirectly or perhaps more delicately. Yes, that might have been better. I'm not usually a hothead, but red mist definitely descended when I saw Roisin lying there. I felt a fool and as if I'd been taken advantage of yet again. And I'd had enough.

Carlos waylays me as I enter the building. 'Kat, I wanted to talk to you about our trip next week to our partner rescue centre in the south.'

'Sure.' Part of me is relieved the conversation with Dexter is delayed a little longer. It isn't going to be pretty, and although I have no problem with owning up and apologising when I'm in the wrong, this is as distasteful as it gets.

Carlos gestures for me to take a seat. I lower myself onto the armchair in front of his desk – no straight-backed office chairs here – and wait to hear what he has to say.

'So, we'll set off about six, as it'll take us a couple of hours' drive. We'll be there for a meeting around nine, then we'll have a large part of the day to study the way they work with their sloths, before we have another meeting with some other rescue centre representatives who are coming from further afield and then we'll head back.' He tidies some papers on his desk but doesn't break eye contact. 'Hopefully, it will give you a flavour for just how far-reaching we intend the project to be and the long-term benefits to the lives of the sloths in the country as a whole.'

I reflect on how different my way of life is now, after only ten days of discovering this sanctuary and meeting Dexter, and pray I can fix things with him so it can continue to be so. I've always wanted to make a difference. In retrospect, I think that's one of the reasons I found it so difficult working in sales. The monotony. The routine. The lack of variety. Virtually nothing in my work life ever changed. The world changed around me, but my contribution didn't change and it was mind-numbingly boring. Now I feel as if what I have to offer has some value, and I don't want to lose that. I set my jaw and press my fingers into my palms; I need to make things right with Dexter.

'Right, can you help Ella this morning? She's doing some data transfer of the sloth adoption information and could use a hand.'

My eyebrows furrow. 'Sloth adoption?'

Carlos smiles. 'Yes. Don't worry. We're not letting the sloths be taken away. This is where sloth lovers adopt a sloth and pledge some funds to help us support the sloth. They get a certificate with its name, a sloth teddy bear and a few other bits and pieces, and we receive an injection of cash which helps keep these guys in medicine for a while and covers some of the sanctuary's costs.'

'Ah, yes, I see.' Memories of TV ads for adopt-a-panda/jaguar/other endangered animal spring to the forefront of my mind. It's similar but on a smaller scale. We're not exactly the WWF here. 'Of course. Where is Ella?'

'In Dexter's office. It's the first time she has worked on this part of the admin, too, so he's been bringing her up to speed.'

I'm finding it hard to swallow, so I simply nod, push out of the armchair and head for Dexter's office. He's not there. Instead, Ella is, alone, sitting on the floor, surrounded by bundles of files.

When I say, 'Hey,' she looks up and bangs her head on the filing cabinet drawer, which is open above her. 'Ow.'

'You OK?'

'Yeah, but I may have a huge bump on it later. So you're coming to help me?'

When I nod, she lets out a long sigh and then beams.

'Glad someone is. This is quite the job. There are records going back years here, and they all need checked and moved onto the new system, or archived as lapsed sponsors.'

I smile. 'It'll be easier with two. Budge up, but let's close that drawer first.'

'Wow!' Ella says as I fill her in on my mistake over Dexter and Roisin. 'No wonder he wasn't his usual cheerful self.'

'It may not be because of that.' I'm trying to cling on to a last shred of hope.

Ella gives me a doubtful look. 'I'd say it had something to do with it. I've seen the way he's been looking at you since you arrived. He's never looked at anyone else like that before. Not even… Sure, there have been other attractive girls who've fancied their chances with him, but he hasn't responded. Roisin, well, she was persistent, but still he didn't bite. I thought she'd given up, but it seems she renewed her efforts when you arrived. I can't believe we all missed it.'

Neither can I. She's always flirting with him. Maybe the others have become immune to it, or perhaps she was even more blatant before.

'Right, I need a break, well, a loo break at least.' I glance at my watch. I've been sorting these files with Ella for almost an hour. 'Back in five.'

As I cross the foyer, I catch a glimpse of Dexter's back as he slips through the door leading to the accommodation blocks. Bingo. I need to get this over with. But as I reach for the door handle, hushed voices from beyond it filter through to me.

'What the hell were you thinking?' Dexter.

A murmured voice. Then its volume rises slightly. 'You prefer that drippy bitch to me? Well, you're welcome to her.'

I freeze. Roisin. Oh crap. I want to turn and run, but my legs won't work, and I need to hear this.

'And how did you even get into my room?'

She scoffs. 'C'mon, Dexter, your lock's been dodgy for ages. You haven't exactly made a secret of it. You must mention it to Victor every second day, yet he never gets around to it. If that wasn't an open invitation, then I don't know what was.'

'Roisin, it was me trying to get my lock fixed. It was not me asking you to spreadeagle yourself on my bed,' Dexter rails. 'Perhaps, in other circumstances, I'd be flattered, but you know Kat and I've just started seeing each other. What the hell possessed you? You're an attractive woman. Why me? Why someone who is already involved with someone else?'

'Maybe I like the challenge.'

Even now there's a come-hither tone to her voice. Does she never give up?

'You're incorrigible,' Dexter says, and there's no humour in his words. 'Do you have any idea of the damage you've done?'

'I'm sure you'll sort it out. If she's who you want. At least I gave whoever did open the door an eyeful. Perhaps I'll work on them instead. They have the advantage of knowing what's on offer. Who was it? Alejandro? Javier?'

He hasn't told her. Oh God. She thinks it was one of the guys because they all share the block. Of course. Why would I or any of the other women be in the men's block? Except me, going to find Dexter. I ease the door ajar.

'Maybe I shouldn't bother with them, anyway. How pathetic, grassing me up to you. If it'd been a proper man, he'd have come in and satisfied me, and let me do the same to him.'

Holy heck. She's some sort of nymphomaniac she-devil. Or just a tart. It's not even lunchtime and she's peddling her wares.

'Are you sure you can resist this, Dexter?' she purrs. 'Are you sure you want to?' Her hands skim her perfect breasts, down over her hips until they stop at the top of her thighs.

A vein pulses in Dexter's throat, but whether with lust or anger it's difficult to tell.

'Roisin, you're making a fool of yourself.' His voice brims with barely concealed anger. 'I suggest if you don't want to be up on a disciplinary charge for sexual harassment and breaking into a co-worker's room, then you stop right now.'

She mutters something unintelligible, but her body language is plain to see. She's like a python poised to strike. A snatch of her words drifts across to me. '…don't know what you're missing.' Then the pitch of her voice changes. 'Don't worry, Dexter. You've made yourself clear. You won't get another chance, though.'

Dexter's body deflates. Relief? Dejection? Did he mean what he said about not being interested?

Roisin heads towards the door and I jerk back, but she stops and spins round to face Dexter again. 'You never did tell me which of the guys was rewarded by seeing me in all my glory.'

God, she never gives up, does she? She's so brazen.

Dexter hesitates for a moment then walks towards her. When he draws level, I can see both their faces in profile. I gasp as he says, 'That's because none of the guys saw you.'

'But…? The door opened … someone came in.'

Dexter nods. 'They did. It just wasn't one of the guys.'

Roisin's face contorts into an ugly mask. '*She* saw me. She opened the door. She was coming to you.'

Dexter remains silent, confirming her assumptions.

Barely a second later, her face transforms back into that of the siren she is. 'Oh, Dexter, it must be wonderful to be so popular. But I can tell you right now, she can't offer you the delights I can. Pity you'll never know now what those are.'

Too late, I react to Roisin moving towards the door. The thud of it as it cracks me on the head makes my skull reverberate before I feel myself slide towards the floor.

Chapter Twenty-one

'Kat! Kat!' The voice is indistinct and sounds far away.

My eyes flicker open then closed.

'Kat!' Dexter?

'Kat! *Oígame.*' Federica?

My eyes flutter open and this time I turn my head to the side as the light is so bright it hurts.

'She's coming round.' Dexter. 'Ella, can you go grab some ice and a cloth from the kitchen, please?'

His steady, assured voice calms me slightly. What's going on? Why do I need ice? Why do I feel dizzy? I start to splutter and warm hands turn me on my side as Dexter says, 'Federica, can you fetch a glass of water, please?'

Moments later, something cold presses against my head. It's both welcome and painful. I can't even work out if it's the ice or the cloth Dexter spoke of.

Ella's gentle voice speaks to me. 'You're OK, Kat. You've had a nasty bump to the head, but a bit of rest and you'll be fine.'

'Bump? Head?'

Like a tsunami, the details come flooding back: Dexter, Roisin, her inappropriate behaviour, her slamming the door open and me not getting out of the way in time. That'll be why they say eavesdroppers never hear anything good about themselves.

Eventually, I sit up, and despite being dazed, with some help from Javier and Dexter, I manage to stand, although my legs are as wobbly as those of a newborn foal.

'Let's sit her in my office,' Dexter says. 'Ella can keep an eye on her. We'll let her rest later, but for now, we have to be sure she doesn't have a concussion. We can't allow her to fall asleep.'

Javier agrees, and between them, they half-support, half-carry me into the office, where they sit me on the old beat-up leather sofa, which is remarkably comfy. Much more so than sitting cross-legged on the floor, back bent over files.

Once I'm in position, Dexter says, 'Ella, I'll check in periodically, but let me know if there are any problems. I have my walkie-talkie.' He gestures to his hip.

Ella nods. 'No problem. I'll keep an eye on her.'

When the guys leave, Ella ensures I'm OK before she sits down in the midst of the piles of paperwork on the floor. 'You gave us quite a scare.'

I try to nod, but it hurts.

'No, keep still. I'll do the talking. You can tell me everything later. Rest, but don't sleep, got it?'

I clear my throat in confirmation.

'Were you just trying to outdo me in the egg-on-the-head stakes?'

I raise a tiny smile as she makes eye contact, but I remember not to shake my head.

'Well, I think you've won the trophy for it anyway.

Right, I'm going to crack on – no pun intended – and just grunt or something if you're not OK. Got it?'

I clear my throat again.

An hour later, it's lunchtime and I'm feeling a little better. Sitting still and regrouping with Ella has done the trick. I'll still need to take it easy for the rest of the day, but I can manage to get up and down without feeling like I'm about to keel over. My stomach's also rumbling.

'Someone's hungry.' Ella laughs. 'Do you think you could keep something down? It might do you some good and it's *enyucados* today.'

'I'll give it a try as otherwise I'm going to keep rumbling. Are these *enyucados* light?'

Ella grins. 'Not exactly. You'll see. Depends how many you eat. It's cassava balls with cheese, butter and eggs.'

My stomach rumbles again. Guess I'm having *enyucados*.

The canteen is half full when we enter and as I take my plate from Sofia, she comments on the bruising that has come out on my head. Since I haven't looked in a mirror, instead washing my hands in the small wash-hand basin in Dexter's office, I had no idea. Sofia holds up a silver serving spoon and I frown.

'So you can check out your reflection.'

'Ah.' I peer into the spoon and recoil at the ugly black bruise that has already formed. 'You might have told me I looked like the Bride of Frankenstein,' I mutter to Ella.

She laughs. 'I'll tell Dexter you're calling him Frankenstein.'

I give her a slight push. 'Shh, he'll hear you.' I glance around. 'On that note, where is he?'

Ella shrugs. 'No idea. C'mon. The *enyucados* will get cold quickly and they're my favourite.'

We sit next to Alejandro – no Roisin, I note – and dig in to our plates of *enyucados*. I can see why they're Ella's favourite. They've clearly been deep-fried, but although they're crunchy on the outside, the inside is soft and gooey cheese.

Roisin enters with Luciana and her face is as dark as the sky on a rainy day. You know the bit before the clouds burst and the deluge occurs? That. I suddenly realise she wasn't around when I came to after being hit on the head by the door, yet she was the one who hit me with it. My animosity towards her ratchets up two notches.

She glowers at me as she sits down. If she clenches her jaw any more, she's going to need serious dental work. I'm guessing she's not impressed at the knowledge I caught her *in flagrante*, after a fashion, instead of Dexter.

But I don't let her spoil my meal.

In the afternoon, I sit in the nursery, taking it easy with Luciana for a bit, giving the baby sloths their milk. It's so relaxing and I catch myself about to drift off a few times. Each of the girls is taking it in turns to ensure I'm definitely OK and not about to pass out at their feet. It's kind of sweet. Dexter also checks in every now and again, but we haven't had time to have a talk, and I can't read him enough to know if we have a shot at sorting things between us. Hopefully, yes, but men are strange creatures. Unpredictable in some areas, whilst predictable to a fault in others.

I'm flagging long before the workday is done and when I see Mariangeles in the rec room in our accommodation block, I say, 'I'm going to skip dinner. I'm still full from the yu-covados?' I've already forgotten the name.

'En-yu-ca-dos,' she corrects me. 'Yes, they're very filling, and delicious. Only Nicolás' mum makes them better, but please don't tell Sofia.'

I smile then make a zipping motion across my lips, sealing them shut.

'See you in the morning. Get some rest.' She hugs me but manages to bump my head with her shoulder.

When I startle at the contact, she apologises. '*¡Ay!* Sorry. I'm so clumsy. Right, I'll go before I inflict any further damage.'

An hour or so later, I'm reclining on three pillows and the book I was reading has slipped down the side of the bed as I begin to doze, when there's a rap at the door.

'It's open,' I mumble. I bet Federica or Ella has brought me a plate of food after all. Honestly, you'd think I need feeding up. I promise, I'm hardly fading away here.

The door opens and Dexter stands framed in the doorway, wearing navy cargo pants and a light blue T-shirt. I straighten up then try to tidy the covers on my bed, which is pointless really; he's seen the state of it already.

'Hi.' His eyes study me as if he's looking for a sign of some kind, but of what I'm not sure.

'Hi,' I reply. Well, I was right about one thing. When he doesn't say anything else, I ask, 'Is that for me?' I gesture to the covered plate he's holding.

He sighs. 'Yes, sorry, Sofia insisted. She didn't want you going hungry.'

I smile. 'Here? As if.'

He grins and it melts my heart. I gulp as I think of how to get us around to the topic we sorely need to discuss. I can't put it off any longer. Catastrophes, in all senses, keep happening the more I delay it.

'Dexter, I just wanted to tell you I'm so sorry I jumped to conclusions.' There's no need to say 'with Roisin', and I can't bring myself to utter her name.

He nods mutely. This is going well … I have no idea if he has any intention of us trying for a reconciliation or not. He's not exactly making this easy for me.

When the silence stretches out between us, I finally say, 'Oh, you can put the plate down on the bedside table there.' Then I realise that makes me sound like I'm talking to a waiter. Gah, why is this so difficult? Relationships should come with a handbook, an encyclopaedia-sized one, so we don't screw things up.

A hint of a smile escapes his lips. He's had the same thought about acting as waiter, no doubt.

But when he has set the plate down, he moves towards me and slowly raises his fingertips to my forehead. I prepare to recoil. It hurt when Mariangeles bumped it earlier. I imagine it will still do.

However, the featherlight caress of Dexter's

fingertips over my bruise is such that I feel no pain at all. Then he bends over and trails gentle kisses over my bruise and the rest of my forehead, before adjusting position slightly, moving back to search my eyes for permission before he leans forward again, but this time his lips meet mine, and it's like every moment has been leading up to this. We've had our false starts, we've slept together, now we've had our first misunderstanding, fight and falling-out, and this is where we kiss and make up. And I'm all for that.

As Dexter deepens our kiss, I shuffle back on the bed towards the wall so he has room to sit down, then he puts his arms around me and the sensation of his heart beating as fast as my own is all I need. No words. No explanations. Just actions.

Chapter Twenty-two

The next week flies past. I'm really feeling part of the furniture now. I know my way around most of the tasks, and no longer need assistance with the majority of them. I've helped release another sloth back to the wild and I've been with Carlos to the meeting in the south of the country, to Corcovado National Park. The drive to the Osa Peninsula was incredible too. It took us about three and a half hours to get there, and after, Carlos insisted we stay a bit longer so he could show me the sights – almost all animal-related, of course.

And whilst I'm loving spending time with the sloths, I can't say it was any hardship to see a jaguarundi for the first time, although it didn't quite live up to its name. I'd assumed it would look like a jaguar, but it was more like a weasel. So, even though it was good to see it, it was a little underwhelming.

However, there were monkeys everywhere. Squirrel monkeys, white-faced monkeys and spider monkeys. Oddly, we didn't see any howler monkeys, despite them supposedly being pretty prevalent on the peninsula. Well, at least I saw those in Manuel Antonio National Park with Dexter.

And then there are all the foods I've been eating.

Chayote, which looks like a fruit but tastes like a vegetable. I think it's a kind of squash. They have a lot of squash here.

Anyway, I feel welcome now – obviously, except for with Roisin, who continues to glare daggers at me at every possible opportunity. I'm sure she also waits around corners to try to trip me up, but I don't care. I got the guy. The guy is into me, and I'm into him, and we're spending pretty much every waking moment, and many of the non-waking moments, together. Whilst it's intense, it sort of feels like we're making up for lost time, plus the whole environment is like being in a pressure cooker, especially with the ravishing Roisin on our shoulders at every turn. Although she's taken the hint, finally, with Dexter, it's like she has the attitude of 'if I can't have him, no one can' and as if she is trying to do everything to sabotage our relationship, our happiness, our enjoyment of being in each other's company, and that of others, as much as possible. She needs to get laid, just not by Dexter. Or she needs to find an interest: take up crocheting, composting, canoeing. I don't care. But she needs to stop bugging us. She's even wheedled her way onto the beach trip Nicolás, Ed, Dexter and I arranged. Ella is coming, too, but the others are staying behind. Someone has to care for the animals, but it's our day off. Roisin switched with Luciana so she could come. Grr.

I'd been looking forward to a day at the beach too. I'm not too old yet to enjoy that kind of life. Volleyball on the beach, lying in the sun with a book, chilling, drinking guaro sours and maybe being brave enough to try the *chiliguaro*, which, legend has it, blows your head off. Although perhaps I'll stick to jaguar coladas. It's like guaro sour, but with passion fruit and cream. Basically, almost a dessert – that works for me!

We're so often dusty and dirty that the idea of sluicing off in the Pacific really appeals to me. And I love to swim. I used to do a lot of wild swimming back home. Probably my only brave trait – at least, my friends thought it was brave. I can't decide if it was brave or stupid, as the water's generally freezing in Scotland. It's the one activity I've missed since I came here, but today we're going to Escondido Beach, or hidden beach, which is not far from the beach where Dexter took me after our night-time walk through the rainforest.

Nicolás and Ed appear not long after breakfast, keen for us all to head off together. We take their car and one of the sanctuary jeeps. The sun is almost blinding in the cloudless sky. I'd say it's going to be a hot one, but every day's a hot one here. Thankfully, my body is more than acclimatised now, but the heat still sucks the air from my lungs sometimes.

Part of me thinks we should be going in the afternoon, since after four is when it starts to cool down, and that's only to around 26 °C. There's a huge difference between that and the 33 °C it will be at its hottest. But I suppose there's a greater chance of rain after that, and it's dark a few hours later, so I guess this is why we're going so early.

I've slathered myself in suntan lotion. I know I won't be able to stomach the relentless sun if I'm lying on a lounger for long, and I'd rather be prepared.

I have my book, and Luciana even lent me a sun

parasol as my skin is so much fairer – so is Roisin's, but I dare say she won't want to sit beside me – and I'm looking forward to chilling and then getting in that water.

We park up and walk the trail until we arrive at the beach, which is gorgeous. The crystal-clear aquamarine water is edged by sand so soft, my feet sink right into it.

Nicolás lays out some blue-and-white collapsible chairs; Dexter, whose hand has been holding mine since we got out of the jeep, sets down a cooler full of beers and soft drinks; and Ed places the diving equipment and snorkels he brought, on the beach beside us.

Dexter kisses me on the nose. 'I'm going to dive with Ed and Nicolás for a bit. You OK to hang here, or do you want to come with?'

I shake my head. 'No, I'm going to chill and read my book. You go.' I lean forward and kiss him on the lips, just as sand blows into my eyes.

'Sorry,' says Roisin, not sounding remotely sorry as she swishes her towel to get the sand off it.

'No problem.' Dexter's tone contradicts his words.

'Dexter, you ready?' Ed calls.

Dexter nods to Ed then turns to me. 'See you later.'

I blow him another kiss and settle back to read my John Grisham. Ella settles down beside me in another lounger and pops her earbuds in. Bliss. I hear a shout and look up, but it's only the boys messing about in the water before they get out far enough to dive. As my attention returns to my book, I catch Roisin scowling at me again. She needs to get a life.

The book's really good, one of his older ones, but

one that somehow I missed. It's set partly in the Cayman Islands. I slide further down the lounger, pulling my navy skip cap, featuring a sloth on it, of course, over my face as my sunglasses aren't quite doing the job. I just want to close my eyes for a few seconds, then I'll strip down to my bikini and go swim in those dreamlike waters.

I must doze as I come to with Ella opening the cool box, and it takes a couple of seconds before I recall where I am. I blink my tiredness away and try to sit up, but my body is sluggish. That's what happens when you relax and you're not used to doing so. If anything, the sun feels even hotter.

'Ella, am I burning anywhere?'

'Hmm?'

'Am I red?' I ask her.

She shakes her head, then I turn and she says, 'Maybe a little here.' She points to my left shoulder.

Damn, I always miss a bit. 'Thanks.' I grab my sun cream and squirt a generous dollop of the factor thirty into my hands then smooth it over my shoulder and over my upper arm. I'll follow Ella's example and have a cold drink, and then I'm going in. The water is too inviting and I'm starting to overheat.

I glance over to where Roisin is lying face down on her sunlounger. I note the factor eight she's using and almost tut. Don't people learn? Well, if she wants to have a face like a piece of dried-out old bark when she's fifty, that's up to her, I suppose.

'Do you want something?' Ella indicates the cooler.

I nod. 'Coke, please.'

We sit and stare out at the ocean, drinks in hand,

and I listen to the rhythm of the waves. The sound of rolling waves has always soothed me and today is no different.

I set down my half-finished Coke and peel off my T-shirt and shorts. Time to go in. 'You coming, Ella?'

'Sure.' She strips down to her tiny bikini. I'd probably wear a bikini like that too if I had more body confidence. Mine covers considerably more, but it's still a bikini.

Against my better judgement, I say, 'Roisin?'

No answer. I try again. Still no answer. Good. I've done my duty, and the good news is, I'm not going to be stuck with her, or have to interact with her.

'Last one in cleans out the cages,' I call to Ella, and she laughs as we sprint as best we can across the sand, straight into the ocean. It's like entering a warm bath after a long day – just with tropical fish for company. I swim for a bit, enjoying the burn in my muscles, then round in circles, Ella by my side. Then I float onto my back, relaxing, until I realise I haven't checked if there are sharks near this beach. When I ask Ella, she shakes her head and tells me not to worry.

'No sharks here, although there were a couple of crocodiles a few years ago.'

That puts me off my stride and I splutter. 'That's not very reassuring, Ella.'

She chuckles. 'You'll be fine. We swim here all the time. Anyway, do you think Dexter would let you swim in unsafe waters?'

If I was on land, I'd shrug. 'Well, at least they're further out. The shark can eat them first.'

Now it's Ella's turn to splutter. 'Charming.'

I smile and continue to swim. I'm heading for the rocks about two hundred metres away. I can't tell you how wonderful it is to be back in the water. This definitely beats the freezing cold Firth of Clyde back home. I mean, I enjoy open water swimming in Scotland, but if it could just heat up by about thirty degrees, I'd be far happier.

This is the life. I smile as my arms slice through the water, then I flip onto my back and drift, paddling with my arms. Not a care in the world, if you forget the earlier mention of crocs.

The cove is beautiful, sheltered, secluded and not very busy. I spot only one other person on the beach now, a guy making a beeline for Roisin. She'll probably lap up the attention. Miaow. Hmm, my run-in with her has awoken my inner bitch. I don't usually consider myself that kind of person – perhaps I'm being territorial over Dexter – but she really does bring out the worst in me. And now I think about it, I haven't noticed the other women at the sanctuary being firm friends with her either. She certainly seems to seek out male attention, and at least the others don't have the problem that she was trying to 'steal their man'.

I reach the rocks and pull myself up on them, admiring the view all around. The sun is unforgiving and the heat warms my skin after being in the water. Droplets of water and salty residue cling to my skin and I can taste the ocean in the air now. Ella prefers to stay at the bottom of the rocks, floating around and around on her back.

Raised voices reach me from the shore and I look over to where Roisin is now standing, feet wide apart, gesticulating like crazy. I can't see her expression from here, but her body language screams 'get the fuck away from me'.

I glance around to see if the guys are back from their dive, but there's no sign of them.

'Ella,' I call down. 'That guy's hassling Roisin, I think. Let's go back.'

Ella shades her eyes with a hand and says, 'I don't recognise him. Yeah, good idea.'

I dive off the rock straight into the water, but on this occasion, I have no time to enjoy the feeling of freedom that comes with swimming in such an incredible location. Much as she's hardly my favourite person, one thing I hate is men pestering women. Even the fact Roisin pretty much did the same to Dexter doesn't stop me wanting to protect her from unwanted attention, especially when she's alone on the beach.

I'm more out of breath than I'd expected when I heave myself out of the water, splashing the final few yards until I'm standing opposite Roisin and the interloper.

They don't seem to have noticed us, they're so focused on their argument. Belatedly, I wonder if she knows him. How will that look, if we interrupt and he's some ex-boyfriend?

Ella stands beside me, but glances at me, as if unsure what to do. I'd forgotten she's only twenty-one. Maybe she doesn't feel confident enough to confront a guy she doesn't know. With a deep breath for courage, I wade in. 'Roisin, everything OK?' I ask, my tone making it clear I know everything isn't OK.

Roisin gives a start. She must have been so

engrossed in her spat with this guy that she didn't hear us approach. In the few seconds it takes her to react, and whilst we were hauling ourselves out of the ocean, I studied her opponent. About five ten, broad-shouldered, handsome, if a little mean-looking. I have no idea how I know this, but perhaps it's the arrogance flooding off him. His stance maybe. The smirk on his lips doesn't endear him to me. He's too sure of himself, and it makes me want to wipe the smile off his face.

It's testament to how uncomfortable Roisin feels in this guy's presence that she doesn't scowl at me, or tell me to get lost; instead she says, 'No, it's not. Some people don't get when they're not wanted.'

I square my shoulders and turn to the guy. 'You heard what she said.'

He gives me a scathing look. 'What's it to do with you?'

'We're her friends. Now, have some self-respect and disappear.'

He sets his jaw and seems ready to challenge me, but eventually he gives us each a long, hard stare then takes a few steps backwards before turning and loping away.

I shake my head after him as he retreats. 'What a creep.'

Roisin looks at me almost with respect. 'Thanks. I'm glad you both came back. I should have gone swimming with you earlier.'

'No problem. And you can rectify that later. I'm sure we'll go back in. Drink?' I gesture to the cooler and she smiles – a rare sight in my company – and says, 'Lemonade, please.'

The three of us sit down on the loungers and chat until the boys come back from their diving session.

As Dexter heads back up the beach towards me, I can't help thinking that today we may have made progress with Roisin, chipped away at her barrier a little, and the realisation sends a warm glow through my heart.

Chapter Twenty-three

'How was your dive?' I ask as Dexter plants a kiss on my forehead and flops down beside me after wriggling out of his diving gear.

'Great. You should do it with me next time.'

I nod. 'I will.'

'So, what have you three been up to?' he asks as he takes a Coke from the cooler and pops it open.

I fill him in on the guy who'd been pestering Roisin.

'She's lucky you were there.'

'Yeah, he totally loved himself. Oh, and I wasn't initially there. I swam to the rocks with Ella.'

Dexter points to the rocks. 'You swam all the way over there? It's quite far.'

I grin. 'Are you patronising me?'

Dexter puts a hand against his chest in mock affront. 'I would never. So, how come you can swim so well?'

'I used to swim competitively when I was younger.'

One of Dexter's eyebrows goes up. 'Really?'

I smile. 'Yeah, really.'

'Get you.' He wraps an arm around me.

'You can test your prowess against me when I go

back out shortly.'

'Oh, I may be too tired. I've been swimming with a tank on my back for an hour almost,' he says, playfully.

I nudge his leg. 'You're just scared I'll beat you.'

'Not a chance. Before you go, though, give me a hand with this crossword.'

'Sure. What you stuck on?'

Once I've corrected the spelling on one of the words Dexter put in, so the answer for his next clue then fits – something I have to do on a regular basis – I grab a water from the cool box and sit back to admire the view. I almost shake my head at how lucky I am, being in this incredible location, with these pristine waters, fabulous company and oodles of sunshine. It's school holiday time back in Scotland now, so it's probably pouring with rain.

Finally, we lie back to relax, or in Dexter's case snooze, but the noise of the seabirds is preventing me from falling asleep, so eventually I drag myself upright again and say, 'I'm going back in. Anyone coming?'

To my surprise Roisin sits up. 'I'll come.' She's not going to try to drown me, is she?

'Ed? Nicolás?'

Nicolás shakes his head. 'Maybe later.'

'Too tired. I'm going to relax for a bit, enjoy the sun,' says Ed.

Roisin glides through the water like a dolphin. She laughs like one, too, I can't help thinking. That said, I haven't heard her laugh much recently. She hasn't had much cause, I suppose.

My competitive streak kicks in and I put on a spurt and overtake her, my body streamlined in the water. I knew that Duke of Edinburgh certification would come in handy one day. I swim and swim and swim and it's so liberating, I'm barely aware of anyone or anything. It's just me and the ocean and the blue sky above. And Roisin, somewhere. She must be a little behind me. I approach the rocks, my hand slipping as I try to grasp hold and pull myself up. As I catch my breath, I scan the horizon – breathtaking. Such a beautiful cove within a gorgeous section of the Pacific. Dexter told me it used to be busier here but the path we took is no longer on the official trail, so although locals know of it, and how to avoid the sections in disrepair, tourists are actively discouraged from trying to reach the beach, which makes it even more of a haven.

I frown. Where is Roisin? I wasn't swimming *that* fast, and I'm hardly an Olympian. I gaze back towards the beach, but can't see her. Did she go back to the beach? Pretend she was coming swimming with me then ditch me? That said, I didn't exactly hang around once we got in the water.

But she isn't on the beach. Panic clutches at my chest and a sense of foreboding comes over me. I dive into the water and head back towards the shore, slowly this time, searching around for Roisin. I can't see her. I tread water for a second and wave my arms to the beach and shout 'Help!' but they can't hear me or see me. I swim again, scanning the ocean frantically. This isn't funny now. I may not be best mates with the girl, but I don't wish her any harm. Out of the corner of my eye, I catch sight of Dexter and Ed entering the water, swimming full pelt towards me, but they're still so far away. Nicolás is sprinting along the beach. What do they see?

And then I see her, or rather, a hand, emerge from the water then vanish again. Without a thought, and training my eye on the spot where the hand disappeared, I slice through the water as fast as I can. The hand comes up one more time then disappears again. I reach the point where I saw the hand vanish, and I dive down below the water's surface. Thank God the waters are crystal clear, but I'm still not a hundred per cent sure on the location. I glance left and right, then I spin around and she's right there and she's starting to bob. Immediately, I spot the problem and I know we're running out of time. Her leg is trapped between two rocks, and at an awkward angle.

With not a moment to lose, I reach her, grab her by the shoulders, point upwards and, all the while holding my breath, wriggle her leg and manipulate it, trying to free it from its prison, but it won't budge. Roisin's eyes start to close. I shake her. I need her to be conscious for this, or we're lost. I lift her head to mine, put my mouth over hers and breathe a breath into her. Hopefully, that will work and sustain her long enough for me to free her leg. If not, we could both be goners. I've watched enough documentaries to think it's worth a try. Her leg will be scraped and sore, but she'll be alive.

With one final yank, her leg comes free, and I drag her to the surface, where we burst through the water and I gulp lungfuls of air into my burning lungs. God, I didn't realise that would hurt so much. Now I just need to keep Roisin afloat and steer her back to the beach. She has gone limp. I hope she's OK. Salty tears prick my eyes. Today can't end like this. Out of the corner of my eye, I see Dexter, Nicolás and Ed racing towards us, and I breathe a sigh of relief, praying they reach us in time.

Dexter reaches me first, then Ed, and wordlessly they take Roisin between them and drag her back to shore, Nicolás staying by my side as we follow them at a slower pace whilst I get my breath back.

When we reach the beach, Ed is doing chest compressions on Roisin and Dexter is on his phone. As I haul my exhausted body out of the water, legs wobbling like I've just stepped off a trampoline after bouncing for ten minutes, a chalk-white Ella is by my side with a towel, which she wraps round me.

Ed administers mouth-to-mouth to Roisin and suddenly she splutters and what seems like gallons of water pour out of her mouth. She chokes and coughs for a few more moments as water continues to come up before Ed finally says, 'I think she's going to be OK.'

Relief swamps me and my shoulders relax.

'The ambulance is on its way,' Dexter says, pocketing his phone. 'She was lucky. You saved her life, Kat.'

'I wouldn't put it like that.' I feel myself colour, but I'm too exhausted to put up any further protest.

Dexter rubs my shoulder. 'I would.'

'So would I,' echo Nicolás and Ed.

Ella stares at me. 'It was a lucky day for our team when you joined the sanctuary.' Then she hugs me, burying her head into my shoulder.

We arrive back at the sanctuary an hour later. I think I'm still in shock. I'm certainly exhausted. Dexter has had his arm around my shoulder or waist almost the entire way, with Ed and Ella driving the jeep and the car. Nicolás went in the ambulance with Roisin, as a representative of the sanctuary, since it belongs to his aunt and uncle.

Sofia comes running out of the main building as we approach. When we all tumble out, she clasps me to her chest. 'I can't believe Roisin has been taken to hospital. You were so brave.' She holds me away from her and looks into my eyes, studying me. 'Are you sure you're OK?'

I nod, feebly. Tired. Overwrought. A tad emotional. Overwhelmed. But definitely OK. And alive. It's times like these that I remember that as well as being incredibly beautiful, the ocean is immensely powerful, and that we are mere specks when compared to it.

'Come. I have made *sustancia de carne*. It will do you the world of good.'

Silently, I follow Sofia. Most of me would like to go lie down in a dark room, but I know she has my best interests at heart, and no doubt the dish she is talking about will make me feel better. I have no idea what it is though, only that the translation is roughly 'meat sustenance'. Distractedly, I think that it sounds hearty.

I stifle a yawn and sway slightly, but Dexter is there, by my side, and promptly steadies me.

Moments later, we're all huddled around one table. Ed has pulled over a few chairs. Carlos is noticeable by his absence, but when Dexter called him to say Roisin was being taken to hospital, he'd immediately asked which hospital, learned that Dexter had sent Nicolás in the ambulance with her, and advised he'd meet them there.

Our little forlorn sanctuary family bustles around, helping Sofia lay the table, serve the *sustancia de carne*, which I discover is remarkably like chicken noodle soup, and settles down, as Victor, Mariangeles, Federica and the others join us.

As I dip bread into the soup, I absent-mindedly note how delicious it is, but I kind of feel as if I'm having an out-of-body experience. The chatter of those around me seems more like a whooshing in my ears and I have difficulty really tuning in, or absorbing what everyone is saying, although clearly the main topic is what happened at the beach.

Somehow I manage to eat the soup, and even some bread, but when I glance at Dexter, his eyes are filled with concern.

He leans into me. 'Do you want to lie down for a bit after this? It's been quite a day for you. I think you might still be in shock.'

I think he might be right. 'That sounds like a good idea.'

When Sofia, who has joined us to eat, sets down some *agua dulce*, I'm already struggling to keep my eyes open.

'Drink. It will help,' she prods gently.

I do as bid and the refreshing *agua dulce* does its work. But I still need that lie-down.

Five minutes later, after I thank Sofia and say bye to everyone, Dexter walks me to my room.

Once inside, he puts his arms around me and leans his chin on my head. 'How are you really?'

I slump against him and all my breath goes out of me. 'Tired.'

He nods. 'That's understandable.' He takes me by the shoulders and moves me away from him slightly so he is looking into my face. 'That was such a brave thing you did, Kat. I hope you know that.' He pauses. 'And it's no secret there's no love lost between the two of you. Truth is, Roisin hasn't done herself many favours generally.'

I remain silent.

'I was so scared when you went down and didn't surface for so long.'

I lift my head slightly, but he goes on. 'I know you said you were a strong swimmer, but swimming and being underwater, for such a long time, are two different things. Years of hanging around with Ed have taught me that.'

I give an almost imperceptible nod as his hold on me tightens and a tear escapes me as the realisation of how differently things could have turned out today hits home.

'I'll leave you to rest, but remember, we're all close by.'

'Thank you.' My throat aches and the words scratch my throat.

Dexter kisses me on the cheek, then as he turns to leave, I call him back. 'Dexter, can you let me know how Roisin is?'

He nods. 'I will. Now get some sleep and I'll check in on you later.'

As I recline on the bed, pulling the cover half over me, my final thought before oblivion takes me is that there are some things bigger than us in life. Somehow, now, our petty squabbles seem so unimportant.

Chapter Twenty-four

'Glad to see you're OK, Roisin,' Dexter says as we walk into the canteen two days later. Unsurprisingly, the hospital had decided to keep Roisin in for observation.

Roisin's face breaks into a huge smile. 'Thanks to you, Kat. I honestly don't know how to thank you. You're a better person than I am. From what Ed and Nicolás tell me, you were underwater for ages trying to get me out.'

I dip my head slightly. 'It probably seemed longer than it was.'

'That's not how they told it.'

When I look up, I try to fathom the expression in her eyes. Surely that's not respect.

'We haven't always seen eye to eye, Kat, and I'm sorry. Stupid to fall out over a man, don't you think?'

I hold my tongue.

She rubs a hand over the back of her neck. 'Anyway, I owe you my life, literally, so anything you need, ask.'

'Ferrari? World peace?'

'Ha! I'm good, but I'm not a magician,' she says. 'But seriously, just ask.'

'No need to repay me, but thanks.'

She hesitates as Dexter wanders over to speak to Sofia. 'And about that other thing…'

When I shrug, no clue what she's talking about, she elaborates. 'Nimble. I'm truly sorry, in all respects.'

We hold each other's gaze for a few seconds then she saunters off towards Victor, who is waiting for her at the entrance to the adult sloth play area.

Dexter and I are sitting with Mariangeles and Federica when Javier comes in. 'Dexter, a call just came in from a couple who've found a baby sloth. They think they saw the mother take off into the trees, but it was too well camouflaged for them to be certain, and they thought it might be injured. They've wrapped the baby in a blanket for now.'

Dexter rolls his eyes. 'We need a better marketing campaign. People are still picking up babies when they don't know that that's half the problem. The mother may never return now. Where is it exactly?'

Javier gives him the address and coordinates and a pulse ticks in Dexter's cheek as he thinks. I can almost see the question marks forming inside his head.

'I reckon that's about half an hour away. Victor, come with me. Luciana, can you redistribute mine and Victor's duties, please, and bring Carlos up to speed when you see him?'

'Sure thing,' Luciana says, scraping back her chair and collecting in the dirty plates and cups.

'Kat, you're shotgun on this. We may need you to take care of the baby whilst Victor and I try to track its mother. Hopefully, she isn't hurt, but there are electrical pylons near those coordinates, and I strongly suspect the baby has fallen from her grasp when she has hit a pylon.'

'What do you need?'

'Nothing. We've got it all in the truck. Let's go.'

As we trundle along the track to the location where the couple are caring for the infant sloth, I take in Dexter's furrowed brow. He really cares about the sloths, and about preserving as many of them as he can.

The heat inside the truck and the events of the past few weeks catch up with me, and as Victor and Dexter converse in rapid-fire Spanish, I feel my body dragged under by sleep. The jolt of the truck stopping and my head hitting the window rouses me, and I wish I'd stayed awake as I'm all groggy now.

A couple who I estimate are in their late fifties, and who have that quintessential British look about their dress – white linen shirts, above-the-knee cream cotton shorts, straw sunhats, and walking sandals – are sitting at the side of the road, a red Mitsubishi SUV off to their right. The woman is holding a baby-blue blanket, and I half-smile at the irony of the blanket's colour. As we approach, her husband comes forward to greet us, whilst she remains seated, as if she doesn't want to disturb the baby.

The man starts to speak in Spanish to Victor, but relief floods his face when Dexter introduces himself and they switch to English, although Dexter does make a point of translating every so often for Victor's benefit.

As Dexter feared, where they found the baby is very close to the pylons. Victor picks up the baby and puts it in the truck bed for safekeeping whilst he and Dexter set off to search for the mother.

I chat with the couple, who only arrived the day

before yesterday, and were astonished to come across the baby. He's a doctor, so his first thought was to care for it.

They seem a decent pair and we swap stories of home and our experiences of Costa Rica so far. They can't believe I gave up my job on a whim to look after the sloths, but the doctor applauds it, says I've found my calling, as he did his. I tell them they don't have to hang around for the others to come back, and that they should go off and enjoy their holiday, but they're determined to stay with me until Victor and Dexter return, as they want to know if the baby gets reunited with its mother.

Half an hour later, crashing in the undergrowth leads me to think we might be in luck, but it's Victor, followed by Dexter, who shakes his head sadly.

'She's nowhere to be seen.'

'We've searched everywhere we can think of,' says Victor, 'but, as you can see, it's like looking for a needle in a haystack.' He points to the tall trees all around us, which stretch out for miles. I note their star-shaped leaves with interest. I must ask Victor what they're called later.

We chat with the British couple for another five minutes or so, then they have a final peek at the baby sloth lying cosied up in the blanket in the truck bed, the woman wishes it luck, and they take off in their SUV.

As the dust from their tyres settles, I look at Dexter. 'What now?'

He gives a sad smile. 'We have a new recruit for the sanctuary. Come on. We'd best head back.'

Once we've secured the baby sloth in the crate, we climb into the truck and my thoughts are full of the baby in its blanket during the ride back. Part of me wants to cradle it on my lap, but I know that's not the best way to care for them. I can't help the human in me wanting to do that, though.

When we arrive back, Dexter says, 'I'll take him to Luciana after we check him over.'

I nod. 'I'll go update Sofia and Carlos and ask what they want help with. See you later?'

His eyes crinkle at the corners. 'You can count on it.'

Victor rolls his eyes good-naturedly. '*Ay, ay, ay,* young love.'

I give his arm a friendly shove and he grins before loping off in the direction of the adult sloth cages.

But when I enter the sanctuary foyer, Carlos is giving a talk to a school group, Ferdinand as ever round him like a belt.

Mariangeles walks out of Carlos' office. 'Hi. Did you manage to find the mother?'

My mouth downturns as I shake my head.

She sighs. 'Happens too often. All we can do is take care of the little one now.'

'Yeah, Dexter has taken him to be checked over, then I think Luciana will be looking after him.'

She nods. 'Best place for him, apart from with his mother, of course. Oh, I almost forgot, a letter came for you.'

I blanch. A letter? From who?

'Let me just go get it.' She spins around and heads into the admin area where we receive and sort the mail.

She returns a moment later, holding a buff-coloured envelope aloft. 'Here you go.'

I resist the temptation to snatch it from her, I'm so curious to find out what it contains and who it's from.

'Thanks,' I say when she hands it over. 'Well, I need to go see Sofia, so I'll catch up with you later.'

'No problem. I have some supplies to order. Roll on dinnertime.'

I laugh. Mariangeles is rake-thin, but she eats like food's going out of fashion.

Before I go to see Sofia, I nip to the ladies. Whatever this is, and whoever it's from, I want to read it in private. No one knows I'm here, except for Mum, Aidan and Becca, and at a push my ex-boss, but he doesn't know where in Costa Rica I am. So why have I received an official-looking letter?

I tear open the envelope, careful not to damage its contents. Inside is another envelope, with my home address on it, bearing the frank of the University of Glasgow.

My hearts leaps then dives. Oh my goodness. The application I made to the vet school. Whereas I ripped the first envelope, here my dexterity deserts me. I fumble with the seal, and finally manage to open it, careful of the precious cargo inside.

Dear Katherine MacDonald

We are writing to inform you that due to an error, you were incorrectly informed the Veterinary Medicine & Surgery BVMS course was oversubscribed. Please accept our apologies for any inconvenience caused. We are delighted to advise you that you have been accepted onto the course, which commences on Monday 11 September...

I'm glad I'm sitting down on the toilet seat lid already. How can life be so cruel? This letter should have arrived months ago if I was going to be accepted. Despair washes over me. I should be ecstatic at this news. It's what I've wanted, but now... I'm settled here, with Dexter, the sloths, the team. The irony isn't lost on me. Last month I was coming for a holiday, to escape my dead-end job and the boredom of my life. Now I live in a sloth sanctuary in Costa Rica and have just been offered a place to study veterinary medicine at Glasgow uni. The beginning of a headache drums at my temples.

I sit for a further five minutes, hoping the answer will magically come to me, but it doesn't and finally I give up for now, tuck the letter into my pocket, wash my hands and leave the ladies.

How I wish I'd told someone now that I'd applied, but I was so afraid of being rejected, and having everyone's pity, that I didn't even tell Becca. What I wouldn't give to have her to lean on now. No, it looks as if this is one dilemma I have to work out on my own.

Chapter Twenty-five

Sofia is happy for the help with dinner, at least, and babbles away to me as I help with the preparations. Meanwhile the letter burns a hole in my pocket and my head continues to throb with the ramifications. I feel like I belong here now, that I've found my place. And frankly, who would want to return to the shitshow that is my life back in Scotland right now? Furious mother. Check. Disgruntled, controlling ex-boyfriend who is incapable of understanding that I really do not want to see him again. Check. Lack of a job to pay the bills. Check. If I go home, I'll need somewhere to live, and it certainly won't be with Mum; she showed her true colours when she took Aidan's side when we split. And it most definitely won't be with Aidan. Becca would put me up for as long as I needed, but that's not the point. Plus, she'll be hurt I didn't mention I'd applied.

I close my eyes momentarily. What a mess. I almost wish I hadn't received the letter, that I hadn't got in. That would be one less decision to make. But I can't un-know what I know now. The question is, what to do about it? Am I on a different planet, living a pipe dream, thinking I can have a long-term-ish future out here in Costa Rica? But then, aren't you meant to make all your crazy mistakes in your twenties and thirties? Aren't you meant to take risks? I'd like to see where Dexter and I could go, especially after the hassle we went through to get to this stage, but am I really going to give up the possibility to go to vet school? Glasgow uni? The thought makes goose bumps come up on my arms.

'Kat. Kat! Kat!' Sofia says finally.

I glance up, startled. 'Sorry, I was miles away.'

'Clearly.' Sofia smiles. 'Can you dish this up whilst I take the rest out of the oven?'

'Sure.' I grab a dishtowel to protect my hands and take the casserole dish Sofia passes me, then I plate up as the hungry hordes descend. Seriously, they're like locusts swarming, or starving hounds at the first whiff of food.

Mariangeles and Luciana are talking animatedly and Roisin stands beside Alejandro as Victor gesticulates with his hands, telling them about some new club opening in town.

When she arrives Federica claps her hands. 'Ay! My favourite.'

I laugh. 'Everything Sofia makes is your favourite.'

'Well,' she replies hotly, 'it's all good.' She's speaking in English. Since we've started practising, it has definitely improved and we're both really enjoying the extra time together, I think.

'I won't argue with you there.' When I've finished serving her, she nudges Mariangeles. 'Hey, you lot, hurry up. Let's eat.'

Mariangeles shoots her a look that could fell a dragon. Fortunately, this is all part of their double act and terribly endearing, and it makes me smile, but I wouldn't want to be on the receiving end of one of her looks, or in her bad books generally. She'd make a formidable adversary. Far better to have her as a friend, a loyal, fierce one – whom I've become very fond of.

Once again my thoughts return to the letter of offer in my pocket. I know I don't need to decide right now, but somehow having no one I can talk to about it is making it far more difficult to deal with. Should I just call Becca, endure her tongue-lashing for keeping it from her for so long and then ask her advice? Or should I puzzle it out on my own a little longer?

Gah! This is driving me nuts. It's even putting me off my meal, and that's saying something.

I smell him before I see him, or rather I smell the cinnamon notes of his aftershave and the hint of fresh sweat as he leans down to kiss my cheek. Dexter. Yeah, like that really helped simplify this situation. Let's throw the hot guy I've fallen for into the mix so I can make a totally rational decision.

'The baby's settling in fine,' he says.

I nod, but his eyes cloud with confusion at my lack of enthusiasm. I'm usually much more upbeat at such news.

'You feeling OK?' he asks. 'You look a bit out of sorts.'

He has no idea.

'I'm a little tired,' I lie.

He notices my three-quarters full plate and frowns. 'You're not eating? You really aren't OK, are you? What's up?'

I shake my head. 'Seriously, I just need an early

night.'

His eyebrows shoot up at that and I suppress a smile. I guess an early night didn't figure in his plans for our evening. He probably had much more adventurous plans for us. Plans I've now scuppered. But I don't think I can act normally around him until I process the contents of the letter, and I need time for that. And a chat with Becca. Oh well, at least I've decided something.

I scrape back my chair. 'I'll see you later,' I say to the girls.

Mariangeles and Federica, who were deep in conversation, as usual, glance up, mystified expressions on their faces. 'Where are you off to?'

I stifle a yawn. 'Bed. I'm shattered.'

Mariangeles' head moves back on her shoulders as if she has been shot. 'Bed? At this time? Are you ill?'

Oh God, this is going to get old really fast.

Fortunately, Dexter intervenes. 'She's tired. Why don't we let her get some rest and we can grill her later?'

Mariangeles casts me a final appraising look and reluctantly agrees, but a hint of suspicion flashed in her eyes as if she knows something is up. There's not much gets past her.

I mouth a 'thank you' to Dexter, then pootle off back to my room.

Once I'm safely inside, and confident in the knowledge they're all having dinner, so I'm definitely alone, I call Becca.

After six rings, she answers. 'It's about time, too. I was beginning to think you'd forgotten about me.'

Becca's tone is joking, but a stab of guilt slices through me. I haven't been as communicative as I usually am. She's my best friend, and we tell each other everything, but somehow life has been very busy here, although I know that's no excuse. Plus, I've had a lot to think about, and that doesn't seem as if it will abate anytime soon.

'Sorry, Becca. Things have been a bit full-on. How are you?'

'Getting my cast off shortly.'

'Oh, that's fantastic. You must be so relieved.'

'You can say that again. I don't know how many knitting needles I've bent trying to scratch my leg.'

I chuckle. 'So have you taken up knitting too during your enforced confinement?'

'Steady on. I'm twenty-nine, not eighty-nine.'

'It's having a resurgence among young people, didn't you know? You could be part of a growing trend.'

'I'm happy as I am, thanks,' she mutters.

I try not to laugh. The thought of Becca knitting has me in stitches – pun intended, but I couldn't resist. It feels good to talk to her, and I needed to chat about something trivial and banal, both to lighten the mood and to pave the way for the much more serious discussion I need to have with her. Plus, I'm not certain how much of a backlash there will be from her at me keeping my university application secret. But since Becca is as forthright as they come, she'll tell me how it is, whether it's what I want to hear or not.

We hit a pause, and deciding this is the moment to come out with my news, I jump right in.

'Becca, I have something to tell you.'

'Oh my God, you're not pregnant, are you?'

'No! Why would I be pregnant?'

'Well, I'm sorry to be the one to tell you this, Kat, but when a man and a woman…'

'Oh, Becca, I do love you, but shut up!'

'You always spoil all my fun,' she murmurs.

'Not true. Right, listen up.' Once I have her attention, I blurt it out. 'I applied for a place at Glasgow uni vet school and I've just received a letter advising me I got in.'

'Vet school? Glasgow uni?' Becca scrunches up her eyebrows as the cogs in her brain whirr and try to compute what I'm telling her.

'Yeah. I kinda have a confession to make.' When she doesn't say anything, I continue. 'I did an access course over the past two years, in the evenings, and because I passed that, I got a place at uni.'

'How on earth did you study for two years without me knowing?' Becca's incredulous expression is priceless and I wish I could snap a photo of her.

I hesitate then admit, 'I think I may have told you I was working an extra shift. Sorry.'

She shakes her head. 'I can't believe you'd keep something so huge from me.'

'I said I'm sorry. Look, I really am, but I didn't want anyone to know.'

'When did you apply to uni?' she asks finally.

I mentally calculate how long it has been. 'Six months ago.'

'Six months ago? Why didn't you tell me?' Indignation punctuates her every word.

I sigh. 'Because I didn't want to feel under any pressure. I didn't really expect to get in, and thought if I got in, it would be a bonus. But to my mind, if I kept it to myself and got a rejection, then it wouldn't be as bad since only I knew about it.'

Becca mulls this over for a second. 'No, I'm not buying it. You should still have told me. We tell each other everything.'

I let out a long breath. 'I know, and I'm sorry. But can we put that to one side for now, whilst we unpack the predicament I'm now in?'

Becca gives me a long look that says she isn't done with me yet, then nods. 'Go ahead.'

'Becca, I've dreamed of going to vet school since I was a little girl. When I didn't get the grades, I was devastated, and then I ended up stuck in the job at Peterson's, a job I wasn't particularly enamoured of, and felt trapped.'

Becca continues to stare at me. 'OK.'

When she doesn't say anything else, I continue. 'And then I came here, on holiday, and life sped up several notches, going from zero to a hundred and sixty in only a few days. I love it here. The sloths. The people. Dexter.'

'Right...' Becca says carefully.

'And now I've been accepted to do the course that I've always wanted, which will allow me to have the career I've always wanted. You know how much I want to be a vet. I just thought it was beyond my reach.'

'Hmm,' Becca says noncommittally. Eventually, she continues, 'I'm guessing Dexter doesn't know you applied to vet school either.'

I shake my head. 'You're the first person I've told.' I pause. 'Becca, I don't know what to do.'

Becca thinks for a moment, pulling her bottom lip between her thumb and index finger as she tends to do when she's deep in thought. 'Kat, I'm sorry. I can't make this decision for you, but what I can tell you is, you'd better tell Dexter, and soon.'

Chapter Twenty-six

Over the next few days, I mull over my options. Ella, I know, has noticed how withdrawn I've become. I feel I'm forcing jollity, as just when I think I've made a decision about my future, a throwaway comment from someone makes me change my mind. How can I not go after the future I'd always dreamed of? Costa Rica is lovely, but am I kidding myself about living here for a sustained period of time? Whereas going to university, studying to become a vet, would provide me with a solid future, a steady income, and then I'd be set up for life.

Becca and I had talked through my options the other night, with her, as ever, the voice of reason. She'd even suggested there may be a similar course here in Costa Rica, yet she wouldn't influence me either way, which frustrated me, despite me knowing she was doing it for my own good. And she's right, it is too big a decision for her to make it for me, and I'm thirty; I shouldn't need my best friend to make my decisions for me. That wasn't really what I was after anyway. I just wanted advice and to discuss my bouncy ball thoughts with someone, instead of simply allowing them to boing around inside my head, driving me to distraction.

And I know Dexter has detected a change in me the past few days, and nights. We've still made love and it has been kind of intense. Sometimes I've had to will myself not to cry as I contemplate whether I can leave, risking everything we have. Will Dexter stay here forever? Will he ever return to Ireland? I don't have any control over his life. I could turn down my place at uni, only for him to say he's going back to Waterford, or moving on to another country in Central or South America. And does he feel as strongly about me as I feel about him? The way he is with me makes me think he does, but I don't know for sure – and I'm too scared to ask. How would that leave things if he wasn't as invested in this relationship as I am? Ugh. My head hurts. It has done ever since the letter arrived. I'd received my acknowledgement email when I applied in January, but then in May, the university notified me that the course was oversubscribed and that unfortunately they couldn't offer me a place.

Is fate playing a hand here? I'm in Costa Rica. The fact the postal service managed successfully to forward my mail here, and nothing happened to it en route, is nothing short of a miracle and suggests the stars were aligning to allow me to have this chance at going to university. And that's all well and good, but it doesn't help me with my dilemma. I love Dexter. I'm also in love with Dexter. And although I've been reluctant to admit this, it's a fact, and I don't know what to do about it.

How can the universe be so cruel – or kind – as to offer me two things I've always wanted at the same time, but which are largely incompatible: life here with Dexter, life at uni back in Scotland? It doesn't seem fair. Maybe I should be grateful, but despite both things being wonderful, given the dilemma it puts me in, I feel as if I'm stuck between a rock and not just a hard place, but a place strewn with broken glass and covered in thorns.

I give a start as Luciana taps on the door then comes into the nursery, where I'm feeding the babies. I like it here, it's so tranquil, but it does give me rather too much time with my own thoughts. I can't escape them, much as I'd like to right now. On the plus side, I can hide away and no one can see the conflicted feelings written across my face.

'Time for me to take over. Lunch for you,' Luciana says, reaching for Bolt.

I pass him over and head to the bathroom to freshen up.

Federica has saved me a spot by her and Mariangeles. They, and Ella, are like the sisters I never had. Federica is the calm, measured one with Mariangeles the feisty, forthright one. She doesn't mince her words. Ella would be the sweet one, the youngest of the group. I don't only have to think carefully about my relationship with Dexter when coming to this crucial life decision, I need to factor my friendship with them into the equation too.

We catch up on each other's day so far and soon I sense Dexter behind me again.

'Hi.' He drops a kiss on my head and swings a seat over from another table as the girls budge up a little to give him room. 'How has your morning been?'

'I've been living it up with Bolt and Rocket,' I say.

He grins. 'You know how to party!'

As we eat, Mariangeles leads the conversation, enthusing over some music gig that's on near the beach at the weekend, whilst Federica tells us that Nicolás has invited us to a party at his – again, although this time for someone else's birthday – the week after next. If it's anything like the party he and Oscar threw me, it will be fabulous.

I zone out partly as I mull over what to say to Dexter. Finally, once the three girls are caught up in talking about the band who's playing the gig – I didn't hear the name – I ask Dexter, 'Have you got ten minutes after lunch? I wanted to talk to you about something.'

He raises a quizzical eyebrow. 'Should I be worried?'

I shake my head. 'No. I'd just like to run something past you.'

He nods. 'Sure. Let's finish this and then we'll go for a walk so we can talk in peace.' His head inclines towards the others, who are half-listening to our conversation. What's new?

Ten minutes later, we head out into the foyer, then pass through into the road beyond.

We saunter along for a few minutes, saying nothing before Dexter turns to me. 'Kat, didn't you want to tell me something?'

I sigh. 'Sorry. I'm just … I don't know how…'

Dexter pales and grasps me lightly by the shoulders, turning me towards him. 'You're not ill, are you?'

Fear flashes in his eyes as he awaits my response,

and I shake my head so he doesn't have to worry about that at least. He audibly exhales, and I sense his relief like it's part of me.

'Thank God for that. So, what's going on?'

We come to a part of the road that has a bench set into the side of it. I've always thought how incongruous a bench is here, because it's not as if many people walk this road. Perhaps it was built for sloths to rest on, or climb on. I smile inwardly at the idea. Anything to procrastinate that little bit more.

'Can we sit down?' I think I might only be able to spit this out if I do.

We both sit on the knobbly old bench, which seems to be fashioned from some sort of tree trunk, without the intervention of a furniture manufacturer to make it smooth and uniform. It makes me wonder who put it here and when.

OK, no more delaying. I take a deep breath in and grasp Dexter's hands in mine. He jerks slightly as if I've given him an electric shock. Damn, I have him on edge now, and that only ratchets my nerves up a notch.

Belatedly, it occurs to me that I may be worrying over nothing. Maybe Dexter doesn't see our relationship as a long-term one. Maybe this is just a little fun to him, and I'm about to make an idiot of myself by going into elaborate detail about the dilemma I'm in. But I won't know if I don't tell him.

'Dexter, you know how I told you I wanted to be a vet?'

He nods. 'Yeah, you said you didn't get the grades to get into uni to do that particular course.'

'That's right. I didn't. But earlier this year, I

applied to do veterinary medicine at Glasgow uni.'

'Right,' he says, letting the word stretch out between us.

'I didn't get a reply. Well, I got an acknowledgement, but not an acceptance,' I rush on.

His shoulders visibly relax, but that's about his only tell. I deliberately leave a pause to allow him to pitch in with his thoughts, but no, it looks like I'm doing this alone.

I steel myself to deliver the final blow. 'The other day I got a letter from home.' I gulp and I'm suddenly aware of the acid reflux in my stomach. Please don't let me be sick. Now is not the time.

'It was from Glasgow uni. An error meant I was wrongly told back in May that my course was oversubscribed.' I pause, letting the implication sink in.

'You got into uni to do veterinary medicine?' Dexter's face lights up.

I swallow hard. 'I did.' I blow out a breath. 'It starts mid-September.'

Dexter reaches for me and hugs me to him. 'Well done. You must be so pleased.' He kisses the top of my head, but it means I can't see his face, particularly his eyes or his mouth, to see if he is genuinely happy or if he's pretending. I don't know whether to be pleased, relieved, or gutted that he's taking this so well. His response was so cryptic.

When we pull apart, I take hold of his hands. 'Dexter, I don't know what to do. It's everything I've always wanted, but now, here, this feels like everything I've ever wanted, too, and now I'm torn.' I leave unsaid that he's all I've ever wanted as well. Let him read between the lines. Surely my feelings for him are plain enough.

We haven't told each other we love each other yet, but I know in my heart, without a single ounce of doubt, that I love this man. And I'm not eighteen any more. I'm thirty. I'm not in the first flush of love, but if my toxic relationship with Aidan taught me anything, it's not to wait. Not to stay in something that's harmful to you, and instead to fight for what's wonderful and worthwhile. But that is making the decision over whether to go to uni or not all the more difficult.

Dexter places one hand against my cheek, looks into my eyes and says, 'You must do what's right for you, Kat. You don't need to rush into it. Take some time to consider what you really want. When do you need to accept your place by?'

I shake my head as if to clear it. I have no idea. That hadn't even occurred to me. I just assumed I pitched up on the day if I was taking the place, that they'd expect me to turn up unless I advise them otherwise.

'I don't know…' My speech falters. 'Dex–' it's now or never. I have to tell him how I feel. I need to know if he wants me to stay. If he doesn't, then perhaps the decision is easier, although I'd still be leaving my sloth family and friends. Maybe I could return … but I know I wouldn't. Once you're on the career path, you're on the career path, and it's hard to step off that hamster wheel.

I take deep, calming breaths as I will myself to say those three little words that mean so much but which are so incredibly difficult to say for the first time.

'Dexter.' I take one of his hands in mine and look into his eyes, willing him to understand what I'm trying to say, what I'm about to say, to give me a sign that I'm on the right track and not about to make a complete fool of myself.

'I–'

A car rumbles towards us. No doubt it's visitors to the sanctuary. But then it draws to a halt, level with us, and a woman rolls down the window. 'Dexter! Just the man I've been looking for.'

Dexter turns around, and his face turns a ghostly white for a second, before he recovers. 'Maite!'

Maite? Maite!

The woman turns off her engine and gets out of the car, coming over and kissing Dexter on both cheeks. 'You haven't changed a bit.' She turns to me. 'Sorry, I'm Maite. I didn't mean to interrupt, but I was on my way to the sanctuary to see Dexter, when I saw you both sitting here.' She turns to Dexter. 'Looking for some peace and quiet, I take it.'

He nods mutely before Maite turns to me. 'We used to come and sit here all the time to get away from things too.'

'Oh, did you work at the sanctuary?' I ask, keen to double-check I have the right person.

She smiles. 'Yes, last year. Don't tell me I'm so instantly forgettable that no one has mentioned me.' She bats Dexter on the arm. 'Aren't you going to introduce us?'

Dexter, for the first time ever, seems lost for words. He runs a hand through his hair, a gesture I've noticed he does when he's nervous. But why's he nervous?

Because he hasn't mentioned Maite to me before?

He clears his throat. 'Of course. Maite, this is Kat. Kat, Maite.'

Maite leans forward as best she can and kisses me on both cheeks. 'Nice to meet you, Kat.' She glances at Dexter. 'When are you free? I need to talk to you.'

There's an undercurrent from Dexter that I can't quite place. He's looking at Maite, but keeps throwing glances at her stomach.

Suddenly, the desire to throw up comes over me. She's pregnant, very pregnant, probably about six or seven months. She wants to talk to Dexter. She worked at the sanctuary last year, only a few months ago potentially. Dexter is looking in alarm at her stomach. Oh my God, she's pregnant and it's Dexter's. That's why she said she was surprised he hadn't mentioned her to me. My vision blurs slightly, although whether from me feeling faint or because I'm having difficulty breathing, I can't be sure. What I do know is I need to get out of here.

'I told Victor I'd check in with him shortly.' A lie. 'I'll leave you guys to talk. Nice to meet you, Maite.' I try and fail not to put emphasis on the word 'talk', then I almost jog back to the sanctuary.

Mariangeles is in the foyer when I rush past to the toilets.

'What's wrong?' she asks but I simply shake my head and race into the bathroom, where I close myself in a cubicle and let the tears flow.

Chapter Twenty-seven

I text Becca. Well, at least I have something else to tell her. She has been texting me every day asking me if I've told Dexter yet about getting into uni. Ha! What news I have for her now. Why is my life like a soap opera? I mean, seriously, how can so much shit happen to one person? I was just about to tell Dexter that I loved him when his pregnant ex turned up. What the actual...?

After taking a few deep breaths, I compose the message.

> *Hi, Becca. You'll be pleased to know I've finally told Dexter. He said I have to do what's right for me. But then — fun fact — his pregnant ex-girlfriend turned up to talk to him and I scarpered. Looks like my decision about uni may have been made for me. Love you x*

For the rest of the afternoon, I walk around on autopilot. I can't settle to one thing, so instead I mosey around the sanctuary doing odd jobs. On a few occasions, I glimpse Dexter with Maite, chatting with some of my friends – Maite's friends – Maite and Dexter's friends. Of course they'll be glad to see her.

No doubt they'll be congratulating her on her pregnancy.

I'm down cleaning out cages with Victor, who is prattling away like a budgie about some cookery programme on TV featuring a chef who makes Victor's blood boil. Victor's busy telling me about all the mistakes the chef made – he doesn't think he did them intentionally – and how he would have made the dish instead. I barely manage a smile at Victor's indignation and supreme confidence in his culinary abilities. I have too many things on my mind.

Becca hasn't texted back either. She's probably working late, but every minute feels like it's dragging. I don't know if Maite has gone, but I did think Dexter might come and seek me out after she'd left, and the fact he hasn't done so makes me think she's still around, laughing and joking with our friends. She seemed like a lovely person, too, and I wish her all the best for the future. I just wish her future wasn't irrevocably intertwined with my boyfriend's.

As I shovel shit, literally, my jumbled thoughts whizz around my head: Dexter, pregnant ex-girlfriend, the sanctuary, my friends here, Becca, Glasgow uni, vet school, my future. Unsurprisingly, I have another headache, but this one's starting to reach almost migraine proportions. I'll need to take some paracetamol or something soon. I'll just finish shovelling shit – what a glamorous life I do have – and then I'll go back to my room to get some. Maybe if I take a break from my chores, I'll be able to think straight too.

'Victor, I'll be back in ten minutes.'

He nods then says, 'Can you send Alejandro down if you see him?'

I pause. That means going into the sanctuary proper. Last time I saw him, he was with Ella in the admin office. I could pretend when I return, I suppose, that I didn't see him, but my conscience won't let me do that. I don't like lying, and Victor's too nice, so I'd feel awful. No, I need to bite the bullet and brace myself for entering the sanctuary.

But Ella is no longer in the office and neither is Alejandro. I stop and listen, but I can't hear their voices over the influx of visitors. I slip into the nursery, where Luciana is feeding Zoom. She looks up as I enter.

'Hi. Have you seen Alejandro?' I ask.

She inclines her head to the right. 'Last I saw him he was with Carlos in his office.'

I thank her and cross the foyer to Carlos' office, but right before I reach it, a familiar voice filters through to me.

'Yeah, I'm taking Maite for a scan on Tuesday. I can't believe it.' His voice muffles slightly, but I just make out 'father' and my stomach clenches again. Any last remaining shred of hope I had that the baby wasn't Dexter's has flown the coop. As the father, of course he's going to the scan. Tears well behind my eyes and my chest tightens. This is it. It's really all over between Dexter and me. How can I compete with an ex who's carrying his baby?

I about-turn and head back to tell Victor I didn't see Alejandro. I can't hang around any longer to hear Dexter talk about going to his baby's scan with his ex-girlfriend, particularly since I don't think she'll be his ex for long.

Once I deliver the message to Victor, I head for my room. As I reach it, my phone rings. Becca. I fumble with the door handle, simultaneously closing the door behind me as I accept the call.

'Hey, Kat. Are you OK?' Her eyes are full of concern.

'No, Becca, I'm not OK at all,' I blurt out, then promptly burst into tears.

Once my snotty sobbing has finished, about ten minutes later, Becca says, 'Look, I know it all seems really bleak right now, but on the plus side, I guess that's your decision made now. And you'd been struggling with it. At least you know now, and not after you'd turned down your uni place. Small mercies, eh?'

I know what she says makes sense, but I can't process that right now. All I can think about is the hot mess of my life and how when I finally found someone worth loving, I was too late. Not only can't I compete with a baby, I wouldn't want to. Without even knowing Maite, I want their baby to have a loving home with two parents. With me losing Dad, the last thing I want is for a baby not to have its father around.

I nod mutely. But I love Dexter. My heart aches, yes, actually aches. It's almost like someone has stabbed me, the pain I feel at the thought of us no longer being together, and the realisation hits me: there's no way I can stay here if Dexter is with someone else. Why, oh why, did I let myself get into this situation?

'Look, you need to speak to Dexter, and when you've done so, call me and we'll talk. If you're coming home, I'm here for you. If you can stomach staying, I'll still be here for you. OK?'

'I love you, Becca, and I'm sorry all I seem to do recently is cry when I'm on the phone.' I hiccough and even manage a smile at this.

'That's what friends are for. Kat, take some time to figure out what you want, then talk to Dexter. Whatever you do, it has to be the right thing for you. I can play devil's advocate and tell you you've always wanted to be a vet, but you know that. Likewise, I can tell you, you deserve someone like Dexter, and that I haven't seen you this happy – today excepted – for years. Certainly not with Aidan. But ultimately the decision has to come from you, from your heart.'

'I know. And to be fair, you were never Aidan's biggest fan.' I give her a watery smile.

'That's because he was a class A dick and took advantage of you at your most vulnerable. After that it was easy for him to continue to manipulate you without you realising that's what he was doing, and you were so grateful for everything he'd "done for you" when your dad was ill and when he died, that you thought you had to put up with his shit forever.'

She finally draws breath, and fleetingly, images of Dad, his blood transfusion and the consequences appear in my mind, but before I can add anything, she continues. 'And you deserve great, Kat, really great. You have a lot of love to give. As your best friend, I know that, and I want that for you. Ask Dexter what he wants. Let him explain this whole Maite situation. It may not be what you think.'

I nod. She's right. I may be getting ahead of myself, so I take a deep breath in, fortifying myself. 'OK,

Becca, I'll talk to Dexter, but first I'll have a real good think about going to uni, too. I need to have all my ducks in a row before we have that conversation.'

Becca grins. 'That's my girl. Right, gotta dash. I have a date in twenty minutes.'

My eyes go wide. 'A date?'

'Yes, you know. That thing where you meet someone and have a drink or dinner, and sometimes end up having a snog, or a bit of–'

'Yes, yes, I get the idea. No need to draw me a picture. Not that you'd be able to engage in any "activities" at the moment, what with your leg in a cast.'

Becca grins again. 'You'd be surprised at how inventive I can be. Last week–'

I hold my hand up. 'Nope, Becca. TMI. I do not want to know. This seems like a good time to sign off. I'll let you know how things go, and good luck with your date. You should have said. Here's me prattling on about my abysmal love life, with all its complications, and you're ready to go on a date, cast and all. Go enjoy yourself.'

'Oh, I will. Good luck, hon. Speak later.' She blows me a kiss and then the screen goes black.

I sit on my bed, my hands tucked under me as I tend to do when I'm thinking through a problem. And what a problem it is. Perhaps the fact Dexter has an ex-girlfriend who has turned up out of the blue and who's pregnant – irrespective of whether the baby is his or not – is a much-needed warning sign to tread carefully. In truth, Dexter and I know very little about each other, or rather, I know next to nothing about his past.

He knows about Aidan, naturally – how could he not – and Dad, but we've never done the previous relationships thing. It felt too soon; neither of us has even told the other we love them yet. It's the university offer that first made this a more pressing issue, of course. If I didn't have to make such a momentous decision – stay or leave – Dexter and I could simply continue at the pace our relationship has been progressing, but the fact that I needed to know our relationship was as important to him as to me has upset that applecart.

I look at my watch and see it's almost dinnertime. I've been skiving off, although I think I'll be forgiven, for longer than I'd meant to. I'll make it up later. One thing about me, I'm not workshy; I just seem to have too much drama going on at the minute. After splashing some water on my face, I head back down to the sanctuary and join the others in the canteen, where the dish of the day is yucca pie. It smells amazing.

Ella is already seated and casts me a worried glance. Maybe my face is still blotchy. Whilst Mariangeles and Federica are deep in discussion with Victor, she whispers to me, 'You OK? I know they're not together any more, but it must have been weird for you to see Maite earlier.'

That's the understatement of the century, but I welcome Ella's concern. She's such a sweet girl and a great friend. I place my hand on hers. 'I'm fine, thanks, but yes, it was a bit of a shock.'

'Didn't you know Maite used to work here?' she asks, keeping her voice low, I guess to avoid being overheard.

'Actually, I didn't know Maite and Dexter were ... Dexter and I didn't ... share info on previous relationships.'

Ella's mouth forms an O then she says, 'That's tough.'

'Yeah.' I give her a sad smile. 'Have you seen Dexter? I wanted to talk to him.'

Ella's face falls. 'Didn't he tell you?'

I frown. 'Tell me what?'

Ella shifts in her chair and her eyes won't meet mine. 'He and Maite have gone out for dinner. They have things to discuss, apparently.'

'I'll bet they do,' I say, thinking of what I overheard about the scan. Why am I kidding myself? There's no question it's Dexter's baby – he and Maite have gone for dinner to talk things through and he's accompanying her to the scan. What else do I need, a blueprint?

'Ella, do you fancy going for a drive later? I have a notion to go to the beach.'

She raises an eyebrow. 'At night?'

'Yeah. Maybe go to one of the bars at Espadilla and have a cocktail, or a mocktail, depending if we can get someone to give us a lift. You in?'

Ella looks me straight in the eye. She seems to be debating something internally with herself, but a second later, she says, 'Of course.'

I smile. 'Great. Let me see if I can arrange for someone to drop us off and we can head off in an hour or so.'

Ella tucks into her yucca pie. I even manage to eat a few bites, although mostly I just move it around on my plate. I wonder if this is the pre-break-up diet. I'd happily retain the pounds I have if I didn't have to go through my current torture. I'm beginning to see a common thread running through my life – drama. Is it normal at thirty to have at the top of your wish list, a nice quiet life?

Once I've eaten enough that I feel Sofia won't question me on it, I take our plates and put them in the dishwasher. As I exit the kitchen, Victor is heading towards the foyer, and I call to him. He turns round and I say, 'I don't suppose you could do me a favour.'

Chapter Twenty-eight

An hour later, Ella and I say goodbye to Victor, who tells us it's no problem to pick us up later, as long as we're not going clubbing. I laugh at that. Part of me feels too old to go clubbing, and the other part of me has absolutely no desire to. That said, things are different here in Costa Rica. It's not an overpriced club like in Glasgow or London, although those do exist, particularly in Jaco, but that's a good hour and a bit from here. Down at the beach, cheerful bars and an eclectic mix of restaurants line the boulevard. Ella and I link arms and traipse into the Sunset Bar, although sunset has been and gone. Ella promised me the cocktails are exquisite. It's not my aim to get blinding drunk, but nicely tipsy sounds like a plan. I haven't managed to make any decisions sober, so maybe with a little alcohol inside me to loosen me up, I'll be able to think straight – ironic though that may seem – or at the very least I'll be able to be honest with myself.

Once I've procured a coco loco for me and a jaguar colada for Ella, we find a table outside. It never ceases to amuse me how many Costa Ricans, and those who live in warm countries, choose to sit inside, when all we Brits want to do is have decent enough weather to sit outside, so I take the opportunity as often as I can. We're not so far from the beach that I can't hear the lapping of the waves, a sound that usually soothes me.

Ella's eyes are on mine. She knows something is up and it's as if she's silently communicating with me to open up. But where to start? With Dexter's impending fatherhood, the fact I've been offered a place at university or that I am having a crisis over whether to leave my adopted home and return to Scotland to study veterinary medicine?

I drain my cocktail and catch the eye of a passing barman. 'Ella?'

She shakes her head, indicating her almost full one.

'Same again, please,' I say to the barman. When he looks at me blankly, I pick up my glass and laugh, suddenly realising how ridiculous it is to ask for the same again when the glass is empty. I scrunch up my eyebrows. 'Coco loco.'

The waiter smiles then inclines his head towards Ella as if to suggest it's not only the 'coco' that's 'loco' but her drinking partner too. I have to admit, I'm feeling pleasantly merry, if not exactly nuts, after my first cocktail. What is it they say? Alcohol enhances your mood. Whilst mine isn't exactly maudlin today, I am resigned perhaps, or pissed off, or at best upset.

My second cocktail swiftly appears and I lean over it, aware that Ella's gaze is still on me.

I raise my eyes to hers. 'Everything's a mess.'

She sits up a little straighter in her chair. 'What's wrong?'

I exhale from deep within my lungs then count off on my fingers. 'I love Dexter and was about to tell him so when his ex-girlfriend showed up. I love it here, in Costa Rica, at the sanctuary. However, I've always wanted to be a vet, and now I've been accepted to a course, in Scotland, that will allow me to pursue that dream.'

I pause for breath. 'Oh, and Maite just happens to be pregnant.'

Ella frowns and then her eyes widen. 'What? And you think it's his baby?'

I shake my head. 'No, Ella, I know it's his baby. He's going with her to the scan. I overheard him saying to Carlos, and he mentioned something about "father". It doesn't take a genius…'

Ella bites her lip, and I feel bad for having unburdened myself to her. She's only young. She doesn't need to be involved in the mess that is my life, but somehow she always seems a wise head on young shoulders, and she always has my back, as do the others. Well, except Roisin, and even she mellowed after the almost-drowning incident.

I can see the cogs in Ella's brain whirring as she frantically searches for another reason why Dexter might be going for a scan with Maite, and why he might have said 'father'. She looks pained, and as if she's scrabbling for an answer. Finally, she says, 'Even if it is his baby, that doesn't necessarily mean things are over between you.'

I arch an eyebrow and Ella deflates before my eyes. She has nothing. She knows, as I do, that this is it. I wouldn't say it has all been for nothing, as I have so many amazing memories here, but is that all I want? Memories? Or do I want to stay here and continue working at the sanctuary?

'What's your heart telling you to do?' Ella asks after studying me for a moment.

'Nothing,' I mope. 'It's broken.'

Ella leans across the table and takes my hands in hers. 'Dexter is another issue. What's your heart telling you about here? The sanctuary? The sloths? Us?'

I swallow for a second. Was it my imagination or did she pack so much significance into that last word? It hits me that Ella is like a little sister to me. That's it. I feel part of a family here, like I haven't done since Dad passed. Mum and I have always been at loggerheads, but never more so than since Dad died, and now with the whole Aidan debacle, it's hard to see us ever reconciling properly, or returning to a place where we're truly there for each other. But here, I have so many possibilities. Sofia is almost like a replacement mum, one who doesn't choose my controlling ex over me; Victor is the uncle figure; Ella the little sister; and Mariangeles and Federica are like my older sisters. Tears sting my eyes and I'm unable to speak for a long moment. Finally, the pressure in my throat subsides and despite my voice cracking, I manage to speak.

'I love it here. I love being with you all, and frankly this feels like home more than home does, even though I miss my best friend Becca.'

She nods at this, but says nothing more, willing me to go on. 'But I don't know if I'm strong enough to stay here surrounded by Dexter every day, possibly seeing Maite and their baby now and again.'

Ella bites her lip but again says nothing, so I sigh and continue as a thought strikes me. 'Perhaps this is the universe's way of telling me I'm supposed to take up this place at university. Maybe it knew I'd struggle with the dilemma and is thus making the decision easier for me.'

Ella nods slowly. 'Perhaps. But, Kat, I believe that we make our own decisions. I think you should talk to Dexter to have a full picture, then you need to make a list, mental or written, of the pros and cons of staying in Costa Rica or going back to Scotland. Plus, you realise we have universities here too? You should look into whether there are any suitable courses.' She pauses for a second. 'I'll be gutted to lose you if you go, but ultimately, you need to do what's best for you. If returning to Scotland and keeping in touch by email, and the odd visit back to see us, hopefully, is what you need, then that's how it has to be.'

I study Ella. 'You know, for someone so young, you're incredibly astute.'

She smiles. 'Yeah, I get that a lot. Old before my time.'

'No.' I shake my head. 'That's not how I see it. You see people, you get them, and you dispense advice very well.'

Truth is, I bonded immediately with Ella. She's the youngest of the girls, but the most switched-on and scholarly. She reminds me of a younger me, although hopefully, unlike me, she'll get the qualifications she needs first time around.

I draw myself up, as if mentally preparing myself. 'Anyway, do you want another drink?' I motion to her empty glass.

'Sure. Same again.'

I order some more drinks from the barman, then turn to Ella and say, 'Enough about my drama, tell me, has Alejandro asked you out yet?'

Her eyes widen and I chuckle inwardly. Even if my life's a mess, I like to think I'm concerned enough about my friends to ensure their love lives are on track, and you'd have to be blind not to have noticed the longing looks passing between those two. In fact, I'm flabbergasted Mariangeles and Federica haven't picked up on it.

An hour later, we decide we've had enough to drink, but I'm not quite ready to go home just yet and I don't think Ella is either. Home. I thought home. Not sanctuary, even though it is for me as well as the sloths, I think, not missing the irony. Well, it was, until all this drama unfolded. But is that a sign? Should I be listening to my Freudian slip? Is Costa Punta my home?

Feeling a little unsettled still, I say to Ella, 'Why don't we go for a walk before we call Victor? It's so beautiful here.' Secretly, I'm also thinking if I do decide I should return to Scotland, then I need to make the most of every opportunity to soak up what this wonderful country has to offer. And I know exactly where I want to go.

'Ella, let's walk along the beach.'

Ella arches an eyebrow. 'In the dark?'

I smile. 'It won't be completely dark.' She frowns, incomprehension crossing her face. 'You'll see,' I say cheerily.

We pay the bill and head down to the beach. As we

leave the promenade and take off our sandals, threading our fingers through the straps, I revel in the sensation of the sand between my toes. It's like powder and so soft we almost slip our way to a more stable part where it's easier to walk. Once we've left the bright lights of the promenade, our eyes adjust to the darkness and then as we round the bend, the bioluminescence stretches out before us in all its glory. I glance at Ella, and see her lips form 'Wow', which makes me chuckle.

'Ella, have you never been here?'

Slowly, she shakes her head. 'No. I usually go to one of the other beaches. It's so busy here during the day.'

'And you've never been here at night?'

'Well, yes, but I've never come onto the beach. And you can't see this from the bar.'

As I look back, I discover she's right. I didn't think about that when I was first here, with Dexter. My throat is dry as I try to push past that thought. We stand together, marvelling at the glow from the bioluminescence. Spectacular is the only word for it. I could never regret coming to Costa Rica, no matter what happens. I would never have seen this. A lump forms in my throat, and this time it has nothing to do with Dexter. I wish Dad could have seen this. He'd have loved it. I wrap my arms around myself, hugging myself. One of the things you miss most about not having close family or a partner is those simple human touches. A hug to tell you everything will be OK. Although, I remind myself, I'm lucky to have the girls here, as they are big huggers. A wry smile crosses my lips, but a shout breaks me out of my reverie. Ella and I whirl round at the same time in the direction of the voice. To my horror, Dexter is making his way towards us, with Maite in tow.

'Ella, I need to use the ladies, desperately. Can you meet me back on the promenade once you've spoken to them?'

Ella is no fool, but my eyes beseech her and she nods, then I hightail it back towards civilisation and the café. I'm not strong enough to face Dexter, nor Maite, not when I'm feeling as raw as I am. Maybe Dexter has brought loads of girls here. What a fool I was to think I was different.

Chapter Twenty-nine

Fortunately, Victor appeared double-quick, once I called him. He didn't need specifics, just told me he'd leave straight away. I managed to compose myself enough in the ladies – so there was some truth in my story after all – to greet Maite and Dexter and paste on a smile worthy of an Oscar-winning actress when I returned to find Ella standing on the promenade with them. I made enough small talk to pass muster, I think, but I was like an automaton, programmed with certain pre-prepared responses. I was never so glad than when the ordeal was over. Sweat ran down my back as I grasped for the right thing to say, when all I really wanted to say was, 'You're having my boyfriend's baby. Congratulations, but your timing sucks.'

When Ella, Victor and I arrive back at the sanctuary, the others are still awake and sitting around the firepit. I try to act as naturally as possible, but it's hard. How can I stay when even seeing Dexter with Maite on the beach provoked such a strong reaction in me? And that's before the baby arrives.

As if sensing something is up, Mariangeles, Federica and Javier circle us as we settle down with the others around the firepit. Mariangeles relays how we got Victor out of a tight spot when we called as they were doing a foodie quiz and he was losing, something that incensed him greatly.

Javier jumps in, 'You know how territorial he gets about Costa Rican cuisine in particular. I think only my mother knows more about it. But Victor doesn't like to be beaten, and for once, I remembered everything she taught me.'

His face breaks into a wide grin as Victor, having parked the truck, joins us. 'Ready to go again, Victor? You're only eight points behind. We waited for you.'

Victor swats the air as if Javier is an annoying insect. 'You got lucky. I'm just finding my second wind. Bring it on. But first, I need a beer.'

'Oh, are you bringing your A game this time?' asks Mariangeles, minx that she is. She winks at the rest of us as Victor doesn't dignify her with a response and instead heads indoors.

'Anyone else want one?' he calls as he reaches the men's lodgings. A few cries of, 'Yes, please,' go up, and I hear his disgruntled, 'Hmph.'

The everyday antics of my adoptive family make me smile and for a nanosecond I forget my woes. Right now, I don't want to think. I've spent too much time in my head already the past twelve hours or so.

When Victor returns, he pulls up a chair and sits down beside me, and the quiz recommences. I chip in where I can, albeit my knowledge of Costa Rican cuisine is still pretty limited. Fortunately, there are some international questions and I manage to redeem myself when Spanish and Italian food questions come up.

It's a good way of passing the time, and I think how wonderful it would be to stay here, doing this night after night, with my friends. The Costa Rican way of life is so chilled, and the weather is warm pretty much all the time. I mean, I don't need to be out sunning myself every day of the week – I'm no sun-worshipper – but I could seriously get used to not having to live through Scotland's inability to abide by the seasons. Scotland is such a beautiful country, probably because of the amount of rain we get; I just wish we didn't have quite so much of it. The lack of torrential rain of a morning definitely sets me up better for the day. It's like those very rare days in Scotland when we get beautiful sunshine and all feels right with the world. That's how I wake up every day here – well, almost. Unfortunately, things can go downhill during the day.

It's not long before tiredness creeps over me and I stifle a yawn as I answer my question on which city Baci chocolates come from. Easy. Perugia. Not so easy, staying awake.

'Guys, I'm going to call it a night. I'm done in.'

Secretly, my emotions are mixed. On the one hand, I'm relieved Dexter hasn't shown up and I've had to pretend everything is OK, but on the other hand, my brain keeps flicking through images of what he and Maite could be getting up to. He is the father of her child, after all.

'I'll come with you.' Mariangeles jumps to her feet, but she has that glint in her eye which means she is about to give me the third degree, albeit in a well-meaning fashion, and I'm not up to it right now.

'No, stay. If we both leave, the teams will have uneven numbers.'

Glancing back at the others, reluctantly she concedes this, and after saying, 'If you're sure,' she sits back down when I nod in confirmation.

As I trudge over to the women's lodgings – hard to summon a skip in my step when I feel like I'm going to the hangman's noose at the gallows – I make up my mind. I know what I have to do.

An hour later, despite my yawns, and wishing I had coffee to keep me awake for this, the deed is done. I've emailed Glasgow uni and accepted my place. I'll text Becca in the morning to avoid waking her. It's nearly six in the morning there, but I know she likes her sleep and I've already broken it too often recently. At least one person will be happy with my decision. It took a while to find flights that weren't extortionate, given I want to leave in a week. I hate letting Carlos and Sofia down, but honestly, I'm not sure I'd be much use to them. The hardest part between now and then is going to be avoiding Dexter, naturally, but also coming to terms with everything I'm leaving behind. I wonder if I can cram in a visit somewhere amazing before I go. There's so much of the country I still haven't seen.

My thoughts turn to Dexter once more. I'm doing the right thing, not just because it's hard for me to see him and Maite together, but if he has a chance at making a go of his little family, then it would be wrong of me to stand in the way of that. I'm not that person.

Next morning, I wake to the sound of voices in the women's rec room. I strain to pick out who's speaking. Roisin. And Federica.

I catch snatches of their conversation '…must be difficult…' Federica. '…it's a complicated set-up, all right.' Roisin. 'Wouldn't wish it on my worst enemy.' Roisin. 'Unsurprising that he'd want to support her.' Federica.

Are they talking about Dexter and Maite? Oh God, I can't even get away from it here. As I sit up and run my hand through my bird's nest of hair, my heart beats faster. This is going to be harder than I thought. How am I going to get through a week of this? Then it occurs to me; how am I going to tell the others I'm leaving? I should really tell Carlos first, since I could be leaving him in the lurch, but my heart knows I need to tell the girls first. Not Roisin necessarily, although things have definitely improved between us since the incident at the beach, but the others are like sisters to me. I gulp. I'd have loved sisters. Or a brother, for that matter. But it wasn't to be.

How to broach the subject of my departure? Mariangeles, at least, will try to talk me out of it. There's always one, isn't there? Always one who won't blindly accept others' decisions when they know how conflicted the person is, and I'm nothing if not conflicted.

I rub my hand over my face. I need coffee. Best to face the music sometime. I'll wait until Roisin has gone. *Because*, a little voice tells me, *you're scared she'll be pleased that you and Dexter can't be together because of the baby.*

With great effort, I will myself out of bed and pad across to the door, from where I hear two other voices mingling with those of Roisin and Federica. Ella. Mariangeles. The whole gang, bar me. Well, here goes nothing.

'Morning,' I say breezily as I enter, wrapping my silk dressing gown around me.

'Morning.' Federica eyes me warily then glances at the rest of the group.

The others bid me good morning, their unsure demeanours almost comical.

'Coffee?' I ask.

'It's made,' Mariangeles pipes up.

I smile as I rest my hand on her shoulder. 'I meant, did anyone want one?'

That earns a yes from Ella, a no from Mariangeles, who raises her cup to confirm she already has a full one, and a no from Federica, whose cup lies empty on the table.

'I'm just going,' Roisin says. 'I told Victor I'd meet him before breakfast. We have that new section of fence to put up.'

Relief washes over me that I won't have to engineer a way to discuss my decision with the others out of earshot of Roisin.

Once she leaves, we all huddle around the round table. Would I be going home if I didn't have a university course to start in September? Who knows? I'll never know what percentage of my final decision was due to the blow that Maite unwittingly dealt me and how much was down to getting into uni.

Ella eyes me uncertainly. It's like she knows I have

a revelation to make. She, more than the others, knows what's on my mind. Has she told them? Gauging from her expression, I don't think she has. I decide to take some of the weight off her shoulders, as I'm sure she feels a little burdened by all of my crap – it's the only word for the collective nonsense that has been my life the past month and a half.

'Guys, I have something to tell you … I'm going home.'

Immediately, there are outbursts and protests and much haranguing in rapid-fire Spanish. It's so quick I don't follow much of it, especially from Mariangeles. I catch snatches of what they're saying, a bit like I did the whispered conversation earlier this morning. I struggle to keep up, until Ella lays a calming hand on Mariangeles and another on Federica. Again, the irony of the youngest being the calming influence isn't lost on me.

'Let Kat explain,' says Ella.

The other two shoot her incredulous looks as if to say 'you knew!'

After they both nod their assent, I begin the tale of how an error led to me being told months ago that I hadn't got into the course to study veterinary medicine. They listen, rapt, jaws falling open, eyes wide, unable to believe I've kept this from them.

'But I thought you were happy *here*,' Mariangeles puts in.

'I am. I was,' I say quickly. 'But things have changed.'

Mariangeles frowns. 'What's changed? You can't leave. I'd miss you too much.'

My heart soars and aches in equal measure. Please don't let her make me cry now.

'And what about Dexter?' asks Federica. 'He'll be gutted if you leave. You're getting on so well together.'

They can't be this clueless, can they?

'Federica, in case you hadn't noticed, his pregnant ex-girlfriend turned up yesterday.'

'Of course I noticed.'

'But they're not together any more, Kat,' says Mariangeles.

Ella, I note, remains quiet. She already heard everything from me last night.

'Well, I'm not going to stand in the way of them raising their child together!' I say hotly. 'That's not who I am.'

Federica and Mariangeles exchange a look before Federica says, 'Do we know for certain that the baby's Dexter's?'

I blow out a breath in frustration. 'Yes! He's going to the scan with her. I heard Dexter telling Carlos yesterday, and he mentioned being the father.'

'He did?' Mariangeles' forehead scrunches up. 'Are you sure?'

About to boil over, I say, 'I know what I heard.'

'What you *think* you heard.'

I jolt upright and spin round to see Roisin framed in the doorway. Unable to help myself, I scowl. 'How long have you been listening in?'

If she's upset at my accusatory tone, she doesn't show it; instead she says, 'Exactly what did you hear?'

'What does it matter? I can't remember the precise order of the words, but I know Dexter's going to the scan with her because–'

Roisin cuts me off. 'Because her boyfriend's away on a business trip to Asia for two weeks, which unfortunately coincides with the time of her scan and she doesn't want to go alone?'

My mouth drops open, as does Ella's.

It takes me a couple of seconds before I'm capable of speech. 'What?'

'Maite's boyfriend works in international sales. He's at a trade show in Hong Kong right now and is doing a week-long tour of Asia immediately afterwards. He couldn't get out of it.'

'Maite's boyfriend?' I parrot back at her.

When Roisin nods, I say, 'And you know this, how?'

'Because I had a thing with her boyfriend's brother about six months ago. Sweet little thing. He couldn't handle me, though.' She smiles.

I try to formulate questions, thoughts, but my brain is having difficulty working. Finally, I manage, 'But why Dexter?'

Roisin smiles again. 'Because despite breaking up, they were always good friends. They didn't break up because they didn't love each other, but because they realised they were better as friends than, well, lovers. They weren't suited well enough for that type of relationship.'

Cogs whirr in my brain, causing me no end of agony. I've jumped the gun – again. I've booked a bloody flight home, without even having spoken to Dexter about all this. I've accepted my place at uni. I cover my face with my hands. Why am I so damned impulsive? Or is it not entirely my fault? Is it more that I've been treated so badly by boyfriends in the past, Aidan, in particular, that I have trust issues? Maybe I don't think I deserve happiness.

Shit! What am I going to do now?

Chapter Thirty

At breakfast, Dexter catches my eye when he walks into the room, then drops a kiss on my head as is his norm of late. I stiffen and his hands move from my shoulders as if I've given him an electric shock.

He swings a chair round to face me and says, 'Hey, how come you ran off last night?'

No matter that he's just being a good friend to his ex-girlfriend, is he really so clueless that it wouldn't occur to him that I'd get the wrong end of the stick or that I'd be hurt, or might require an explanation prior to him going out all evening and night with his pregnant ex? Particularly given the conversation we'd been in the middle of when we were interrupted by her pulling up in her car.

'How's Maite?' I ask in as restrained a manner as I can. Although I know I'm the one who will be backpedalling shortly, my mood hasn't altered enough not to be a tad snippy still.

He smiles. 'She's good. Looking forward to having her baby.'

Immediately, I note his usage of 'her baby'.

'How far along is she?'

'Twenty-eight and a half weeks. Don't forget the

half, she told me.' He grins.

I force my tone to remain neutral. 'So, was it a shock her appearing here, pregnant?'

His brow furrows. 'It was kind of a shock her turning up at all, pregnant or not. I knew she'd been seeing someone, but I didn't realise it was so serious. And she never mentioned in any of her texts that she was pregnant. I guess she wanted to tell me face to face.'

'Or show you,' I mutter under my breath, thinking of how obvious it was the moment she stepped out of her car.

Dexter's brow furrows deeper. 'Is something wrong, Kat?'

I sigh. 'Can we talk later? I don't want to discuss it here, and we do need to finish our chat.'

'Right. Sorry, I got so swept up in Maite's sudden appearance, I wasn't thinking straight. So much so, I left my phone here in the canteen, too. I couldn't even text you yesterday. Then when I saw you and Ella on the beach, it was like providence.'

Not from where I was standing it wasn't; it was torture. Before I knew he wasn't the baby's father, naturally.

I wait to see if he answers my original question. Eventually, he cottons on to the fact that I'm looking at him expectantly.

'Yeah, sure, I have a meeting with Carlos after breakfast, but let me come find you straight after.'

When he leaves, I pick at the breakfast Federica has set in front of me, although I don't taste a single bite of what I manage to swallow.

After breakfast, I head off with the girls to carry out our morning chores caring for the sloths, doing admin and ordering in medical supplies. However, before we can go our respective ways, Mariangeles tugs on the hem of my shirt. 'What are you going to do?'

When I shoot her a quizzical glance, she says, 'Now you know Dexter's not the father. Does that change things for you about returning home?'

'I already accepted my place.'

'And?' Mariangeles prods. I know she means it in the way of 'so what, that doesn't matter, you can email them and tell them you've changed your mind', but I choose to be obtuse and say, 'And booked my flight.'

She tuts, clearly not impressed at my deflection and swats a hand through the air. 'Details.'

I feel myself visibly deflate in front of her. If I deflate any further, I'll be like a tyre that reversed over a six-inch nail. It's not lost on me that much of this mess is of my own making. I'm not denying responsibility, but I do wish life had dealt me a different set of cards, and the ability to think things through before doing anything rash. Like accepting a place at uni or booking a flight home without discussing it with my boyfriend first.

Mariangeles grabs me by the forearms and looks intently into my eyes. 'Kat, do what makes you happy, but really think about it. And know that we all consider you family.'

'You're not making this any easier, you know,' I say with a wry smile.

She beams. 'I wasn't trying to. I don't want you to go, but if this is what you need to do, do it. But first, you need to have that chat with Dexter.'

The blood drains from my face as I reflect on what that will entail. 'I know. Mariangeles, do me a favour and keep me busy, talk to me about anything except me and Dexter until he comes looking for me. I feel as if my head is about to go boom.' I splay my hands to show exactly what would happen to my head.

She takes me by the elbow, steering me towards the nursery. 'Luciana has gone home as her mother isn't too well, so we're on nursery duty.'

I don't know whether this is the best task ever or if I'm likely to bawl my eyes out and become a snotty mess at the thought of having to leave the baby sloths in a week. *Dig deep, Kat.*

Steeling myself, I follow Mariangeles to where Carlos is surveying Zoom. Oh crap, I haven't told Carlos yet, and I didn't tell the girls not to tell anyone, although I'm sure they won't. But now I feel awful that I've told them, when I haven't even told Carlos I'm possibly leaving in a week.

I think of the British Airways e-tickets in my phone and am overcome with guilt.

'Morning, girls. How are you today?' Carlos asks as he makes notes on one of the sloths' charts.

'Good, thanks,' I manage. *Liar.*

Mariangeles provides a more involved response, asking how Zoom is doing and who Carlos thinks will be next to be released into the wild. They chat for a few minutes then Carlos takes his leave as he says he's meeting Dexter.

Mariangeles and I go through the motions of checking on the sloths. Well, I go through the motions, doing everything automatically. Mariangeles is probably showing her usual care and attention. We chat about Costa Rica and Scotland as we feed the babies, not once mentioning Dexter, or the fact I may be returning home within a week.

Finally, the door opens and Dexter pops his head round, flashing me a huge smile, which makes my heart simultaneously do handsprings and sink like an anchor.

'You got ten minutes?'

'Yep.' My voice comes out as a squeak.

He looks at me curiously, but his lips curl up at the edges. Oh crap. This is going to be harder than I thought.

We head through the foyer and out to the rear of the sanctuary, where we all sat around the firepit last night, except Dexter, who was still out on his nocturnal jaunt with Maite. And why *were* they out quite so late? I can't help wondering indignantly.

'I feel as if I haven't seen you for ages.' Dexter slips his arm around my waist and pulls me towards him for a kiss, but I pull back.

Hurt and confusion replace his smile and I feel bad that I'm the cause.

'I think it's best if we talk first,' I say eventually.

We perch on a couple of chairs, noticeably not next to each other, but opposite. It's almost like one of us is interviewing the other.

'Kat, you clearly have something on your mind, and I don't think it's only your uni place, is it?' Dexter says pointedly.

I rub my fingers through my hairline, something I do when I'm stressed. 'No.'

Dexter waits patiently. I don't think I can tell him now that I love him, although I do love him. So instead I blurt it all out, the raw, uncensored truth.

'Yesterday afternoon, I had no idea whether to stay or go. Then Maite showed up, pregnant. I overheard you talking to Carlos about going to the scan. I heard you say "father" and assumed that meant you were the father.' Heat creeps up my cheeks and I risk a glance up at Dexter.

His mouth forms an O, then a flash of anger crosses his face. 'You thought… You thought *I* was the father? Do you really think I'd leave my pregnant ex-girlfriend to do all this alone?'

I shake my head vigorously. 'No. Not that. Never that.' I pause to regroup a second, droplets of perspiration trickling down my back. 'I thought you didn't know, and you were being presented with a "fait accompli" from a past lover.'

'How very French,' Dexter says drily. 'Sorry to disappoint.'

I flinch at his snarky tone, but I'm determined to get this over and done with. Sure, he's angry, but yesterday I was distraught and destroyed.

'When you didn't come back or contact me yesterday after Maite's visit, I jumped to the wrong conclusion.'

'I came looking for you, but I couldn't find you.' His eyes meet mine. 'Wait. You really thought I was the father?'

I bite my lip then say, 'Yep, and I was…' gutted, desolate, lost, devastated '…confused.'

He quirks an eyebrow, but I hurry on. 'I didn't

think I could stay here. I thought my position was now untenable. You'd have your ready-made little family unit, and I'd be surplus to requirements.'

Dexter places his hand over his jaw and mouth, almost as if he's trying to hold the words back and his anger in check.

But there's more. 'I debated every scenario, every way, and I do mean every, that this...' *farce* '...situation could have, and I came to the conclusion that I couldn't come between you and Maite and the baby, and that the best thing was for me to return to Scotland.'

I pause. Dexter is looking at me intently. He lifts his chin slightly, an indicator I should continue.

I gulp then say, 'I replied to the university, accepting my place.'

Dexter's Adam's apple bobs, but it's the only outward sign he gives that he's either not pleased at the news or that it surprises him.

I inhale a deep breath, as surreptitiously as I can, and say, 'Then I booked a flight home. I leave next week.'

A pulse ticks in Dexter's cheek, but he says nothing.

Eventually, my patience gives out. 'Aren't you going to say anything?'

He raises his eyes to meet mine, pain and anger vying for top billing. 'I think you've already said everything, don't you?' He stands and without a backward glance strides off towards the sanctuary.

Chapter Thirty-one

For a few moments I sit rooted to the chair in a daze. What just happened? I'd expected some sort of reaction from Dexter, not this non-reaction. It's almost insulting. Fury boils up from deep within me. Aren't I worth fighting for? Maybe he isn't the right man for me if he's willing to give up on me quite so easily. I bat aside the thought that the same is true of me, and I'm being hypocritical. That's not the point here.

My breath comes in heaving gasps, and it gives me no pleasure to know I've probably done the right thing in booking my flight home and accepting my university place. Everything here is so transient, after all. Just when I thought I had my future here mapped out, it's up in the air again.

Well, I guess there's only one thing for it: I need to tell Carlos and Sofia. I hoist myself out of the garden chair and head back indoors towards Carlos' office. But before I can reach it, Mariangeles appears as if conjured by some magician's trick. I have no idea how she manages to materialise out of thin air, but she's always there. Perhaps she has the gift of invisibility or super speed.

'Well?' she asks. 'How did it go?'

Numbly, I say, 'It didn't.'

She frowns. 'You didn't tell him? Whyever not?'

I give a small headshake. 'No. I did tell him. He didn't react. Didn't fight for me … for us.' I mumble the last part almost to myself.

Mariangeles guides me into the admin office. 'I think you'd better tell me everything,' she says in a tone that brooks no argument.

It doesn't take me long to fill her in. When I've finished, she shakes her head. 'Do you know something? I want to knock both your heads together. He is as stubborn and pig-headed as you are impulsive.'

She's not the first to call me that.

'So, what now?' she asks.

I sigh heavily. 'I was on my way to tell Carlos and Sofia.'

'No, no, no, no, no!' She wags a finger at me. 'Not yet. Let's see if we can sort this out.'

'Mariangeles—' I look her directly in the eyes '—what exactly do you think there is to sort out? Maybe if Dexter had given even the slightest indication that he cared one way or the other if I stayed or not, we'd have a chance. Perhaps I would turn down the opportunity to go to uni if I felt he reciprocated my feelings, but from where I was standing – or sitting – during that conversation, the traffic was all one way.'

'And I'm telling you, you're wrong,' Mariangeles insists. 'I was here when Maite and Dexter were together, and I never saw his face light up when he was with her, the way it does when he's with you.'

I grit my teeth at the unfairness of it all. 'Then he has to do something about it. As things stand, I fly home a week today. And personally, I don't see anything changing. I'm grateful for your support, Mariangeles, more than you'll ever know, but I think you may be wrong about this one.'

'I'm never wrong,' Mariangeles mutters under her breath. 'You'll see.'

'Maybe, but it's only fair I tell Carlos and Sofia now.'

Mariangeles takes my hands in hers. '*Chica*, please, leave it at least until tomorrow.'

'Then I'm not even giving Carlos and Sofia a week's notice. I can't do that. My conscience won't let me.'

Mariangeles growls in frustration, actually growls. 'Give it until dinner then, please.' She looks into my eyes so earnestly, I can't say no.

'Fine. Dinnertime. Right, I'm off to ask Victor to give me some work, to keep me as far away as possible from Dexter hopefully for the rest of the day.'

Mariangeles mumbles something noncommittal and goes off in the opposite direction to me.

As I walk down to the sloth enclosures, I ring Becca. Immediately, her face pops up on my phone. Video-calling is the best, except when you have bad news to impart. I hadn't managed to text her earlier to tell her the latest drama, so I'll fill her in on all of it now, plus the outcome. Job done.

'Hey, Kat, how's it going in the Rich Coast?'

'It's been better.'

Most people would think, "What now?" but Becca outright says, 'Oh, what now?' Her directness is one of the things I've always loved about her.

'Hmm, where to start? Well, as you know Dexter's pregnant ex-girlfriend turned up and I thought it was his baby, but it wasn't, so in a fit of pique – I guess – before I knew it wasn't his baby, I emailed the uni and said I'd start in September and then booked a flight home.' I finally pause. 'Yep, that's about it, in a nutshell.'

Becca gapes. 'You did what? Why? Didn't we discuss this already and you were going to talk this through with Dexter like adults?'

I blow out a breath. 'Yeah, well, that horse has bolted.'

'Jeez, Kat, I can't leave you alone for two minutes.'

'I forgot to ask. How was your date?' I deflect nicely.

'Oh no, no, no, no! You're not getting away with it that easily.'

'What? I'm just showing some interest in your life. You have to deal with my dramas all the time. I thought maybe you had some of your own, I could help with.'

'Kat, stop it! This is serious. Much as I'd like you to come home from a "having my bestie here" perspective, you have to resolve the situation in Costa Rica first, before you can move forward. Did you even talk to Dexter?'

My hand flies to my mouth. 'Oh my goodness, I'm so sorry.' My voice oozes insincerity. 'I almost forgot the best part.' I pause for a second, collecting my thoughts. 'Didn't I say? Oh, when I told Dexter that I had assumed the baby was his, and that I'd booked a flight home and accepted a place at uni, he said nothing. Noth-ing. And when I asked him if he had anything to say, he said, and I quote "I think you've already said everything, don't you?"'

I wait for Becca's outburst, but when her reaction comes, it's not what I was expecting.

'Is it any wonder, Kat?'

'Sorry?' It's amazing how much outrage I manage to fit into one word. Becca's my best friend. Surely she isn't taking Dexter's side in this.

'Kat, I love you, but sometimes you can be so stubborn and blind to what's going on around you. By your own admission, you jumped to conclusions. You didn't give the poor guy time to respond, to explain what the situation was with Maite. You did your usual, and it's not completely your fault. That muppet Aidan has a lot to answer for. He's knocked your self-confidence and your faith in men.'

I go to interrupt but she holds up a finger to silence me. 'No, you need to hear this. But Dexter isn't Aidan. I don't even know him, but he sounds like a decent guy from what you've told me. The complete antithesis to Aidan. And, he's supporting his pregnant ex-girlfriend, even though the baby isn't his. That sounds like a pretty responsible man to me.'

She draws breath and I start, 'But, Becca, you–'

'Kat. You haven't told each other you love each other yet, but you've assumed he was shagging Roisin and you've thought he had got someone pregnant and was in a jam. But on both occasions, you didn't talk it out with him until it was too late. How am I doing so far?'

I bristle slightly then gulp and say hesitantly,

'That's reasonably accurate.'

'And now you've told him you've accepted a place at uni, on a different continent, and even booked a flight home, without having any type of discussion with him, or allowing him to explain. Have I got that right?'

I nod numbly.

Becca stays on the line, but says nothing more, until finally I crack. 'I've screwed up, Becca. Once, I might have been able to come back from, but twice? Everything you've said is true. I made assumptions based on the worst-case scenario, when Dexter had given me nothing but reasons to believe in him, believe in us.'

'Kat, I'm going to contradict myself here, but do yourself a favour, instead of just asking for my advice, this time I strongly recommend you take it.'

'I'm sorry.' I'm on the verge of tears, and I hate myself for being so needy and pathetic. I don't know what's going on with me.

'And stop bloody apologising. Go and sort it. Now I'm going to go, because sometimes I need to be cruel to be kind. Call me back once you've spoken to him. Good luck.'

She hangs up and I stare at the phone in shock. I know Becca's forthright, but part of me feels that was a step too far, even for her.

Once I've recovered from the way Becca spoke to me, I return to the sanctuary – Victor will have to do without me for a little longer – but I can't find Dexter anywhere. I bump into Mariangeles, too, but she hasn't been able to track him down either.

I try calling him. Nothing. I try texting. Still

nothing.

Finally, I go to see Carlos, who is in his office, sifting through a pile of paperwork, Ferdinand, as ever, close to him.

'Kat! What a lovely surprise. What can I do for you? Come in and sit down.'

'Thanks, but I'm not stopping. I'm going to help Victor in a sec. Have you seen Dexter? I needed to catch up with him about something.'

Carlos gives me a long, hard look, not an unkind one, but searching and knowing. 'I'm afraid you've missed him. He asked for a few days' emergency leave. He left about ten minutes ago.'

It's all I can do not to rant and rail against the injustice of it all. Whilst I was getting a lecture from Becca, Dexter was hotfooting it out of here. Great. What now?

'I don't suppose he said where he was going, did he?'

Carlos shakes his head. 'No, he just said it was something urgent, and I didn't ask him any questions. I know if he wanted me to know anything or wanted my advice, he'd say so.'

I can't help thinking Carlos' comment is a little pointed, as in, I'm prying too much. Trying not to show my disappointment, I say, 'OK. I'll catch up with him later.'

My fingernails dig into my palms as I walk out of Carlos' office. I don't recall the last time I felt this despondent. I honestly don't know what to do. My duty is here, at the sanctuary, at least until I leave, but part of me wants to track Dexter down, although the fact he's not answering his phone gives the impression he doesn't want to be found.

If Dexter's really away on leave, I can't hang around. I won't give Sofia and Carlos only a few days' notice that I'm leaving, nor will I not tell them, when the girls already know – it's not fair. I just need to decide exactly when to tell them and how.

All day, I startle whenever I hear a beep, wondering if it's Dexter finally responding to my texts or calling me, but it never is. At dinner, I sit with the others, feeling sorry for myself, but trying to pretend everything is OK. I told Mariangeles that Dexter has gone away and neither she nor Ella or Federica can think where. And even if he is with Maite, that's not a bad thing, as he's helping a pregnant friend in need whilst her partner's away. I don't begrudge him that – now – but I wish I had a way that we could talk, cards on the table, and work through our problems.

I texted Becca. I couldn't face her berating me again. I know she did it for the right reason, but I can't deal with it at the moment. I told her Dexter had taken off and that I'd missed my chance to have that chat.

And I've come to a decision. After dinner, I'm going to tell Carlos I'm heading home. I can't sort things with Dexter if he's not here, and if he wasn't willing to stick around to try to repair things between us, then what's the point? Maybe I should begin to look forward to the new start and challenge back home – the chance finally to go to university – something I've never had. A new experience. New friends. New potential boyfriends.

But I don't want new friends, or a new boyfriend. I want the ones I have here. Ideally, I'd like Becca to have a portkey so she could zip back and forth between Costa Rica and Scotland so I wouldn't miss her. That is, as long as she isn't going to be quite as direct as she was earlier, although that was purely a one-off to sort me out. Still, in the absence of the portkey or the portal, I'd settle for my Costa Rican crew. But that possibility is looking less and less likely.

I don't even manage my dessert. *Empanadas de piña.* I nibble at a piece of the pastry and the pineapple tastes heavenly, but I simply can't swallow it.

'*Chicas*, wish me luck. I'm going to tell Carlos.'

Ella's mouth downturns, Mariangeles grasps my hand and Federica shoots me a pitying look. Yeah, they can tell how this is going to go down: like a lead balloon.

Carlos is walking to his car when I accost him. I'd clocked him leaving the canteen and wanted to get him on his own.

'Carlos, do you have a minute?'

He turns, but his usual smile is absent; instead he adopts a wary expression as if he already knows I'm about to tell him something he'd rather not hear.

'*Venga*, let's sit by the firepit. We can talk there as the others are still at dinner.' He ushers me towards the chairs that encircle the fire. It's not lit at the minute, so I pull my cardigan around me as I take a seat.

'Carlos, I'm really sorry, but I'm leaving.'

His eyes don't show the shock or surprise I'd expected. Did Dexter tell him? But if so, why didn't he tell me so earlier when I asked about Dexter's whereabouts?

When he says nothing, I go on. 'I've been offered a place at university to study veterinary medicine.'

He steeples his fingers under his chin. 'Congratulations. I'm happy for you.'

'You are?' I try but fail to keep the incredulity out of my tone. 'But why? Aren't I leaving you in the lurch?'

Carlos smiles. 'Kat, it has been a pleasure to have you here, however temporary. I would never stand in the way of one of our volunteers going off to do their own thing again, especially when they're improving themselves.'

Personally, I'm not sure university is an improvement on living in Costa Rica and working in a sloth sanctuary, but I keep shtum.

'Kat, how could I be cross at you wanting to work and train with animals? This way you'll be realising a dream. A lifelong dream?'

'Since I was little.'

'See? I couldn't possibly be mad at you. I'll miss you, as will we all, but you must do what's right for you.'

His words echo those Dexter spoke to me right before Maite pulled up in her car, and what the others have been saying since.

'Well, thanks for being so understanding. I-I-I've booked a flight. I'm afraid I leave a week today.'

'In that case, we'll have to make the most of you being here for the next week.'

'I'm sorry about the short notice,' I say, fidgeting

with the hem of my T-shirt.

'Kat, in life things happen for a reason. You came to us for a reason. Maybe your mission has been accomplished. Don't worry about us; we'll be fine. We always are.' He pats my hand in a fatherly fashion. 'Now go and enjoy what time you have left with us.'

I nod mutely and smile at him, too caught up in my thoughts to muster anything else.

Chapter Thirty-two

The next few days fly past, as we care for the sloths, a man down, with Dexter still absent. It's obvious to me that Dexter does more than the job of one person, as it's so noticeable when he's not there, and part of me wonders if Carlos was just saying they'd cope no problem when I return home, to stop me from feeling so bad.

Knowing Dexter had told Carlos he would be gone for a couple of days, I finally stop checking my phone or glancing up when a car rumbles along the road towards the sanctuary, instead focusing my energies on making the most of these final days with the sloths and my adoptive family and friends.

Two days before I am due to fly home, I wave Carlos and Sofia off as they leave for a trip to Quepos.

An hour later, a taxi draws up to the sanctuary, and Dexter steps out, wearing faded jeans and a red checked shirt. He looks like a wrangler on a Texan ranch.

I've decided I want to make things right with him before I go home, even though any romantic relationship between us is over. However, I don't want to pounce on him the minute he steps over the threshold. Instead, I wait until I bump into him naturally. I'd imagined that would be in the canteen, but I'm wrong.

'Kat.'

I look up at the sound of his voice. I didn't hear him come into the nursery. I've been busy with Bolt. A jolt of electricity courses through me as his eyes meet mine; however, it's not a jolt of attraction, but alarm. He still takes my breath away, but it's the pain and sadness in his eyes that I note.

'Dexter.' I gulp past the bowling ball blocking my throat.

He scrapes a hand through his hair. I've never seen him look so wretched, not even when we argued about the Roisin debacle.

'So you're really going?'

My eyes search his and I nod mutely, which elicits a long sigh from him.

'Dexter, I want you to know I'm sorry.'

His eyebrows raise at this. 'For what?'

Now it's my turn to sigh. 'Where do I start?'

He gives a sad smile. 'The beginning's usually the best place, I find.'

My lips lift slightly at the corners. 'I'm sorry I destroyed everything between us by jumping to conclusions and by being so bloody impulsive. Becca's not pleased with me either.'

'Things must be bad.' His eyes crinkle at the corners.

'Yes, we don't argue often. In fact, we never argue,' I realise. 'But she was pretty vehement when we last spoke. She made it clear to me that just because I've had reason to be wary in relationships in the past, I shouldn't have foisted those issues onto our relationship. She's right, and I'm truly sorry.'

Dexter dips his head in acknowledgement. 'Thanks. For what it's worth, I'm sorry too. I should have been more sensitive to the situation with Maite. It simply didn't occur to me, as I knew I didn't see Maite in that way any more, plus I obviously knew I couldn't be the father. The timings weren't right.'

'I know that now, but when your face went white on seeing her baby bump when she got out of the car, I assumed the worst.'

He smiles. 'You did. You added two and two and got five.'

I give a wry grin. 'Yeah, I tend to do that a lot. Dexter, I wish things could have been different. I'll always … always … care about you.'

His face shutters over momentarily. Damn. I've said the wrong thing again.

'And I you,' he finally says. He clears his throat. 'So, are you looking forward to starting your course?'

I haven't even thought about the course, or much about what will happen when I return home. All I know is I have no idea where I'm going to live, beyond on Becca's couch for the first week.

Whilst I'm here, I'm in a kind of limbo, and Dexter's disappearing act added to that. And now he's back. Will the next two days stretch out interminably between us like some sort of protracted torture, or will it whizz past because the face of the man I love is ever-present and I'll be subjected to seeing him constantly, fully cognisant of the fact that soon I'll be leaving him and there's nothing I can do about it? My chance has passed.

I want to indelibly imprint his face in my mind, forever, however painful it may be. The long, straight Greek nose, the satin soft eyebrows whose shape is far better than mine, annoyingly, and the sandy blonde stubble.

Despite him appearing drawn, the heavily stubbled look suits him, although I'm not sure whether he has adopted it through lack of self-care the past few days or by design.

Belatedly, I realise Dexter is still waiting for an answer. 'Honestly, I haven't even thought about it.'

He straightens at that and shoots me a quizzical look.

'I've not exactly had much headspace,' I confess, and he nods slightly as if he understands.

Silence descends between us, and it's me who eventually breaks it. 'I hope you'll be happy. I really wish that for you.'

He regards me for a long moment, then says. 'And me for you. I–'

His phone rings but he ignores it. His eyes remain on mine. 'Kat, I…'

He looks like he's debating something with himself and can't quite commit to getting the words out. Finally, he says, 'I wish we had more time. I–'

His phone rings again. 'Sorry. I need to take this. That's the second time Carlos has called in a few minutes.'

I nod and wait for him to leave to take his call, but

he stays put. Answering, he says, 'Carlos?' but the jovial banter I expected between them after Dexter's few days away isn't forthcoming, and I glance up to see Dexter has a grave expression on his face.

'Of course.' He signals to me for pen and paper, which I grab from a nearby table and hand to him.

He scribbles furiously and then listens for another few moments before hanging up.

His hand shakes as he tears the piece of paper from the pad and puts it in his pocket.

A horrible feeling unfurls in my stomach. 'Dexter, is everything OK?'

'No, that was the police. Carlos and Sofia have been in an accident. They're being taken to hospital in Quepos by ambulance.'

My hand flies to my mouth and I think I'm about to throw up. No! God, no. Nothing can happen to Carlos and Sofia.

Instinctively, I reach out and touch Dexter's arm. 'Did the police say what happened?' I want to ask how critical they are, but I'm afraid of the answer.

He shakes his head. 'They weren't very clear on the details. All they said was Carlos and Sofia were alive but had been in a three-car accident on the road to Quepos.' His voice cracks as he says the last part and my fingers find his.

'They'll be OK.' I look him in the eye. 'They will. They have to be.'

He bobs his head automatically. 'We have to find Javier. The police tried his number first, but his phone was switched off. I'm their other emergency contact, so they called me.'

'Which hospital are they going to?'

'Max Teran Valls. It's a good hospital, so that's a relief.'

My heart rate dials back a notch. Dexter looks like a million things are going through his mind right now, so I say, 'You go find Javier, I'll let everyone else know what's happening, presuming that's what you want.' I wait for his confirmation.

He nods, so I continue, 'Then I'll meet you at the truck. I'm coming with you.'

'You don't have to do that,' Dexter protests.

I lay my hand on his arm again. 'I want to. Carlos and Sofia are almost like replacement parents to all of us.'

He nods again. 'OK. Call me if you see Javier before I find him, or if anyone knows where he is.'

'I will.' I follow him out of the nursery and hear Federica say, 'Are you OK, Dexter? You don't look well.'

He draws up short at that and Federica visibly startles.

'Have you seen Javier?' he asks her.

Federica shakes her head. 'What's going on? Is everything all right?'

'Go,' I tell Dexter. 'I'll explain to Federica.'

Dexter doesn't wait any longer and leaves the foyer, eyes scanning as he goes, on the lookout for Javier.

'Federica, where is everyone else?'

She frowns. 'Mariangeles and Ella are doing admin, Victor's mucking out, Alejandro's constructing something in the outdoor sloth play area and Roisin nipped out for some groceries. Why?'

'Let's go see Mariangeles and Ella, then I'll tell you.'

We head for the admin office where Ella is sitting at one computer with Mariangeles at the other. Both glance up as we enter.

'Hey, *chicas*.' Mariangeles' smile is bright until she reads our faces. Ella's eyes are wide with concern.

'What's wrong?' Mariangeles asks.

'That's what I asked,' says Federica, framed in the doorway beside me.

'Have either of you seen Javier?' I ask.

Ella shakes her head, but Mariangeles replies, 'He was going diving with Ed and Nicolás today, I think.'

Oh shit.

'Do you know when he left?' I press.

Mariangeles shrugs. 'A little after Carlos and Sofia. Why the sudden interest in Javier's movements?'

'Give me a minute, then I'll explain. I need to call Dexter first.' I fumble with the keypad of my phone, searching for Dexter's name.

'Dexter, Javier went diving with Ed and Nicolás. Try their phones. Let me know if you get them. I'll be at the truck in five minutes tops.'

When I end the call with Dexter, my three friends are staring at me wide-eyed and their expressions mirror the fear I feel in my gut.

'Tell us what has happened,' says Mariangeles, her voice trembling.

I take a shaky breath in. 'Carlos and Sofia have been in an accident. They're on their way to hospital now.'

'*Dios mio.*' Mariangeles blesses herself, whilst

Federica's look of horror says it all, and Ella blanches.

'What happened?' Mariangeles asks once she has composed herself.

'We don't know yet. All the police could confirm was that they were alive and on their way to hospital.'

'We have to tell Javier. *Ay*, he's at the beach with the guys,' puts in Federica.

'Dexter and I will go get him. His phone was off. That's why the police called Dexter.'

Comprehension crosses their faces.

'Can you all manage everything between you? Sorry, I know I'm the newbie, soon to be…' I'll have to postpone my flight. It hits me with a clarity I've seldom possessed. There's no way I can return to Scotland knowing Carlos and Sofia are incapacitated. Certainly not until I know the extent of their injuries. Depending on their severity, it could be weeks, months before they can get around independently. I give myself a little shake. I need to stop catastrophising. For all we know, they may simply have whiplash, although honestly, that's not how it came across when Dexter was on the phone with the police.

My phone rings. Dexter.

'I called Nicolás. They've just come out of the water. We're going to pick Javier up on the way. Can you meet me at the truck now?'

I hesitate for a split second, translating the unspoken message in his instruction. It doesn't take two of us to drive to the hospital. In fact, I'd probably be more use here. No, there can only be one reason Dexter has asked me to come: He needs me there.

'I'm on my way.' I hang up and turn to the girls.

We share a group hug, and for some reason I feel the need to reassure them. 'They're both going to be OK, got it?' Somehow if I say that aloud, it's as if a higher power will listen and it will all be fine. Let's hope I'm right. With an extra hug to a now tearful Ella, I jog to the sanctuary entrance and out into the car park where Dexter is starting the engine.

As I swing myself into the seat next to him, he shoots me a grateful look. He doesn't say anything, but he doesn't need to. We both need to concentrate on what lies ahead. Now is not the time for talking. Best to keep our energy for later, when we meet Javier, then hopefully Carlos and Sofia.

It's not long before we pull into the beach where Ed, Javier and Nicolás were diving, but it felt as if the journey took hours. Javier's face is ashen and I instinctively envelop him in a hug after Dexter greets him. Nicolás' face, too, is drawn, his eyes red.

Javier sinks down in the front seat, deep in thought as we rumble away from the beach and along the highway towards the hospital. Nicolás and I sit in relative silence in the back as I will the truck to go faster.

The one godsend is that Javier wasn't too far away today. I know he, Ed and Nicolás have gone on some dives much further afield in recent weeks.

Twenty minutes later, thankfully, we arrive at the hospital, where I go directly with Javier and Nicolás to reception to see what they can tell us whilst Dexter parks the truck. As I cast my eye around the waiting room, the only piece of good news is that it isn't that busy. Maybe that bodes well for Sofia and Carlos.

My heart aches for Javier as I witness him try to be strong when he must surely be falling apart inside. I put my arm around his shoulder and he leans into me, clearly appreciative of the support, both mentally and physically.

By the time Dexter joins us, a doctor is talking calmly to Javier and Nicolás and inviting them to follow him into a side room. Oh God, this is bad. That's the relatives' room. Isn't that what they do in medical dramas when the news is bad? When someone … I can't bring myself to say the word which springs to my lips. No, I've got to keep thinking positive, particularly for Javier's sake. It's just fear getting the better of me. They're not even my parents and I'm terrified. Perhaps it's because I've already lost one parent and know how devastating it is.

We still don't even know what exactly happened. What caused the accident. Who caused the accident. If there were any other people injured. What type of injuries they've sustained. Crikey, I'm thinking like an American crime drama. Sustained. Oh, here we go. My mind is going off on a tangent to prevent me thinking too hard about the possibility of Carlos and Sofia being hooked up to machines and tubes.

Then the doctor comes back out of the relatives' room with Javier, who looks dazed, and Nicolás, who has his arm round his cousin's shoulder. Dexter and I both move towards them in synch.

We wait for Javier to speak. His voice cracks with emotion and then he bursts into tears, as Dexter sweeps him into a hug and I hold them both. It can't be. And both of them? Two of the most wonderful people on the planet. What kind of god would take them so soon? Especially with all the good they do and how kind they are. *The same god who took your dad too early*, says a little voice.

In between us, Javier snuffles then composes himself. 'They're in ICU. Mum has a ruptured spleen and Dad has punctured a lung.'

Suddenly, that seems like the best news I've heard in years. Next to me, Dexter sags with relief. I'm sure he thought the same as me when Javier broke down – that his parents were gone. At least now they have a chance. Their injuries are significant but they're alive.

Javier looks at Nicolás. 'They've said we can see them for a little bit.' He turns to Dexter and me. 'Sorry. It's only family for now.'

'We understand, Javi. We'll wait right here, and we'll be here for you both when you come back,' Dexter says.

'And if they can hear you, send them our love,' I add.

He nods mutely then heads with Nicolás in the direction of the ICU.

As they walk away my phone rings. Assuming it's someone from the sanctuary, I answer, but it's Becca, video-calling me.

'Hey, checking in to see how you're getting back from the airport on Friday.'

Oh no. Worst possible timing. Becca starts rabbiting on about how we're going out on the town when I get home, and that now I've made the decision to come home, I need to forget Dexter, move on. Cringing, I turn the volume down a little, hoping Dexter didn't hear.

Eventually, I interrupt, as Becca is on a roll and doesn't show any sign of stopping.

'Becca, can I call you back? It's not a good time. Carlos and Sofia have had an accident. I'm at the Emergency Room now with their son, nephew and Dexter.'

'Oh my God!' blurts Becca. 'Are they all right?'

I shake my head. 'It's too soon to say.'

Flustered, she says, 'Well, keep me posted.'

I hang up and turn to Dexter, who looks even more crushed than before. Did he overhear or is he simply, and understandably, worried about Sofia and Carlos?

Dexter sits down on the hard metal bench chairs, his hands laced together, his elbows on his knees and his head hanging down through them.

I do the only thing I can: I try to comfort him by slipping my arm around his back, so he knows I'm here for him. I say nothing and we stay like that for a few minutes.

As I sit there in the silence, I know one thing for sure – I can't go home. Not now. Not yet.

Chapter Thirty-three

Sirens wail, monitors beep, alarms go off. When we arrived, in the rush to learn news of Carlos and Sofia's conditions, I hadn't thought of how the last time I was in a hospital was when Dad died. Suddenly, grief hits me like a tsunami, and tears slide down my cheeks as I sob silently. I remove my hand from Dexter's back to wipe them away, causing him to look up at me. Alarm registers on his face.

'Kat, they'll be OK.'

I say nothing; I'm not able to. So he takes me by the shoulders and turns me towards him. 'This is one of the best hospitals in Costa Rica. They're in safe hands.'

I nod, but still say nothing. How can I explain that whilst I'm worried about Carlos and Sofia and the extent of their injuries, I'm having some kind of flashback to Dad's death, Dad being in the hospital, Dad never coming home again?

All I want to do is bury my head in Dexter's chest and feel his arms around me. I know that would provide me with some reassurance right now, but it's no longer his place to be there for me in that way, and I don't have the right to ask. Plus, it wouldn't be fair.

As if reading my thoughts, he sits up, and

awkwardly, since we're sitting side by side, his arms encircle me, then he leans forward into me so that the only place my head can go is on his shoulder.

This is not the action of a romantic partner but of a good friend, and I accept it as such.

Tension drains out of me as I relax into him. It feels so right being here, so right that we're supporting each other in this way. If only we – for that, read *I* – hadn't screwed up our relationship. Maybe we could have had a shot. A real chance.

When we finally break apart, Dexter looks into my eyes with a tenderness that makes my heart stutter, and says, 'You OK?'

I nod as he moves a strand of hair from in front of my eye.

Somehow as we return to sitting side by side, Dexter's hand is in mine, in a show of support. And I'm glad, as the stark, clinical nature of the hospital waiting area and the corridors off of it continue to remind me of Dad, but with Dexter here with me, the grief I feel is surmountable.

Suddenly, I sit bolt upright. 'We need to call the others. They still don't know what's going on.'

Dexter rolls his eyes as if he can't quite believe we forgot. 'I'll call the sanctuary; you call Ed.'

After half an hour or so, Javier and Nicolás reappear. Javier's face is pinched and grey.

'Mum was awake, but Dad was asleep, or so heavily sedated he couldn't hear me.' His voice cracks and he visibly crumples. This time it's me who supports him first. 'They looked so awful, with all those tubes coming out of them, and with so many bruises and cuts.'

'Do we know what caused the accident yet?' Dexter asks.

Javier shakes his head. 'No, but the police were talking to one of the doctors about it, and the doctor told them I'm their son. They've asked me to let them know when they're in a position to answer questions. The doctor wouldn't let the police question Mum yet.'

Dexter and I both nod. Javier stumbles over nothing, and as Nicolás puts a hand on his arm, I realise how unsteady he is on his feet.

'Javi, Nicolás, do you want me to get you something to drink?'

'Yes, please.'

I head over to the water dispenser and fill a cup for each of them then take them back to where they have sat down beside Dexter. As I reach them, I hear Dexter tell Javier not to worry about the sanctuary, that he has it in hand, and we'll help them through this. He's so calm in the face of this crisis, so practical, it makes my heart swell with love for him.

'You concentrate on your parents, for now,' is the final thing Dexter says before I pass the water to Javier, who glances up and gives me a wan smile. 'Thanks.'

Later, once Javier has been able to see Carlos awake and ascertain that his father is stable, we all head back to the sanctuary so Javier can get some rest before he returns to the hospital in the morning. The nursing staff agreed to keep him updated on any change to his parents' conditions.

When we pull into the staff car park, light still shines out from the sanctuary building. All the visitors are gone for the day, but I spot Victor heading towards us, arms swinging purposefully.

His already lined face appears to have developed a few more lines since I saw him last, with worry evident in every crease.

'Any news?' he asks Javier as we stride towards him.

'They're stable at the moment, but the doctor wasn't able to talk about prognosis or length of recovery yet,' Javier says disconsolately.

Victor rubs his chin as he absorbs the information. 'C'mon, let's get you something to eat. I know most of your mother's dishes off by heart, so I've cooked dinner. Ella and Federica handled lunch.'

Of course. With Sofia out of action, someone will have to cook the meals, possibly for some time to come. Well, cooking's something I'm good at; I can certainly help with that. I'll talk to Victor about it later, because much as I'm happy to muck in and do the heavy stuff, I can't work at the same pace as Victor, so short- to mid-term we need him back at least partially fulfilling his usual role. A slight smile dances on my lips despite the circumstances. I can just imagine Victor in his element in the kitchen. I also wonder if he'll stick to Sofia's recipes, or branch out with his own ideas.

The momentary distraction helps release some of the day's tension as we head towards the canteen where Alejandro is helping ladle out what looks like a hearty soup.

We each take a plate and my mouth waters as I inhale the beefy aroma, and suddenly I realise how long it has been since breakfast. My stomach chooses that moment to rumble and Victor laughs.

'It's not the same as Sofia's, but my *sustancia de carne* isn't half bad, even if I say so myself.'

Indeed, his beef soup hits the spot, although I note the veggies he topped it with are different to those Sofia uses.

Everyone else waits for us to eat before delving into how the patients are faring, and it's with a tentative collective sigh of relief that we all proceed to dessert, once Javier and Dexter have answered everyone's questions and concerns.

'Victor, can we talk after dinner?' Dexter says. 'We'll need to come up with a plan for feeding the troops going forward.'

Victor nods, as if he'd expected the suggestion.

An hour later, we sit round the firepit, subdued, but doing our best to keep our spirits up for Javier's sake. He hasn't heard anything else from the hospital, which we all tell him is a good sign.

Victor is sitting with Javier and Nicolás, Dexter is talking to Mariangeles, and I am two seats away from him, chatting with Federica about what the next day will bring. Chores are being reallocated to allow for the impact of the unexpected events. One thing is for sure; Carlos, in particular, would want everything to continue like clockwork at the sanctuary, and for us to take care of his beloved sloths. Rocket was supposed to be released into the wild tomorrow, but we're postponing that as we're all a little too unsettled. We can delay that a few days. It's the only thing that Dexter appears to be allowing to deviate from the norm.

Dexter leans over to me. 'Kat, I'm so sorry, but could you take a taxi to the airport on Friday? I don't think we can afford anyone to be away from the sanctuary for that long.'

The penny drops for me. I haven't told Dexter I'm staying. I'd almost forgotten I was intending to go home. That plan seems such a long time ago. I look into his eyes. 'Dexter, I'm postponing my flight. I can't go now. Not until Sofia and Carlos are home.'

Dexter stiffens. 'You're not leaving?'

'Yes. And what's more, I can cook, so I'll help Victor with the meals.'

For the first time all day, the hint of a smile plays on Dexter's lips.

'You're really staying?'

I hold his gaze. 'I'm really staying.'

His eyes light up then I say, 'For now anyway.'

He hesitates a second then pats my arm. 'Thanks, Kat. That's good of you.'

Wait, what? Is that it? Yes, I'm doing it for Sofia, Carlos and the sanctuary, and no, I don't harbour any illusions about us getting back together – sadly, that ship has sailed – but I'm part of the team. We're all pulling together. But maybe some tiny part of me wanted him to be glad, not just in his role as the sanctuary's deputy manager, that I was staying, but as someone he had a connection with, and who shared his bed, not so very long ago. My spirits plummet as quickly as they rose earlier, and it's with relief when Javier says he's going to call it a night that I tell him I am, too.

The next couple of days pass quickly; with so much to do and so few bodies to do it, free time is scarce. There are still group visits, school visits, educational tours, an infant sloth rescue, an adult sloth rescue, we finally release Rocket into the wild, plus the general upkeep of the sanctuary, caring for the sloths, cooking for everyone – fortunately Victor and I have developed a fluid routine that works, but it still takes up a huge chunk of time. There's barely a moment left over for us to do much but eat, sleep and shower.

Javier visits his parents daily, and we've all agreed that once we're allowed to, we'll visit them on rotation. That way Sofia and Carlos will have lots of new faces to see and all the sanctuary chores will be completed on time, and hopefully we'll manage to keep their sanctuary ticking over just as they like until their return.

After I postponed my flight, by a month, life has continued pretty much as if I hadn't been intending to return home at all. Well, with one exception: Dexter and I are friends, but nothing more. Although I've felt wistful on many occasions about what could have been, usually immediately before I go to sleep, I haven't had any indication from him that he'd like the status quo to change. Even with my protracted stay at the sanctuary, there hasn't been the slightest hint that he'd like our romance to get back on track.

The day of Maite's scan came and went, with Dexter absent for most of the afternoon. Strangely, it didn't negatively affect me; instead, it consolidated my belief in him as a truly wonderful human being and a good friend – one I'm leaving in a few short weeks.

I suppose I really should start thinking about my future back in Scotland. As things stand, I'll be starting uni only a few days after I return from Costa Rica, given my new flight booking, and I still haven't sorted out anywhere to live past Becca's sofa for the first week.

Somehow, being stuck in this limbo of not returning to Scotland when planned is preventing me emotionally from moving forward, with regards to Dexter and leaving the sanctuary family and the sloths behind, and from beginning to focus on my upcoming studies and my lack of abode.

I'm trying to make the most of my extra time in Costa Rica, but something's missing. It's not only Dexter and me not being back together, or any hint of that being on the horizon at any point. I've accepted now that we'll only ever be friends, however painful that may be. No, it's more connected to the fact I know I'm going home for sure. Before Sofia and Carlos' accident, it was a fait accompli, but because I decided to delay my return, for some reason it seems more final now. More certain. I know it's odd, but I can't help it; it's how I feel.

I don't actively try to avoid Dexter, but I do find it difficult to be around him, so it's good in some respects that we're all so busy, as our paths don't cross too much for any length of time, except at mealtimes. He gives me instructions and tasks and is perfectly pleasant with me, but I sense he's guarded, as I am too. How I wish I knew what was going on inside his head, or maybe it's best I don't know.

I'm adding some small logs to a new sloth play area that's being constructed – the sanctuary is sadly at the highest capacity I've seen since I arrived, so we're planning ahead – when Dexter's navy cargo-panted legs appear in my line of vision. I straighten up, to see him standing, keys in hand.

'What's up?' I ask.

'Sloth rescue. Up near Jaco. The others are busy. I wondered if you wanted to come.'

Well, I'm not about to say no in any respect. He's my boss, and maybe some time alone is what we need to get past the awkwardness that still hangs between us, unresolved. I do, however, inwardly bristle slightly at the fact I appear to be last choice.

Without giving away any hint of my mixed feelings, I say, 'Sure. Let me just wash up.'

When we're in the truck five minutes later, Dexter puts the radio on and we fall into an uncomfortable silence – well, for me it is, at least. Shortly afterwards, I glance at my watch. Ten minutes have passed. Time is barely moving. It's over an hour to our destination. This is excruciating. Finally, I crack and latch onto safe ground: the injured sloth.

Dexter fills me in on all the known details and then lapses into silence again. So much for my opening gambit.

I fold my hands in my lap and stare at them as if willing them to provide answers for how to endure this journey. A couple of times, I sense Dexter's eyes on me, but I don't dare look up to check.

'Kat. I'm sorry.'

What? I finally look up at him and his eyes are so full of sorrow, if I were standing I'd be undecided whether to take a step back or move forward to give him a hug.

'What for?'

He exhales heavily then glances at me. 'I should've realised that Maite turning up pregnant could have been misconstrued, but you see, I knew that the baby couldn't possibly be mine.' He looks awkward for a second then says, 'The timing wouldn't have worked, by several months.'

My brow furrows as he goes on. 'Even though she worked here up until the end of last year, we weren't "together" in that way by that point. Our relationship ended early last year.'

The penny drops for me. He knew he could never have been the father, hence it didn't occur to him that I might think that.

'But I realise now,' he goes on, 'that Maite turning up out of the blue, pregnant, and my reaction, could have made you think otherwise, and I'm sorry I wasn't clued up enough to consider that.'

I bite my lip, mulling over what he's saying.

He sighs. 'And when you assumed the baby was mine, I was so shocked that you would think I'd do that that I overreacted.' He gives me a sad smile.

'I'm sorry, too. I also overreacted,' I say, mirroring

his expression.

'Anyway, I wanted to clear the air. I don't want things to be "difficult" between us.'

I nod. 'No, I don't want that either.' But where's the mention of him wanting to give it another go? For a moment, I had a glimmer of hope.

He smiles at me again, but this time there's warmth instead of sadness in his smile. 'I'm so glad we sorted that out.' He pats my arm and it's as if he has scorched my skin, yet he seems unaware.

Dexter turns back to the road and focuses on the sat nav's directions. I'm about to see if I can find an in to return to the conversation about 'us' when the phone rings.

'Hi, Javi,' Dexter replies, putting him on speaker.

As Javier fills Dexter in on the latest from the hospital, I think, once again we've missed our chance to rekindle our relationship.

We arrive at the site in Jaco, but this time there's no person physically waiting with the sloth, or indeed anything to show us exactly where the sloth is except the approximate location Dexter received from the caller. When we get out of the truck, I note how the sky has darkened. I've been so lost in thought since before Javier's call that I hadn't even noticed. Now, however, I feel that change in the air, smell the petrichor, and I know it's about to tip it down. Question is, can we find the sloth before that happens? I glance down at my skimpy vest. That wasn't the best planning, but then I didn't plan it – Dexter came to find me whilst I was building the play area, so I was kitted out properly for that, just not particularly well for this, if the weather turns.

'This way,' says Dexter, looking at the GPS coordinates he has been given.

I follow him into the undergrowth, past groups of tall trees, although I don't think these are water apple trees. We sweep around, but I can't see any sign of the sloth. Or any sloths.

'Damn it,' says Dexter, just as the first large drops of rain hit my bare shoulders.

'What's wrong?' I ask.

'I think the GPS coordinates must be off slightly. It happens sometimes near trees and tall buildings.'

That doesn't sound good. 'So what do we do?' I ask as the rain comes down in vertical sheets, bouncing off the rainforest floor.

Dexter blows out a breath. 'We have to search a wider area. You have your phone on you, right?'

'Yes.' I pat down my pockets to double-check.

'Good. Let's try walking in a fifty by fifty metre radius. If nothing, try seventy-five, then out to one hundred. I'll go this way.' He points to the left. 'And you go that way.' He points to the right. I know it's probably south by southwest or something like that, but I can just about manage left and right. Fortunately, he's not going to be too far away. A couple of hundred metres max.

'Phone me, or shout if you have no reception, if you find the sloth,' Dexter says.

'OK.' I head off, scanning the trees and the ground. I can't help wondering how exactly the caller saw the sloth, if we can't see it out in the open. I suppose it could have crawled a little way by now, and it has taken us over an hour to get here.

I try fifty metres, then seventy-five, but the rain is really hammering down now, and despite it being warm, it's not very comfortable, and it's also making it exceedingly difficult to see anything. I'm just about to give up and redraw my radius to a hundred metres when I spot something moving in the undergrowth. My first thought is it's the injured sloth. Then I have a moment's panic where I consider it could be a wild beast, possibly even a predator, and it might eat me.

As I clear my soaking wet hair out of my eyes, I make out its shape more clearly. It is a sloth. I call Dexter. No reception. 'Dexter!' I shout. I wait. Nothing. 'Dexter!' I shout, louder. Damn it. He clearly can't hear me over the driving rain. Still nothing. I go to shout again, but then a noise behind me startles me, and I whirl round to see Dexter, his shirt sticking to his body, and despite the circumstances, a jolt of lust shoots through me.

'I'm here. Did you find it?' he asks. For a millisecond, I can barely answer him as I can't tear my eyes away from the water dripping from his hair, down his face, sliding into the collar of his shirt.

I gesture to where I can see the sloth, just peeking out.

Dexter approaches it tentatively. It's a few months old, at best guess. But it seems to have blood on its fur, near its stomach.

'Kat, can you get the med kit from the truck?'

I sprint back to the truck, grab the med kit and jog

back.

'I don't know what has caused these wounds,' Dexter says. 'But it looks like a predator. He could have been lying here since last night if it was an ocelot or puma.'

I shiver, thinking again of my concern at the rustling in the undergrowth. Seems it wasn't misplaced. I dread to think what I'd have done if I'd come face to face with a puma or ocelot. Screamed probably.

I watch as Dexter expertly handles the animal, tending to its wounds as best he can with the med kit, then he tells me to stay with the sloth, whilst he fetches the cage. When he returns, he's even wetter than before as the rain hasn't halted. I can only think what a sight I look.

Once the sloth is safely settled in the truck, Dexter turns on the heater to try to dry us off as we make the journey back to the sanctuary. I'm not sure it does any good, as I'm shivering. I can't wait to have a hot shower then put some dry clothes on.

Dexter calls the sanctuary on the way back and preps Victor to take over when we arrive so we can go freshen up.

As we swing into the sanctuary car park, the rain suddenly stops.

Mariangeles greets us as we come in the back way. 'What happened to you two? You're like drowned rats.'

'The rain was a little heavy out towards Jaco,' I say, looking down at my vest top, which I realise to my horror is see-through when Mariangeles folds her arms discreetly over her own chest and raises her eyebrows meaningfully at me.

Fortunately, Dexter's attention is elsewhere. 'I'll take this little guy to Victor,' he says.

'I'm going to grab a shower,' I tell Mariangeles. I'll catch up with you afterwards.'

The hot water streaming over my skin is balm to my soul after how shivery I felt following the rescue. I open the bathroom door and am about to cross to my room when I see Dexter bending down. It looks like he has dropped something, but what is he doing here? My breath catches in my throat as I note the hard lines of his body, which are clearly visible since he's only wearing a towel on his lower half, and lust unfurls inside me again.

'Dexter?'

'Kat!' He straightens up and clasps a bottle of shower gel to his chest. 'Sorry, I didn't mean to startle you. Our showers aren't working. Alejandro's away to get a plumber friend to take a look. Mariangeles suggested I use the girls' ones.'

I bet she did. Matchmaking witch.

'I think it's me who startled you.' I laugh, but I notice his eyes drinking me in. It seems I'm not the only one affected by our state of undress.

We hold each other's gaze a little longer than necessary, then Dexter waves his shower gel at me in a goodbye. 'I'd best get dressed.'

As he walks away, back towards the men's accommodation block, I can't help the longing that pulses through me. I didn't imagine how he looked at me. I know I didn't. He apologised earlier about overreacting to my getting the wrong end of the stick about Maite's pregnancy, and I apologised too. So what's holding him back? I stand there for a moment, thinking how I will never understand men, then I wander off to find Mariangeles.

Chapter Thirty-four

Ten days after the accident, we're finally allowed to visit Carlos and Sofia. I almost feel like a child on Christmas morning, at the prospect of seeing them soon. Dexter and Mariangeles are the first to go visit after Javier and Nicolás. I've been keeping busy with running the kitchen, doing my best to recreate Sofia's recipes under Victor's tutelage, to a certain extent, although we alternate who takes the lion's share of the cooking, given we need to focus on the other sanctuary tasks. Victor, as I suspected, is in his element. He's been coaching me, too, and I've already learned so much in ten days. Only three more weeks and I'll be heading home, with an impressive culinary education, a heavy heart and leaving behind some of the best friends I've ever had.

We all spend the evenings around the firepit, in the two rec rooms or occasionally going further afield to the promenade at Espadilla beach, having a cocktail or mocktail, as the mood takes us.

When I'm not cooking during the day, I spend my days in the adult sloth play area, or in the nursery, and I name two more sloth rescues. Swift, the one I rescued with Dexter the day he apologised, and Lightning. I'm grateful to have had the opportunity to name a couple more, but saddened at the realisation they'll probably be my last.

Finally, it's my turn to visit Carlos and Sofia in hospital. Roisin and I have come up together, so we can visit them alternately, given Sofia's in a women's ward and Carlos is in a men's, so it's not exactly as if their beds are next to each other and they can share visitors.

Sofia's face radiates with pleasure when I knock on her room door and go in. 'Kat, it's so wonderful to see you.' As I reach the bed, she cups my face in her paper-thin crepey hands.

'And you. These are for you.' I hold out the bouquet of plumerias I brought from the garden at the sanctuary. She takes them and presses the delicate blooms to her nose, inhaling their sweet scent.

'Oh, thank you, Kat. This is like a little piece of home.' She casts her eyes around the room. 'And whilst it's nice here, it's a bit clinical.'

I sweep my eyes over the bed, the bedside cabinet, the monitors, the straight-backed chair and tray table and have to admit she has a point.

Plumerias are the flowers I spotted when Dexter first showed me the female accommodation, although I didn't know what they were called then, but they fast became my favourite flower – their fragrance sings 'tropical paradise' and I'm so pleased they've added a sparkle to Sofia's day.

'How are you feeling?' I ask as I take the flowers from her and place them on the table.

She gestures to her body. 'Physically, I've been better.' Then she taps her head. 'Mentally, I'm good, because I know you and the others are looking after the sanctuary so well. Everything from caring for our precious sloths to looking after our extended family. I hear you're helping feed them up.'

I smile. 'As best I can. Victor's been guiding me.'

'And no better a guide could you have. He knows his stuff.' She leans forward slightly then winces. Clearly, she hasn't fully recovered yet. 'If he keeps going like this, he'll steal my culinary crown.' I grin and she pats me on the arm. 'But joking aside, he's a fabulous chef, as I'm sure you've discovered.'

'I have indeed.' I tell Sofia, at her request, all of the dishes he has cooked and what he has taught me, and how I am going to recreate them when I go back home if I can find the ingredients.

By the time it's my turn to visit Carlos, I'm loath to leave Sofia. She is such a positive person that perhaps it's unsurprising she became my replacement mother figure so quickly after I arrived at the sanctuary.

I text Roisin that we should swap now, then I hug Sofia goodbye and tell her I'll see her again soon. She says, 'Hopefully, I'll be home next time.' I agree that would be preferable, but that also reminds me that my time here is drawing to an end and I gulp past the lump in my throat.

'How is he?' I ask Roisin, when I meet her in the corridor a few minutes later.

'In good spirits. Maybe a little tired now. I wouldn't advise staying too long.'

'OK. Sofia's doing well. Talking of coming home,

although as far as I know none of the doctors have suggested that yet.'

'Sounds like Sofia.' Roisin grins. 'She'll be going crazy sitting still for so long.'

I laugh. 'Something like that. Right, I'll see you in–' I check my watch '–half an hour, back here.' I indicate the row of metal chairs where Javier, Dexter, Nicolás and I sat on the day Sofia and Carlos were admitted.

She heads off to Sofia's room. As I walk away, I can't help but think how much Roisin has changed in the two months I've been here. She's like a completely different person – concerned and compassionate. Perhaps a brush with death will do that to you.

When I enter Carlos' room, initially I think he has fallen asleep and that Roisin's warning about him needing to rest is right; however, his eyes flutter open the moment I sit on the burgundy padded visitor chair next to him.

'Kat. So nice to see you.' His eyes shine with warmth and it sends a warm glow all the way through me to the tips of my toes.

'You too. I take in the yellowish bruising on his face and arm, and wonder at how much worse it was in the days following the accident. Dexter had spoken of angry purple bruising and a black eye from where the airbag hit Carlos in the face.

'How are things?' he asks.

'Good.' I guess he's just making small talk, so I oblige, although I'm sure Roisin has filled him in already.

'And Dexter?' He raises an eyebrow.

'Dexter … Dexter's taking care of everything, as you'd expect.'

'Hmm.' He studies me for a long moment. Finally, he says, 'And what about you and Dexter?'

Wrong-footed, I say, 'Me and Dexter?'

Carlos nods but waits for me to continue.

'Dexter and I…' I scan the room, looking for some inspiration, but nothing occurs to me. 'We're getting along better now.'

'Hmm,' Carlos says again. 'You know, Kat, I want to thank you first of all for deciding to stay to help us out. It means a lot to Sofia and me.'

I bat my hand through the air. 'Don't give it a second thought. I was needed, and I was happy to help. Anyone would have done the same.'

Carlos frowns. 'Would they have though?' He thinks for a second. 'I'm not so sure.'

I go to play it down again, but Carlos raises his hand to stop me. 'Kat, don't waste this opportunity. Tell Dexter how you feel.'

When I'm about to protest, Carlos gives a slight shake of the head. 'Men can be very stupid about showing their feelings, or what they're thinking, but do you know what?'

I wait, ready to see what pearls of wisdom he's about to impart.

'So can women. Dexter cares about you, deeply. Make sure when you leave, you've left no stone unturned regarding your feelings for each other and pursuing the chance you may have of happiness together.'

I fidget, not sure what to say. I'd hoped after the recent rescue that something more would have come of the time we spent together, particularly after his apology and the bumping into each other in the accommodation block in our towels, but he seemed to retreat again after that. If he still has feelings for me, he's doing a pretty good job of hiding them.

'Sorry, I've probably overstepped the mark, but when you're older, you realise it's easy to waste time, and not appreciate it, until you no longer have it, and by that point it's too late.'

His words bring Dad's early passing to mind. Time ran out too soon for him, and he had so many things he still wanted to do.

I nod. 'Thanks. Maybe I will talk to Dexter.'

Carlos changes the subject, perhaps sensing his work on the topic of Dexter is done, and I tell him about Lightning and Swift. Any mention of the sloths makes his face light up, but never more so than when he talks of Ferdinand.

Carlos talks of Ferdinand with such fondness and pride it almost makes me cry, and I turn my head and rearrange my hair, as I cough-sniff to hide my emotion.

When it's time for me to meet Roisin and leave Carlos to rest, I can tell he needs it. He's yawning a little and his eyes drift closed. As I go to kiss him on both cheeks before leaving, he does, however, have the energy to say, 'Remember, talk to Dexter.'

I smile. He's indefatigable in his efforts to matchmake. 'I will.'

I kiss his forehead and head back to the foyer where Roisin is waiting.

Chapter Thirty-five

Roisin and I are comparing notes on how we think Sofia and Carlos are doing, strolling towards the hospital exit, when a voice shouts, 'Coming through!'

We each move to one side of the wheelchair that's being wheeled through the front doors, with a heavily pregnant woman panting, her long hair all mussed and strewn across her face, her forehead sweaty with exertion. I'm just thinking 'remind me never to get pregnant' when I spot who's wheeling the wheelchair.

'Dexter!'

Both he and Maite glance up at Roisin and me, just as Maite lets out an ear-piercing scream.

'Is there anything we can do?' I ask.

Dexter scans the foyer then heads to the reception desk, calling back over his shoulder. 'Just get back to the sanctuary and take care of things with the others in my absence.'

Roisin and I return to the car, where shellshocked, I put the car into gear. Maite's baby's coming. Early. Too early. Her boyfriend was supposed to be back, wasn't he? Or did he have to go on another business trip? Whatever, thank goodness Dexter was on hand. She looked like she was about to give birth in the foyer.

We arrive back at the sanctuary and fill the others in on Carlos and Sofia's progress and the fact we met Maite and Dexter in the hospital.

'She's only thirty-two weeks.' Mariangeles' face is creased with concern.

'It's early but babies can survive from much earlier these days,' Federica reassures her.

When we turn in for the night, Dexter is still noticeable by his absence. Part of me wants to text him to check everything is OK, but the other part doesn't want to intrude, especially in case everything isn't. Poor Maite. When you're pregnant, I imagine all you think about is the beautiful little bundle of joy at the end of it, and maybe you give some thought to the endless nappy changing, sleepless nights and lack of social life that will follow, but you probably don't spend much time wondering if the baby will come early and what the ramifications may be.

Next morning, at breakfast, Mariangeles beams. 'Maite has had the baby. A girl. Pilar. Four pounds two ounces.'

'That's a relief.' I sigh. 'That's not too bad a weight for a baby of thirty-two weeks. I worked with a woman whose thirty-five-week baby was only three pounds fourteen ounces.'

Federica pours herself some coffee. 'Yes, that's very positive. What else does she say?'

Mariangeles raises her head from her phone. 'No, it's Dexter who messaged me from Maite's phone. She's sleeping. She must be exhausted and have asked Dexter to handle her messages. They're both doing well, but Pilar will be in the neonatal unit initially.'

'That's good,' says Federica. 'What about her boyfriend? Where is he? I'm guessing he's away for work again if she called Dexter.'

Mariangeles is mid-chew, but when she finishes she confirms, 'Yes, he was in Copenhagen and should land later today. Obviously, they weren't expecting the baby to come so soon.'

Ella pipes up. 'Has anyone told Carlos or Sofia? They'll be delighted for Maite.'

Mariangeles shakes her head. 'Unless Dexter has found time to visit them, then no. Or perhaps he has texted them. No matter, I'll let them know in case they don't already.' She taps away on her phone and then beams as Victor places food in front of her. I grin. The way to Mariangeles' heart is definitely through her stomach.

As we set off for the day's chores, Federica walks with me. 'Kat, can I ask you something?' she says in English.

'Sure' I say, wondering what's coming.

'Do you think my English is improving?' she asks, her voice filled with uncertainty.

'Most definitely.' I grin at her and she grins back, then I sling my arm around her shoulder and we head out into the foyer together.

Three days later, Sofia is finally released from hospital, and four days after that Carlos is too. The sanctuary comes to life again in their presence, almost as if without them its soul was missing.

It's wonderful to have them back. Even though they're both under doctor's orders to take it easy for the next month or so, they're back at the heart of things, and where they belong, and that's all that matters.

I never did manage to have that conversation with Dexter; with Maite going into labour and giving birth shortly afterwards, there simply hasn't been time. And now it's just over a week until I leave. I didn't tell anyone what Carlos said to me about Dexter, so the girls are busy organising a final hurrah for me, at the sanctuary, of course. Everyone is invited: Ed, Nicolás, Oscar, as well as all the sanctuary family. It'll serve as both a goodbye for me and a welcome back for Carlos and Sofia, but the more I think of it, and of leaving, the sadder I feel.

It's the day before I'm due to leave. Things have been … difficult, to say the least. I've tried to take my mind off the Dexter situation by dealing with the practicalities that need seeing to back home: arranging somewhere to live after the first week, buying my books for my course, checking all of the announcements from the university, double-checking my flight details.

Everyone is preparing for the party. They want to make it a real celebration, even though it feels like underlining the final stage in a chapter of my life when I'm not ready for it to end yet.

Mariangeles, Federica and Ella, and even Roisin, have gone all out, decorating the firepit area and inside the two rec rooms; they're now festooned with multicoloured bunting and garlands. They don't quite have the raw materials Nicolás had at his disposal for my surprise birthday party, two months ago, but they've done an excellent job nonetheless.

Carlos and Sofia are well enough to sit in a high-backed chair and an armchair that Javier has deemed suitable and which he and Ed have carried out of Carlos and Sofia's living quarters.

Since I'm the guest of honour, I make sure to arrive first, with the girls. Carlos and Sofia are helped out to the firepit area next, by Javier, and Nicolás, who has just arrived with Oscar, Ed and Gloriana.

Victor comes round asking everyone what they want to drink and Alejandro starts up some music, whilst Mariangeles and Federica begin dishing out snacks.

Dexter hasn't arrived yet, and for a moment I wonder if he simply won't show up. I'm sure this must be a bittersweet moment for him too. I know he told me to do what was best for me, even before the misunderstanding over his and Maite's relationship and the baby being his, but we were close, even if now we're just friends. Plus, it's not like I'm only moving down the road. I checked. Five thousand, two hundred and eighty-five miles isn't exactly insignificant.

I glance over at Carlos and Sofia. Sofia is cackling with laughter and Carlos leans in towards her, says something, which makes tears of mirth run down her face. I'm happy to see them enjoying themselves. Particularly after recent events. Carlos catches me watching them and crooks a finger at me.

I head over to him, to check if he wants his drink

refilled, and lean down to hear him over the music.

'Did you ever speak to Dexter?'

I look into his eyes, which are so full of wisdom, then shake my head. 'I didn't get the chance. You remember that was the day we met him at the hospital when Maite had gone into labour.'

Carlos waves his hand through the air, dismissing my argument. 'It's never too late, you know.' He glances around. 'Where is he, anyway?'

I shrug. 'I don't know. I haven't seen him–'

'Kat, can you help me a moment?' Mariangeles asks as she struggles with a tray of wine glasses, one precariously hovering near the edge.

'Sure.' Taking this as the moment to seek my reprieve from Carlos, I shoot him an apologetic smile and follow Mariangeles to the bar area Javier and Alejandro constructed earlier, where I accept the glass of wine she pours me.

'It looked like you needed rescuing,' she says.

'I did. He was asking me about Dexter.'

Mariangeles' eyebrows shoot into her hairline. 'Dexter? I thought you had both put that to bed. Pardon the pun.'

'We had … have,' I assure her.

'Is there something I should know?' Mariangeles asks, arching an eyebrow.

'No, of course not.' Suddenly desperate to escape from Mariangeles' probing questions, I excuse myself, on the pretence I need the loo, which is true, but it's also a good get-away-from-Mariangeles card.

As I walk out of the toilets, I run into Dexter. Literally. Like straight into him. Oof!

'Sorry.' He smiles. 'I was lost in thought.'

I can't help wishing I knew what he was thinking about, but I'll bask in the warmth of that megawatt smile any day. It has been missing too often lately.

I smile back and go to move, but he says, 'Kat...' and I stop. A myriad of emotions flickers across his face and I wonder what's coming next.

He takes my arm gently. 'I want you to know that I wish things had been different for us, too.'

That's it? Somehow I feel even more deflated than before he said that.

But he goes on, 'I'd take you to the airport, but I think it would be too difficult.' He looks at me ruefully, and just like that, my insides melt. They'd started to freeze over at his previous sentence, but his admission shows me he does care.

I nod. 'I understand. In fact, I'm taking a taxi as I hate goodbyes, and I know the girls would have me in floods if they came to see me off. They've offered, but I've turned them down. I have a cab coming in the morning.'

'Oh!' He looks wrong-footed, and I wonder if it was something I said. Damn, here's me thinking *he* has said the wrong thing. 'Anyway, I'll miss you and I wish you all the best.'

Well, that's drawn a line under that then. Those words are pretty definitive.

He leans in to give me a hug. God, he smells so good. It would be so easy to kiss him from this position, but that's not what this conversation's about, not where it's leading. We break apart about ten seconds later, yes, admittedly, a few seconds longer than would be usual for a platonic hug, but then when has anything been usual with us? Since I found Roisin naked in his bed, life has been a little bit of a rollercoaster for us both.

'Thanks. I'd better get back, and you'd better…'

'…go to the toilet?' His lips curve slightly. Perhaps he realises this is not the most romantic of endings.

'Quite. See you.' I skip, actually skip, back to the others as if I'm delighted with what has just transpired, when nothing could be further from the truth.

The party is fun. How could it not be, with the girls organising it and Victor making the snacks. The music is good, the company is fabulous, the food is amazing, but my heart isn't in it.

I decide I need a little time to myself, so I let myself into the nursery and sit on the sofa, with my glass of star fruit wine, at peace, watching the babies sleep. I'm going to miss them so much, and I'm not only talking about the pups. Tears prick the back of my eyes and this time I let them flow.

Voices come from outside the door, and I hope I'm not in trouble.

Ah, no, it's just Mariangeles. Probably Federica's with her. They're joined at the hip mostly. But the next voice I hear is Dexter's.

'I *have* tried.'

'Not hard enough, obviously.' Mariangeles.

'She's made it quite plain she's going.'

Uh-oh, nothing good ever came of eavesdropping. I more than anyone else know that.

'Did you tell her how you feel?' Mariangeles hisses.

'Yes. I told her I'll miss her.'

'Dexter, oh my God, why are men so stupid?' She lets forth a torrent of words whose meaning I can't even guess at, her flow of Spanish is so rapid.

'Mariangeles. Leave it. It's done. We had our chance.'

And just like that, he has given up.

'You should have told her. Carlos told you to. I told you to. God, even Victor told you to. Why are you being so stubborn?'

Dexter's voice is a whisper. 'Because it hurts too much when the other person doesn't feel the same way.'

'*Ay!* But she does. I told you she does.'

'But she hasn't told me. She's had every chance. Three little words. That's all it would take. And anyway, I don't want her not going to uni because of me.'

'Oh my God, I give up. She's a big girl, who can make up her own mind about whether to stay or go. But with regards to saying those three little words, it works both ways, Dexter. Take the initiative. Don't wait until it's too late.'

'It's already too late.' I hear footsteps moving away then a few seconds later Mariangeles muttering mild obscenities under her breath then more footsteps going in the other direction.

I sit there, my heart beating so loud I feel it whoosh around my head. Three little words. I love you? Could it be anything else? Why would he expect me to say them first? I was about to, though, wasn't I? That day on the bench when Maite appeared, when I was telling Dexter I'd got into uni. My head starts thumping and I don't know if it's because of the wine, the stress and sadness at leaving or what I've overheard.

In a daze, I make my way back to the party, pasting a smile on, pretending everything's fine.

'Ah, there you are,' Nicolás says. 'I've been looking for you so we can dance.'

'Oh, no, Nicolás. I…' But he ignores me, taking me by the hand and signalling to Oscar to cue the music. Immediately, a salsa tune comes through the speakers, and Nicolás leads me – he's an excellent dancer. Soon, he's whirling me around and my flippy black dress is flying up like I was born to do this. It feels amazing. I'm so glad Nicolás is an expert at this, as, much as I love this type of dancing, I'm not particularly good at it, but with Nicolás as my lead, I don't come across as a total fiasco. In fact, I'd go so far as to say I'm actually not too bad. Praise indeed.

The music changes to a song with a slightly slower tempo, and just as I'm thanking Nicolás and about to walk away, Nicolás says, 'There you are, right on time.'

I turn to see Dexter, who, by the startled expression on his face, has been ambushed. Nicolás takes me by the hand, kisses it, then offers it to Dexter. I've half a mind to tell him I'm not a prize cow ready to be handed over to the new owner, but when Dexter takes my hand, all reason goes out of the window. This could be the last time I'm ever close to this man, this man who picked me up, literally, when I fell; who kissed me until I begged him to stop; and who made love to me until I pleaded with him *not* to stop. Ever.

Our eyes meet, and I see there what I imagine Dexter sees in mine: desire, love and ... hope?

As we dance and sway to the beat of the music, which though slow, eventually builds to a crescendo, Dexter's lips almost brush my ear. Was he trying to kiss me? But then as we complete the dance, I'm sure of two things: one – he whispered something to me, and two – he said 'I love you'. But I don't think he intended me to actually hear him. He said it so softly, it was almost like a caress.

As he spins me away, then close to him, I look up into his eyes, which are partially covered by his hair flopping into them, and try to decipher what lies beneath. Did I imagine that he told me he loved me? Have I wanted to hear those words from him for such a long time that I've conjured them up in my mind?

The music ends and as our eyes meet again, Dexter smiles and thanks me for the dance, then turns away, disappearing into the hustle and bustle of the party. And now I'm even more confused than before.

Chapter Thirty-six

Next morning, Dexter isn't around. No one knows where he is. I had a fitful night's sleep, lying awake thinking of Dexter in his bed just across the garden in the men's accommodation block.

Victor has done us proud on the breakfast front, and he has even made me a packed lunch – bless him – as he doesn't trust airline food. I hate to tell him I won't get through customs with it, but neither will I waste it. I'll eat it in the queue for Security, if I have to.

I have just enough time before my flight to say goodbye properly to all the sloths, particularly Flash, and then thank and hug every one of my sanctuary family. I feel as if someone is carving holes in my heart with a scythe. It was bad enough last night when I said an emotional farewell to Ed, Oscar, Nicolás and Gloriana, but today seems too much to cope with.

Now I'm really glad I chose to take a taxi. I look at my watch. It's almost time. Where the hell is Dexter? I know he couldn't face taking me to the airport, but I thought he might at least show up in the foyer like everyone else. I'll be absolutely gutted if… Here he is. Finally. He heads straight for me.

'I don't like goodbyes, so let's just say "hasta la

vista".'

I smile. 'You forgot the "baby".' I can't help but channel Arnie in *Terminator* when anyone says 'hasta la vista'. It was one of Dad's favourite films.

He grins, and I'm glad our final exchange has been a humorous one and we're parting on good terms. Then I realise that this will be the last time I ever see him and my throat constricts.

He hands me a book. Crossword puzzles. 'For the plane journey. To make it more bearable.'

'Thanks.' I know I was his crossword partner, helping him out when he mucked up the spellings, but it seems such a banal gift after everything we've shared.

The taxi beeps its horn outside. 'Right, this is me,' I say. I'm about to break down; I know I am. I need to get out of here before I start sobbing.

Rather than endure the pain of hugging and kissing everyone again, I wave as Victor helps me out to the cab with my bags.

'Bye, everyone. I'll email! Take care. I'll miss you.'

There are so many shouts of love and support and tears, too – from most of my sanctuary family – that my vision is blurred before I reach the cab.

'Bye, Victor.'

'Remember, cook the *sustancia de carne* fifteen minutes longer than Sofia's recipe,' he whispers, and I can't hold back my smile. God, I'm going to miss them all.

The cab pootles down the road and I wave frantically for about twenty seconds before I turn to face the cab driver, who eyes me curiously.

'I hate goodbyes,' I explain.

He nods. 'Me too. And I see far too many of them.'

'I can imagine.'

I settle back in my seat, my bag in my lap and the crossword book Dexter gave me still in my hand. Too big to put in my cross-body bag, I curse myself for not putting it in my suitcase.

We're picking up speed now and the palm trees and water apple trees that have formed my daily landscape are soon whizzing past as we make our way towards the airport.

My phone pings and I dive in my bag, hoping Dexter has had some last-minute epiphany, but it's a text from Mum.

Safe flight, Kat. Looking forward to seeing you, Mum.

I smile as I think of how different things were a few weeks ago. Rational thought returned to her, eventually, and she apologised for the things she said, particularly about Dad turning in his grave. And she seems to actually be happy I'm coming home, and not just so she can tell me working out here was a half-baked idea at best, an insane one at worst. Plus, she gave me a piece of good news, recently. I'm not sure whether she thought it might make me want to rush home to try to patch things up with him, but Aidan has a new girlfriend. The fact all I feel is relief speaks volumes, and it will make my re-entry to Scotland and my old life marginally more palatable.

I decide I may as well start one of the crosswords since I still have a long way to go to the airport. But when I open the book to the first page I notice some of the letters have already been filled in. 1 Across. Bear named after US president. Easy. Teddy. Frowning, I see only the T is filled in. Why would someone – presumably Dexter – only put in the first letter, or fill it in at all, particularly if he was giving it as a gift?

Another letter has been filled in. Again another first letter. E. I check the clue. Spiny anteater. Echidnea.

Further down, I note another letter on the left. A. 14 Down. Capital of the Netherlands. Well, that's Amsterdam.

On the right, another letter. 27 Across. M. Clue. Italian dictator. Mussolini.

And one final one, right near the bottom. O. Clue. Type of theatre production. Opera?

But why have these letters, only the first letters of the words, been filled in? I squint, trying to figure it out. TEAMO. Team-o? That doesn't make sense. I look up, trying to work it out. Then I see a tiny furry bundle by the side of the road and shout, 'Stop!'

'*Dios mio*,' says the cab driver. 'You almost gave me a heart attack.'

'There's a sloth by the kerb. It's injured. Adult. About three years old.' I break off, realising that I'm talking to the driver as if he's one of the sanctuary staff. 'Give me a minute. I need to call the sanctuary.'

'OK, but he's not coming in my cab,' the driver warns.

'I know. It's OK.' I turn away to make the call. 'Dexter? Oh, thank God! There's an injured sloth lying at the kerb on the road about half an hour from the sanctuary.' I give him my approximate location and tell him I'm with the cab driver. He asks to speak to him and I hand the phone over.

I hear the cab driver say 'yes' a lot and then he

passes me back to Dexter, who gives me instructions on what to do until he arrives.

Dexter has told the driver to wait, apparently, so once I've done what I can to make the sloth comfortable, without handling it too much, my mind turns again to the team-o conundrum. Meanwhile, I keep an eye on the sloth for signs of laboured breathing or further distress.

On the off chance, because it's driving me mad, I say to the driver, 'I don't suppose you know what 'teamo' means, or if it means anything in Spanish, do you?'

'Team-o? No. How do you spell it?'

'T-E-A-M-O.'

The driver grins. 'Not "team-o" but "*te amo*".'

My jaw drops. Oh my God, of course. How could I have been so stupid? That's why Dexter gave it to me as I was leaving. I didn't imagine the words he whispered to me last night; I just didn't confirm that I'd heard them, as I wasn't sure. He does love me. *Te amo*. I love you.

I smile so widely the driver grins at me again. 'Looks like it's your lucky day,' he says. 'Is this him?'

I turn to see Dexter striding towards me from the sanctuary truck. I didn't even hear it draw up, I was so lost in my own little world – at the realisation Dexter loves me. I needed a sign and now I have two.

As Dexter reaches me, scrutinising me, probably wondering why I'm smiling when I've just told him I've found an injured sloth, I throw myself, yes, I do, actually throw myself, into his arms and say, 'I love you, too.' Four words, not three little words, but since he only used two, I felt justified in adding the extra one.

He sets me down. 'Good, because I love you,' he says, overemphasising the words and pointing to himself then forming a heart shape with his fingers and pointing at me.

The cab driver whistles and I flush red, but I don't care and neither does Dexter, as he kisses me softly at first then more deeply until the driver shouts, '*Ay*, remember, there's an injured sloth here.'

'Good point,' I say, recovering, and smoothing down my hair as Dexter steps away, still holding my hand, and moves forward to assess the sloth.

As I watch Dexter gently and carefully deal with the sloth, one of a species I love, I know, with one hundred per cent of my being that I have everything I need right here at Costa Punta: the sloths, my sloth family, and of course, Dexter.

Chapter Thirty-seven

Three months later

'Becca, come on. If I can do it, you can,' I call.

'I'm not bloody going up there, and definitely not down there. I'll stay and have some après-ski.'

'It's not a ski resort, Becca. It doesn't have après-ski.'

'Well, that's a bit of a letdown,' she shouts back.

I laugh. It has been great having Becca here. She was disappointed at first that I wasn't coming home, and the uni replied saying I could defer my place or reapply at a future date if I should change my mind, but I won't. I get to study animals – sloths – firsthand here. I don't need a degree to do that. I gain so much on-the-job knowledge from doing what I do day in, day out; that's a far better education and much more useful than sitting in a tutorial or doing exams. I can always return to studying in the future. And I'm already in at the animal end of the action.

Plus the scenery's not too shabby. I finally made it to the Monteverde Cloud Forest. Our planned trip kept being pushed back for one reason or another, but now I'm here and it's every bit as spectacular as I thought it would be. It really does feel as if I'm in the clouds, and a little mist has shrouded our view, on and off all morning. We already completed one of the trails and crossed the most amazing suspension bridge so we could see some of the incredible species on offer here, although I admit the crossing was a little scary.

The orange-bellied trogon was a particular favourite, mainly because of its long, cool name, and the three-wattled bellbird – now that's an odd-looking but still beautiful bird, with its chestnut lower half and its white head and breast. I'm beginning to think they don't go in for short names here, though, but they're so wonderfully descriptive, I don't care.

Talking of scenery, the view's not too bad either. Dexter walks towards me and enfolds me in a hug. 'Is Becca moaning again?' he asks.

'She is. She's a total lightweight.'

'I am not,' she yells.

'Go down then,' I shout up to her as my fingers find Dexter's and I clasp his hand in mine.

'Not a chance in hell!'

For someone usually so fearless, she sure is spooked by this zip line.

'We're leaving you here then until we get back,' I call.

'Sounds good to me,' comes Becca's voice.

I laugh. 'Looks like we're on our own. You ready?'

Dexter grins. 'Yep. Ladies first.'

I shoot him an incredulous look. 'You're really making me go first?'

'I am.'

'In that case, wish me luck.'

'Good luck.' He kisses me one more time, a long, lingering kiss which is featherlight and leaves tingles on my lips after we break apart.

I check my harness. I'm good to go. Then I push off, down over the jungle. '*Pura vida!*' I yell. What a rush! The jungle canopy zooms past me and I plummet towards the ground.

When I land five minutes later, my first thought is 'let's do it again'. Moments later, Dexter lands behind me, and I give him a long, lingering kiss until Alejandro, Ella, Mariangeles and Mum encircle us in a group hug. Yes, Mum. She decided when I chose to stay, and told her I'd pursue my veterinary studies here, too, that she was coming to visit. What an experience. What a life. I'm so lucky. I came to Costa Rica on one adventure, and ended up falling into another. Finally, I've found my place in the world and I couldn't be happier.

***

COMING 23 SEPTEMBER 2025!
A Taste of Christmas Spirit

Pre-order here: https://books2read.com/u/4997jw

And if you haven't already read *The Leap Year Proposal*, you can order it here now:
https://books2read.com/u/3kj7AG

Author's Note

I hope you enjoyed our little visit to Costa Rica. I loved it when I visited and I hope to return and that I manage to see many more parts of this beautiful country. I love sloths – you can probably tell! They always seem to be smiling. I can honestly say I did more factual research for this book than I have for any of my other books. I kept going down sloth-shaped rabbit holes, as I found out more about these delightful animals. Plus, once I discovered more about the areas of Costa Rica I'd visited, and those I hadn't, I wanted to know more. I hope you did too, and my most sincere hope is that reading *You Can't Hurry Love* has made you want to book a plane ticket! I also loved learning more about Costa Rican food as I wrote this book. I was in a state of permanent hunger and was more than a little miffed that I couldn't get all the ingredients here in the UK, at least not readily.

You Can't Hurry Love is the first in a new series, the Dream Destinations series. I am very lucky that I have travelled a lot, both for work and pleasure. So, expect more stories set in far-flung, dream destinations.

Susan x

Did you get your free short stories yet?

TWO   UNPUBLISHED   EXCLUSIVE   SHORT STORIES.

Interacting with my readers is one of the most fun parts of being a writer. I'll be sending out a monthly newsletter with new release information, competitions, special offers and basically a bit about what I've been up to, writing and otherwise.

You can get the previously unseen short stories, *Mixed Messages* and *Time Is of the Essence*, FREE if you sign up to my mailing list.
www.susanbuchananauthor.com

Did you enjoy *You Can't Hurry Love*?

I'd really appreciate if you could leave a review on Amazon or Goodreads. It doesn't need to be much, just a couple of lines. I love reading customer reviews. Seeing what readers think of my books spurs me on to write more. Sometimes I've even written more about characters or created a series because of reader comments. Plus, reviews are SO important to authors. They help raise the profile of the author and make it more likely that the book will be visible to more readers. Every author wants their book to be read by more people, and I am no exception!

The Leap Year Proposal

When three women meet at a mutual friend's hen weekend on the Scottish island of Arran, they get more than they bargained for when one of them has the genius idea of proposing on 29 February, like the age-old Irish tradition.

High-flying businesswoman Anouska and boyfriend Zach are deliriously happy and madly in love. If only they had more time together. But now she's pregnant and doesn't know how to tell him, since having kids hadn't featured in their plans.

Dog walker Jess lives with her childhood sweetheart, but they're already like an old married couple, without the romance, or the wedding, or the ring. When Mark doesn't propose on New Year's Eve, Jess is gutted and decides to take matters into her own hands.

Ellie and Scott still live apart after six years, and his lack of commitment is a sore point. She's up for a huge promotion which involves moving country. It's make-or-break time. She needs to know he's worth turning down the job for.

The women meet weekly, helping each other with decisions big and small, becoming each other's support system in the run-up to 'the big ask'.

Will love conquer all or will their hopes and dreams come crashing down around them?

The Christmas Spirit (book 1 in the Christmas Spirit series)

Natalie Hope takes over the reins of the Sugar and Spice bakery and café with the intention of injecting some Christmas spirit. Something her regulars badly need.

Newly dumped Rebecca is stuck in a job with no prospects, has lost her home and is struggling to see a way forward.

Pensioner Stanley is dreading his first Christmas alone without his beloved wife, who passed away earlier this year. How will he ever feel whole again?

Graduate Jacob is still out of work despite making hundreds of applications. Will he be forced to go against his instincts and ask his unsympathetic parents for help?

Spiky workaholic Meredith hates the jollity of family gatherings and would rather stay home with a box set and a posh ready meal. Will she finally realise what's important in life?

Natalie sprinkles a little magic to try to spread some festive cheer and restore Christmas spirit, but will she succeed?

Just One Day – Winter (book 1 in the Just One Day series)

Thirty-eight-year-old Louisa has a loving husband, three wonderful kids, a faithful dog, a supportive family and a gorgeous house near Glasgow. What more could she want?

TIME.

Louisa would like, just once, to get to the end of her never-ending to-do list. With her husband Ronnie working offshore, she is demented trying to cope with everything on her own: the after-school clubs, the homework, the appointments … the constant disasters. And if he dismisses her workload one more time, she may well throttle him.

Juggling running her own wedding stationery business with family life is taking its toll, and the only reason Louisa is still sane is because of her best friends and her sisters.

Fed up with only talking to Ronnie about household bills and incompetent tradesmen, when a handsome stranger pays her some attention on her birthday weekend away, she is flattered, but will she give in to temptation? And will she ever get to the end of her to-do list?

www.ingramcontent.com/pod-product-compliance
Lightning Source LLC
Chambersburg PA
CBHW050613170726
48283CB00001B/222